BOOK 2
PART 1

TEANCUM

THE GHOST SOLDIER™

AUTHOR:
JASON MOW

ILLUSTRATOR:
GABE BONILLA

ETHOS™
PRODUCTIONS

Teancum: The Ghost Soldier Part 1
Author: Jason Mow
Illustrator: Gabe Bonilla
Graphic Design: Nicole Bonilla

For information regarding permission, please email info@ethospro.com.

ISBN 978-0-9905953-1-1
First English Edition, September 2017
Printed in the USA

DEDICATION

This book is dedicated to the brave men and women who took a vow and stand watch against evil. Remember my brothers and sisters, the Sheep Dog answers to the Good Shepherd, not the flock.

Contents

PREFACE

The War Chapters Series of books are based on characters appearing in the Book of Mormon—a volume of scripture of The Church of Jesus Christ of Latter-day Saints. In our book, as in the Book of Mormon, the characters frequently affirm their faith and commitment to the Savior, Jesus Christ. We think the messages of faith, honor, courage and sacrifice in these stories are universal and should appeal to everyone, regardless of religious belief.

While we hope this book contains insights that will help the reader in their effort to better understand the great messages contained in the Book of Mormon, this book is a work of fiction by its author. It is not produced, endorsed or aided by The Church of Jesus Christ of Latter-day Saints, or its leadership, in any way. While the author is a faithful member of the church, this book should not be used in the place of true scripture study, prayer and reflection. These books are meant to serve as catalysts to inspire readers in their efforts to further study the war chapters in the Book of Mormon.

There are plenty of theories as to where the Book of Mormon lands were located. There is not, as of yet, a definitive location acceptable to the majority of historians. We are not endorsing any of these theories. While we are using the actual place names from the Book of Mormon, there are also some fictional places the author has created for the benefit of the story. Any geographical similarity to existing locations is purely coincidental.

The label "War Chapters" is often used to describe the long period of war, civil war and social upheaval that is described in the book of Alma, chapters 43-62, in the Book of Mormon.

ACKNOWLEDGEMENTS

The journey I took while writing book two of the War Chapters series was such an amazing adventure. There were so many people who came into my life along the way. You all inspired and pushed me to tell this story. I know I can't possibly acknowledge everyone who had a hand in this process, but there are a few I would like to give my thanks to.

To Nikki, my beautiful new bride. When you found me I was a shell of a man. You gave me the inspiration to heal and push myself towards greatness. I want nothing more than to be the man you deserve. To your children and extended family, I say thank you for making me and my family feel welcome among you.

To Gabe and Nicole Bonilla. Thank you for not rolling your eyes in front of me when I would come up with some of my crazy ideas or say "I am still working on the book." You and the support staff at Ethos Productions are the true heroes of this story. Gabe, your artwork can say more in one page then I can in a hundred pages of written words. Nicole, you are the creative engine that runs this whole operation. Thank you all.

To my editing staff, Sandra Bonilla, Katey Bersch, and Jenna Roundy…You would think that after writing my first book I would have learned to spell, punctuate and form a complete sentence…but no. Your patience with me is the stuff of legends. I am so grateful for your time and talents. This would have been monumentally more difficult without you three ladies.

To Nick and Rachael…my Prince and Princess. You two are my heroes. Daddy loves you both more than you will ever know.

To all of my friends who stood by me during the most difficult time in my life I have ever experienced. I cannot express enough my love and gratitude to you all. I will not forget your loyalty. Mine is a debt of honor.

To my fans…..I know book two will be a reward for your continued excitement and enthusiasm for the stories in "The War Chapters!"

Honor, Courage, Strength, Discipline.

For Liberty!!!

–Jason

Speaking of Teancum:

"He had been a man who had fought valiantly
for his country, yea, a true friend to liberty."
−Alma 62:37

General Mormon, Chief Commander of all
Nephite forces about 385 AD

CHAPTER ONE

BLESSINGS

It was still an hour before dawn, but the air was electric with anticipation. All the family members, the servants and most of the ranch hands were now awake and had gathered in the great dining hall to await the news. The dining hall, like the rest of the house and the entire cattle ranch, was large, spacious and reflected the expensive but functional taste of the owners. The elderly patriarch and master of the house paced back and forth in front of the fireplace that was burning brightly with a new fire. His tall frame and striking facial features contrasted against the fire's light. The look of concern and worry could easily be traced in the lines and wrinkles of his weathered face. His wife, elegant and graceful, even at this early hour, was sitting in a large plush chair close to the hearth trying to feel the fire's warmth and casually fussing with the her long braids of dark hair.

"Tum," the lady of the house spoke with a gentle voice, "Please bring me a blanket, and inform Seppi we will be breakfasting early today."

"Yes, my lady," a tall, thin and regal looking man in his late fifties responded. He raised his hand signaling to a young girl wearing a plain homespun apron, standing in the shadows, to come to him.

"Deliver the message about breakfast to the kitchen and fetch the lady a blanket;" He paused to look back at the distinguished gentleman still pacing in front of the fire; "Also, bring the master his sleeping robe and tell Seppi to boil up some of his herbal teas." He dismissed the young maid who hurried off into the shadows of the grand house.

"Pilio, please sit down. You're going to wear a hole in the floor if you don't stop pacing." The regal lady gestured to her concerned husband.

"I sent for the doctor two hours ago, where could he be?" he responded in an impatient tone. The groans of a woman in labor could be heard echoing through the great hall. "Shouldn't you be in there with her?" Pilio questioned his wife.

"I have been up with her all night," she responded in her usual calm and sophisticated manner. "The midwife and the nursemaid are with her now. I am resting and will return when the doctor arrives. Now please, come sit next to me," she said while patting the seat of a chair next to her.

The groans of labor rang out again. Everyone in the room turned to face the closed door from where they came.

"The poor thing, I know she wishes Kail was here with her," Pilio said with sympathy while accepting his robe from the young housemaid, putting it on and tying the sash around his waist. "What she ever saw in that common soldier I will never know...."

"They are in love, Pilio. Your daughter knew what she was getting herself into when she married Kail, and"...She paused to look him in the eyes, "he is an honorable man and soon to be the father of your first grandchild. Besides, you were a young soldier once... remember?"

He knew instantly he had almost crossed the line. He too had been a young and brash soldier, much like his son-in-law. She was right, as always, and in her gentle way she reminded Pilio of his own past. Grabbing her hand he kissed it gently and responded, "Of course, my dear Saria, I am sorry for speaking ill of him." Another set of groans came from the next room. "I am just worried for Rachael and feel a bit helpless." He took the blanket from the servant girl and wrapped it around his wife's legs. Looking into each other's eyes, he smiled as she stroked the stubble on his cheeks with her hands.

This was a conversation they had shared several times, starting the first day their only daughter, Rachael, brought home the young warrior to meet her parents. Although Kail was an officer in the army, Pilio did not like him. Kail was from a poor family and a bit rough around the edges. But Saria instantly saw in him what Rachael saw. He was a good, honorable man as well as a good soldier. She knew Kail would make Rachael very happy. So, as with most everything else in his life, Pilio bowed to his wife's good judgement and welcomed Kail into the family.

The duties of a Nephite soldier had taken Kail away from Rachael before, but never for this long and never as far away as he was this night.

Even if the message of the impending arrival of his first child got to him quickly, it would take Kail several days to get back to the ranch. Pilio had sent word of the coming birth to the local garrison commander several hours ago when the labor pains started. Pilio and the commander were old military academy classmates and friends. Pilio was hoping he could get word to Kail and arrange for Kail to take leave and return to be with his new family.

"My lady, the cook informed me she will need a count of those staying for breakfast," Tum spoke in a quiet tone behind Saria. Saria turned in her seat to face the head servant.

"Have her make a grand breakfast that will include the family, the entire staff along with the doctor, if he ever arrives." She smiled at her husband. He smiled back. "This is a special occasion. Breakfast will be served here, in the dining hall, and everyone is invited to partake." She rose from her chair as she spoke, gesturing to the servants and staff standing around the perimeter of the room. Out of love and respect for the grand lady of the home, everyone including Pilio, stopped what they were doing to face Saria as she stood.

"That is most generous, my lady," Tum responded. "A special occasion, indeed!"

"Tum, I'll leave it to you and Seppi to work out the details. I have a feeling I will be involved in a more pressing matter." She spoke as cries of labor rang out again from the other room.

An excited and breathless male servant barged in from the back of the room, "My lord, the doctor has arrived!"

"It's about time," Pilio gasped. "Quickly, show him in."

The servant disappeared down the dark hallway from which he had just emerged, returning seconds later holding a small oil lamp, guiding a middle aged man into the dining hall. The doctor was of average height with graying hair, and tired blue eyes. He was carrying a large bag with a bundle of cloth under his arm. His clothing and general appearance looked neat and clean, but his eyes gave way to the truth; he was tired, so very tired. There were several sick people in the village. He had been up all night tending to them. The early and unexpected arrival of Rachael's first child meant he was going to miss a few more hours of sleep. He knew this but maintained his professionalism as he greeted Pilio, Saria and the rest of the family.

"Doctor, thank you for coming so quickly," Saria spoke as she held out her hand to greet him.

"An exciting morning, yes?" he responded while shaking hands with Saria then Pilio. "Is the midwife with her now?" he asked Saria in a matter-of-fact tone.

"Yes, and I think the pains are coming very quickly. Not much longer now."

"Excellent! Just in time I think. Shall we go in, my lady?" he questioned Saria.

"Yes, this way, please." She gestured toward the door in the far corner of the hall. Without another word, the two walked to the door, letting themselves in, just as Rachael let out a fresh round of cries.

With the door shut behind them, an odd silence fell on the dining hall. Pilio was left standing alone by the fire as the rest of the gathered staff in the room looked to him for instruction.

"Well," he said clearing his throat, "I guess we wait for breakfast or a baby." There was a light chuckle from the group as Pilio turned back to look at the roaring fire.

"Very well!" Tum exclaimed after clearing his throat, "It's almost dawn, and some of you have chores to do." He looked at the stable boys whose job it was to milk the cows and fetch the fresh eggs for the kitchen. "We can't enjoy breakfast unless you see to yours, lads." The two young boys quickly broke for the back of the great house and to the stables. Tum turned to the remainder of the group, "The rest of you will assist Sappi in the kitchen or ready the dining hall for our feast."

The staff all slowly started to move out of the hall when Rachael's cries suddenly became more intense. Everyone stopped and looked at the closed door. Pilio was beside himself with worry. He was wise enough to know that even under the best of conditions childbirth is dangerous for both the mother and child. He knew Rachael was young, healthy and strong and the doctor was now with her, but the cries meant his only daughter was still suffering. Before he realized it, he was standing next to the door trying to hear the conversation going on inside. He could make out the doctor and Saria giving Rachael encouragement and telling her to push. Rachael, in turn was moaning and grunting under the pains of delivery. Tum walked up to his old master and friend and the two made eye contact. Tum could see the anguish in Pilio's eyes and he put his hand on Pilio's shoulder to try and comfort him. They were both mature men and had faced pain and suffering before. This was different; Rachael was precious to both of them. It is difficult for a man to stand by and do nothing when a loved one is suffering, even when that pain is a natural part of childbirth.

As they stood in silence, the doctor's voice could be heard giving Rachael more commands, "Push now, my lady…one more big push!" There was one last exhaustive scream, then the unmistakable sound of a new baby crying and gasping air for the first time.

"This is a blessed day!" Pilio exclaimed as relief and fatigue swept over his body. Tum and Pilio grabbed each other's shoulders and shook while laughing with delight at the sounds of the new baby coming from inside the room. Several of the staff were crying while others were clapping for joy at the news the new child had finally arrived.

"Go tell Seppi and the rest of the kitchen staff the baby has come," Tum ordered one of the maids still standing in the hall.

"Sir, she is going to want to know if it's a boy or girl," the young maid responded.

Tum turned to face Pilio who blinked several times and nodded. It was his right, as master of the house and grandfather of the newest member of the family, to enter the room to investigate. Taking a deep breath and squaring his shoulders, Pilio knocked three times on the hard wooden door. Not waiting for permission to enter, Pilio gently pushed the door open and stepped inside.

Rachael looked exhausted but was beaming with joy. "Daddy!" She half cried and choked when she saw Pilio standing in the doorway. Saria was sitting on the edge of the bed next to Rachael dabbing a cool wet cloth on her forehead. She looked up and smiled a broad toothy smile.

"Come in stranger and meet your grandson." Saria spoke with a song in her voice. She continued to beam with joy as she looked back down at the bundle of swaddling blankets wrapped tightly around something in Rachael's arms. Moving a bit of cloth with her hand Saria put her pinky finger down by the blanket and a tiny hand grasped it tight. "A strong grip, that's a very good sign." Sarai whispered. "Wouldn't you agree, doctor?"

"Yes, a very good sign." The doctor spoke wihtout looking back while washing his hands in a large basin of water. The midwife handed him a clean towel and he dried his hands as he walked over to where Pilio was standing.

"Is everyone fine?" Pilio questioned under his breath as the doctor approached.

"Yes my old friend, mother and son are the picture of health." He put his hand on Pilio's shoulder. "But you look like you're about to burst."

"I did nothing but wait outside and I feel completely spent. I can't begin to understand how she must feel," Pilio responded as he jerked his head toward Rachael.

"I will take my leave and give you some time with them. I will be right out here if you need me. Congratulations, my lady." The doctor spoke as he moved past Pilio and bowed slightly to Rachael. She smiled a grand smile full of gratitude at the doctor and he exited the room to wait in the great hall with the rest of the staff.

"Daddy, come and meet your new grandson," Rachael beckoned. Drawing a deep breath, Pilio moved forward toward the bed. With every step, the love and joy he felt for his family grew until his chest felt as if it would explode with pride.

Reaching the edge of the bed, he bent over and gently kissed Rachael on the forehead. He could taste the accumulated salt from her sweat. She had been in labor for hours and the sweat stains on her sleeping gown, pillows and sheets were a testament to her effort.

Looking up he held out his right hand and lovingly stroked Saria's cheek. They looked into each other's eyes and smiled. They had been a couple for so long they did not need to speak. Words were useless at this moment, but the feelings of love flowing forth spoke volumes.

"And who is this?" Pilio said as he looked down at the new baby while moving some of the blanket away from his face. "Does the young master have a name yet?" He asked Rachael as he looked into her beaming face.

"We wanted it to be a surprise." Rachael said, speaking for Kail in his absence. "I was reading in some of the old books at the library of the High Priest and I found a word that meant 'brave of heart' in the old language. I thought it would make a great name if we had a son. I told Kail what I found and he agreed."

"What is it dear?" Saria questioned with the tone only a loving mother can have.

"Teancum ... his name will be Teancum," Rachael said as she drew her new child closer to her heart.

"Teancum," Pilio echoed back. "A fine name for a fine boy. Let me hold my grandson." Pilio gently moved his hands under the new baby.

"Careful, dear, watch his little head," Saria commanded in a soft tone.

She was never far away from her role as the mother and caregiver of the home.

Pilio took the new baby and held him in both arms. "A fine boy," he whispered, and then giggled with surprised excitement as the baby grabbed Pilio's finger and held it tight. "He does have a strong grip... that is a very good sign," Pilio said looking up at Rachael. "He will be a warrior like his father."

Rachael gave her father a look that reflected her love and respect, even though she knew he was being a bit silly. "He has not even survived his first feeding yet. Maybe we should wait until he is a bit older before we decide his fate."

"Spoken like a true lady of the house." Pilio smiled and winked at his wife. He carefully returned the newborn to his mother's arms and kissed her forehead again. "Who wants to tell the staff the good news?" he asked the two women.

"Mother will you please inform them for me? I don't think I can find the strength to get out of bed right now" Rachael spoke.

"Of course, my dear child. You rest. I will take care of everything." Saria stood up from the bed and walked toward the door. Just before opening it she turned back to her child. "You spend a few moments with your new little prince, I will return with food. Then we will get you cleaned up and the two of you can take a well-deserved nap."

"Thank you mother, I would be lost without you." Rachael gasped as she choked back the tears of gratitude. She was loved, and she knew she was loved. Rachael was also blessed. Her family was rich and powerful. On her father's cattle ranch, she lived better than most others but was raised to be humble and respectful. She was taught by her parents the value of a hard day's work. She never took her position as the oldest child of Lord Pilio and Lady Saria for granted. She was so happy that she now had the opportunity to share that happiness with her new son, Teancum. "Any word from Kail?" Rachael inquired, already knowing the answer.

"No my child, not yet." Pilio returned to his role as father figure. "Rest assured, he will come home just as soon as he can."

Rachael held a brave smile, but there was a hint of sadness in her eyes. She missed her husband. They had been trying to have a child for some time, and she wanted him home to enjoy this moment with her. She knew with all her friends, family and the many dedicated servants surrounding her, she would never be lonely. But for one brief moment, sitting there holding her new son without her husband at her side, she felt truly alone. Shaking off the emotions, Rachael sighed and put on a brave smile and said, "Well then, we will just trust in God that Kail will be home soon."

CHAPTER TWO

BETRAYED

"Lieutenant Kail…Lieutenant Kail?" The young soldier called out several times as he moved around the stables full of horses, while several Nephites tended to the animals. He was too young to be involved in the fighting so he did his duty by helping out where he could until the time came when he could take up arms for his country. Today, his duty consisted of running messages around the camp for the commander. As he moved around the stables, men were brushing and feeding their horses while others worked on the horseshoes and saddles. A large cart full of hay was blocking the way so the young soldier had to move around it as he called out.

"Over there," one of the older soldiers pointed to a wooden corral just outside the stable doors where several more men had gathered to watch as a wild horse was running, kicking and jumping in anger at being locked up for the first time. The young messenger nodded in thanks then moved quickly to deliver the message.

"Lieutenant Kail?" He asked as he approached the group of men. The boy did not know Kail by sight, but had heard his name when he listened to other soldiers talk at chow time or at night when they would gather around the fires.

Kail was young, still learning his role as a Nephite army officer but he was respected by his men. He was willing to learn from the seasoned vets as well as listen to his superiors as they instructed him in the ways of a warrior. Kail was strongly built, and often won the impromptu wrestling matches that would spring up among soldiers who were testing their skills. He was a good runner along with being a skilled swordsman. The word was quickly spreading that Kail was an officer of some merit, whom others could follow and trust.

"Here!" Kail called out as he raised his hand to signal to the young messenger his location among the men watching the horse in the corral.

The boy ran up to Kail rendering a proper salute. "Sir, the commander requests your presence in his tent right away."

Kail nodded that he understood the message while starting to move toward the stable. "What's going on, sir?" An older sergeant asked as Kail walked past. "I don't know, sergeant; the old man needs to speak to me. Finish up with the horses then get the men to chow. I'll be back as soon as I can."

"Yes sir," the soldier replied while watching his young lieutenant walk off toward the command area of the camp.

"Where is the lieutenant going, Sarge?" A second soldier asked.

"The commander needs to see him. If they are transferring him, I'm gonna be upset," the sergeant lamented. "We finally got a decent officer commanding this platoon. I just might retire if they ask me to break in another new lieutenant."

The command area was dominated by a large oval-shaped tent with several battle standards flying near the entrance. The area around the tent had several smaller tents set up, along with a very large shade tarp built between some trees with tables and chairs under it. A set of wooden picket barricades were erected surrounding the command tents. They were more to keep unauthorized personnel at bay than actual protection from an assault. The only entrance to the command area and the commander's tent was guarded by several armed Nephites with others walking the inner perimeter. Kail walked up to one of the guards manning the post at the entrance. The guards saluted Kail and he responded with his own salute.

"Lieutenant Kail reporting to the chief captain as ordered."

"Wait here, sir, while I inform the chief captain of your arrival." The guard moved swiftly to the command tent as Kail looked over the other guards at the entrance. A short time later, a tall older man with salt and pepper hair exited the tent, followed by a second, well-dressed officer, as well as the original guard.

"Let him through!" The older man called out. The guards at the main entrance instantly responded to the commander's voice. Kail stepped past the guards. He saw the commander waving for him to follow, as he and the well-dressed officer walked to the shade tarp.

Kail caught up to his commander standing ramrod straight as he saluted. "Lieutenant Kail reporting as ordered, sir."

The commander returned the salute then spoke, "Lieutenant, thank you for coming so quickly. Please, have a seat."

"You only sit if it's bad news," Kail thought to himself. "Thank you, sir," he said out loud as he took a seat across the table from his boss. He tried not to show emotion but the look of concern was starting to spread across his face. "Sir," Kail continued, "If this is about a transfer, I would like to stay with my men."

"Relax, Kail. It's good news," he responded as he held up a parchment "I was given a message from the garrison commander at Zarahemla. It says that your wife went into labor. Considering how long it takes to get messages out to the frontlines….well, Kail. I think it's safe to say, congratulations— you're a father."

Kail was numb. Then gradually, he felt a wave of relief cross over him as he tried to focus on the words he just heard come from his commander. "Really? Wow, I am a father!" he said, breaking all military protocol with his question and response. The old commander smiled, letting that slide, considering Kail was both a very good soldier and now, a new father.

"Here you go son, directly off the scribes' desk," he said as he handed Kail the parchment with the message scrolled on it. Kail read it over three times, slowly mouthing the words before he looked back up. 'Sir, I…" But before he could continue, the commander held up his hand to slience him.

"I know what you are going to say Kail, and the timing could not be better. This is Captain Kalup, the army paymaster for this section." The chief captain pointed to the well-dressed officer sitting next to Kail. Kail nodded acknowledging the man. "Sir, it's a pleasure to meet you."

"Congratulations, lieutenant," Kalup responded matter-of-factly as he extended his hand to shake Kail's. "The chief captain tells me you are from this area, and you know your way around the mountains and trails that lead back to Zarahemla."

"Yes sir. I was born here and spent most of my youth earning money hunting wild game, then selling the meat and pelts in the grand market."

"Excellent!" Kalup responded and looked back at the chief captain.

"Lieutenant Kail, you and your men are being temporarily reassigned."

"Sir?"

"I need you to take a squad of your best men and escort Captain Kalup, along with what remains of his payroll chest of gold coins, back to Zarahemla. Take the safest route you can find, but avoid contact with anyone. When you deliver him to Zarahemla, send your squad back here. Then you are on a two-week leave to tend to your family. At the end of the leave, you will meet Captain Kalup and his new armed escort, then deliver them with the pay chest safely back here."

Kail blinked several times as the words "two-week leave" echoed in his mind. Catching up to the conversation, he shook his head to clear his mind. "Is there a problem, sir? Why do you need a new escort?"

Captain Kalup answered that question. "One of my escorts was in league with the Sons of Nehor. He led us into an ambush. They got the payroll chest and killed all my men. I barely made it out with my life," he lamented as his voice quivered slightly. "We need to get these taxes, which I collected from the local leaders, back to Zarahemla. Then a new payroll needs to be distributed. There are young soldiers who are going without pay. We need to go as soon as possible to help them feed their families. Do you understand, lieutenant?"

"Sir," Kail looked back at his commander with a questioning look on his face. "Don't you think the bandits will be looking for him to return? Maybe we should take more than a squad of men. If we see signs of them along the road, we could track them down and rid ourselves of these criminals."

"Now, Kail." The old leader smiled like a caring father. "While I do appreciate and respect your motivation, the captain feels, and I concur, it is more important we get the pay to the soldiers so they can feed their families than it is to hunt down the bandits. There will be time enough for that later." The old commander paused then looked Kail right in the eyes. "You don't want to be responsible for the children of those brave warriors going hungry because you wasted time looking through the vast forests for a few robbers, do you?"

Something was not right— Kail could feel it. Why would the chief captain, who is charged with keeping the peace and protecting the Nephite citizens from harm, not want to deal with criminals like the infamous Sons of Nehor? The army had policies and procedures in place to deal with an unforeseen lapse in pay. The local elders could be called in to help tend to the needs of the soldiers' families. Army rations could be used, and hunting parties organized to bring in extra food. Why would he allow a second chest of gold to be sent out when he knows there are bandits in the area? But Kail desperately wanted to go home to see his wife and newborn child. If he pushed the issue, he might be replaced by another officer and lose this chance to take leave. He was just a young, new lieutenant and did not want to make waves so he kept his questions and concerns to himself.

"No sir," he sheepishly answered.

"Very well then," Kalup quickly responded as he stood up. "Lieutenant Kail, I will see you and your squad of men here in the morning at first light. We should get an early start. We have a hard ride ahead of us." He smiled then walked back toward the command tent without asking the chief captain for permission to be dismissed.

Kail crinkled his forehead and looked at his commander in a silent question as to why he allowed that disrespect from the captain. Waving his hand to dismiss the look by Kail, the old soldier stood up and spoke as Kail quickly stood out of respect. "You have your orders, lieutenant. Go with God. You are dismissed."

"Kail stood up, saluted and said, "Yes sir, thank you sir," and instinctively he turned to leave. He took a few quick steps toward the gate but slowed his pace when that feeling he had that something was not right came over him again. He turned back to look at his commander and saw him walking briskly toward the command tent.

"It's just your nerves," he told himself then took two deep breaths to calm his emotions. The breathing did not help. With his head down, he slowly walked back to his men while searching his thoughts for the answers to his questions.

The two men stood in the shadow of the tent door watching as Kail walked out past the guards and back toward his men. "He is a good soldier," the old camp commander said. "Do you really need to kill him?"

"As long as he does not interfere, we will spare him," Kalup responded, almost hissing his words. There was a tense pause as the chief captain took a long deep breath. "Relax," Kalup continued as he slapped the old man on the back and tossed a bag full of coins into his hands. "You are part of the Sons of Nehor now. Enjoy your newfound wealth and let us worry about the details."

Kalup rushed out of the tent and walked to an open grassy area just outside the picket fence. He turned to face a thick stand of trees just west of the encampment, he then grabbed his war cloak and flung the end of it over his left shoulder. Deep inside the tree line, two figures watched Kalup, crouched in the tall grass and bushes. They were wearing dark, hooded clothing with their faces obscured from the sunlight.

"There is the signal," one of the hooded men said in a whisper. "He is saying they will leave at dawn."

The second man just smiled, exposing a row of rotted teeth, and replied, "Excellent."

THE SONS OF NEHOR

Kalup was becoming impatient watching Kail and his men make the final preparations for the mission. The sun had almost fully risen in the eastern sky. He felt they should have been moving an hour ago. "What is the holdup, Lieutenant Kail?" Kalup barked as he looked out the window of his small but ornately covered carriage.

"As soon as the water barrels are full, we will move out, sir. I apologize for the delay." Kail was trying to be calm and patient with Captain Kalup but he was becoming unbearable. Kalup was a garrison soldier and had been gifted with a political appointment to the rank of captain. He did not earn the title through hard work, living a soldier's life. His military rank had come through his personal connections while drawing in favors. He was not used to a rough field environment. Kalup was used to being pampered, not being exposed to the elements for such long periods of time. He did not understand that plans made in the field don't always work out as intended. Delaying their departure to ensure there was enough water for the trip was sound judgment, and Kail was not moving his men until he was sure they were ready.

"He's getting a little testy. I guess he does not like waiting," one of the soldiers said under his breath to the squad sergeant as they checked the ropes holding the water barrels to the pack horse. "Looks like the lieutenant is getting a little frustrated with this peacock," he continued whispering to his sergeant.

"This will be over soon enough," the sergeant responded matter-of-factly as he tightened the knots holding the barrels. "There are worse assignments than escorting one pompous fool with his chest of gold coins back to Zarahemla. Besides," he smiled to the young soldier, "when we get there, I'm sure we can find a reason for us to stay a few nights in the capital." They both smiled at each other while continuing to work.

"Are we ready?" Kail asked as he walked up to the two soldiers.

"Yes, sir," the sergeant responded. "I just checked the knots myself. We are ready to go."

Kail replied, "Excellent. Tie those pack horses to the back of the carriage. Let's get moving before he has a stroke." Kail gestured toward Captain Kalup who was still sitting inside the carriage, slapping at flies buzzing around him.

"Saddle up men. Let's move!" Kail shouted as he reached for the reins of his own horse. "Two days' hard ride will put us in Zarahemla." Kail gracefully swung up into his saddle and spurred his mount over to Captain Kalup. "We are ready to move out, sir, with your permission…?"

"Of course, lieutenant, move your men forward. Tell the driver I want to stay in the middle of the formation with my cargo."

Kail looked at his soldier that was assigned to drive the carriage. The soldier looked back, giving a nod of understanding, then rolling his eyes back to his commander. Kail winked at him. They both understood the unspoken frustration with Captain Kalup.

Kail turned to his men who had moved around him. "I will take point. We are not going to take the main road back. You two are with me. He pointed to the closest two soldiers to him. "Sergeant, you stay with the carriage." Kail continued to issue his orders. "The rest of you form up behind the carriage. Keep a sharp look out. Let's not make it any easier for the bandits." Kail moved his horse assuming his place at the front of the column. The rest of the soldiers followed him down the dirt road toward the lush mountains knowing Zarahemla was on the other side.

After two hours of steady movement, the column came to a fork in the road. Kail knew this area very well, and was happy to be back in the woods and wilds of Nephite lands. Raising his right hand up to signal the others following him to stop, Kail then moved his horse back to the carriage to speak to Kalup.

"What is the holdup, lieutenant?" Kalup asked in a bored tone.

"Sir, we have come to a fork in the road. I just wanted to show you on the map where we are and what path we will be taking."

"Don't trouble me with the details, lieutenant. Your job is to get me there as quickly as possible and in one piece.… Now, do your job," Kalup barked in a contemptuous tone while waiving Kail away from his carriage window. He then sank back inside the darkened passenger compartment.

Kail sat motionless on his horse for several seconds trying not to lose his composure. HIs disdain for Kalup was continuing to grow.

"Your orders, sir?" the sergeant asked as he rode up next to Kail.

"The road less traveled," Kail said as he moved back to his position at the head of the formation. Signaling for his men to follow, Kail spurred his horse down the right fork in the road. The carriage lurched forward with the band of soldiers quietly following their leader.

As the carriage started to move down the right fork, Kalup quietly opened a small hidden compartment in the armrest of the carriage. Inside the compartment were several stones the size of peach pits. They were painted bright white. Kalup removed one of the stones, then carefully opened a small hatch in the floorboard of the carriage. Kalup dropped the stone down through the opening. It landed in the middle of the path. One of the soldiers following the carriage looked down and saw a white painted stone lying in the roadway. Thinking it was odd, he looked more closely as his horse slowly walked past. Puzzled by its appearance and location in the middle of the path, the soldier thought it strange, but shook off the thought while continuing to move down the road. The caravan continued out of sight from the painted stone.

There the stone waited, alone in the middle of the path, until several minutes later the two hooded men who had been watching Kalup from the trees the day before, rode to the fork in the road. They spotted the stone in the right fork. One of the men dismounted his horse and picked up the stone. Then looking down on the ground he found the fresh tracks from the carriage and escort. Standing up, the man turned to look at the other hooded man still sitting on his own horse.

"They are taking the mountain pass," he spoke in an even tone.

"Good! We can hit them as they try to cross the stream where the large tree was struck by lightning," the second hooded man spoke as he took out a small patch of parchment to write a quick message. He handed the message to the first man who then walked to his own saddle bags, and removed a small wooden cage from inside the bag, covered in a cloth. Taking off the cover, he exposed a messenger pigeon to the sunlight. The small bird squawked, flapping its wings in protest to the sudden change in its environment. The man with the birdcage rolled the small parchment message tightly and stuffed it inside a tiny metal tube attached to the pigeon's leg. Removing it from the cage, he took the bird in both hand. Holding it out in front of him, he tossed the bird into the air, watching it circle several times in order to orientate itself with the sun and the surroundings. The bird then took off like a stone shot from a sling. The men watched it fly away until they lost sight of the bird as it flew over the trees.

"The others will get the message and be ready for them at the crossing in the morning," the man still sitting on the horse spoke with no emotion.

"What now?" the second man who launched the bird asked.

"We follow the carriage and enjoy the show." He smiled a wicked smile.

The two men then continued their slow progress down the right side path following Kail, his men, and the large chest of Nephite gold.

Kail and his men camped at a spot he knew, passing a restless night. Kail was feeling more confident with each mile travelled, but couldn't shake his original feeling of unease. The morning air was clear and cool. Kail was raised in the lowlands but never got used to the cool of the mountains. It always fascinated him when he was hunting as a young man how on some mornings, he could see his breath as he talked while around the fire or when he exhaled. This morning was no exception. Kail enjoyed a bit of mental release as he stood motionless next to the newly lit fire, warming his body and breathing in and out while watching long bands of steam come from his mouth. Around him, his soldiers were rolling up their sleeping mats, making the final preparations to continue their journey to Zarahemla.

Kail learned a trick from an old sergeant when he first started out as a young soldier. "Everyone takes their turn on watch, lieutenant," the old sergeant counseled. "Because you are in charge, you make the schedule. You can pick your time for watch. I would recommend you take the last watch of the night before everyone gets up. That way, you can clean yourself and roll up your sleeping mat while everyone else sleeps. Then you will be up, ready to supervise and lead, when the rest of the troops are waking up." Kail had always followed this advice, and it had helped to make him a successful leader in the field. This morning was no different.

He was up and warmed by the fire before anyone else was awake.

"Good morning, lieutenant," Captain Kalup burped as he drained his soup from a metal cup. The sudden arrival of Kalup caught Kail off guard. He was a bit startled by his presence and jumped slightly.

"Sorry, I did not mean to scare you," Kalup said with a mocking tone in his voice.

"No sir, you caught me thinking of home," Kail quipped with a hint of shame at allowing a soft garrison soldier to sneak up on him. The two stood looking at each other for several seconds as Kalup waited for Kail to do something. Kail couldn't hide the puzzlement on his face. Finally, Kalup broke the moment.

"I guess you don't salute superior officers in the morning where you are from?" Kalup said sarcastically.

"Sir, you don't salute any officers in the field," Kail responded back with a bit of contempt of his own in his voice. "If the enemy is watching, they will know who the ranking officers are and will try to kill them first if they attack." Some of the other soldiers snickered and looked away. This was common knowledge among any combat soldier. Kalup was neither a good soldier nor experienced in combat and he knew it. But it was the look in Kail's eye that gave Kalup reason to feel ashamed. Kail narrowly looked at him as if to say, *Pathetic, even a new soldier fresh from basic training should know that. Why don't you?"*

Kalup stood motionless, blinking several times, trying to come up with a response to the correction Kail just gave him. He knew Kail was right and he felt embarrassed. The truth was, Kalup was not a field soldier and Kail was. Of course, Kalup felt he did not belong among this band of low-ranking rabble. He was from a very rich family, with power and influence, and it was beneath him to sleep outside and eat food cooked over a campfire. He was embarrassed he had been corrected in front of the men by Kail, concerning something so basic. Failing to find the right words for a reply, Kalup frowned, turned and walked back to his carriage, muttering to himself.

As he walked away, the soldier who was assigned to drive the carriage moved up next to Kail.

"Don't worry, sir," he said in a quiet tone. "He's just grumpy and his backside is probably a bit sore from the ride yesterday....for some reason." He chuckled as he continued to speak, "I hit...I mean the wagon ran over every pothole and bump in the road on the trail yesterday, and I have a strange feeling it will do the same today."

Kail snickered under his breath then gave the soldier an *"I know nothing about it, but I approve"* glance.

Kalup held his emotions in check until he was safely back inside the carriage and out of view from the rest of the squad. "Stupid Kail..." he pouted like a spoiled child, as he sat down on the bench seat. "We are far from the enemy lines and in no danger!" he whispered loudly as he angrily tossed a small pillow across the inside of the covered carriage. "He should have saluted me; I'm a captain. He is supposed to salute me. He did that on purpose. He is trying to humiliate me and gain favor with his men. Well, I will show him," Kalup sat plotting in his mind. Now that he was working for the Sons of Nehor and was so close to becoming a full-fledged member of that secret criminal group, he had scores to settle and Kail just earned a spot at the top of the list. "We will see who gets the last laugh," he whispered as he smiled and thought about revenge. "The Sons should hit the caravan sometime today. Then we will see how brave a soldier you really are." Laughing to himself, he flung open the curtain covering the side window of the carriage. "Lieutenant Kail!" he barked. "I want this caravan moving right away. That's an order!" He pulled himself back inside and jerked the curtains closed. Sitting back in the seat he smiled again to himself and took a congratulatory sip of his soup.

"Let's go, boys." Kail said, just out of earshot. "One more hard day's ride and we're done with him." Kail clapped his hands to get the soldiers moving. The squad quickly finished breakfast, saddled their horses and were ready to begin the last leg of their journey.

Several hundred yards away, on the top of a rocky rise overlooking the mountain road and the small clearing where Kail and his squad were camped, the two hooded figures who were following the caravan lay prone behind a pile of rocks. One of the men was sleeping face up, wrapped in a light blanket and softly snoring. The second man was looking down at the camp, watching the Nephite soldiers prepare for travel.

The one, who was watching nudged the sleeping man. "They are getting ready to move." Then he took a big bite from a hunk of jerky.

Snorting and rubbing his face, the sleeping man came back to life and looked over the rocks hiding them from view.

"It's about time," he groaned. "Remind me to thank Kalup for making us sleep on the rocks, out in the cold air, without a fire or hot food."

"Be patient. When we get our hands on that chest of gold coins, you will be sleeping on a feather bed, served food by lovely maids," the man chewing a mouthful of jerky responded. "As far as Captain Kalup is concerned, the boss likes him, so as long as he is useful to the brotherhood, he is not to be touched."

"The boss may like him, but some of us don't appreciate his attitude."

"He is a peacock, no argument there, but… he did deliver two chests full of gold, just like he promised," the first spy spoke as he pointed down to the carriage as it started to move down the dirt path with Kail and his men. "Let's saddle up. They will be at the ambush point in two hours."

The two men grabbed what meager belongings they had with them and slunk out of sight back down the far side of the hill where they had tethered their horses.

Kail and his men had been on the road for a while when Kail noticed something strange about Kalup. He had been sitting in his carriage not doing or saying anything for the entire morning, then quickly, he began acting very nervous. Kalup kept poking his head out of the windows of the carriage, as if looking for something. He asked Kail, two separate times, if Kail had taken a different path or changed the route.

"No, sir. We are still on the same mountain path we have been on all morning long," Kail responded a bit sarcastically. There was a pause as Kail watched Kalup shift in his seat and again look out of the window. "You seem nervous, captain. Is everything ok?"

"Lieutenant Kail, you need to worry about your own skin," Kalup curtly snapped back. Kalup suddenly realized he might have just said too much and quickly sank back inside the dark recesses of the covered carriage.

Hmmm, that was odd, Kail thought to himself. He played the scene over and over in his mind as he tried to make sense of what just happened. As he was working it out in his mind, one of his men riding point came up to Kail and said. "Sir, there is a stream ahead we are going to need to cross."

Putting Kalup's odd behavior in the back of his mind, Kail ordered, "Show me," as he galloped off with his scout.

As the two soldiers rounded the bend in the path, they came to the edge of a wide but shallow and slow-moving stream.

"Look at that," Kail pointed at the massive tree nearby that had been split right down the middle with charred bark on both sides. "Lightning?"

he asked the other soldier with him.

"Yes, sir, that would be my guess."

"That's a shame; it was a really big tree. It looks like that tree was there long before Father Lehi crossed the ocean." Kail sat and examined the dead tree as the carriage and the rest of his squad of soldiers rode up to him.

"Your orders, sir?" The sergeant asked out of formality. He already knew the answer. Kail was a by-the-book kind of soldier and this was a standard crossing. He knew what Kail was going to say before he said it.

"Let's do this by the numbers, sergeant. Take one man, check the depth of the stream to see if it's crossable. Scout the other side and then report. The rest of you, take up a perimeter around the wagon."

"Yes, sir," the good sergeant responded with a gleam in his eye. He knew deep down that being predictable is not always a bad thing when you are a competent and well-trained soldier like Lieutenant Kail of the Zarahemla legion.

Taking one of the other soldiers with him, the sergeant quickly guided his horse across the shallow stream. "This is a good spot to cross, lieutenant," he hollered back after stopping mid-stream and carefully examining the streambed.

"Okay, check the other side!" Kail shouted back. The sergeant nodded and spurred his horse toward the far bank. Reaching the other side, the two soldiers walked out of the stream and followed the bend in the road. As they continued down the wide dirt path and around the corner, they were quickly out of Kail's view, blocked by the thick vegetation. Kail sat motionless on his horse for several seconds, waiting for the scouts to return. The heat of the day was starting to bear down on the back of his neck, and because they were so close to the water, there were small bugs that were attracted to his skin. Kail removed his helmet to wipe the sweat out of his eyes and brush away a pesky fly that kept trying to land on his face. With his helmet off, Kail was now able to hear all the birds in the trees and the frogs croaking down by the water. As he sat enjoying nature's grandeur, the symphony of sounds suddenly stopped. There were no animal noises coming from the forest. No buzzing of insects or birds chirping. Everything became quiet and it quickly made him uneasy. Something was also spooking his horse. His mount could tell something was wrong and started to shift its weight and flick its ears back and forth while neighing loudly.

"Whoa boy…easy," Kail reassured his horse while patting it on the side of its neck. The other horses began to act spooked, as well. They all knew something was very wrong.

With a loud swoosh, a large black arrow came flying from the brush near the water's edge. The arrow struck the carriage driver in the center of his chest, pinning his body against the front wall of the carriage. With blood spurting from the wound and his mouth, the driver grasped at the arrow shaft sticking out of his body. But it was no use; he slumped forward onto the arrow, dead in a matter of seconds. Kail was too schocked to move for a moment and jerked the reins of his horse to spin him around.

"Ambush!" Kail shouted but it was too late. Two more arrows came screaming in from the treeline, striking the two soldiers positioned at the rear of the carriage, knocking them both off their horses. Kail pulled his sword and spurred his horse toward the carriage. "Captain Kalup!" Kail yelled trying to get Kalup's attention. Kail felt an arrow go streaking past his face as he moved up next to the carriage. The two remaining soldiers still with Kail were also moving toward the carriage when a shout went up from the trees. Several hooded men, all bearing weapons, burst from the shadows toward Kail and his men. Kail quickly looked across the wide stream, hoping his sergeant was aware of the ambush and was returning to help defend the lives of his soldiers. All he saw was a lone hooded man standing on the far bank of the stream, holding the reins of the two horses belonging to his sergeant and the scout who had gone with him.

"Defend the wagon!" Kail shouted to his two remaining soldiers. The Nephite soldiers closed the distance between each other and positioned themselves for a defiant last stand.

Six hooded men in dark clothing approached the carriage in a semi-circle with their weapons out. They were slowly closing the distance when Kail challenged them, pointing his sword. "Are you prepared to die for a few gold coins? Because I am prepared to kill you for them!"

The six men stopped advancing and held their ground. Thinking he had just gained a few seconds Kail banged on the carriage wall with the hilt of his sword. "Captain Kalup, are you okay?"

Kalup appeared in the window of the carriage. "Just do what they ask, lieutenant."

"They haven't asked anything, sir. They just killed my men," Kail responded.

"I mean, when they ask for the money, just give it to them." Kalup replied dismissively. He smiled nervously and sank back inside the carriage.

Kail knew instantly he had been set up and Kalup was in on it. His men were dead because this coward loved money more than the lives of his fellow Nephites. Cursing out loud, Kail turned back to his men. "Stand your ground!" he ordered.

"No one else needs to die, lieutenant." The voice came from the bushes behind the carriage. The two men who had followed the squad from their base camp walked out from behind the carriage along with two more hooded men who both had black arrows nocked in thier longbows. The spokesman for the attackers paused and waved his hand at the men surrounding them. "We are the Sons of Nehor and we only want the gold. Give it over and you and your men can go free."

"Five of my men are dead because of you and that cursed chest of gold. What about them? Are they free to go?" Kail barked back, his horse stomping and snorting at his tension. "You murdered them for money. You will answer for what you have done!"

"Yes, I had those men killed, and it was for the gold." The hooded man nodded slightly and the two archers quickly aimed and loosed their large black arrows at the two remaining Nephite guards. The arrows found their marks and both soldiers were struck mid-chest. Mortally wounded, both men fell off their horses and landed hard on the road.

'No!" Kail screamed as he saw the last of his men die.

"All I want is the chest of gold, lieutenant. Move out of the way and you will survive this." The leader spoke in a even, dangerous tone as the two archers loaded more arrows. The hooded men on the ground repositioned themselves closer to Kail.

There is no way I am getting out of this alive, Kail thought to himself. *I am a witness to their crimes and I know Kalup is involved.* Kail spun his horse around in a full circle to assess his position. "Surrounded," he whispered. *Forgive me, my darling wife*, Kail prayed as he asked the universe to beg his wife's forgiveness for refusing to comply with these robbers, resisting evil to his last heartbeat. Taking a deep breath Kail resolved to fight his way out of the trap and try to make it to Zarahemla to find help. "Kalup, you coward, this is far from over!" Kail shouted, then spurring his horse hard in the flanks, causing the animal to rise up

on its hind legs. Before Kail could make a move to try to fight his way free, Kalup opened the carriage door and struck Kail on the back of his helmet with a wooden club. Kail felt the impact and almost instantly lost consciousness. Falling face-first off his horse, Kail hit the ground completely helpless.

"It's okay now…I got him." Kalup smiled as he waved the club in the air to show the bandits. There was no reaction from the bandits, Kalup sat back down, feeling a bit embarrassed for trying to gain their approval. Dropping the club on the floorboard of the covered buggy, he swung the carriage door all the way open and tried to pull out the large money chest. It was too heavy for Kalup to move easily. He grunted and strained as he tried to get it out. As he struggled with the chest, the bandit leader and his henchman walked up to Kail, still unconscious and lying at the feet of his horse.

"This is a good horse," the hooded leader said as he inspected the animal. The henchman bent down to Kail's body and removed his satchel and personal coin purse. After kicking away Kail's sword and taking his knife out of his weapons belt, the henchman checked to see if Kail was still breathing.

"Is he alive?" the leader asked as he rummaged through Kail's saddle bags.

"Yes, he still breathes," the henchman said before looking up at Kalup. "Why did you not just kill him?"

Kalup blinked several times, swallowing hard. Kalup knew that deep inside his soul he was a coward. He needed to establish dominance with these ruffians before they turned on him. All he had ever done, up to this point in his life, was talk about how strong and courageous he was. He knew he was not a warrior or even a good man, but he was a captain in the Nephite army and these bandits did not know he gained that rank through bribes and favors. Letting them assume he was a warrior was fine with him. Trying to sound confident, he cleared his throat, "You're the hired thugs, not me. If you had done your job right the first time this would not have happened." Kalup jumped out of the carriage and with all the arrogance he could summon, walked past the bandits. "There is your gold. Tell your masters that I have delivered as promised."

"Where are you going?" the bandit leader asked as Kalup walked past him moving toward one of the pack horses tied behind the carriage.

"I'm hungry, I want to eat," Kalup replied with even more arrogance.

Kalup untied a sack from the bundle of items strapped to the pack horse and reached inside. Pulling out a large apple, Kalup chomped down and chewed as he walked back past several of the hooded men. "Go on," Kalup mumbled with a mouth full of apple, gesturing with his hand back toward the carriage. "Get your gold. I have things to do."

Every bandit turned to look at the leader who was still standing next to Kail's horse. They could all feel the contempt and arrogance coming from the Nephite soldier and they all wanted to kill him for it. The leader made eye contact with his men and nodded toward the covered wagon, silently telling his men to fetch the gold and whatever they wanted to steal from the dead Nephites.

"What are we going to do with this peacock?" the robber who took Kail's things whispered to the leader.

"Leave him to me," was all the hooded man said.

The two bandits shared a wicked smiled as they both contemplated the plans they had, not only for Kalup but for all Nephites, if they did not comply with the Sons of Nehor and the wishes of their secret society.

"Okay boys… let's get the swag," the henchman called out to the other hooded bandits. A cheer went up from the robbers and they moved toward the carriage to gather up the stolen gold. In his excitement, one of the robbers moved past Kail, who was still unconscious on the ground and struck Kail's back with his foot. The jarring bump from the robber quickly brought Kail out of his unconscious state and he opened his eyes. Keeping himself still, Kail tried to assess the situation and looked around as best he could without moving his head too much. Wincing in pain from the blow to the back of his head, Kail realized all of the bandits were looking inside the carriage and no one was watching him. He saw his horse standing a few yards away. *If I'm going to escape, it's now or never*, he thought as he turned his head a little more to look around again and ensure there were no bandits watching over him. Convinced he was unguarded, Kail slowly and carefully curled his legs up to his chest and gently moved to his knees. Trying to stay low, and not draw attention, Kail got to his feet and started to carefully move toward his horse. He was two steps away from his mount when Kalup looked up and saw Kail moving toward his horse.

"Hey…hey, he is escaping!" he shouted with his mouth still full of apple as he ran toward Kail, fumbling with his sword.

Kail quickly jumped up on his horse and grabbed the reins. Pulling hard on the left rein. Staying low in the saddle, Kail spun the animal around and kicked hard into its ribs. The robbers all dropped what they were holding and ran after Kail, shouting and screaming as his horse leaped toward the stream bed.

"Get your bows. Shoot him!" the bandit leader ordered as he grabbed the two archers pushing them toward where they had left their weapons. The two hooded archers stopped trying to chase down Kail and ran back to where they left their bows. Kalup, still holding his half eaten apple, ran to the edge of the stream and tried to get in between Kail and his escape route. Waving his sword in the air and shouting, "Stop!" Kalup shouted, hardly presenting a difficult obstacle. Kail was moving at a full gallop when he reached Kalup. He kicked Kalup square in the face with the heel of his sandal as he rode by. Kalup's nose exploded from the impact of Kail's foot and blood spattered over his face. Flipping backward from the impact, Kalup did a complete reverse somersault, landing in the shallow water and mud of the stream. Kail's horse did not miss a beat hitting the water at a full gallop, crossing the shallow part of the stream in several strides. Kail smiled to himself as he looked back and saw his pursuers had stopped when they reached the water. "Get around the bend in the road and we will be safe," he said to his faithful horse.

The two archers reached their bows and spun around to face Kail as he fled across the water. Loading their weapons, they judged the distance and speed that Kail was traveling, as well as the flight time for the arrows. Both men adjusted their aim so the arrows would strike where they thought Kail would be, not where he was. They only had time for one shot each. After adjusting their aim, they both let their arrows fly.

Kail was almost at the bend in the road and was tucked down low behind his horse as it charged forward at breakneck speed. His face was rigid with determination and his eyes were locked on his one goal: to get back to Zarahemla and tell his chain of command of Kalup's murderous treason.

The large black arrow struck Kail in the center of his back, right between his shoulder blades. The impact of the arrow and the sudden blinding pain caused Kail to let go of the reins and lurch forward in his saddle, nearly falling off the galloping horse. At the last possible second, Kail reached out and gripped the horse's mane with both hands and held on as tightly as he could. The well-trained horse felt the shift in Kail's weight and the tensions on the reins loosen. Sensing that something was

42

wrong with his master, the horse quickly slowed down to a walk. Kail struggled against the pain and internal damage caused by the arrow in his back as he pushed and twisted to regain his proper seating in the saddle. Gasping for air Kail grabbed the reins again and urged his horse forward. "Got to keep moving," he whispered with real agony in his voice. Kail knew he was just a few hours away from Zarahemla and the bandits would be pursuing him. "Come on, boy," Kail said as he clicked his mouth and slapped the reins down. "Just get me home," he ordered his faithful horse. Kail could taste the blood in his mouth and felt the struggle for his body to get enough air in his lungs. Kail knew deep down he was a dead man and it was just a matter of time now before either the arrow or the bandits finished the job. As the horse loped on, the pain in his back intensified his resolve to survive long enough to see justice done.

Back at the stream, Kalup rolled out of the mud and groaned as he brought his hands up to his injured face. "My nose!" he shrieked, as the bandit leader walked up to him with a horse in tow.

"You should have killed him when you had the chance," the hooded man said matter-of-factly as he handed the reins of the horse to Kalup.

"What is this?" Kalup asked as he spat blood on the muddy ground and looked up at the robber.

"Go after him and finish the job."

"Why me?" Kalup whined as he gestured to his broken nose as if to say he was too injured to chase after Kail.

"Because he has seen us and can expose our entire brotherhood," the dark-spirited leader hissed as he walked around Kalup, who was still sitting in the mud and shallow water. "Now get up and go after him!" he barked as he kicked Kalup in the small of his back.

Instinctively, Kalup jumped up and turned to face the robber. "Who do you think—" Kalup's voice was caught in mid-sentence as the bandit leader grabbed him by the throat with his right hand and locked his fingers around Kalup's windpipe. Kalup's eyes went wide and he gasped and grabbed at the bandit's arm with both of his hands. Squeezing tightly and pulling Kalup close to him he spoke with utter contempt, "Think about it, that Nephite has seen us and knows who you are. If he makes it back to Zarahemla alive, he will tell everyone. Either you kill him and keep our brotherhood a secret or I will kill you both to keep our secret. Do you understand?"

Kalup tried to answer but no air was escaping. He could only gag and spout a gurgled "Yes."

Releasing his grip and pushing Kalup down into the water, the dark leader turned and walked back toward the carriage. Stopping a few feet away, he turned to his trusted henchman who was standing and watching. "Go with him to make sure the job is done. No more mistakes, no more weak links," he ordered. The two robbers made eye contact and the subordinate nodded to his master, then turned to fetch a second horse.

Kalup moaned under his breath while pulling himself up and out of the shallow, muddy water. The pain from his broken nose was intensified as the blood that was cut off from the choking grasp around his neck came rushing back to the injury. This whole experience was the most intense thing he had ever dealt with. He could feel his eyes tearing up. There was fresh blood all over his face and tunic. Struggling to get to his feet, Kalup started to get the feeling he had made a terrible choice by betraying his country and taking up with these criminals. But he knew there was no turning back now. Kail knew Kalup was in league with the Sons of Nehor, and he was galloping toward Zarahemla to tell everyone about the murderous ambush and that Kalup had betrayed the Nephite people. "I have no choice now," Kalup thought out loud and breathed deeply when he realized he would need to kill Kail to keep his secrets. Finally on his feet, he walked out of the muddy shallows and into the stream until he was waist deep in the lazy flowing water. The cool refreshing feeling of the water helped him somewhat recover as he washed the mud and blood off of his face and hands.

"Get on the horse, Kalup," the henchman barked as he dropped the reins down on Kalup's head.

"It's Captain Kalup," Kalup replied curtly while brushing the reins off his head and looking up at the bandit.

"No. Not anymore— now you are just a murderer, like the rest of us." The bandit smiled a rotten, toothless smile. "Now move!" he barked, spurring his mount forward toward the opposite side of the stream.

CHAPTER FOUR

TROUBLE AT THE CROSSROADS

Rachael was pacing back and forth in front of the fireplace, in the great hall of the ranch house. It was very early in the morning but the house was alive with activity. Today was the day young master Teancum was to be blessed by one of the priests at the temple in Zarahemla. Going over her list of tasks in her mind, Rachael reflected on what she had done so far to make her baby ready for the short but momentous trip to the city. Checking her bag she mumbled, "Okay, he has been fed and changed, I have his blankets, changing rags, and the aloe for his skin." She picked up a small object from one of the chairs, "and the rattle from your grandfather," she continued as she shook the small toy in front of the young child. Teancum was awake and lying quietly, swaddled in a large blanket on top of a pillow on the floor.

"Rachael?" Her mother called out as she entered the hall, "do you want to carry Teancum or use this cradle board?" She handed Rachael a small bundle that resembled a pack with a leather wrap and leather bindings laced across it.

"Do you think he is big enough to be in there?" Rachael asked while looking at the baby carrier.

"Of course dear, let me show you." Saria put the baby carrier on the floor next to young Teancum.

"The secret is stuffing the bottom with a blanket," she said as she looked back up at Rachael, then grabbed a blanket out of the bag, "like this."

Saria expertly placed the blanket in the bottom portion of the cradle board, then picked up Teancum. "Now, he will be all cozy and warm," she said in a soft, happy voice as she smiled at Teancum and gently laid him inside the large leather folds. Quickly rearranging him in his swaddling blanket, she then overlaid the leather wraps and laced up the bindings. "There... he is all set. Now you can walk through the city with both arms free." Saria instructed Rachael on how to put the cradle board on her back just like a backpack, without disturbing the baby. Ensuring the straps were secure around Rachael's shoulders and inspecting the final product, Saria gasped as she looked at Teancum. "He is just an angel. With all this excitement and getting ready for his first trip to Zarahemla, our little prince has fallen asleep." Saria softly kissed Teancum's little forehead and then gently spun Rachael around. Locking eyes and passing love between them, as only a mother and daughter could, the two most important women in Teancum's life smiled at each other. In the background, Pilio's voice could be heard telling them the carriage was ready. Saria kissed Rachael on her forehead.

"I wish Kail were here," Rachael whispered with moist eyes.

"I know you do, dear. I'm sure he misses you both and he will be here just as soon as he can," Saria responded in a gentle and comforting tone.

"Saria, please, we have an appointment with the priest at the temple and we cannot be late," Pilio said as he stuck his head into the hall, beckoning his wife and daughter to hurry along.

"Coming, my dear husband." Saria's tone was playfully condescending, and it made Rachel laugh. Pilio just shook his head then moved back toward the main entrance to the house.

Stepping out into the morning sunlight, Rachael realized this was the first time she had left the ranch property, or even spent any real time outside since the birth of Teancum. Shading her eyes from the sun, she moved with Teancum strapped to her back, through the open courtyard toward the waiting carriage.

Tum was waiting at the side door to the large carriage next to a small wooden step. "My ladies," he spoke in his monotone manner "would you care for the top cover on the carriage?" Tum extended his hand to assist both Saria and Rachael into the seats of the carriage.

"I think the sunlight and fresh air would do us both a bit of good, don't you agree mother?" Rachael spoke as she removed her baby carrier gently setting it right next to her on the seat.

"Yes...yes I do. Thank you, but no Tum, we shall keep it uncovered for now," came Saria's reply.

"As you wish, my lady." Tum turned to a second wagon behind the carriage and pointed. "I shall be in the second wagon if you need me." Looking around, Saria quickly noticed that Pilio was not with them.

"Tum, where is Lord Pilio?"

"My lady, he is saddling his horse," he responded in a slightly disapproving tone while clearing his throat.

"Tum, I thought we agreed with the doctor to limit his riding. He is not getting any younger."

"Yes, Lady Saria, that is what the doctor suggested, but…."

His words were cut short as Pilio rode up next to the carriage on a large, spirited black stallion. "Easy boy," Pilio said with a happy voice as he tried to rein in the mount, trying to get him to stop moving. "A fine morning for a good ride," he continued while smiling at his wife and struggling to control the animal. Her frown told him she was not pleased.

"Pilio!" she half-shouted. "If you're going to defy the doctor's orders and all good judgment, at least ride your older walking horse, the quiet, old painted mare!"

"This one could use a good walk. Besides, he and I need to work out a few things along the way." Pilio smiled as the horse turned completely around with him jerking on the reins. That's when Saria saw Pilio's large sword strapped to his side.

"And why do you carry your sword?" she asked. "Are we going to the temple for your grandchild's blessing or to war?"

"What kind of a man cannot and is not ready to defend his family? Off we go!" Pilio bellowed as he kicked the excited horse in the ribs and took off down the gravel courtyard path toward the main road like a stone from a sling.

"That man!" Saria gasped out of frustration, shaking her head. "Tum, let's be off before that old fool hurts himself again."

"Yes, madam," Tum quickly replied as he stepped back from the carriage, signaling for the rest of the attending servants to finish their tasks. Tum was not about to take sides between the master and the lady of the house.

There was a crack of a whip and the party was off as both wagons moved down the gravel road toward Zarahemla and the temple of God.

Kail was slumped over the saddle and barely alive. The large black arrow was still sticking from his back, blood drenched his clothing and ran down both arms. His horse had slowed to a walk as rider and mount emerged from the tree-covered trail, onto open ground. The horse continued for several more steps while Kail desperately clung to the animal's mane to keep from falling off. Half-delirious, Kail was unsure how long he had been riding or exactly where he was. He was sure he had lost consciousness at one point, and he fought against the lightning bolts of pain accross his back as he tried to lift his head to account for his location.

"Good boy," he whispered faintly as he patted the neck of his horse. Following instincts, the horse had taken Kail to a crossroads, then stopped to wait for his master to tell him which road to take. Kail gently looked around and found he was in the intersection of the mountain trail and the main merchant road that leads to Zarahemla. With a weak tug, Kail pulled on the right reign and the horse began to move down the wide and well-maintained road. "Not far," Kail whispered as he urged his horse to keep going. *Two more miles, soldier*, Kail spoke to himself in his mind. *Hold it together for two more miles.*

Not long after he turned onto the main road, the sounds of the hooves clapping the ground at a full gallop could be heard echoing across the open ground from behind Kail. "They found me," he gasped and reached for his belt in a fruitless attempt to grasp his missing sword.

"Soldier!" Pilio called out from behind as he pulled up on the reins of his running horse next to Kail. "You are wounded. Let me help you." Pilio was shocked at seeing an injured man on the road, so close to the city. His mind raced to make sense of what he had just came upon.

In his delirium, Kail was sure his mind was playing tricks on him. The voice calling out to him was his wife's father, but in the fog of pain and blood loss Kail was unsure. "Father Pilio?" He questioned with a breathy gasp.

"Gracious heavens!" Pilio exclaimed as he realized who the wounded man before him was. Jumping from his horse, Pilio ran to Kail's side and grabbed the reins to control Kail's horse. "What happened boy....who did this to you?"

Kalup and the dark hooded bandit reached the edge of the clearing and stopped. They could just make out Kail with the arrow in his back on the road before them.

"Let's finish this," Kalup said under his breath. He starteded to move forward. "Wait." the bandit put out his hand and graped Kalup's tunic. Kalup stopped and impatiently looked back at the bandit who had a hold of him. There was an awkward pause as Kalup waited for a response from the bandit. The bandit only stared out ahead and held very still for several seconds then pointed across the open ground toward the distant sounds of a galloping horse. "We are not alone," he hissed.

Scanning the area in front of him, Kalup saw Pilio galloping along the main road, coming to a stop next to Kail. Kalup turned back to the bandit with a question in his eyes. "Kill them both. Now!" was all the bandit said.

With darkness and contempt in his eyes, Kalup spurred his horse forward to kill two innocent men in the name of greed and power.

"Easy, lad, easy." Pilio gently helped Kail down laying him on his side.

Kail knew they were in danger and tried to get the warning words out but the pain of being moved was too much. "Am...bush," he managed to push past his teeth as he choked on some blood, pointing to the faraway tree line. Pilio looked in the direction he was pointing. Scanning the trees Pilio saw Kalup emerge on his galloping horse heading directly towards them.

Pilio could see the approaching rider wore the armor of a Nephite army officer. "It's okay Kail, it's just another Nephite soldier coming this way. You are safe." Pilio moved back to his own horse and quickly pulled the saddle off. Grabbing the blanket cover and his saddle bags, he quickly moved back to Kail. Pilio covered the lower half of Kail's body with the blanket and rested his head on the saddle bags. "Rachael is right behind me with a wagon. We will get you into the city in no time and get you fixed up. Don't you worry."

Hearing that his wife was close and knowing the great danger they were in, Kail tried to get up, but his body convulsed in pain. "Stay still boy!" Pilio ordered as he held Kail down. Pilio looked back up to see Kalup riding closer.

"Help, over here!" Pilio called out, thinking that Kalup just happened to ride by and that he could be trusted and helpful. Pilio was so focused on Kail's condition, he did not notice Kalup's horse was winded and that Kalup had came from the same direction Kail did.

Realizing the old man helping Kail did not know about the events at the river crossing, Kalup feigned surprise at the scene. "I am Captain Kalup of the Zarahemla legion. What has happened here?" He asked as he stopped his horse next to the two men.

"He is wounded, he said there was an ambush." Pilio's voice was shaking. "Please help me…he is my son-in-law and his family is in that wagon." Pilio pointed back behind him to a distant wagon coming down the main road.

That's just great! Kalup yelled in his mind. *More witnesses. I need to do this quickly and get away before the wagon arrives.* Kalup slid off his horse and walked toward Pilio. "Of course, I will help you, fetch your horse." Kalup motioned to Pilio to turn around and get his own horse. Pilio turned away from Kalup and started to move toward his mount. He took about three steps and stopped, *Wait, why do I need my horse?* As he started to turn back, Kalup struck him in the head with a large rock he'd found lining the roadway. Pilio dropped to the ground, unconscious.

"No!" Kail cried out faintly as he watched his beloved father-in law fall to the ground.

"Had to be the big bad soldier boy hero…didn't you?" Kalup challenged as he turned back to Kail who was trying to get up. "All you had to do was give up the money… Was it worth all of this?" Kalup paused. *The wagon is getting closer*, he thought as he looked back over his shoulder. "Maybe I will let your family live…or maybe I will sell them as slaves to the Lamanites. No matter— enjoy your last breath of mortal air, my friend." Kalup drew out his short sword and raised it up over his head as he stood over Kail's wounded body. Drawing in a deep breath and with fire in his eyes, Kalup spat, "I pledge eternal loyalty to the Sons of Nehor."

Pilio was trying to regain consciousness when he heard Kalup shout his bold oath. Instantly he was snapped back into reality and reacted out of pure instinct. Rising to his knee, Pilio pulled out his sword and in one motion slashed with all of his might at Kalup's legs. The tip of the sharp blade easily cut deep wounds across the back of both of Kalup's legs. The sudden intense pain and loss of balance caused him to drop his blade and sent Kalup tumbling to the ground crying out in agony. Pilio, his own head bleeding profusely from the wound caused by Kalup's rock, tried to stand but was still too weak. All three men were lying on the ground, suffering from their own injuries, each one wanting to kill another, but no one was able to get up and finish the job. The first one to stand would be the victor.

"What is that, mother?" Rachael squinted under the bright sunlight as she shaded her eyes with her hand trying to see what was going on at the crossroads. Saria was holding little Teancum when she looked up to see what Rachael was looking at. "I don't know. Driver, can you see there…is someone shouting?"

"I'm sorry, ma'am, but my eyes are bad in bright light," he replied.

"Tum has excellent vision….Tum!" Rachael called out as she turned to the wagon behind her and pointed. Tum stood up on his seat to gaze over the first wagon. "It's Master Pilio's horse, but I can't see him!" He shouted back with concern in his voice.

Panic shot through Saria's mind. "Driver, go faster!" She ordered and secured Teancum back into his cradle board. The teamster slapped the reins down hard on the backs of the draft horses pulling the carriage and shouted, "Yah!" Everyone in the wagon lurched back as the horses raced ahead. In less than a minute they reached the crossroads.

The dark-hooded bandit had seen the whole scene play out from his place hidden in the trees. He took in a long breath of air and let it out in frustration. He watched with disgust as Kalup was bested by an old man while he was trying to kill Kail. Now, as two more wagons full of witnesses approached the scene, the bandit knew he had to take matters into his own hands. "If you want something done right…" he whispered to himself. Guiding his horse to the right, he got off the trail and skirted the tree line to avoid detection.

"Pilio!" Saria shouted as she leaped from her still moving wagon. Showing the athletic ability of a woman half her age, Saria ran past the horses to her injured husband. Pilio was just getting to his feet when Saria arrived at his side. "Pilio, my husband…did you fall?" She questioned with tears in her eyes and reaching out to help him find his balance.

"Stay back, woman!" Pilio, his eyes burning with rage, pushed her away and barked with an authority in his voice that Saria had not heard for decades. "This man attacked me!" Pilio snarled as he wiped blood from his eyes and held up his sword and moved toward Kalup. Kalup was lying on his side, whimpering like a beaten dog, while desperately trying to stop the blood flowing from his wounded legs. Holding out one of his blood-covered hands, Kalup begged for his life. "Please, don't kill me!" He begged. "I was blackmailed by the Sons of Nehor!" Kalup sheepishly pointed toward the wood line. "They are watching!" Pilio's blood ran cold at Kalup's warning. He turned toward the unseen enemy in the trees and instantly knew they were all in mortal danger.

"Pilio...?" Saria called out. She knew her husband well enough to know his mannerisms and moods. She could tell that in a heartbeat he had changed from outraged to frightened. "What is happening?"

Tum was next by his side, followed by the wagon drivers who were holding clubs. Tum was holding a small dagger and trying to make sense of the scene before him. "Master Pilio, you are injured!" Tum's voice was soft but demanding. "What has happened here?"

Pilio's mind was racing; he was trying to process all that had just happened. "Where is Rachael?" He whispered.

"She remained in the wagon with master Teancum," Tum answered with a questioning tone while pointing back behind him.

Pilio shouted past Saria and Tum. "Rachael, bring water and a blanket!" Rachael handed Teancum to a nursemaid and moved to fetch the requested items. He turned to Saria and pointed, "It's Kail!" Saria gasped, holding her hands to her mouth as she gazed down at Kail's wounds.

"We are in danger here and must move quickly," he said. The military leader in him was coming back now. "Saria, help Rachael tend to Kail. Tum, get a rope and bind that man's hands," he said, pointing to Kalup. He pointed to the two wagon drivers, "You help Tum, and you fetch all the horses," he ordered. "We need to get everyone on the wagons and moving to Zarahemla. Kail needs a surgeon and we are in very real danger out here. Move!" he commanded. The men scattered as Pilio barked orders. Saria moved and stood over Kail trying to make sense of what she was seeing and feeling. Then she remembered that Rachael did not know who the wounded soldier was. Looking up, Saria saw Rachael running toward her with a small wool blanket and a water skin. Saria did not know if Kail was alive or dead. Looking back down at the arrow in his back, she saw blood oozing from a reopened section of the wound. "If blood is flowing the heart is still beating," a voice from her past rang in her ear. As a young Nephite woman she had learned some basic medical aid to be an effective wife and mother. Setting bones, stitching wounds, soothing burns and making herbal teas was part of the life of a woman in her time. "He is alive," she gasped with joy and relief in her tone.

"Mother?" Rachael called out as she got closer to Saria. Saria moved away from Kail and grabbed Rachael by both shoulders. Looking into her eyes, Saria knew now was not the time to panic or lose control. Saria knew Rachael was strong, but she had never faced death like this. With the hard and firm voice only a mother could deliver, Saria spoke in an even tone. "Rachael, you must be strong. It's Kail."

"What....what are you saying?" Rachael was confused and questioned with panic building behind her eyes. She looked past her mother and down at the pitiful sight before her. It was her beloved husband, wounded and dying. "No!" she screamed, desperately trying to push past Saria.

"Rachael, you must be strong for him!" Saria spoke in Rachael's ear as she pulled Rachael close to her, holding her tightly. "He needs you to be strong for him," she repeated in a soothing voice while hugging her oldest child. "Gently now, wash his face and give him some water while I cover him with the blanket."

With tears rolling down her cheeks, Rachael hesitantly moved closer to her man. "Is he alive?" She choked out as she knelt down and brushed his hair away from his face rubbing his cheek with the palm of her hand. His skin was a deathly grey and he hardly seemed to be breathing.

"Yes, he lives, but he has lost consciousness. We must get him to the surgeon. The wound is to his back, so we must take care in moving him." Saria snapped into her role as the mother and instructed Rachael on how to care for this combat wound. "Do not disturb the arrow. The surgeon must cut around the shaft and remove the point or it will cause greater injury. Never pull it out, unless you have no other choice." Saria moved to continue instructing Rachael. "Clean around the wound as best as you can. Only give him sips of the water. Do not let him take full drinks of water or eat anything." Saria moved to Kail's back. "Pack silk or cloth around the wound and bind it tightly to stop the blood flow." Saria then covered Kail with the blanket. "Keep him warm and dry. It will help fight the fever that will come."

Rachael was numb, trying to follow along and help the best she could. Her mind was clouded with emotion and fear. This was her husband, the father of her child, and her future. How could this be happening to her? How did he get wounded? Who did this to him? Saria saw that Rachael's mind was losing focus. "Rachael!" she barked. "Concentrate...we must help him."

"Yes, mother," Rachael responded and refocused her efforts on helping her husband.

"Pilio," Saria shouted as she stood up, "we need a wagon over here. Quickly now!"

Pilio waved his hand in response to Saria's request and instructed the driver who was securing the horses to move a wagon closer to Rachael.

Tum made quick work of binding Kalup's hands. He was not discreet about his disgust for Kalup and made it very clear when he cinched the ropes down around Kalup's arms and hands. Tum then cut large sections from Kalup's own cloak and tightly wrapped them around Kalup's legs to help control the bleeding. Kalup winced in pain from the rough treatment at Tum's hand.

"Stop your bellyaching, you cowardly dog," Tum whispered as he pulled the knot tight on one of the leg wraps. "You're lucky we don't leave you for the ants and the crows."

"Please…I was blackmailed. It was the Sons of—" But before Kalup could say any more, Tum stuffed a bit of rag in his mouth muffling his words and then wrapped a second section of rag around Kalup's head to keep the rag in place.

"All of you come and help lift my son-in-law into the wagon!" Pilio ordered. Everyone moved toward the back of the wagon now positioned next to Kail. With all hands helping, Kail was picked up as gently as possible and placed on his side in the wagon. Rachael got in next, followed by Saria, as the maid who was still holding a sleeping Teancum moved to the far corner and out of the way.

Pilio then turned to Tum and pointed to Kalup. "Help me put this sack of rubbish in the second wagon, and hurry, we must be off. Quickly now."

Tum and the two drivers moved to where Kalup was lying. The four of them picked up Kalup and dropped him in the back of the second wagon like a sack of potatoes. With a muffled scream Kalup cried out in pain. One of the drivers snickered, "Beg padon, my lord. He slipped out of my grasp." Pilio smiled back, then moved to his horse.

"My lord." Tum handed Pilio a long strip of cloth from Kalup's cloak gesturing toward the wound on Pilio's head.

"Thank you," Pilio responded as he took the piece. Walking over to the first wagon, Pilio handed the cloth to Saria who quickly used it to bind up the cut on the back of his head. Mounting his steed, Pilio drew out his sword, then he spoke, "Zarahemla is only two miles away. We are still in danger here and must move quickly but carefully. Everyone keep an eye out for trouble. I will follow behind and stand ready to defend you if need be. Drivers, if there is trouble, everyone stays in the wagons and ride away as fast as you can. I will hold them off to give you a chance to escape."

"No, Father!" Rachael cried out. She was still not sure exactly what happened or how Kail ended up at the crossroads with an arrow in his back. Now her father was riding around with a bleeding wound to his head and his sword out like a crazed war captain barking orders, fleeing from some unknown danger.

"Do as I say, child, and tend to your husband, now…move out!" Rachael blinked several times and sat back down next to her husband. Pilio had never spoken to Rachael in such a sharp tone. It was a lifetime ago when he commanded men at arms as a Nephite army officer and she had never seen this side of him. Rachael was overwhelmed and started to cry. Saria moved next to her and put her arm around her shoulders.

"It's not you," she whispered into her daughter's ear. "Father is just concerned for our safety and is concentrated on getting us all home in one piece." Quickly deflecting the issue Saria continued, "Let me help you with Kail."

Both wagons lurched forward and moved at a good pace toward the protection of the walls of Zarahemla. The bumps in the road were not helping, but it was urgent they find a doctor as soon as possible. Pilio and his large horse were riding a wide protective circle around the two-wagon convoy carrying his family. Like any devoted father, he was prepared to face any enemy and die, if necessary, to ensure his family's safety. One good man fighting for his family and his home is more dangerous than five thugs. He knew it and was hoping the unseen bandits knew it.

The dark bandit did know that fact. He saw how Pilio was guarding the wagons and he knew it was useless to try to attack out in the open. Moving along the tree line, the Son of Nehor kept a close eye on where they were going. He knew that Kalup would tell all of the bandit clan's secrets to save his own skin. "Coward," he spat on the ground while thinking about how much trouble Kalup had been from the first moments he approached the Sons and asked to join their secret society. Going over several possibilities in his mind, he kept coming to the same conclusion. *I must kill Kalup and that Nephite officer before they can speak with the authorities. That means ambushing them at the gates of the city,* he thought to himself. Unable to come up with an alternate plan, the bandit spurred his stolen horse through the trees in an attempt to reach the gates of Zarahemla first.

THE DARK ASSASSIN STRIKES

As the wagons reached the massive gates of the capital city, Zarahemla, Pilio could see a long line of merchant wagons waiting to be inspected by the guards. Keeping contraband out of the city was a thankless but very important job. It fell to the city's armed security forces to enforce the laws. Pilio knew if he waited for his turn in the inspection line, Kail might die. He also knew he had a wounded Nephite officer bound and gagged in his second wagon. Pilio had to think fast. He rode up to the second wagon and looked down at Kalup. Making eye contact with Kalup, Pilio spoke, "Do you hear me?" He asked. Kalup nodded his head. "Good. My servant is going to remove your gag."

"My lord …?" Tum interrupted.

Pilio held out his hand asking his old friend to be silent. Tum nodded and remained silent.

"He is going to remove your gag. You are going to act like you are unconscious as we pass through the checkpoint. If you raise the alarm or try to signal for help, I swear by the four winds, I will chop off both of your hands and feet before anyone can come to help you. Do you understand?" Kalup could see in Pilio's eyes that he was not to be trifled with. He meekly nodded his head that he understood. Pilio turned to Tum, and Tum removed his gag.

"Water,…please?" Kalup gasped thorugh a dry, scratchy throat. Tum looked up at Pilio and Pilio nodded back. Tum turned, grabbed a half-full water skin and pulled out the stopper. Tilting his head up, Kalup allowed Tum to pour a small quantity of the liquid into his mouth. Swallowing hard Kalup whispered, "Thank you," then closed his eyes to fake an injured sleep. Pilio gave Tum a hard look and jerked his head toward Kalup as if to say, "Watch him." Tum understood and pulled what remained of Kalup's cloak over his bound hands. Then Tum pulled out his small dagger and hid it behind his leg out of sight of the gate guards.

"Father, what's happening?" Rachael called out as Pilio rode past the first wagon toward the waiting guards at the main gates of the city.

"It's all right child, we will be moving shortly," Pilio responded without looking back at her. Rachael looked down at her hands, noticing her husband's blood on her skin and clothing. A wave of helplessness crashed over her and she started to cry again. Sitting back down on the wagon bench she was sobbing quietly when a weak voice broke the sorrow-filled air.

"Where am I?" Kail demanded just above a whisper.

"Kail...?" Rachael called out. "Kail, I'm here!" She cried as she dropped to her knees and moved to look at Kail's face.

"How...?"

"Shhh, my love, don't talk. You are wounded and we are at the gates of Zarahemla, trying to find you a surgeon."

"Rachael.....how?" Kail moaned.

"It's okay; I'm here with you now, my love." She brushed the hair away from his eyes again and tried to smile for him. She looked up, trying to tell her father that Kail was awake but he was too far away. "Mother... Kail is awake!" she exclaimed as she turned back to face her. Saria handed little Teancum back to the maid then knelt down next to Rachael.

"Don't let him move or try to get up. Kail...," Saria spoke in an even tone, as she bent over his head and spoke directly to him, "Kail, dear, you must not try to move. Hold still until the doctor can help you."

"Water."

"Rachael, moisten his lips." Saria motioned to the water skin next to Rachael's leg. "Kail, you must hold on a bit longer, help is coming," she answered back as Rachael dabbed a wet cloth across his parched lips.

Saria looked back at the second wagon and called out to Tum. "Tum, Kail is awake. Please go tell Lord Pilio to hurry."

"Yes, madam," Tum responded. Tum looked down at Kalup and kicked him in his ribs. Kalup's eyes shot open. "The deal still stands, you hold your mouth closed or we will show no mercy." Tum handed his dagger to the driver who stuck in into his tunic belt. Tum jumped down from the wagon and looked up at the driver. "Keep him quiet," he ordered.

"Yes, sir," the driver responded while patting the knife in his belt and looking down at Kalup. "He's not going anywhere."

"Lieutenant," Pilio called out to get the attention of the officer at the guard post. The soldier heard Pilio's call and turned to face the regal man on horseback.

"Yes… what is it?"

"My name is Lord Pilio and I have found two wounded Nephite soldiers by the crossroads. They are in my wagons and need medical attention right away!" Pilio pointed back to the end of the long row of wagons still trying to get into the city. He knew the one man who attacked him was an army officer and tried to kill his son-in-law. Pilio did not know who to trust so he kept the information vague.

"Sergeant, come with me!" the army officer called out to his next in command. "Show the way, sir." He gestured to Pilio to lead them to the wounded soldiers.

The dark bandit came out of the wood line and slunk his way behind the merchant shacks that lined the main road near the gates of Zarahemla. Dismounting, he walked his horse around the riff-raff and trash heaps that always seemed to gather in places like this. Looking between and through the shacks and thatch roofed stores he could see the two wagons he had been stalking, stopped behind a long line of wagons trying to enter the city. He watched as one of the men got down from the wagon and walked up to the first one. He then saw the driver of the second wagon look down into the wagon and pat his knife. *Kalup must be in the second wagon*, he thought to himself. *That lone man is guarding him, and all of the women are tending to our boy hero in the first wagon.* The bandit looked up toward the gates and saw Pilio talking to an army officer standing near the gates and pointing back to the wagons. "Now," he said out loud. "It must be now." Quickly scanning his environment, the bandit found just the things he needed to help him commit his heinous crimes.

One of the small shops next to where the bandit was standing was a lamp oil merchant. From his vantage point behind the thatched hut he could look through the rickety old stand at the old man inside the store. The shopkeeper was fast asleep. Using his refined skills at burglary, the bandit crept quietly into the shop, past the sleeping owner. Inside he grabbed a large jug of lamp oil as well as an unlit torch. Walking out into the sun-soaked main road leading to the gates, the clever bandit walked along unnoticed with the rest of the Nephite citizens who were moving around the market place. The bandit held the jug in one hand while he walked toward the wagons. He casually pulled out his flint and steel from a pouch on his belt. From many years of criminal behavior, he knew that if he acted natural no one would think twice or give him a second look. With his dark cloak and hood on, no one could clearly see him to identify him later. He just needed to get a little bit closer to those wagons and to those blasted people who interfered with their plans. The killer could feel his heart racing in his chest as he got closer to the wagon carrying Kalup.

The anticipation of killing was always a rush for him. *This weak and pompous society will blow over like a pile of dried leaves for the Sons of Nehor*, he reflected as he smiled getting ever closer to his prey. "They are cowards, weak and ignorant...Look at them," he spoke to himself under his breath. The contempt for those walking around him grew to a fever pitch as he looked at the people moving and shopping with no idea a murder was about to happen right before their eyes. As the hot blood pulsed in his veins, the bandit felt the euphoria of the bloodlust overtake him.

This is what being a god feels like. Not those soft, stupid emotions they talk about in the weak, Christian church with their so-called, one true God. No... it's power and control, which is what this world is all about, and I have it. Any feelings of mercy or hope for humanity were long ago lost to this man. He sold his soul for a few gold coins when he took the blood oath to the Sons of Nehor. Now, as he reached the back of the wagon holding the wounded Kalup, he was almost frothing at the mouth with hate and rage. As he looked into the back of the wagon, he made eye contact with Kalup who was lying on his side and covered in his own blood. Kalup tried to move but he was in such pain and he was still bound by the ropes. "Please ...help me," he whispered to the bandit. Smiling at his helpless victim, the dark one set the jug of oil down on the ground. Pretending to adjust his sandals, he bent over. Taking the flint and steel in his hand, the bandit quickly lit the torch, then picked up the jug of oil. "Kalup...you have been found unworthy of our love," the bandit hissed then dumped the entire contents of the jug over Kalup's body. Kalup could taste the strong bitter oil in his mouth and knew instantly what was about to happen. "No!" he cried out, but it was too late. The bandit dropped the lit torch onto Kalup's clothing and he instantly burst into flames.

The wagon driver was distracted as he watched Pilio ride to the gate, but turned back to hear Kalup cry out. The sudden rush of intense heat and flames caused the driver to instinctively jump from the wagon. The flames and commotion spooked the horses pulling the wagon, and with no driver to calm them, they bolted uncontrollably toward the city gates. Kalup was screaming as he burned alive in the back of the out-of-control wagon. Everyone, from the tower guard to the smallest child in the market, stopped what they were doing and turned to watch as the horses pulling the burning wagon ran down the street. Moving quickly out of their way, the people and wagons made a wide path for the chaos to travel down. The driver, who jumped from the burning wagon, was joined by the driver of the first wagon as they both ran after the burning fiasco to try and save the horses.

Everyone was looking in the opposite direction at the burning wagon as the bandit moved to the back of the next wagon holding Kail and his family. In one smooth motion the murderer jumped into the wagon and stood over Kail. He pulled out a long, serpentine-shaped blade from under his dark cloak. The shape of the knife was like a snake with the open mouth of the serpent molded into the hilt. This was the weapon of a Nehor assassin. The sudden appearance of the armed dark stranger caused Tum to turn back around. Tum saw the killer's blade and lunged forward to try to stop the assassin as Rachael and Saria cried out for Pilio. With one smooth motion, the bandit struck Tum on the face with the back of his hand as Tum was trying to move closer. Tum was caught off balance and got knocked off the wagon, his body hitting the ground with a thud.

Pilio heard his family yelling out for him as they also tried to stop the murder of their beloved Kail. He could see Rachael and Saria grabbing at the arms of the bandit trying to keep him from hurting Kail. Pilio tried to move his horse toward the wagon but a large crowd of people had gathered around him when they moved to make way for the burning wagon.

"Move! Out of my way!" he shouted as he tried to maneuver his way around the frightened onlookers.

As they tried to stop the assault on Kail, Saria and Rachael found out quickly they were no match for the bandit. Try as they might, he was just too powerful. His true size and strength were hidden beneath his dark and menacing robe and hood. Swatting them away like pesky insects, the bandit readjusted his footing and positioned himself over Kail for the death blow. Kail was now lying on his left side in the fetal position too weak to resist. In his last defining act, Kail raised up his right hand to try to stop the knife.

Looking down the road toward the gate, the bandit could see Pilio had moved free of the crowd and was now galloping toward him. Pilio had his sword out and at the ready while the foot soldiers, who manned the gate, were running behind him. "Fools," the murderer whispered with a smile on his face. With his teeth clenched, the bandit hissed, "For the Sons of Nehor!" and he plunged the long knife deep into Kail's ribs.

Kail gasped his death pangs and both Rachael and Saria cried out helplessly as they watched Kail's murder. The bandit stood up and made eye contact with Pilio as he charged forward to the rescue of his family. Not wanting to be anywhere near Pilio or those soldiers, the bandit reached for his prized snake-shaped blade. As his hand reached the hilt of the crafted weapon, he felt the tip of the wagon driver's riding whip break across the flesh of the top of his hand. Gasping in pain, he pulled his hand close to his chest and looked up. There he saw Saria holding the small whip in her hands. It was her desperate attempt to keep the hooded bandit away from Kail. She whipped it at his eyes and shouted, "Get away from him, you monster!" The bandit flinched and moved to the back of the wagon to avoid the whip.

He bent over and snarled at the two women, "How dare you!" Then he saw Pilio was getting closer. He looked down at his blade and leaped from the wagon. He had to make a quick escape or risk capture. He landed hard on the ground and ran toward the confusion and maze of the back alleys behind the merchant shops.

Pilio made it to the side of the wagon just in time to see the murdering bandit round the corner of a shop and disappear. "Over there!" he shouted to the running guards, pointing with his sword. "The man in black went around that shop!"

Not missing a beat, the soldiers were in full pursuit cutting through the screaming crowds, past the wagons, running at top speed to try to catch the assassin.

Rachael was the first to move toward Kail. Slowly, and still in complete disbelief over what she had just witnessed, she got close to him, but did

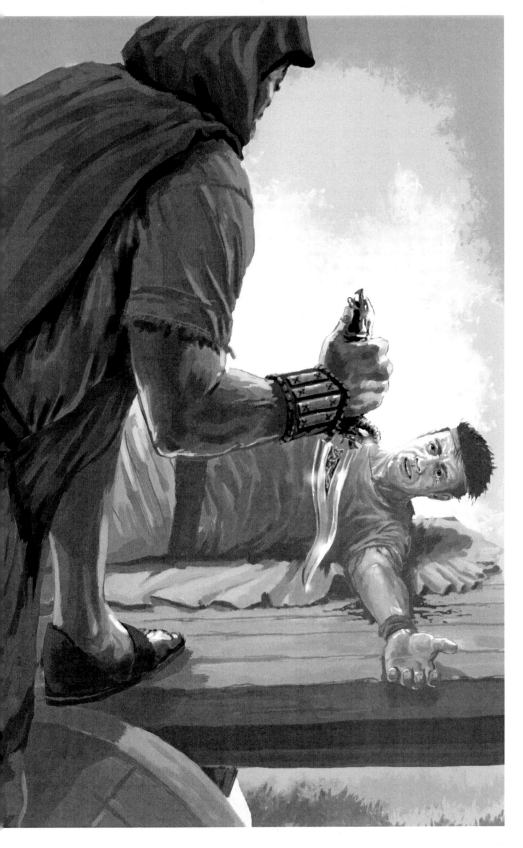

not know what to do. Fumbling with her hands and crying, she tried to reach for the dagger still protruding from the side of his chest. Catching herself before she pulled it out, she then tried to reach for the arrow still in his back. Still not sure what to do, she moved closer to his face and whispered in his ear, "My darling, I love you." Her tears dropped onto his pale skin. She wanted to hold her husband, but he was close to death now and she was in shock.

"My child," Kail weakly croaked.

"Mother!" Rachael cried when she heard Kail's request. She turned to see where her baby was.

"Here!" Saria said as she handed the cradle board, with little Teancum still inside, to Rachael. Teancum was awake and looking around, startled by the noise and confusion all about.

Rachael took the baby carrier, laying it flat on the floor of the wagon in front of Kail's face. Moving the blanket away from Teancum's head, she gently spoke while choking back more tears, "Here is your son, my love."

"Name?" he gasped with the last few breaths left in his wounded body.

"Teancum, his name is Teancum." Rachael was barely able to control herself as she sobbed out the words.

Kail tried to reach out to touch his child, but he could only move his hand a few inches toward the boy. Saria, seeing Kail struggle to reach out, bent over and gently moved Kail's hand the rest of the way and set the his hand down next to Teancum's face. Kail managed to weakly rub his finger along Teancum's cheek and stroked the soft skin of his only child. "My son," he sighed as a tear fell from his eye. Looking up into Rachael's eyes, Kail mouthed the words, "I love you." Then gasping twice, Kail stopped breathing and the light in his eyes went dark.

Rachael wailed, her scream echoing off the city walls, while reaching for the comfort of her mother. Pilio had watched the entire event transpire from his horse. Blinded with rage and vengeance, he cried out, spurring his horse toward the market. Pilio was going to find the killer and make him pay for what he had done to his family.

The bandit was running as fast as he could down the back alleys, through the shops and shanties, trying to lose the soldiers persuing him. He was not running blindly, but looking for something while he quickly moved. Coming around a corner, he spied the exact thing he was looking for. There, lying on the ground next to a small smoldering fire, was a homeless beggar, drunk and filthy. Quickly the bandit pulled the large black robe over his shoulders and off his body. He had on plain homespun clothing under the robe, and he stuffed the black garment into an empty rain barrel. Grabbing the drunken man's dirty blanket, the bandit sat down next to the beggar, wrapping the blanket around his shoulders and over his face. He knew he had to control his breathing or the soldiers would know he was the killer. Taking several deep breaths in and out, the bandit quickly slowed down his body's need for oxygen. He then calmly reached for the half empty jug of wine in the drunk's hand and took it. The beggar was too inebriated to complain. The bandit took a quick drink, sloshed it around in his mouth and spat it out on the ground just as several soldiers rounded the corner stopping right in front of him. He slowly lowered his head to avoid making eye contact with one of the soldiers. *You are just another drunk,* he told himself as he slipped into character.

"Which way, Sarge?" One of the soldiers asked while gulping for air.

"Spread out and search by twos," the soldier commanded. "You two, that way." He pointed with his sword at the first two soldiers next to him. "You two, in the shops…start asking if anyone saw where he went."

Without questions, the young soldiers moved to perform their duty. The bandit peeked up ever so slightly to get a better look at the soldier giving orders in front of him. In one glance he knew this soldier was not to be trifled with. He was large and powerfully built. His armor bore the markings of a combat veteran and his sword was well made.

"You there, beggar," the Sergeant had turned and noticed the bandit peaking up at him.

The bandit's blood went cold. "Yes, my lord ?" he slurred.

"I am not your lord," the impatient warrior spat back. "A man came running through here. He had on a dark cloak. Did you see him?"

"My apologies, sir…" The bandit felt the tension in his chest release when he realized the soldier did not recognize him. "I did see a man like that come running through here just a short time ago. Went that way, he did." The bandit pointed down the alley with the jug of wine sloshing in his hand.

"How long ago…speak!" the soldier ordered as he kicked the bandit's foot.

"Can't say for sure." He held out the jug. "Strong wine… weak mind." He snickered and pretended to burp.

Gasping with disgust, the sergeant called out to his men. "Soldiers, report!"

"Nothing here, Sarge." One set responded. "No one saw anything in here," the second set called out as they quickly exited a merchant shop.

"Right," the leader answered as he pointed down the road in the direction the bandit had shown. "Keep moving that way, asking the people as you go, if they have seen him." He turned back to face the drunk. Pulling a small coin from out of the pouch sewn into his tunic, the sergeant flicked the coin toward him. "For the information," he whispered.

Instinctively, the bandit quickly grabbed for the coin and caught it in mid-flight. "Thank you, sir." He smiled.

The sergeant trotted off several steps down the alley behind his men when he suddenly stopped in his tracks. *That was a good catch of that coin for a drunkard...He was pretty quick,* he thought to himself for a second then remembered seeing sweat coming off the beggar's forehead. The voice in his head shouted at him *That's the guy!* Gasping, he drew his big sword and turned back around to confront the beggar. All he saw was an empty blanket lying on the ground and an empty jug of wine on its side. The man under the blanket was gone.

Pilio searched for several more minutes before accepting the obvious: the dark-cloaked assassin had escaped. Making his way back to the road, he could see several more soldiers had arrived along with a contingent of high-ranking officers and city officials. The noise, confusion, wagon fire, and now murder of two Nephite army officers outside the main gates of the city had aroused the attention of the city's leaders. Several of them were standing just out of reach of the wagon where Rachael continued to wail and Saria tried her best to console her. Tum, still bleeding from the backhanded strike to the face, left the company of the soldiers and walked the several yards to meet his master. Tum was ashamed he was not able to stop the attack. He was no warrior, but he was a man. A man with a single duty, to serve his lord and lady, and in his eyes, he had failed them both.

Tum reported the sad news of Kail's fate to Pilio. "I'm sorry, my lord. Kail..." Tum swallowed hard and choked on the next words, "he is gone." There was shame in his voice and head was bowed.

"That murdering scum!" Pilio spat out the words like he was looking the bandit in the eyes. "God will avenge this family!" He put his old sword back into its sheath and climbed down from the horse.

Pilio could see that Tum was ashamed for failing to protect Kail. Without a word, Pilio put his hands on his old friend's shoulders looking deeply into Tum's sad eyes. Much can be said without the spoken word. Eye movement, gestures, body language, nonverbal communication are common with men of action and those who are as close as Pilio and Tum were to each other. After looking Tum in the eyes for several seconds, Pilio gently shook his old friend's shoulders and pulled him close for an embrace. Pilio did not blame Tum for the death of his son-in-law. There was only one man who Pilio blamed. Pilio knew that Tum was not a warrior, but he did try to make a stand against the assassin. He showed true bravery—being scared and still taking a stand. Not everyone would have the courage to try and stop a Nehor assassin. Pilio knew that. He loved and respected Tum now even more for it. Without a word spoken, Tum was relieved; his lord and master had forgiven him for failing. He responded with a weak smile and quickly bowed his head. The two men turned and walked toward the wagon and the heartbreak awaiting them.

A very large crowd was gathering around the sorrowful scene. Several of the city's guards were trying to force the onlookers back. Pilio and Tum tried to make their way past the crush of people when they were stopped at the perimeter by a guard with a spear in his hand.

"No further!" the guard ordered as he held up his hand to signal them to stop moving forward. "There is nothing more to see here." The attitude was not personal. The guard had been trying to keep the gawkers and onlookers at bay for a while, and now two more unknown men suddenly appeared, trying to get closer to the crime scene.

Pilio opened his mouth to protest but he was quickly interrupted by a voice coming from behind the guard. "It's okay, soldier…let those two men come forward." Pilio looked past the guard and saw the army officer he was speaking to earlier by the gate wave to him to come forward. The guard moved his body out of the way and Pilio and Tum briskly walked past.

"Thank you, lieutenant," Pilio said as he approached the group of men standing off from the wagon.

"My deepest regrets to you and your family, my lord ," the frustrated young officer said. "That your wife and daughter had to witness this senseless act of violence is a true shame."

"I was not completely truthful with you at the gate, lieutenant," Pilio remarked without taking his eyes off his wailing child and his beloved wife. "That soldier in the wagon is my son-in-law and that is his wife and new child."

"Good heavens!" the lieutenant gasped. His shoulders sagged. He lowered his head as he turned back to face the wagon.

"Father…!" Rachael cried out when she saw Pilio standing a few feet away. She held out her arms, silently begging him to come and hold her. Her face was flushed red and stained from the tears.

Pilio's heart broke for his grieving daughter. He moved to the side of the wagon reaching for his princess. He gently lifted her out of the wagon and held her in his arms. He was devastated. She was so delicate and vulnerable— how could he have let this happen to her? Tum was by his side. He reached up to help Saria out of the wagon. Saria had removed young Teancum from his papoose and was holding him close to her chest. When she stepped down she moved close to Pilio, wrapping her free arm around them both. The three of them, as well as the baby, became one, as each both gave and received the love and tenderness they so desperately needed.

The scene of pure emotion was too much for most of the onlookers to bear. Women in the crowd were openly weeping and several of the soldiers had to turn away to avoid being seen shedding tears in public. The only person watching the scene, unaffected by the sorrow was a figure of a man standing in the shadows of a merchant store a good distance away. The shadows cast a long and dark cover over his face and a hint of a smile as he paused for a moment to admire his work.

The funeral had all the pageantry of a true military affair: Soldiers in full armor marching, banners blowing in the wind, important men giving speeches about duty, honor, and country. Quite an event for those who were watching it unfold. For those attending because Lieutenant Kail of the Zarahemla legion was a friend, brother-in-arms, or family member, the funeral was heart wrenching. The noise, confusion and discomfort of the funeral procession was affecting young Teancum. He was crying in his mother's arms. Rachael had not slept in days, and her eyes were dark and hollow. The expression on her face made her thoughts appear as if they were thousands of miles away.

Pilio and Saria did their best to comfort her and see to her needs, but the wound to her heart was beyond healing. The words from the preacher, as he stood over the grave, rang hollow in Pilio's ears. The holy man spoke of Christ's eternal love, that families would someday be together forever and how learning to forgive those who wrong us in this life would lead to our salvation. But the pain he felt in his heart while he held his only daughter was boiling up inside of him.

Forgiveness… He thought to himself as he bit down hard to hold back his emotions. *The men who did this attacked my family.* He wrapped his arms around his wife and grieving child and gave them both a gentle embrace.

I believe in God… He looked up as the preacher was finishing his remarks. *But those Nehor are monsters and must be destroyed.*

Pilio reflected on his past life. He had been angry when he was young. He was angry at his family, angry at his own father for never understanding him, and for pushing Pilio to do things he did not want to do. He knew his own father had been trying to prepare him to be a nobleman who could continue the family legacy, but Pilio chafed under his rules and prohibitions. Instead, he wanted adventure and excitement, not lessons and lectures. He ran away to the army to get out from under his father and be his own man.

Saria had seen his anger in their youth, but believed that she could help him overcome it. She loved his passion and he loved her calm. She became the rock to steady him. She knew how to weather the storms of anger that sometimes overcame him. He knew if he did not change his ways, he would lose the love of his life to the bitterness of his past. So Pilio accepted Christ into his life and let the eternal powers, and the love of a good woman, heal his heart. He softened as fatherhood came, and over time, he'd come to believe he was past those feelings.

Now, many years removed from the angry young soldier he once was, Saria and Rachael had given him a reason to change and become a good father and man of God. But he realized at that moment that deep inside, there was still a fire burning.

At the end of the ceremony, condolences were given to the family and pleasantries were exchanged. Then they were left all alone on the hill under the ^solemn oak tree, standing at the side of a freshly dug grave with a large river as the distant backdrop. Now that all of the commotion had calmed, Teancum had fallen back to sleep, and Saria had managed to rescue him from his mother's grasp. Pilio was standing behind Rachael as she looked down at the freshly-dug brown dirt covering her slain

69

husband's body. Saria was standing next to Pilio, rocking baby Teancum, and quietly humming her favorite hymn. After several long moments of heartbroken silence, Saria looked at Pilio, making a gesture with her head, suggesting he take control of the situation and comfort his daughter. Pilio nodded sadly. His broken heart felt even more pain with the realization he was lost in the moment, feeling hatred towards other men, instead of caring for his child. He stepped forward to stand next to Rachael. After standing beside her for several more seconds, he put his right arm around her shoulders to pull her close to him. Rachael was too numb to cry any more tears. She calmly accepted her father's overt expression of love, allowing him to hold her by his side.

"What am I going to do now, father?" She whispered.

"We are going to take this one step at a time, my little dove," he whispered back. His anger was like acid burning in his mouth. He had not called her that pet name in quite a while. For a brief moment, it made both of them feel a little better to reflect on a happier time.

"Is God punishing me for some unknown sin?" she questioned with sadness. "I know all things are in His hands and we should trust in His wisdom and mercy." She was emotionally struggling with the enormity of it all— life, death, raising a fatherless child, finding hope and a purpose to go on. Her uncertain future was weighing down on her.

"No." Pilio released his grip from around her shoulders and turned her to face him. "This was the act of savage, evil men and God will avenge you." Pilio responded with a firm, fatherly voice. He pulled her in close to his chest, holding her tightly. "You will have justice, in this life, or in the life to come. I swear it." Pilio felt his blood rising, pounding in his ears. He couldn't help the harshness in his tone, and he felt his grip on Rachael's shoulders grow uncomfortably firm. He willed himself to relax, to calm the anger welling up inside at the injustice of his daughter's pain. Rachael had a worried look on her face as she saw her father clench his jaw and close his eyes. She knew her father well enough to know he was calming himself, and he wasn't mad at her.

"What of Teancum, Father... What am I to do? How am I to raise him?"

"Teancum is my only grandson. He is my heir and the young master of my house," he said, looking down into her eyes. He knew he needed to calm himself and be the father that Rachael needed. "He will be raised to be a mighty man. He will go to the finest schools, have the best tutors, teachers and scholars I can find. He will be raised as a man of wealth, power and influence among the Nephites." Pilio let go of Rachael reaching for both her hands. Holding them in his own hands he continued, "And one day, he will know the story of his brave father, Lieutenant Kail, the mighty Nephite warrior who gave his life so that his wife and son might live free." Pilio smiled down at his grieving daughter and Rachael gave a broken smile in return.

Teancum was getting hungry and started to fuss. Saria moved closer to the two of them as all three looked at Teancum.

"I can't do this alone." Rachael began crying again as she took Teancum from her mother.

"Child, you will never need to bear this burden alone. We will always be here for you, and through our faith, we will find hope." Saria smiled at Rachael, but she knew it would be a long, hard road to peace, even with God's help. Saria was the anchor of their family. Her strength and motherly goodness were like a beacon for her husband and only child. Her testimony of the living God and His plan of happiness had carried her and her little family through hard times before. Now she was doing what she did best— radiate love, stability and compassion.

"This is not the end of it." She smiled and covered Teancum's head with his blanket. "Remember what the scriptures say: 'He will wipe away every tear and lead us to the waters of comfort'." Rachael smiled at her mother, it was one of her favorite passages of scripture. She'd often heard her mother recite it to herself in quiet moments and to others they would visit. Her mother often visited members of the community who were sick or suffering. The gifts of food and goods were never as appreciated as Saria's calm demeanor, and words of comfort. She would open the scriptures and share her faith with them, even when they weren't believers. It worked now as it did then. Saria's words and gentle touch calmed Rachael as she stroked her daughter's dark hair. "Let's go home."

The three of them took one last look at the fresh mound of dirt, then turned to walk back to the waiting wagon.

CHAPTER SIX

TEANCUM BECOMES A MAN

One grows up fast when living and working on a cattle ranch at the edge of the frontier, in the land of Zarahemla. Teancum learned from Pilio's example the value of a hard day's work at a very young age. As soon as he was old enough, Teancum was up at dawn and working with the others to manage the ranch. From shoeing a horse, to harvesting grain, to mending fences, Teancum was not spared from hard labor. As Teancum got older, each day, after a hearty lunch, Teancum studied while the rest of the ranch hands returned to their duties. Good to his word, Pilio had brought in the most accomplished instructors his money and influence could provide who taught Teancum math, science, religion, language and reading, economics, politics, athletics, music, military history and tactics. It was not long before his teachers realized that Teancum had a gift. He could understand and retain his lessons quicker than their other students. His teachers would only need to show him literature once and Teancum could recite it back to them. Teancum could also demonstrate a new skill or trade like a seasoned craftsman with very little practice. Teancum had a gifted mind, a strong body and a big heart.

As a result of his hard work, good, wholesome food, and living in a loving environment, Teancum grew to be very strong in mind, body and spirit. He grew taller than most of his friends, and inherited a chiseled jaw line. He also had dark, intense eyes and jet black hair, just like his father. He would wrestle with the other boys his age and challenge them to foot races or to see who could swim fastest across the many lakes dotting the countryside. But the one thing he loved the most was spending time with his grandfather Pilio. Pilio was a wonderful role model for Teancum. Pilio was loved and respected by everyone who knew him. Watching his grandfather work and intermix with others, Teancum soon learned why Pilio was held in such high regard. Pilio was a just and honorable man, who loved and feared God. He treated everyone, even the lowest stable boy, with respect and kindness. As he grew older, Teancum noticed that when Pilio would speak about the troubles caused by the criminals who lived in the mountains, Pilio would grow cold and his words would become sharp and full of hate. His grandfather had little patience or respect for those who would usurp the laws and live outside the bounds of honorable men. Pilio always seemed ashamed if Saria heard him speak words of hatred for those who were responsible for the pain that his family had suffered. There was an unspoken understanding between the two. With one look from Saria his heart would soften and his demeanor would change back to the Christian man he tried so hard to be.

Teancum knew it was wrong to hate. He was taught this by his grandmother, and the priests on the Sabbath. But he felt his grandfather's same rush to anger and often dreamed of him and Pilio punishing the men who had so wronged them. In his daydreams he would find them and knock down their hideout, then toss them into the air with a single blow from his grandfather's sword. The boyhood fantasy faded over time, but he always held onto hope he might someday be able to fulfill his grandfather's wish. Pilio showed Teancum how to be a proper gentleman, and how to treat women and girls with respect but that was not all, he also explained why men of honor act a certain way. "Teancum," Pilio called out to his young grandson while they worked with the horses one day. "Do you know why I insist you stand up every time your grandmother or mother enters the room?"

Teancum stopped spreading hay on the stable ground and turned to look at his grandfather. "No sir, I just figured that was what we do." One of Teancum's favorite games with Pilio was to see who could stand up first whenever his mother Rachael, or grandmother Saria, entered the room.

"That is true. It is what we as men of honor, do." He chuckled while taking his floppy sun hat off and walked toward Teancum. "But haven't you ever wondered why? Have you ever wondered why I do certain things, like wait until Grandma has taken her first bite of food before I take mine?" Pilio sat down on a log bench next to Teancum gesturing for the young man to sit down next to him.

For most people this would have been an awkward interruption to a long work day, but Teancum admired and loved his grandfather. Sitting with him in the cool of the shade, listening to Pilio explain the mysteries of life was one of Teancum's greatest joys.

"You mean, like how you always let Grandma get in the carriage first, and how you hold the door open for her and the other ladies at church?"

"Exactly," Pilio complemented Teancum on his observation and deduction skills. "That, and doing many other things is one way we, as men, show our love and respect to the women in our lives. It is also how we show God how thankful we are for creating such a beautiful and mysterious creature as a woman." He leaned in and playfully bumped Teancum with his shoulder.

Teancum chuckled. He was old enough now to recognize the difference between a man and a woman. And he was old enough to find attraction in the opposite sex.

"The love and respect of a good woman is a gift from God," Pilio continued. "But it is a gift you must earn every day of your life, or it will be taken away from you." He looked into Teancum's eyes to emphasize the point. "Not just women, but the elderly and children too. We never put our hands on a person out of anger or vengeance, unless it's self-defense." Pilio gently punched Teancum's upper arm and they both had a quick laugh. "We never speak cruelly to others or belittle anyone in any way." He pointed his finger at Teancum. "Remember, everyone you meet is a master at something you cannot do. Everyone is better than you at something, so a true man of honor will treat everyone he meets with the same level of respect." Pilio sat back looking straight ahead. Taking a deep breath, Pilio continued his lesson. "A man of honor will always put the needs of his family first and you should never put yourself in a position where you would take from them. Just like the scriptures say, one day God will sacrifice himself for all of us. So we, as true men of honor, must follow his example and sacrifice for our families and those we love. If He is willing to die for a sinner, then we should be willing to live with honor for our families, yes?" He looked down at Teancum.

"Yes, sir," Teancum responded while wondering why Grandfather was telling him these things now.

He quickly received his answer.

"Teancum, I will not always be around to set the example for you and teach you how to be a man. You must set yourself upon an honorable path and never give up your values and morals. You are of my house and my blood. My name is known throughout the land as someone with honor and integrity. You will soon carry my name and be the master of all you see." He swept his hand in a wide arc across the front of his body to stress the point to Teancum. "There is much that is expected from the grandson and heir of Lord Pilio." He looked back at Teancum and raised his eyebrows in question.

"Yes, sir." Teancum would begin to understand what this wise counsel truly meant years later when he was reacquainted with his childhood friend, Hanni.

Hanni was the daughter of the military commander of the Zarahemla legion, and one of Pilio's oldest friends. Hanni and Teancum grew up around each other, but at the time, Teancum was too young and adventurous to notice her. He had often been annoyed by her following him around and he would run and climb trees to get away from her. Instead of being deterred, she found it a wonderful game, and he was often frustratingly outsmarted by her. Even though he saw her as a pest, she saw something in him, and never forgot it.

Teanum had all but forgotten her by his teens. It was not until Teancum was older, when he and his family attended a celebration at the commander's home that fate and love caught up with him. They were welcoming Hanni back from spending two years away serving the poor and needy for their church. Teancum had protested, asking why he needed to be there. It was all forgotten in an instant. For Teancum, it was love at first sight when Hanni walked into the room for her grand introduction. Teancum could not believe the woman in the fitted, ornamental gown standing at the far end of the great hall, being presented by her father was the same pigtailed girl who would push him into the lake. It snatched the very breath from his lungs noticing just how beautiful she was. Her long, light brown hair was draped over the back of her shoulders, her full red lips and those deep blue eyes that danced in the evening light made Teancum's heart skip a beat when they made eye contact and she smiled at him from across the room. Teancum felt his face go flushed with hot blood racing through his veins as Hanni made her way across the great hall toward where he was standing. Swallowing hard, looking away and shifting his feet, Teancum tried to shake and hide the emotions he was feeling. Rachael and Saria were standing next to Teancum. They could see Hanni's acknowledgement of young Teancum and the physical effects Hanni had on him. Making eye contact and silently acknowledging they both just saw the same thing, the two most important women in his life smiled at each other.

"Go and say hello," Rachael whispered in his ear. Teancum turned to face them both.

"It's the proper thing to do," Saria continued in an instructive voice.

"What should I say?" he sheepishly asked.

"Try saying, 'Hello, Hanni. It's nice to see you again'," Rachael responded while fussing with Teancum's tunic and hair.

"Okay," Teancum said after taking a quick gulp of air and blowing it out past his lips. Finding his courage, Teancum started to turn around. He had no idea Hanni had walked up and was standing right behind him. He turned around and there she was, facing him. Lurching in surprise, Teancum knocked over the cup of fruit juice Hanni was holding in her hand.

"Oh! I am so sorry," he gasped as the cup rolled across the marbled floor, clanking, and spilling its contents. Hanni let out a laugh as she grabbed for Teancum's hand using him for a bit of balance as she jumped and moved to try to avoid the spilled liquid. A few others nearby glanced over and chuckled. Teancum was mortified and at a loss for words. His face was turning several shades of red as he gasped and choked on his own breath, searching for something to say.

Hanni, seeing Teancum was quickly losing control, knew if she did not act fast, this entire night would be lost. "If a bit of Father's special papaya juice, spilling on the floor is the most dangerous thing I face tonight, I will be very happy," Hanni giggled and winked as she grabbed Teancum's other hand moving them both away from the spill. Still holding Teancum's hands, she moved him around the waiters as they quickly cleaned the mess off the floor. Once they were clear of the fuss over the spilled juice, she pulled him closer and they looked into each other's eyes. "Thank you, brave sir, for saving me from the evil fruit juice," she playfully whispered.

Having caught his breath, Teancum weakly responded, "I'm so sorry about that. I am such a clumsy…" He smiled and continued speaking to her with a nervous tone. "Hi… Teancum. It's nice to see you again."

She smiled, giggled and cocked her head to one side. "Teancum, don't you mean, 'Hi Hanni, it's nice to see you'?"

Blushing again, Teancum opened his mouth to say something, but she raised her hand pressing her finger against his lips to cut him off. "Shhh…you can make it up to me by asking me to dance with you."

"Dance with you…?" Teancum was completely overwhelmed by her presence and the intoxicating aroma of her perfume. He was having a very hard time processing what had just happened.

"Why yes, I would love to dance with you," she replied, without missing a beat, pulling Teancum toward the gathering crowd of party attendees, waiting for the next song to start from the minstrels. Moving toward the center of the dance floor, Teancum looked back at his mother and grandmother. They were both smiling at his look of panic and waved as he was pulled out to the dance floor.

"She seems nice," Rachael said.

"I don't know who I feel sorrier for," Saria added, "you or him."

Rachael turned to face her mother and closest friend. "What do you mean, Mother?"

"Planning a wedding is a very time-consuming affair," Saria continued with a big smile and a wink.

"A wedding? Mother, please, it's only one dance," Rachael responded with exasperation.

"I will remember you said that." Saria nodded across the room at the two youngsters dancing. Rachael turned to see Teancum laughing and spinning Hanni around to the rhythm of the music. There was a sudden sting of sadness in her heart as she watched her only child quickly slip away from her and into the arms and life of another woman. This moment had been inevitable, and Rachael welcomed the future knowing the only thing that mattered to her was Teancum's happiness. She wiped a tear from her eye and looked up into the night sky. Somewhere, up there, her sweet Kail was watching and smiling back at her.

From that day on, Teancum and Hanni were always together. Riding horses in the wide meadows, walking through the markets of Zarahemla, reading to each other on the large porch of his ranch, picnics, holiday gatherings. It quickly became common and expected to see them together. So it was not a real surprise that when everyone was gathered at the city's main pavilion for the grand feast of the harvest moon, Teancum planned to ask Hanni's father for his blessing to marry her.

Guests at the feast bustled around them, but Teancum hardly noticed. Teancum had reason to be nervous. Hanni's father was a gruff and stern military man. He commanded the legendary Zarahemla Legion and had a way of looking at someone that could make them fear for their very lives. He never let an opportunity pass to remind Teancum that Hanni was his baby girl. Teancum glanced nervously over towards the table where her father was conversing with other guests.

"You will do fine," Hanni said as she straightened Teancum's clothing and kissed him on the lips.

"You know, he really does not like me," he responded to her encouragement, feeling less than confident in the outcome of his impending conversation with her father. He was nervous and his whole demeanor showed that fact.

"Nonsense," she smiled back. "Why, just yesterday he commented about you at breakfast."

"Really, what did he say?"

"Oh, it's not important what he said; it's the fact he was talking about you to me."

"Not important!" Teancum gasped. "I'm about to ask his permission to marry his only daughter. I think whatever he said about me is very important!"

"Well…" she paused and tapped her lips with her finger, "I think it was something about finding you face down in an unmarked grave…. or something like that," she said simply as she went back to fussing with his buttons.

"What…?"

Hanni could not keep a straight face any longer, and burst into laughter. She could see that Teancum really was nervous and she was not helping the matter. She had enough fun at her love's expense. "I'm just fooling with you, my darling. He thinks you're a fine man, and so… do…I." She kissed each cheek and then his nose between each pause. "Now, go and ask him for his blessing before someone better comes along and sweeps me off my feet."

Teancum smiled at that. Hanni and Teancum were soul mates and madly in love with each other. She had known they were destined to be together long before Teancum did. Even at a young age, she was in love with the dark haired prodigy. She even told him, on more than one occasion, when they played together as children, "I'm going to marry you,

Teancum." But he was too busy being a boy to listen or understand. Now that he was finally in her arms, she was never letting go. She was going to love and honor him forever, bear him strong sons, lovely daughters and be his truest, most trusted friend.

"Go," she whispered with one more kiss for luck and then gently pushed him toward her father's table.

As commander of the Zarahemla Legion, Hanni's father always had several well armored and dangerous looking guards close by. Unless they were family or a trusted advisor, no one even got close to him without their approval, and Teancum was no exception. By now, the guards all knew who Teancum was and that he was courting the commander's daughter. This fact did not sit well with the men of the legion who looked upon Hanni as either their little sister or were secretly in love with her. The soldiers would remind Teancum, every chance they got, that he was not a warrior and he better mind his manners around Hanni. Tonight was no different as the captain of the guard met Teancum at the end of the long table where the commander was sitting, talking with some of Zarahemla's wealthy and influential citizens.

"Young Master Teancum, what brings you here tonight?" The large and annoyed officer inquired as he stepped into Teancum's way. He was tall and imposing with his armor and war cloak on. "If you're looking for the servants' entrance, you go out the main doors and around to the back of the hall."

"Good evening, Captain," Teancum smiled, trying not to make eye contact while responding in a very non-confrontational tone. He knew this was just part of a game they started playing with him a long time ago, but it was getting a bit old. Teancum was the grandson of Lord Pilio and the heir to the largest cattle ranch in the land. He had every right to be at the event and walk freely around the room. He knew the soldiers were jealous of his wealth, his education, his position in life and what he had with Hanni. But he also did not want a confrontation with them. Teancum had tried his whole life to avoid confrontations. He was physically strong and in great condition, but Teancum lacked the emotional strength to stand up for himself. Pilio tried to be a good male role model but for Teancum there was a hole in his heart that only a father could fill. This void left him feeling unsure and always trying to avoid the hard choices in life. He never really had the confidence to stand alone on his principles. He would avoid confrontations or use humor to get out of the emotional conflicts that life would present.

"So…Out the main doors and around to the back? Great, I will be sure to tell your men where they can find work when they are done defending the commander from the old, overweight and pompous of Zarahemla." Teancum patted the guard on the shoulder. "Very dangerous work indeed. You're doing an excellent job, Captain; I might even write you a nice letter of recommendation someday. Now if you would be so kind, I must speak to the commander," he continued as he tried to get past the guard.

The soldier nudged Teancum into some chairs and said, "Wait here." He turned to speak with his commanding officer. The soldier's pride was hurt with Teancum's insults, but he still had to do his duty. Walking up next to Hanni's father, the guard whispered into his ear. Turning around in his seat, the commander looked bored as he spoke to the guard. They shared a quick laugh then he waved Teancum over. Teancum knew they were laughing at him because he was no soldier and they'd probably shared some joke at his expense. The only thing that made him move forward was a quick glance back at the love of his life. She was standing partially hidden behind a large pillar, and when she smiled and waved at him, he found the courage to continue.

Teancum walked up next to Hanni's father as he continued to speak to the crowd gathered around him. "Ladies and gentleman, may I present young Teancum, the oldest grandson of Lord Pilio and Lady Saria."

Teancum knew most of the high-born citizens gathered before him, so introductions were not needed. But this was just one more game the commander was playing with him. It gave the appearance that Teancum's status in life was not that important or of any concern to the commander or to anyone else, for that matter. So, out of courtesy, he was obliged to introduce Teancum to those with whom he was speaking. Hiding his emotions once again, Teancum played along.

"My lords and ladies, good evening." Teancum bowed slightly at the waist. "Commander," he continued as he turned to face Hanni's father, "I apologize, but may I have a word with you in private?"

"A private matter, how intriguing," he smirked as he addressed those around him. "Come, walk with me on the balcony, Master Teancum," the old soldier continued with a hint of impatience in his voice. "Do please excuse me," he said to the others around him as he stood up from his chair and bowed. Those he addressed bowed back and moved away to enjoy the festivities. "Captain, have someone bring us some refreshments on the balcony. I have a feeling we are going to be out there a while."

"Yes, sir," the guard force leader barked back as he glared at Teancum.

The long running game of insults between Teancum and the soldiers continued as Teancum looked back at the soldiers and spoke, "A large cup of the fruit juice and a plate of cheese and bread for me…for you, sir?" Teancum addressed the old commander as he moved toward the doors of the balcony.

"The same for me…and some broiled meat."

Teancum turned back to look at the soldiers who were now foaming with anger at Teancum ordering them around like the cooking staff. "You heard the man! Quickly now, off you go," Teancum smiled. One of the soldiers, who looked especially angry, lunged toward Teancum but he was stopped by the captain of the guard. "You have a job to do soldier," the captain spoke in a controlled tone to the angry soldier.

"Yes, sir," the soldier replied, glaring at Teancum while heading for the kitchen to fetch the refreshments.

"What is it, Teancum?" The old soldier said in a direct tone. His back was to Teancum as he leaned out over the balcony railing staring out into the hot night. The evening wind rustled his war cloak.

"Well sir, there is no other way to say it, so I will just come right out and speak the words." He took two quick breaths for courage. "I love your daughter and she loves me. I want her to be my wife. I am asking for your permission to marry Hanni."

The commander stood completely still for what felt like ages. No movement, no emotions, no sounds. Teancum was not even sure the old man was breathing. After a very long an awkward silence, Teancum spoke.

"Sir…?"

Waiting a few more seconds, the commander slowly moved his right hand from the railing toward his waist line. Teancum was relieved there was some sign of life but quickly became afraid that he might be reaching for a weapon. Looking around for the closest exit, he took two steps back readjusting his stance, just in case he needed to make a quick getaway.

"I have waited for this moment for a while now. I have something for you," he said to Teancum in a deep slow tone.

Oh no, Teancum's mind was racing. *This is it. He is going to try to kill me. Get ready to move and run!*

As the old soldier slowly turned, it looked like he was grasping the hilt of his big sword, getting ready to pull it out. But to Teancum's great relief, instead of a weapon, he pulled a small leather pouch from under his sash.

"This is a necklace that belonged to my mother. It is a family heirloom that has been passed down for hundreds of years. I am told it was brought over from the old world by one of Ishmael's daughters....Lily, I think her name was Lily. The one who married Father Sam." He looked into Teancum's eyes to see if he understood the importance of the jewelry. Teancum blinked several times and was still processing the fact that he was not going to be killed by the large soldier. The commander continued shaking his head. "But no one knows for sure." He opened the top of the pouch and pulled out a silver braided chain with a medium-sized ruby set in a silver disk. The disk had two small Egyptian hieroglyphs, one representing the symbol of a man and the other a woman, on either side of the gemstone. "It is supposed to bring luck to whomever possesses it on their wedding day. I don't believe in all that hocus-pocus nonsense, but Hanni knows about this necklace and she loves the romantic story behind it." He put the necklace back into the leather pouch and handed it to Teancum. "Give this to her as a token of my response to your request. She will understand what it means."

Things were still a bit unclear for Teancum. "Is...this a yes?" He questioned as he held out his hand for the pouch.

"You're a good boy, Teancum. You care about my daughter very much, even a blind man could see that. Her mother and I have had several long conversations about you and Hanni." He moved closer to Teancum and put both his hands on Teancum's shoulders. Squeezing firmly, he continued, "If you ever do anything to hurt my daughter, I will personally pull your spine out." He smiled and squeezed very hard on Teancum's shoulders. Looking Teancum right in the eyes, he took a deep breath and continued, "Yes, you may marry my child."

Teancum grimaced at the pain in his shoulders. "Thank you, sir, I won't let you down."

"I know you won't," he smiled, as he released the pressure on Teancum's body.

The commander's security chief and his squad all stood just outside the balcony, waiting for the commander to return. The soldier who left to fetch the refreshments returned with a large tray of food in one hand with two goblets and a jug of juice in the other. "Captain, I have the food that was requested, and something extra for your good friend, Teancum."

The captain turned around with a puzzled look on his face. "What do you mean 'extra'?"

The soldier set the tray down and walked up to the captain. "Sir, would you please hold this cup?" He handed the cup to the officer and then pulled something out of his tunic pocket. "I found it just outside the kitchen doors." He held up a large dead cockroach. Smiling, the soldier dropped the dead insect into the cup, then poured the thick fruit juice in, filling it to the brim. "A little extra protein for the growing boy."

The captain snickered in approval of the disgusting prank. The rest of the guards, standing around the two men, joined in the laughter, thinking about Teancum drinking the bug-flavored juice. "Allow me," the Captain said as he took the tray of food and the drinks from the other soldier, then walked out onto the balcony. This drink he wanted to personally serve to Teancum.

The captain led the procession of guards as they all walked out onto the balcony, just as the commander released his grip on Teancum's shoulders.

"Sir, the food and drinks you requested."

"Excellent timing, captain, bring them here," he said, gesturing to a table next to him.

The captain set the tray down, quickly grabbing the two goblets. He handed the one with the roach in it to Teancum and the empty glass to the commander. As the captain was pouring the juice into the empty cup, Teancum wondered why he got his glass first and why it already had liquid in it. *Military courtesy was that the highest ranking officer gets his glass first. You never pour anything into an officer's glass without first asking permission....Something is up*, he thought. Teancum looked down into his goblet then back at the soldiers standing behind the captain. They all were smiling and looking at him. One of them even gave a thumbs up and pointed to Teancum's cup while another made a drinking gesture.

They put something in my drink! The realization shot through his mind like an arrow. *I can't let them know I'm on to them...but how can I turn this around?* Teancum's mind was racing when a devious plan came to him.

The old commander raised his full goblet and gave a toast to Teancum and his health. But just before he took his first drink Teancum interrupted.

"Sir..." He cleared his throat as he was thinking about his next move.

"During my studies, I came across an Old World tradition that I think is appropriate for this occasion."

"Really?" His soon to be father-in-law lowered his glass. "Do tell."

"As a symbolic gesture," Teancum could not believe he came up with this so quickly, "the father of the bride-to-be and the groom-to-be exchange goblets the first time, after the consent to marry is given, then they both drink the entire contents in one big gulp." Teancum looked back at the soldiers standing behind him whose facial expressions ranged from disbelief to sheer horror.

"No, sir. Not a good idea!" The captain called out as he reached for Teancum's cup. Teancum refused to relinquish his cup.

"Nonsense, I like that idea, the symbolism…. It's kind of like I'm giving you what is mine," he said as he pointed to his goblet. "My daughter, and in return you give me something back." He then pointed to Teancum's glass. "Like grandchildren, ha!" He reached for Teancum's cup and gave his in return.

The captain was beside himself. "Sir! I…" But it was too late. The old man raised up the cup with the dead cockroach and exclaimed, "To my grandbabies!" Then he drank the entire contents of the goblet in one large gulp, insect and all.

"To my future children and your grandbabies!" Teancum responded and winked at the captain as he drank from his clean cup.

Some of the soldiers just stood and gasped. Two soldiers succumbed to their gag reflexes as they started to dry heave watching their commander swallow a large dead cockroach whole. One soldier just turned and walked away. The captain was stunned into silence and could not move, his mouth gaping wide open. *How did that prank go so badly, so quickly?* he wondered.

The old commander finished his drink in one big gulp and smacked his lips. "Very good juice. Thank you, captain." He handed his empty glass to the leader of his security detail.

"Yes captain, a very good glass indeed," Teancum quipped with a not so subtle hint of sarcasm in his tone as he handed his cup to the officer.

"Now…" the old soldier barked as he grabbed Teancum by the back of the neck, shaking him slightly, "Where is my daughter? I'm sure she is lurking around here somewhere."

"This way, sir." Teancum pointed back toward the doors leading back into the great hall. The two men started to walk toward the doors and

Teancum looked back at the captain and squad of soldiers still standing in disbelief.

"Have a good evening, gentlemen," Teancum smiled as he waved goodbye as he and the commander walked through the doors.

The whole squad stood frozen, looking at each other in complete silence, pondering how their prank went so very, very wrong.

A cheer of joy and delight echoed through the hall as Hanni wrapped her arms around her father's neck, kissing his cheek. She was overjoyed with the news of his consent. She hugged him and jumped up and down all while squeezing his neck. Hanni's mother had just arrived and Hanni turned to tell her the good news. "He said yes, mother!" Hanni shouted. Her mother joyfully wiped away a tear as she hugged Hanni, and looked at Teancum. Teancum smiled, bowing at the waist, as a sign of respect for Hanni's mother. He stood a few paces away allowing Hanni and her parents to enjoy the moment. The three of them all came together in a family embrace, then Hanni reached out for Teancum's hand. Taking two steps toward Hanni, Teancum grabbed her hand. He was quickly pulled into the family embrace.

"Your mother— where is she, is she here tonight?" Hanni's mother asked as she released her hold on both Teancum and Hanni while looking around the hall.

"No, ma'am. She was needed at the ranch and left this morning, but she eagerly awaits word on tonight's outcome," Teancum responded while readjusting his tunic. "It is calving season and we have many cows ready to give birth. I must return in the morning to assist, but that should give my lady and Hanni some time together to start working out the wedding arrangements." The two women hugged again and smiled at each other. They were both thinking the same thought: how much fun it will be to plan a grand wedding.

"So, Teancum?" The commander spoke after clearing his throat, "What are your plans for the future? Are you going to remain at the ranch and take over for Lord Pilio when he retires?"

"Well, sir, the ranch will stay in the family. That I can promise." He gave the commander a reassuring nod. "It is good you are all here. Now, I have some more good news." Teancum turned to face Hanni. He grabbed both her hands looking into her eyes. "I just got word today," he smiled into her eyes, "I have been accepted into medical school at the King's Royal Academy of Medicine."

Hanni's eyes grew wide and her mouth opened in a gasp. She let go of Teancum's hands and covered her mouth with both of her hands letting out a muffled scream. "The King's Academy….They said yes?" She whispered in excitement while bouncing up and down.

"Yes, my love." He smiled wider and nodded. "I'm going to be a physician."

It took a second for Hanni to completely process what he had shared. The thought of what had happened broke slowly across her mind. "I'm going to marry the man of my dreams, and he is going to be a doctor." Her deepest wish was coming true. Screaming, Hanni jumped into Teancum's arms. With tears of joy running down her face, she embraced him with all the passion and feeling that only someone truly in love could do. "I'm so proud of you. I will love and honor you forever," she whispered into his ear. Teancum hugged her even tighter as she said those words. He was starting to realize his own dream was coming true.

"A doctor…Well done, my boy, well done," Hanni's father said as he patted Teancum on the shoulder. Hanni and Teancum let go of their tight embrace as Teancum turned to face his soon to be father-in-law.

"Thank you, sir," Teancum responded as he offered his hand to the old soldier. Hanni's father slapped the hand to one side. Grabbing Teancum around the neck, he gave Teancum a very strong embrace. Teancum's face was turning a bit red from the pressure around his neck, Hanni had to intervene before Teancum passed out from the lack of blood flow to his head. Laughing, the old soldier let Teancum go, moving out of the way to make room for his wife. Bowing, he relinquished the position of his dominant presence and succumbed to the majesty of his own soul mate's allure.

Hanni's mother was next to address Teancum. "Congratulations, Master Teancum," she spoke in her ever-present, regal demeanor as she stepped forward offering her right hand to Teancum. She was very much a proper Nephite lady, much like Teancum's grandmother. Taking her hand ever so gently and bowing slighting before her, out of respect, Teancum assumed his role as a young Nephite man of honor addressing a woman.

"Thank you, my lady," he said in an even tone. "You honor me with your encouragement and support."

"Nonsense," she replied, as she took her left hand and touched Teancum's cheek. "It is you who honor this family. You are a good and honorable man. You make Hanni very happy. What more could we ask for in a son-in-law....?" She looked at Hanni's father and smiled. He smiled back. "Welcome to the family." She finished and unexpectedly reached out to Teancum for an embrace. Teancum blinked several times and took a half step back. This caught him off guard. Until today, he had never been less than an arm's length from her since he had known her. Now, she was offering an embrace...this was definitely a day to remember. Moving gently and not knowing exactly what to expect, Teancum positioned himself between her arms while carefully wrapping his arms around her upper back. She wrapped her arms around his neck giving him a quick squeeze. It felt awkward, but Teancum was just glad she allowed him to be that close to her. They embraced for several seconds and she was the first to release. Stepping back, Teancum bowed again and spoke,

"With your permission, my lady," he spoke with a slight bow of his head, "I have much to do. I must make ready for my return to the ranch in the morning. I would like to spend what little time I have left today with Hanni."

"Yes, of course," she gestured with her hands, "go with our blessing. Please, give my regards to your mother and grandparents. Tell them they are always welcome in our home."

"Thank you, my lady, I will tell them." Teancum then turned to face Hanni's father. The emotions of the moment had left her father's face and he was again the stern warrior.

"By your leave, commander?" Teancum asked respectfully while standing up straight. Teancum was not in the army but this man before him was responsible for the lives of everyone in the city. His reputation preceded him as a true warrior, a man of honor and high moral integrity. And he was still the father of his bride-to-be. Showing a deep level of respect to Hanni's father was expected from a young Nephite like Teancum and it is what Teancum gave.

"Granted. Go with God's blessings, lad," he responded to Teancum in a very militaristic tone. "Tell your grandfather he is welcome at my table for the military games next month."

"I will, sir. Thank you." Teancum bowed and turned to face Hanni. Her face was flushed and her cheeks were streaked with the salty stains from her happy tears. Smiling, he took the few steps to be at her side. Taking her hand, they started to walk away when Hanni broke free from

Teancum's grasp and ran back to hug her parents one more time. They all embraced and Hanni could not help but shed more tears of joy.

"Remember to be home before the night watch closes the main gates." Her father repeated those infamous lines she had heard hundreds of times before. Hanni and her mother shared a quick glance and an unspoken joke between them.

"Dear," Hanni's mother spoke to her husband while she gently stroked his muscular arm. "Hanni is nineteen. She is going to marry soon."

Looking at the two most important women in his life, the commander knew he was outmatched. Recognizing the wisdom in his wife's gentle words, he conceded his point and smiled. But deep down inside his heart, Hanni would always be his little girl, no matter what. "Enjoy your evening with Teancum."

"Thank you, Daddy." She kissed him on the cheek then quickly walked back to Teancum. Teancum watched, understanding what was happening. He was letting her go. He and the old soldier made eye contact and nodded to each other. Nothing else needed to be said between two men of honor.

Grabbing Teancum by the arm, Hanni spun him around and they joyfully walked toward the center of the city.

"So, what's on the agenda?" she asked after they walked several paces.

"Dinner? I did not want to eat the food at the party from your father's table."

"Why not?" she asked in a curious tone.

"I'll tell you later." He smiled.

The commander and his wife stood watching as Teancum and Hanni walked around a corner and out of sight. Once they were gone, he grabbed his wife around her hips. Pulling her close, he stole a kiss and the two embraced out of pure joy for their only daughter and her bright future.

"You are happy about this?" she questioned her oldest friend and life partner.

"He is a much cleverer boy than I had given him credit for," he responded with a bit of mischief in his tone.

"Oh, do tell!" She was curious.

"Well…" She gently placed her arm in his. They started to walk back to the party as he explained the joke his guards attempted to play on Teancum with the bug in the drinking glass. The old commander was an excellent soldier and was always aware of his surroundings. He knew something was going on the moment the captain of the guard walked out onto the balcony. So he was impressed in how Teancum had seen right through the prank and turned the tables on the guards. As they walked farther away, no one could hear what they were saying, but if someone was watching, they would have seen him make a gesture like he was drinking something and she yelped in disgust. He laughed out loud as she playfully slapped his arm.

Teancum left the city very early the next day and rode his horse directly to the ranch. Every time he made the trip down the wide and well-used merchant road, he would stop at the crossroads marker where, years ago, Pilio found Kail mortally wounded. He would pay his respects to the memory of his murdered father. Dismounting from his steed, he walked over to the large familiar grouping of boulders just off the road, and found his spot. His horse didn't care about the importance of this place. He was busy chomping away at the green grass growing around the large rocks.

"She said yes, Father." He smiled, still holding the reins to his mount while looking up into the bright mid-morning sky. "I think you already knew that." Smiling he looked back down at the ground. He went to church out of obligation and he knew the teachings. He knew his mother believed Kail's spirit was always close by, but did he know it? Teancum was not sure. But he did like to think that his father was watching over him.

"Sometimes, I feel overwhelmed and wish you were here to guide me. Grandfather is doing the best he can, but I know he is getting old and tired." Teancum sat still for a moment and thought about his life. He smiled again as he reflected on how blessed he truly was. This was a beautiful day and the first of his new life. He was engaged to an amazing, beautiful woman and he'd been accepted into a prestigious medical school. He may be without a father but that did not mean he was not adored by those around him. His mother, his grandparents, Hanni, and now her parents too. As he sat there on the rocks, he felt the warmth of their love grow in his heart as real as the warmth of the sun on his face and the fresh breeze gently blowing his hair. Closing his eyes, he lifted his chin and took in some deep breaths. All was right in the world for Teancum and he was enjoying this special moment. Teancum kept his eyes closed to bask in the feelings of peace. As he sat in quiet stillness, the image of a tall, well-built man with dark hair standing in front of him, came into his mind. It lasted only a few seconds but Teancum saw the man look down and smile at him as he sat on the large rock in the mid-morning sun.

The man mouthed one word. *Courage*. It gently sounded in Teancum's ears and he quickly opened his eyes. But, the vision was gone.

"Father?" The word escaped Teancum's mouth before he had a chance to think about what he had said. Standing quickly to check his surroundings, Teancum saw he was alone, except for his hungry horse. Confused as to why his master suddenly stood up, Teancum's trusty mount looked up at him. They stood still for several seconds, looking into each other's eyes then Teancum playfully spouted, "What are you looking at?" The horse stood still for a few more seconds, flicked its ears then went back to ripping the fresh grass from the ground. Feeling a bit foolish, Teancum snorted under his breath, shook his head and sat back down. Teancum thought about the single word the unknown personage spoke to him.

"Courage," he had said out loud. Leaning back, he closed his eyes and said the word over three more times. "Courage to do what?" He asked out loud. As he pondered this thought, his horse walked in front of him snorted and dug at the ground with its hoof. "Ready to go, big boy?" Teancum asked as he stood up and moved to climb into his saddle. Teancum stood beside his horse, patting its neck. "Please don't tell the other horses that I am seeing visions and talking to myself...Okay?" The horse moved its head toward Teancum, brushing up against him as a sign of affection. "All right," he said as he swung up into the saddle, "let's go home before mother sends Tum out to search for us." Making a clicking sound and giving the reins a shake, Teancum urged the large animal forward and back onto the merchant road.

Teancum was still a half a mile away, but he could hear the ringing of a large metal gong that was set up near the main entrance of his home echoing across the green meadows and through the ancient trees lining the pathway. Someone had spotted him coming up the road. The ringing was to announce to the entire ranch the young master had returned. He smiled to himself as he thought about what his return meant. Warm embraces, a grand feast, and a long sit by the hearth's fire awaited, while he would tell everyone about his engagement to Hanni and his appointment to the King's College of Medicine. Crossing through the tall stone and wood archway, Teancum entered the grounds of the ranch itself, stopping to enjoy the view before him.

The main house dominated the open landscape with a wide open, grass meadow in front and a large barn and several utility buildings to the side and rear. Teancum always loved the view of the property from the gate. Most of the trees had been removed to make room for grazing land, but the house itself had several massive, ancient trees around the perimeter for shade. The barn's design matched the home in color and shape. It was big enough to house several horses as well as store feed and farming supplies. There was a millhouse with a large stone that was set up to be turned by a donkey or horse. There was also a metal shop, wood shop, and root cellar, which had been buried to help keep it cool for food storage. Three small cottages and a bunk house were set up in the back of the property for the families and single men who worked on the ranch. The main house was large but not audacious. It was a two-story home of wood and stone construction with a porch that wrapped all the way around the structure. Teancum could see smoke coming from the kitchen chimney and he knew lunch was not far behind. The young boy ringing the metal gong had stopped as several people came out to the front of the home to see who was approaching. Teancum could see his grandmother standing on the porch wiping her hands with her apron. He smiled and waved to her as he continued forward. Teancum always admired the fact that his grandparents worked alongside the paid help to manage and run the ranch. They were a very respected, rich and powerful couple and did not need to exert themselves. But there they were, up nearly every morning, Pilio in the large garden or working the cattle. Saria, managing the house and the affairs of the ranch. Everyone knew who was really in charge. Pilio would play along, but he knew his place. He was the lord and master but this was Saria's house, her garden, and her ranch.

The same boy who was ringing the bell was waiting for Teancum at the foot of the front steps leading up to the main doors. Teancum stopped, dismounted from his horse and handed the reins to the boy.

"Hello Kip...." Teancum said as the boy took the horse. "Brush him down and store the saddle in the tack room. One fleck of hay and one bucket of oats for his dinner, please."

"Yes sir," the young boy responded as he led the big horse to the barn.

"Kip, please bring Master Teancum's saddle bags inside and put them in his room," Tum called out as he stepped out from the front door and stood next to Saria.

Teancum nodded to Tum as he walked up the steps and into the waiting outstretched arms of his loving grandmother.

"Hello, Grandmother," Teancum gently spoke as he wrapped his arms around her then gently squeezed.

"You are home at last," she happily responded.

Letting go, Teancum looked around. "Where is Mother?"

"She is in the garden with Lord Pilio. The grasshoppers came early this year. They are doing what they can to save the corn," she responded as she smiled and looked up into his dark eyes.

"Tum, how are you?" Teancum acknowledged the head servant and old family friend.

"I am well, Master Teancum. Thank you for asking," he responded with a slight bow to his head. There was no need for the overt courtesy. Tum was just as influential in raising Teancum as anyone else on the ranch. But Tum found joy and great pride in excelling at his chosen profession as the servant to Lord Pilio and Lady Saria. He was well compensated for his talents and skills in caring for the family as well as helping Saria manage the ranch. But it was the love that everyone felt from Tum that made him indispensable to the ranch.

"Lunch is almost ready," Lady Saria spoke. "Why don't we go around to the garden to see your mother and grandfather? I will have the noon meal served on the back porch," she spoke as she took Teancum's arm then turned to look at Tum. Tum took the verbal clue to change the eating arrangement and bowed to the lady.

"Very well, my lady," Tum responded. "Welcome home, Master Teancum."

"Thank you, Tum…It's good to be home." Teancum held his arm in the proper escort position as Saria grasped tightly to it with both hands. She was moving a bit slower now but still had the fire and presence of a true regal Nephite lady.

They both walked around the side of the big house on the wrap around porch.

"You look a bit tired, Teancum. Is life in the city disagreeing with you?"

"No Grandmother, life in Zarahemla is fine. I was up late last night finalizing some personal matters."

"Nothing bad I hope?" She questioned as they continued to walk.

"No ma'am, just the opposite. Actually, it's some very good news."

"Well, are you going to share this news?" She asked while shaking his arm slightly.

"I was hoping to share it with the whole family after dinner tonight." He paused, "With your permission, of course."

"Teancum." She playfully scorned and waved her hand in front of her body while speaking, "You are the heir to this entire estate and all your grandfather's wealth. You hardly need my permission to speak to the family."

They stopped near the back doors of the ranch. Teancum waved to his mother, who was standing in the garden in rows of chest high corn stalks. She was in her favorite summer dress with her hair pulled back and covered with a scarf to keep it clean and to keep the sweat out of her eyes. She excitedly waved back shouting behind her, "Father, he is here!"

Dinner that night was a grand feast of lamb and venison with fresh vegetables just harvested from the garden, with watermelon and sweet bread for dessert. It was such a nice evening that Lady Saria had dinner served on the back porch. Everyone on the ranch was invited to join them and partake.

"A very pleasant evening for eating outside," Teancum said as he fumbled with his food. He was nervous and excited at the same time while waiting for the right moment to make his grand announcement.

"Not much longer; the weather is going to change. I can feel the cold coming on in my bones," Pilio responded to Teancum as they sat next to each other during dinner, making small talk.

One of the ranch hands' wives had just given birth. Rachael was sitting next to the new mother while holding the new baby, gently rocking it to sleep. "What a good baby," she observed as the infant lay quietly in her arms, wrapped in a light blanket, eyes open, and looking around.

"He is now that I finished feeding him." The new mother looked happy but exhausted. "Give it a few hours, my lady. He will be crying loud enough to wake the dead."

The two women had a small laugh while they continued talking softly about motherhood.

Teancum took a bite of food and chewed while he looked around the large table at everyone who was important to him in his life. Then he remembered there was someone missing, someone who he was madly in love with and desperately wanted to share moments like this with.

Quickly swallowing the bite of food in his mouth, Teancum stood up and cleared his throat.

"Can I have everyone's attention please?" he asked in a polite tone. He turned to look at the head of the table. "Grandfather, with your permission, may I make an announcement?" He knew what the answer would be, but etiquette and good manners required him to ask permission from the master of the home.

"Of course, Teancum. Please." Pilio held out his hand, gesturing for Teancum to continue.

"Thank you, sir." Teancum nodded his head to his grandfather then continued. "Mother." He looked at her and acknowledged her as she continued to gently rock the newborn. "Grandmother." He turned and made eye contact with his sweet grandparent. "Family and friends." He raised up both hands to show he was addressing everyone else sitting at the table or standing nearby. "I have some wonderful news I want to share with my family and dear friends. As you all know, it has been recommended by several of my tutors that I should seek a profession in medicine. Well, I applied to several good schools to do just that, and yesterday," he paused as he pulled out a parchment from inside his tunic holding it up for all to see, "I was given word that I was accepted into the King's University of Medicine, right here in Zarahemla."

There was a collective gasp as everyone reacted to the amazing news. Rachael quickly turned to the new mother sitting next to her to give back the baby. She wanted to get up and approach her son, but before she could get out of her seat, Teancum held up his hand to signal her to stop. "Mother, wait, there's more."

Rachael sat up straight in her chair with both her hands clasped in front of her. You could see the excitement in her eyes. She was hoping it was about Hanni.

"When I got the news that I was going to be a physician, I knew my life would not be complete unless I had someone to share my life and good fortune with." He stopped to look at his mother and was beaming from ear to ear as he continued to speak. Rachael was bouncing in her chair. "Yesterday, I asked Hanni to be my wife..." He paused for effect. "And she said yes."

"Yeaaaaa!" Rachael threw both of her hands into the air shrieking with excitement. She was out of her chair, moving toward Teancum before he could ready himself. She wrapped both her arms around his neck.

"I'm so happy for you both," she was crying as she embraced her only child, tightly. Pilio and Saria both got up from their chairs and moved to be next to Teancum. They also wanted to congratulate their oldest grandchild but Rachael was not letting go. The rest of the ranch staff, with their families, were all excited and talking amongst themselves about the news. They all knew and liked Hanni very much. They had all known her as a young girl, visiting the ranch. She had left them all with the impression she was a kind and generous young lady.

Rachael finally let go, stepping back and wiping tears of joy from her eyes. Saria and Pilio both give their congratulations, then Tum was the next to speak.

"Congratulations, Master Teancum," he said as he put forth his hand to shake. "Have you set a date for the wedding?"

Teancum took his hand and shook it. "We were thinking about having it after the New Year. This will give Hanni and her mother time to work out the many details. By then, I will have one session of schooling completed."

"And the celebration? Where were you thinking about having that?" Saria spoke without missing a beat. If there was going to be a grand party, she was going to be involved in the planning. It was the only way to ensure the event was up to her standards.

"Well…." Teancum knew his family very well. He knew the answer before she asked the question, but he needed it to feel like it was her idea to make it work. "We thought about having it here, but figured it would be too much trouble, and the guests would need to travel all the way out here…." He paused as he looked at Pilio.

Pilio gave him a look that told Teancum he knew exactly what Teancum was up to, and he was not happy about it, but he would keep quiet. Teancum gave a quick smile back. They both knew Saria well enough to know what was going to happen next.

"Nonsense!" Saria sounded almost insulted. "You will have the celebration here." She actually put her foot down as she spoke. "We will arrange for wagons to bring all the guests from the city and return them when we are done." She looked at Pilio for assurance that he was in agreement.

Pilio knew better than to argue and quickly nodded his head. "Excellent idea," he smiled. He then gave Teancum a menacing look. Teancum just winked back and smiled. He knew he was going to pay for this later, but right now he was enjoying the moment.

"Well, we have much to discuss. Pilio dear," she turned around to speak directly to her husband. "We should go to the city to visit with the commander and his wife. There is much to arrange, and a short time to do it."

"Yes dear, absolutely," Pilio smiled again as Saria walked past him. He looked back at Teancum and pointed an angry finger at him. Teancum covered his mouth to keep from laughing.

"Come Rachael, I have several ideas already swimming around in my head. We should go write them down," Saria said as she walked away from the table.

"Now you have dragged me into this," Rachael whispered to Teancum as she moved past him to follow Saria inside the house.

Pilio held up two fingers in front of Teancum. "That's two of us now." He smiled. "You're running out of friends very quickly around here, mister."

Teancum snickered and shrugged his shoulders.

"Teancum," Pilio put his hand on Teancum's shoulder, speaking loud enough for the rest of the staff to hear. They all saw what had happened and were enjoying the exchange between the two men. "You take charge of the dinner cleanup and see to the dishes personally." Pilio then held out his arm to escort Rachael from the table. Smiling and winking at Teancum, Rachael took his arm and the two walked into the house to join Saria.

Tum walked up to Teancum as Teancum started to stack the dishes on the table. They made eye contact. "It was worth it," Teancum snickered as he lifted a stack of plates taking them to the cleaning sink.

It was a cool, crisp morning as the servants finished loading the rest of Teancum's bags into the wagon. Refusing to succumb to the coming fall season, the sun was just starting to come up over the eastern horizon, desperately trying to warm the open fields and wooded valleys of Pilio's ranch. The few fluffy clouds in the sky were changing colors from white to purple, to a warm red as the morning sun's rays pierced the blackness.

"I'm so proud of you," Rachael spoke into Teancum's ear as she hugged him tightly. This moment had been a long time coming and Rachael was doing her best not to cry. Pilio and Saria stood next to Rachael, waiting for their turn to say their goodbyes to their oldest grandson. Saria was wrapped in a large blanket and Pilio had his arms around her shoulders rubbing them for warmth.

"He has become a very handsome young man," Saria bragged as she looked up into Pilio's eyes.

"Yes, he has," Pilio responded as he exhaled.

Rachael held on to Teancum as long as she could, then, her calm exterior belying her turbulent emotions, she let her boy go, knowing the next time they met would be for his wedding.

Teancum took one step back looking deeply into his mother's eyes. "I will send word as soon as I'm settled." He smiled and rubbed her shoulders. "It's alright mother, I'm just going back to Zarahemla, not to the Land of Desolation."

Rachael cocked her head to the side and spoke. "Don't worry about me," she said as she patted his chest with the palm of her hand. "You just come back home when you can." She sniffled and wiped her nose with a handkerchief. "You are going to be an excellent doctor. Now say goodbye to your grandparents and be on your way."

Teancum smiled again and turned to face Pilio and Saria. With his arms wide open, Teancum walked toward them. Saria grabbed him around the waist and Pilio wrapped his arms around Teancum's neck. The three embraced each other and shared a quiet, loving moment. "Make us proud, Teancum," Pilio said as he looked Teancum in the eyes.

"Yes sir, I will."

"Do you have everything you will need?" Saria asked like a true grandmother while fussing with the lapels of Teancum's coat. "Yes, ma'am. I think so," Teancum responded with a hint of hesitation in his voice. Taking a deep breath, he continued to answer his grandmother. "I don't know what to expect, so I guess I'm as ready as I can be."

"You will be just fine, son." Pilio interrupted.

Saria gave Pilio a soft slap on the chest. "Let me finish," she warned him playfully. "You will be just fine." She shot a look at Pilio. "You are a brilliant, handsome, strong young man. You are loved and now you have someone to love. What more could we ask for in a grandson?" Saria hugged Teancum again and Pilio patted his back. "Now go," Saria sniffled, "before I change my mind and make you stay here with us forever." She smiled as she gently pushed him away from her. Teancum took two steps back and smiled at his grandparents. Rachael had moved up next to Pilio and Saria. They all shared a last quiet moment together.

"I must be off," Teancum finally said and he smiled at his mother as he picked up his personal bag, flinging it over his shoulder. He could see the tears freely flowing down Rachael's' face now, and it was breaking his heart, but he knew he must leave. He moved quickly, hugging his mother one last time.

"Go," she whispered into his ear. "Make me proud."

Teancum looked into his mother's eyes, then smiled. "I will, mother, I will." With that, he quickly turned and moved to the small wagon, tossing his bag in the back with the rest of his belongings. Jumping on his horse, he was on the road before anyone could change his mind.

Pilio, Saria, and Rachael all stood huddled together against the crisp morning air, watching their pride and joy as he disappeared past the stone archway and around the bend in the road. There was a very old pain in Rachael's heart, slowly making its way to the surface. A pain she had not let herself feel in many years. Pilio was the first to sense a change in Rachael. Her posture, demeanor, even her breathing patterns were changing.

"What is it, my princess?" he asked in a loving, fatherly tone.

"I really miss Kail right now." Rachael half choked with emotion as she spoke. Saria put her arms around Rachael.

"We all do." Saria smoothly rocked Rachael back and forth. "He would be so proud right now, seeing his only child leave to start his amazing life." Rachael nodded in agreement while trying to breathe through her congested nose. "Let's go back inside and enjoy a good breakfast together, shall we?" Saria continued.

"Wonderful idea," Pilio said as he gently guided the two women toward the main doors of the ranch house.

CHAPTER SEVEN

HANNI

L ife at medical school for a first-year student was very difficult for most. A vast majority of the young students were from wealthy and privileged families who could afford to pay the high cost of an excellent education. Those students from rich families were raised in a pampered environment with servants and very little personal responsibility. Hard work, and the demanding expectations of being a medical student attending the King's College of Medicine, was an unwelcome and troubling surprise. Teancum was from a very rich and influential family. In fact, one of the most influential in the entire land. But, from the day he could walk, he had been taught the value of a hard day's work. He'd been taught to respect others, especially his elders and those in positions of leadership over him. So it was no surprise that it was very apparent to the teaching staff and upper classmates that he was exceptional in almost every way. His grandfather Pilio was trained at the Nephite military officer's academy. Out of the service, he continued to live his life in a disciplined way. He passed those disciplined ideals onto Teancum who had been instructed, at a young age to always make his bed and keep his room clean and orderly.

"By making your bed and insuring your room is clean before you leave for the day, you have accomplished something good, and that sets the tone for the rest of your day," Pilio would instruct young Teancum as he helped the young boy make his bed and pick his belongings up off the floor. "Then at the end of a long day, when you're ready for bed, you will end your day looking at and enjoying the fruits of something you have successfully done. It sets the groundwork for you to enjoy a successful life."

Teancum took to these good habits like a fish to water. It did set the tone for his new life and the way he approached his learning. Up in the morning before the others, Teancum was clean and ready for the day while his classmates grumbled and fussed just to get out of bed. His study habits reflected Teancum's desire to excel and before long he had memorized several key aspects of his medical training. The more he studied, the more he knew. The more he knew, the better he became at the healing arts. It was not long before Teancum was leading study groups and tutoring his fellow students. Teancum was honored to be asked by his classmates for advice and help. He freely gave of his time and was very generous with his knowledge and understanding. It was unheard of for a first year student to be so advanced in the training. This did not go unnoticed by the instructors. In fact, the only thing in Teancum's life that distracted him from his studies was Hanni.

She would visit him whenever possible. She wanted to spend every waking moment with her love, but with making the wedding plans, her employment with the charitable organization she worked for, and trying to find time to meet between his classes was difficult. That is why she relished the Sabbath day. This was a day without the distractions of Teancum's schooling or her employment. They could just be a couple. Teancum would join her for Sunday breakfast with her family, then they would sit together for worship service and slowly walk back home when it was over. Hand in hand, they would always end up taking the long way around, to sit under a tree, or walk through the grand markets of Zarahemla, talking about the future and plans for their lifelong happiness. Dinner on those nights in Hanni's home were always an affair. The commander and his wife would entertain the powerful and influential from all over the province. Teancum was introduced as their future son-in-law to the elite of Zarahemla's society. He was quickly making acquaintances with those of power in politics, the military, religion, and high society. He was raised to be a proper man of honor on Pilio's ranch and blended in seamlessly with those around him. He was charming, witty, gracious and above all else, polite. This did not go unnoticed by those in power. There were toasts between men of power to a bright future for this tall, handsome lad, the heir to Lord Pilio and Lady Saria, and the newest member of the garrison commander's family.

After months of planning and waiting, the grand day had finally arrived. The wedding of Teancum and Hanni had grown to become the event of the season, with anyone who was anyone in the land of Zarahemla being invited. Pilio, Saria and Rachael had arrived in the great city the day prior and were the honored guests in Hanni's home. Teancum was still living in the college dormitory. He was up early, as usual, finishing the packing of his personal belongings and taking inventory of his life to that point.

With the help of some of his classmates, Teancum carried his bags to the main courtyard of the school and into a waiting wagon. Standing near the back of the wagon was the headmaster of the medical college. At the suggestion of Hanni's father, a few weeks ago, Teancum had extended the headmaster and his wife an invitation to the wedding and celebration.

"Good morning, Headmaster," Teancum called out as he lugged his bags toward the waiting wagon.

"Young Teancum, good morning and congratulations again on the fine match you have made." It seemed the headmaster was a bit star struck. He was not very high on the list of important people in the city. The man was as thin as a stick, with a hawk nose and big feet. He always had an arm full of books or papers and moved like he was late to something. He was quite socially awkward, to say the least, so a personal invitation from the groom to the wedding of the season was a big deal for him. "Do you have all your belongings?" He asked as he watched Teancum and his friends load the wagon.

"Yes, sir. Thank you again for everything," Teancum responded as he held out his hand to the school master.

Eagerly shaking Teancum's hand, the headmaster responded, "My pleasure, and thank you again for the invitation." He pulled Teancum closer speaking in a low tone. "My wife has been walking on clouds ever since you gave us the invite." He winked and patted Teancum on the back.

Teancum smiled back. "My pleasure sir." There was an awkward silence as the man continued to hold on to Teancum's hand and smile at him. "I do need to get going," Teancum said with a bit of awkward humor in his tone. "There will not be a wedding if the groom does not show up."

"Yes...Yes, of course." The headmaster released his grip, moving to allow Teancum to move toward the wagon seat. Teancum shook hands and hugged his school chums, then jumped up into the passenger seat next to the wagon driver.

"Do you know where to go?" he asked the driver.

"Yes, sir," the driver mumbled. It was still early for him and he had not yet had breakfast.

"Good, let's go....quickly please," Teancum whispered as he looked over his shoulder one last time, waving to his schoolmates and the headmaster.

The teamster slapped down on the reins and said, "Yah!" The old dark horse lurched forward. They were off to the large house belonging to the garrison commander.

Hanni had been scrubbing, curling and primping, dressing and undressing for almost twelve hours. She was exhausted, hungry, frustrated, and most of all, wishing she could see her beloved Teancum. "Well, it's a foolish tradition, if you ask me," she responded to her mother as she looked into a mirror, fussing with her hair. The debate over why she must wait until the actual marriage ceremony to see him had been raging for about twenty minutes.

"My dear, traditions are very important to our culture," Hanni's mother grunted as she struggled to put on a shoe. Her new custom-made shoes had just arrived. They were just a bit too small for her feet, but she loved the way they complemented her new gown. Standing and grimacing painfully, she held out her hands for balance as she admired them and continued, "We honor our heritage by following those traditions. You will definitely feel different when it's your child sitting here making the final preparations to get married."

"I suppose so," Hanni sighed as the hairdresser finished braiding her hair. Hanni's mother moved next to the hairdresser, taking the long white ribbon off the table. The hairdresser bowed, moving so the lady could put the final touches of the hair design by tying the big bow at the bottom of the braid. She then inserted small white flowers in a cascading design down the long braid.

"It's all done. Let's see how it turned out." She took a step back, putting her hands down to her sides.

"Well, Mother?" Hanni took a breath and spoke. "What do you think?" Hanni carefully stood up, turning around to face her mother and the other women in the bride's preparation room. Her dress was magnificent. It was a layered gown, made of light woolen cloth, bleached to a snowy white and tailored to contour her feminine shape. It was adorned with accents of small clear stones that sparkled in the light. Her veil was a thin lace shawl that rested on her shoulders until the last moment when her head would be covered for the ceremony. Her long, hair was braided in a single strand of large loops down the center of her back and tied off with a white bow. Resting on her head was a finely crafted tiara made with her favorite small white flowers ringing the outside, the same flowers that were flowing down her hair. Around her neck was the heirloom necklace her father gave Teancum the night he asked for her hand. Hanni was nervously fumbling with the small icon on the necklace as she waited for her mother's acknowledgement. She looked like an angelic princess and the gathered women in the room all let out a collective gasp. Wiping a single tear from her eye, Hanni's mother tried to comment, but words were escaping her. She was overcome with emotion and moved to hug her only daughter.

"You are so precious. I hope Teancum understands how truly beautiful and special you are." Hanni's mother was not able to contain the flow of emotions, and she started to sob great tears of joy.

"Mother!" Hanni cried out as she felt the wave of emotion and started to cry, herself. "Please stop," she begged, as she fanned her eyes to try to dry them. "I can't get married with bloodshot and watery eyes." They both laughed at the moment together as the rest of the women came in close to inspect the dress and partake in the moment.

Teancum was more anxious than nervous. He had been standing at the front of the large chapel near the stone and wood altar for about ten minutes, waiting for the ceremony to start. Everyone he knew was in attendance sitting on the bench seats or standing around the outer edge, and there were many more whom he did not know. Friends and distant family members of both families, citizens of Zarahemla, several men in their military dress uniforms. This was a very large crowd and the longer Teancum stood in front of them, the more uncomfortable he became. He was wearing a new fitted overcoat that matched Hanni's snow white dress. It had small carved wooden toggles running down the front and his breeches were a soft tan leather. He wore a red sash across his chest and the emblem of his clan was pinned to his left breast. Unlike the Lamanites, the traditions of the clans had all but faded from the Nephite nation, but just like Hanni's family, Teancum's family was steeped in traditions. Through Pilio's side of the family, Teancum could trace his heritage all the way back to Father Jacob, Nephi's oldest son. As tradition held, Jacob was the first off the boat from the old world and the first person from the original family to walk upon this Promised Land. That relation was a point of pride for Teancum, and he wanted to honor that heritage today. The cut of the coat he was wearing accented Teancum's broad shoulders and athletic build. Combined with his dark hair and piercing eyes, he made a very handsome groom.

Teancum had been standing there awkwardly for so long, he felt like he should say something to the gathered group. He looked to Pilio who was sitting in the front row, next to Saria and Rachael, for silent guidance. Pilio nodded and held out his hand to calm Teancum, signaling him that everything would be fine, to just be still and wait. Teancum was letting his emotions overwhelm him. He was starting to sweat, fidget and shuffle his weight back and forth on his feet but was saved at the last second by the musicians in the back playing the music announcing the arrival of the bride. Everyone in attendance stood and turned to look to the rear of the hall as Hanni made her entrance.

The procession started with the priest and his attendants, draped in their robes, leading the way down the center aisle, followed by the flower girls and Hanni's young nephew as the ring bearer. Then came the bride. You could see Hanni's smile and the light in her eyes through the veil. She was radiant and beaming with happiness. This was her moment and she was glowing. Teancum felt a lump of emotion in his throat as he looked at his new bride walking toward him. Hanni's father had her arm and was escorting her to the front of the chapel. He was outfitted in his dress uniform, an ornate dress sword, and all his medals and awards decorating his chest. Hanni's mother, looking elegant and regal, was walking behind them. She was escorted by four Nephite soldiers from the security detail, also in full dress uniforms. One of them snarled at Teancum as they made eye contact. Out of spite, he winked back only infuriating the soldier more. Teancum blinked several times and realized he would be playing this game with the guards for a very long time. Teancum focused on his bride and felt again like the awkward kid at the harvest dance when he had been reacquainted with Hanni. She was so beautiful and she made him so happy. He locked this moment in time into his memory and prayed to never forget how perfect she looked.

The priest took his position and the commander escorted Hanni up next to Teancum. The old soldier stood staring into Teancum's eyes for several seconds. Then, bowing his head he reached down, took Hanni

by her delicate hand placed her hand into Teancum's, and covered both hands with his own. Grasping them tightly, the commander smiled with his misty eyes then let go of his daughter's hand.

"She is yours to care for and protect now, son." He spoke quietly and emotionally. "Go with my blessing."

"Yes sir, thank you, sir." Teancum whispered, bowing his head.

The commander stepped down and took his seat next to his wife. She covertly passed him a handkerchief, which he used to carefully dab the tears from his eyes.

The high priest that officiated the wedding ceremony was a kind and regal man who commanded much respect among the Nephites. He stood at the head of the altar, inbetween the bride and groom. He raised his arms and gestured to the couple, then looked out at the gathered family and friends.

"My dear brethren and sisters, we gather here to honor this sacred moment, where this couple will make sacred vows before God and this congregation to love and honor one another." He paused to look kindly at Teancum and Hanni. "Love has brought them together, but," he looked at Teancum, "it is only through God's help they may see themselves through the trials to come."

Trials?

Teancum felt oddly troubled at his words, but the priest shifted his gaze and began to speak to the congregation. Teancum felt the corners of his mouth pulling down to a frown, then he looked over at Hanni and her beauty completely drained his mind of worry. The priest spoke of hope and excitement for their future. He spoke of this as their first great step toward someday becoming an eternal family and their opportunity to carry on their love forever in God's grace. All nodded in agreement with him, especially Teancum's mother, whose eyes glistened with tears. How dearly she looked forward to the day she would be reunited with Kail. The priest looked at Teancum again. "Are you ready?" he said simply.

Teancum took a calming breath, looked into Hanni's eyes and smiled. "Yes." He said to his bride. "I am ready to be yours for all time."

The wedding itself was over far quicker than Teancum thought it would be. Before he realized it, he was saying "I do," and it was done.

He was in such an emotional haze, he did not even remember the words the priest said. But it did not matter. It was over and she was his for all time. There were handshakes, slaps on the back, and hugs from many people. Hanni and Teancum were enveloped by family and well-wishers, but all they wanted to do was get out of the chapel and move on with their lives. However, the festivities were far from over. Outside, waiting to caravan the entire wedding congregation to the ranch, were more wagons and buggies than could easily be counted. With the precision of a military operation, the wagons moved and guests were loaded as quickly as possible.

While the guests were loading into the wagons and the preparations were being made to move all the guests to the ranch, Teancum and his new bride finally had some time to themselves. They quickly changed into more appropriate traveling clothing. Their bags were packed and moved to their wagon. Standing with their arms around each other, they looked into each other's eyes, enjoying their first moments of marriage.

"I love you so much," Hanni whispered into Teancum's ear. "You have made me so happy."

"I will try to do the same every day from now until the end of time. I will make each day better than the last one for you, my queen," Teancum whispered back. They continued to kiss passionately while holding each other so tightly that time itself had no meaning.

After a few moments, Tum appeared at the end of the hallway. He saw Teancum and Hanni at the other end, still kissing while embracing fervently. Clearing his throat, he tried to get the attention of the newlyweds. He realized it was not working, so Tum resorted to calling out to them.

"Master Teancum?" he called. "Master Teancum, your mother has sent me to inform you the wedding caravan is ready and waiting for you and Lady Hanni." He gave Teancum a wry smile

"Um, Thank you, Tum, we will be right out," Teancum said, trying to compose himself, without taking his eyes off of his precious new wife.

"And Lady Hanni, may I be the first to congratulate you and compliment you on your fine wedding dress?" Tum continued in his proper manner. He knew there was a timetable for the festivities and they needed to get things moving right away.

They parted so Hanni could thank Tum for the compliment. After she said thank you, Teancum and Hanni smiled at each other and Teancum leaned in for yet another kiss.

"Master Teancum, did you remember to pack your school books?" Tum queried. He was teasing the two lovebirds now. But he still needed them to get into the wagon.

"You are not going to let us alone are you, Tum?" Teancum lamented.

"Your grandmother, Lady Saria, has made it quite clear regarding the timing of this wedding feast."

Teancum finally pulled away from Hanni and they smiled at each other. "Tomorrow will be about just the two of us," he said to Hanni.

She smiled and patted him on the chest. "Deal. Now let's get this over with." She grabbed his hand and the two of them walked down the hall toward Tum and the waiting wagons.

Teancum and his new bride were seated in the lead wagon. The train of followers behind them spanned for a mile. The trip seemed to last an eternity. Teancum loved feeling the warmth of Hanni as she leaned on him. They arrived at the ranch as the final preparations were being laid out. In the grassy, open area in front of the house, several large tarp coverings had been erected to form plentiful shade. Under each tarp, several chairs and a large table covered in finger foods were waiting for the guests to sample while they mingled. A smaller shade tent had been set up just off to one side of the others. Under that tent were minstrels playing music for all to enjoy. The wagons were unloaded as efficiently as they had been loaded in the city. The guests enjoyed a splendid day wandering the ranch, dancing, reacquainting, and congratulating the two families on the fine match. Speeches were made, toasts were given and wedding gifts were stacked on the porch of the grand home. Hanni was not accustomed to being the center of attention of so many people. She was in heaven and Teancum enjoyed watching her revel in the spotlight.

With about one hour of sunlight remaining, Lord Pilio stood on the porch and rang the metal gong by the front door to gain everyone's attention. "Ladies and gentlemen, may I have your attention?" It took a few moments for the merry crowd to simmer down and turn to face Lord Pilio. "From the bottom of our hearts, Lady Saria and I want to say thank you all for coming to our home and helping us celebrate this most wonderful occasion." The crowd cheered, raised their glasses and applauded. Pilio held up his hand to let them all know he was not done speaking and he wanted to continue. "My thanks go out to our brave garrison commander and his lovely wife for their consent to allow my oldest grandson, Teancum, to marry their beautiful daughter, Hanni." Pilio gestured with his hand toward his new in-laws. Those in attendance turned to clap and shout praises to them. The commander and his wife stood and waved to the crowd. After a few moments, the crowd quieted down and turned back to Pilio. "I am sorry to say we have come to the end of this day's festivities. If you have made arrangements to travel back to the city in the caravan, and you want to make it back before dark, you must start loading up now." The crowd let out a sigh and started to move toward the waiting wagons. Pilio finished his address. "Thank you all again for coming. Please, take what food you want for the ride home and we will see you all very soon. Good night."

With that, the party had ended. Pilio and Saria moved to where the passenger wagons were being loaded. With Teancum and Hanni, they personally said goodbye to as many of the guests as they could. The sun was starting to go down when the last of the guests had pulled out the main gate. Teancum stood with Hanni by the gate, his arm around her waist, the two of them waving goodbye to the last wagon.

"I don't know if I have the strength to walk back to the house. We may just as well sleep on the ground right here tonight," Hanni said as she rested her head on his chest. She had gotten up long before dawn to get ready for the wedding and now that the day was all over, she was exhausted.

"My lovely bride," Teancum said as he kissed her forehead, "it is unfortunate that you are too tired to walk back to the house. Wait here. I will fetch a blanket for you with which to sleep." She playfully slapped his chest. "It will be lonely without you in my bed tonight, but I will manage somehow," he changed his tone to be more dramatic as he finished talking.

Hanni gasped and playfully tried to push away from Teancum. "No." She jokingly fought with him. "You don't deserve me."

"You are right, my love." Teancum swept her up into his arms. "I don't deserve you." He kissed her lips. "But I will spend the rest of my life trying to prove to you that I do." He carried her all the way back to the ranch house in his arms, her head resting on his shoulder and her arms wrapped around his neck.

The time they spent together on the ranch was magical. Hanni took to ranch life like a duck to water. Like clockwork, she was up at dawn, dressed and ready for the morning chores. She worked hand in hand with Teancum, learning everything she could in the short amount of time she had about how to manage such a large ranch. Even though it had been some time since she'd been there, she still remembered most of the ranch workers' names. But now she was invested in seeing the ranch remain a success and was determined to do her part.

"I think I could be very happy living here," Hanni told Teancum as the two of them lay next to each other on a blanket in the middle of a wide meadow. They had gone for a horseback ride that morning to check on some of the cattle, then decided to stop there for lunch.

"I have noticed that you have taken to this place quite well," Teancum responded. "I do miss the simplicity of the life and the quiet of nature when I am in the city."

"You need to go back to school tomorrow," Hanni pointed out.

"Don't remind me," Teancum groaned.

"We can still live with my parents in the city while you finish your training, but I want to come out here to visit as often as possible."

"Yes, ma'am," Teancum whispered as he turned his head to kiss her cheek.

"And, I want twelve children," Hanni blurted out.

"What?"

"Eleven boys and one baby girl."

"Eleven…what?" Teancum gasped.

Hanni covered her face and started to giggle. Teancum realized she was joking with him. He grabbed her by the waist and started to tickle her. The two wrestled in the grass until they were both exhausted. Holding each other closely, they both were breathing hard until they each slipped into a peaceful sleep. Teancum had been asleep for about thirty minutes when the buzzing of a pesky insect woke him. The noisy thing was hovering around his face, so Teancum slapped it away with his hands. He was awake now and sat up, being careful not to disturb Hanni. Looking down at the most precious thing in his life, Teancum smiled as he watched her sleep. She was curled up on her side, facing him, with her arms under her head for support. He was so in love with her and he felt so happy at that moment to have someone to share his life with. As he sat looking at her, a gentle gust of wind blew across the meadow making some of Hanni's hair cross over her face. Teancum tried to gently move the hair back but accidently brushed his finger against her nose. It startled Hanni to feel Teancum's finger against her skin. She woke with a bit of a jolt.

"Oh! I'm sorry, my love," Teancum apologized as Hanni looked up at him. "I was trying to move the hair from your face."

Hanni closed her eyes, smiled and groaned as she stretched out her arms and legs. "How long were we asleep?" She asked, yawning while covering her mouth with her hands.

"I think for around half an hour, maybe more," he responded, while having a sympathetic yawn of his own.

"The horses?" Hanni asked as she tried to sit up.

Teancum looked over to the other side of the big tree providing them some shade. He saw their two saddled mounts still tied to the big branch that was hanging low to the ground. They seemed perfectly content just standing in the shade while waiting for Teancum and Hanni to climb back on.

"Right where we left them, my queen."

"Good," Hanni spoke as she slowly tried to get to her feet. "It would be a long walk home with you carrying me on your back."

"What!" Teancum barked as he playfully tried to grab Hanni as she stood. She squealed as she jumped out of his reach.

"Missed me, slowpoke!" She laughed and started to backpedal as Teancum got to his feet. Teancum crouched down like a wrestler, and then charged at Hanni. She tried to avoid his grasp but she was laughing hard, and really did not want to try that hard, any way. Teancum scooped her up in his arms, flinging her over his shoulder. He spun Hanni around, several times, in the air.

"Your horse awaits your command," he shouted as he bounced and spun his love around the meadow.

"Put me down," she playfully cried out. "You are going to make me sick!"

"Okay," Teancum responded as he came to a stop but still held on to her, "but it will cost you a kiss." She slowly slid off his back and landed on her feet facing him.

"Just one?" She asked as she passionately kissed her man several times. They held each other in their arms. The feeling of love was almost intoxicating.

"I love you so much, Teancum. You have made me a very happy woman," Hanni gushed.

"I love you too, Hanni," Teancum smiled with eyes as well as his mouth.

They stood for a few more moments in each other's arms, her head resting on his chest, his hand stroking her long hair.

"We should probably start heading back. Mother will send out a search party if we don't show up soon," Teancum laughed. They both realized their alone time had run out and it was time to return. They walked, somewhat sadly, hand in hand, back to the blanket and quickly gathering up their belongings. The items were stowed in the saddle bags and the two were up, on the horses, and moving back to the house.

CHAPTER EIGHT

LIFE BEGINS

The rest of the ride home was uneventful, as was the remainder of the evening. Early the next day, Hanni and Teancum were up with the sun, loading the small wagon with their trunks and personal items. It was time for Teancum to return to school, but no one really wanted him to go back to the city.

"Be careful, my child. Take good care of him," Rachael spoke into Hanni's ear. While at the ranch, Hanni and Rachael had grown very close and they felt a closer bond growing.

"I will, Mother," Hanni said as she smiled at her new mother-in-law. "Lord Pilio, Lady Saria," Hanni bowed slightly as she turned to face the two. "Thank you so much for your hospitality and love over these last few weeks. You have truly made me feel welcome and a member of this family."

"My dear child," Saria held out her arms beckoning Hanni to come closer. Hanni obliged and the two warmly embraced. "You are family now and welcome here anytime."

"It was our sincere pleasure to have you here on the ranch. Lady Saria is correct, you are now family and will always be welcome," Lord Pilio spoke next as he held out his arms to Hanni. Hanni was so happy to know she was considered family and loved by these people. Everyone on the porch had tears in their eyes as Hanni said her goodbyes. Turning to Tum and the rest of the ranch staff, Hanni was graceful and proper as she addressed them, thanking them for their efforts in making her feel at home.

As she finished speaking, Teancum dashed up onto the porch exclaiming, "We are all ready to go." He quickly made his round of goodbyes and embraced his mother and grandparents. "We're off," he said, as he took Hanni's arm and escorted her to the wagon seat. He knew if he did not get moving, Hanni just might decide to stay at the ranch, while Teancum would be forced to go back to Zarahemla alone and spend the next session of his schooling without her. He made one last quick pass around the wagon, checking the tiedowns, and ensuring the rope connecting his riding horse to the back of the wagon was secure. Satisfied that all was in order, Teancum climbed up next to Hanni, in the seat, and grabbed the reins. "We will see you all in a few months!" he shouted and waved to his family, still standing on the porch. Hanni also waved goodbye, but she was choking up with emotion and did not speak. She did manage a teary smile and a brave look as Teancum clucked to the horses and slapped down on the reins to get the beasts to move.

Teancum could see Hanni was crying so he put his arm around her shoulder for comfort. "It will be okay, my love. We will return for winter break. The time will fly by and you will be right back here. You will see."

"I miss your family already. They were all so good and kind to me," she said, sniffing and wiping her tears with her hankie. "This place is so different from the city. I don't know if I will like living there now that I had a taste of this life."

"I don't care where we live," Teancum reassured her as he hugged her a little tighter. "As long as we are together, everything will be okay."

The two of them made their way down the wide and well-used merchant path back to the main gates of the massive city, and to Hanni's family home. Because Hanni's father was the commander of the Zarahemla legion and high protector of the city, the home where he lived was inside a sprawling military compound in the heart of the oldest section of the city. He had made arrangements for Hanni and Teancum to live in the compound. A small bungalow had been made available for the new couple, near her parents' house. They quickly unpacked the wagon and secured their personal belongings inside. It was just after lunch when Hanni and Teancum had reached a stopping point with their unpacking and decided to walk around the compound to get a feel for their new home. There was nothing pleasant or homey about a Nephite military camp. It was very clean and everything was in order, but there was no life or warmth to it. Hanni was accustomed to the life and did not realize how different it was from the life on the ranch until she was showing Teancum around the camp. She found herself almost apologizing at times to Teancum for the utilitarian and homely environment in which they now lived.

"That is the main soldier barracks," She pointed to a large block shaped building with few windows, "and over there are the bathhouses and latrines," she grimaced while pinching her nose, to let Teancum know the odor was not too pleasant over there. As they walked, it seemed like every soldier they passed knew Hanni and would greet her. It was starting to upset Teancum to see so many, big, strong men come up to her and acknowledge her.

"Silly boys," she said. Hanni could sense this was making Teancum uneasy so, she took him by the arm, "My love, don't worry. Remember, I grew up here. They are all like brothers to me. There is only one man I want to be with." She stopped walking and turned into his arms. Kissing Teancum she smiled. "Come, let me show you the market that is just outside the compound gate." He felt a little bit better after the kiss, but he still watched the soldiers out of the corner of his eye as they walked past.

That evening, Teancum and Hanni were invited to join her parents for dinner. The conversation was light. The food was simple, plentiful and full of flavor.

"Teancum?" The commander questioned as the attending staff removed the dishes from the table. "You look to be in excellent shape. Why don't you join me and the other soldiers tomorrow in morning calisthenics before you head off to classes? They say a good morning workout stimulates the mind and it might help you with your studies."

Teancum stole a quick, concerned look toward Hanni. He was not afraid of hard, physical work. On the contrary, life on a cattle ranch is a daily workout unto itself. He was worried this might be a setup and he did not want to look foolish in front of Hanni's father or the other soldiers.

"An excellent idea, Father," Hanni said while nodding her head back toward Teancum. "This will give the two of you a chance to bond and Teancum can meet some of the men."

"Outstanding! It's settled then." He slapped the arm rest with his hand. "Teancum, you can meet me on the parade ground for the morning flag ceremony; then we will have a grand workout," The commander smiled as he spoke and drank from his large goblet.

"Yes sir, thank you sir," Teancum responded while shooting Hanni a concerned look. He had a bad feeling this would not end well. Hanni gave Teancum a subtle wave to tell him everything would be okay then she went right back to speaking with her mother.

Great, Teancum thought to himself as he smiled back at Hanni and her father. He swallowed the rest of his comments with a big gulp of water from his cup.

Teancum hardly slept that night in grim anticipation. He was up before dawn and dressed in some loose-fitting clothing. He had lit a single candle and was moving around the small bedroom, searching for his clothing while trying not to make a sound and wake Hanni.

"Morning baby," Hanni spoke in a raspy, tired voice.

"I'm sorry, did I wake you?" he asked.

"It's okay. I wanted to get up and see you off on your first day anyway," she responded as she rose from the bed, stretching her hands over her head.

"I don't know how long this thing with your father is going to take, but I would like to sit and enjoy some breakfast with you before I go to school," he said as he put on his sandals. "I won't see you all day and I don't know how long I will be able to last without looking into your eyes." He smiled as he reached across the bed to kiss his wife on the cheek.

"That would be nice," Hanni yawned, covering her mouth while turning away from Teancum. "Sorry... morning breath," she giggled, then stood up from the bed. "Now, you need to get out there and be in place before the banner raising." She grabbed him by the arm with one hand and the small candle with the other. Walking him toward the door she continued, "If there is one thing I have learned by living on a military base, it's that it is very disrespectful to be late to morning formation or walking around when they raise the King's banner. Now, shoo! I will have something to eat waiting for you when you get back to change for school."

She pushed Teancum out the front door as he turned to speak, "But what if...?" He was cut off by Hanni putting her finger to his lips. She knew he had self-doubt about not being a warrior, especially around her father and the other warriors. Exercising with other strong men was far outside his comfort zone. Her intuition told her this would be very good for him to experience and she tried to be as encouraging as possible.

"I love you, my dear. You are a strong, well-conditioned and intelligent man. You will do just fine." She smiled and gave him a quick kiss. "I believe in you. Now go, have some fun playing outside in the dirt with the boys."

"Funny," he said as he turned and started to walk toward the group of men gathering in the distance on the grassy parade ground.

Teancum was standing at the back of the formation of soldiers as they stood at attention and saluted in unison as the King's banner was raised up the large pole in the center of the camp. A lone horn player stood off to one side and played the familiar tune to alert everyone in camp the banner was up and the day's business on the army base could commence.

The commander walked out to the front of the formation and addressed the gathering, "Good morning men!" he bellowed.

"Good morning sir!" was the thunderous response.

"Gentlemen, we have a guest joining us today for our morning physical training." The commander gestured to the back of the formation and some of the men turned their heads to see Teancum standing there looking very out of palace. "He is new to these parts, so I thought we could give him a tour of the city!"

There was audible snickering and some laughter from the ranks of men. Teancum sighed as he smiled wanly back at the commander, *another joke at my expense.*

"First sergeant!" The commander called out for the ranking noncommissioned officer of the company of soldiers to report to his location. A very fit-looking middle-aged man stepped out from the first row of soldiers and moving quickly, he stood in front of the commander and sharply saluted.

"First sergeant reporting as ordered, sir!"

The commander saluted back. "First sergeant, put them in columns of two and march them out the front gate!" The commander turned and barked out to the troops, "I will lead them today."

"Sir, yes sir!" The experienced soldier saluted again. He knew something was up but did not know what to expect. He had a slight grin on his face, thinking it might have something to do with the commander's new son in-law joining them today.

"Alright you dogs!" The sergeant shouted as he turned to face the formation, "Attention!" In unison the disciplined men of the Zarahemla legion gathered on the grassy parade ground, brought their heels together, their arms to their sides and stood as straight as spears.

They all knew what command was coming next. They had done this every morning for years. "Right face!" The command of execution was given and, as one unit, they all turned and faced to their right.

"Columns of two from the left…forward…march!" The sergeant snarled out the movement command. The formation was broken down into four rows of men. The first two rows of soldiers took their first step with their left foot, marching forward in rhythm and time. The second two rows waited until the first two rows had marched past then they fell in line, right behind them. This created two long columns of men marching as one toward the main gate. The First Sergeant called out cadence to keep everyone in step.

Teancum did not know what to do. He stood and watched as the soldiers moved past him. *I guess I follow,* he spoke to himself, confused on what to do next or what to expect. Moving quickly, he fell in line behind the last soldier in formation, trying to keep in step. As they marched forward, they sang songs of battles and feats of valor all while keeping in step with the rhythm of the song and each other. This was a new experience for Teancum. He was really starting to enjoy it. It made him feel like part of a unit.

They reached the front gate and Teancum could see his father-in-law moving up to the front of the formation. He reached the head of the two columns, looking over his left shoulder he waved his arm forward then shouted, "Follow me, boys!"

Every man in the formation shouted out their war cry and the commander took off at a dead run through the center of the city. Keeping in formation, all the soldiers of Zarahemla ran after their commander, joining him in a crazy game of follow the leader.

Teancum blinked in surprise as the men in front of him took off running. "Here we go!" Teancum whispered. Taking a deep breath he lowered his head and ran after them.

They sprinted for approximately four hundred yards through the sparsely populated streets of Zarahemla, following the old, but very fit commander until he reached the first obstacle. It was a low stone wall about three feet high. The commander leaped over the top of it without breaking stride and continued on at a good running pace. Teancum sprinted as hard as he could, passing a few of the men along the way. He reached the wall, jumped over the top while trying not to get in the way of the other soldiers, but also trying to keep up. The commander ran a few hundred yards more, then reached the edge of the temple grounds. There were benches set along the cobblestone path that circled the walls of the temple itself for people to sit and enjoy the gardens that lined the path. The commander ran up to the first set of benches then dropped to his belly. Crawling under the closest bench, he was up and running before the first set of soldiers could reach it. The space under the bench would only accommodate two men at a time, so several of the soldiers broke from the main group, finding other benches to climb under. Teancum saw some of the soldiers in front of him angle for a set of benches not far from him and headed that way. He ran to the bench, hitting the ground just as those in front of him had cleared the obstacle. He crawled under it and was up quickly and moving.

"Just getting warmed up!" One skinny soldier shouted as he ran up next to Teancum.

"Can't wait to see what's next!" Teancum shouted back breathlessly.

They followed the commander around the entire perimeter of the temple grounds, climbing under and jumping over benches along the path, laughing and cheering each other on as they went. As they were running along, Teancum realized with some pride he was keeping up with most of the soldiers and even out-performing some of them.

The commander made a hard left at the next cross street, climbed up and over a wagon that was parked in the street near a merchant shop. The mule pulling the wagon was unfazed by the fact so many men were jumping and climbing around him. He just stood there, tied to a post, periodically looking behind him and minding his own business.

"He's heading for the main gates!" someone shouted from the crowd of soldiers around Teancum.

"Is that a good thing or a bad thing?" Teancum gasped.

"You will find out very soon," another voice called out to answer his question. Several soldiers laughed when they heard the response.

Another hard left and Teancum could see the open gates in the distance. The commander was still running ahead of the pack, but Teancum was quickly gaining on him. The streets were starting to fill up with people, horses and wagons. The formation was now broken up. Soldiers dodged around civilians and livestock just trying to keep up. The commander reached the gates, then ran to the right where a set of switchback stairs had been constructed to help the soldiers get to the top of the walls quickly. The stairs were made of wood with a sturdy railing to keep someone from falling to the ground. The commander started to climb the stairs, but he did not take the traditional route to the top. Instead using the steps, he started to climb along the outside of the stairs, on the railing itself, pulling and swinging, clinging and grasping. The leader of the soldiers made his way up the outside of the stairs and to the top of the wall. Shouting down, he challenged his men to follow him. Teancum was now near the front of the formation and watched as several soldiers tried to make their way up, following the commander's lead. It was Teancum's turn. He grasped the closest hand hold and started to climb. He was surprised how easy it was for him to maneuver around the wood railing while making his way to the top. He even passed some of the more athletic-looking soldiers who were having trouble on this obstacle.

It's just like climbing one of the giant trees back home, he thought as he continued to climb. *Three points of contact at all times. Hold with your hands, push with your legs...no problem.* He reached the top faster than he thought he would. The commander was already running, again, along the catwalk and yelling to the men to follow him. Teancum could tell the pace had slowed but the men kept moving. He was starting to feel the effects of the running and climbing on his muscles but he knew he had plenty of reserve energy still inside of him.

The commander ran along the top of the massive wall, passing soldiers who were on duty standing watch. Those soldiers were catcalling, waving their weapons in the air and cheering as their brothers-in-arms ran past them. Teancum continued to gain on the commander, passing those soldiers who were getting tired and slowing down. He estimated they had run for another four hundred yards when they reached a section of the wall that was being repaired. New stones were replacing ones that had cracked. There was a robust scaffolding system with rope pulleys erected near the wall to lift the new, larger stones into place. The commander shouted for the workers and soldiers around the construction site to move out of the way. Not stopping his momentum, he lept from the wall, grabbing one of the large, sturdy ropes on the scaffolding pulley system. Dangling high above the ground, The commander started climbing down the rope, hand over hand, until he reached the bottom. Landing on his feet, he was off like a rabbit while his men stood at the top of the wall

looking down at him.

"Crazy old fool," one soldier spouted as he gasped for air.

Teancum looked around at the men standing next to him. No one had tried to climb down after the commander. Not knowing what else to do, Teancum took two steps back and then rushed forward, jumping with all his might while flailing his arms out for the same rope. His hands slid across the rough rope and it burned his fingers. He grasped the thick rope and held on desperately to keep from sliding. His body momentum caused his legs to swing out away from the wall and he almost lost his hold on the rope. Catching the rope with his legs, Teancum was able to quickly climb down, hitting the ground with a backwards roll. His hands were still burning from trying to grip the rope. Teancum got to his feet, staggered forward, as he looked at the palms of his hands. They were glowing red hot and pulsing with pain. "That's going to leave a mark," he spoke to himself as he tried to find his balance and keep moving forward. The rest of the men on the wall followed him down.

This went on for another hour as the commander found strange obstacles and buildings to climb up and over, things to jump across, mud to crawl in and long sections of road and spaces to sprint. When Teancum finally re-entered the gate at the army barracks, he was exhausted, covered in mud and bleeding from scrapes to his knees and arms. He was among the first group of soldiers to make it back and when he arrived, he saw his father-in-law, still muddy and wet, standing in the middle of the grassy parade ground holding a big wooden training sword. There was a large rack full of additional training swords next to him.

"Grab a sword, gentlemen, and find a sparring partner!" he shouted to the soldiers as they arrived back at the field. In pairs and small groups, the soldiers broke off and started to spar with the wooden swords. Teancum could tell they were all physically exhausted. He did not understand why the commander was pushing them so hard without a break. He walked around the men and stood next to his father-in-law to watch as they simulated attacking and defending with the training swords.

"Sir, could you explain the reason for the weapons training right after that intense exercise?"

The old commander look pleased as he turned to address Teancum's question. "You cannot tell the enemy you are too tired to fight. I want these men to know what they are capable of and to push their bodies past the breaking point in training so they know they can handle the stress of combat."

Teancum looked at the fatigued soldiers just going through the motions of sparing. Some of them were not really trying at all, but just carelessly flinging their training swords in the air, in a vain attempt to look like they were giving an effort. This seemed like a useless endeavor. *If you are going to train, then you should train to do it correctly*, he thought to himself. But he was not a soldier and he was in no position to tell the garrison commander how to ready his troops for war.

"Do you want to go a few rounds with me?" The commander asked as he held out a wooden sword for Teancum.

"You have a bit of an advantage over me, sir." Teancum smiled and laughed nervously as he held both of his hands up. "I am thankful and honored you asked me to join you and your men this morning, but I do need to go get cleaned up and get to my classes. It is my first day back and I want to make a good impression."

"Well, you certainly made an impression on me this morning," The commander replied. "Well done." He slapped Teancum's back and a small cloud of dust and grime came off his shirt. "Study well."

"Thank you, sir," Teancum replied. He felt awkward and did not know what else to say. "I will give Hanni your regards." He bowed slightly to his father-in-law then turned to walk away.

Arriving back at their small home, Teancum was greeted by Hanni at the front door. She was trying not to laugh at his pathetic appearance, which resembled a dirty and mangy lost dog that had come to the front door begging for food. She felt sorry for Teancum but could not help herself. She covered her mouth as she tried to stifle her giggling.

"It's not funny," Teancum said, as he removed his muddy shoes and pulled off his shirt.

"Oh baby, I'm sorry," Hanni replied, with sympathy in her voice. "Go around to the back door. I will fetch some warm water to wash with, and aloe for your scrapes," pointing toward the side of the house. Teancum walked slowly around to the back door.

Teancum made it to his first class, just in the nick of time. Moving gingerly so as not to aggravate his already battered and bruised body, he found a seat near the front and sat down as the instructor entered the room. When he realized who the teacher was, Teancum, along with the rest of the class, groaned under their collective breath. This teacher's reputation preceded him. He was a hard instructor who did not give his students any slack.

"Welcome back, students," the teacher called out as he entered the classroom. He was an older gentlemen with a receding hair line and pudgy face. "Most of you had me for Introduction to Anatomy last session, so I will dispense with the introduction and we can get right to it." He dropped his supplies onto the desk then turned to look over the gathered students. "Right…Master Teancum." He pointed right at Teancum. "Please, come forward and name for me the internal organs of the human body, in descending order, from the neckline to the pelvis."

"Blast," Teancum lowered his head, whispering under his breath. Taking a deep breath and wincing from the pain of trying to get out of his chair, he shuffled forward and stood next to the instructor.

"Welcome back, Master Teancum," the teacher spoke in a low tone.

"Thank you sir," Teancum responded with a slight hint of sarcasm in his voice. He stood for several seconds, trying to recall the lessons from last session, but the pain and fatigue he felt from the morning exercise with the soldiers was messing with his concentration.

"We all have other classes to attend today, so whenever you are ready." The other students snickered a bit.

"Yes, sir, sorry sir," Teancum responded. He was embarrassed. Teancum needed to focus. He knew this information. He had a powerful mind and could recall most everything he had learned, experienced or read. *I need to block out the distractions and see the images in my mind*, he thought. Breathing deeply and closing his eyes, he cleared his mind and suddenly the outline of the human body appeared in his mind's eye. One by one the organs appeared in their rightful place so Teancum was able to recite them in exact order. When he was done, Teancum opened his eyes and looked at the students sitting before him. The snickering had stopped. They were impressed, hardly any of them could have done that.

"Nicely done," the teacher commented. He was also impressed with Teancum's ability to retain information. "It is nice to see your grades for the last session were not a fluke. Please take your seat."

Teancum moved back to his chair and sat down. As he was adjusting his seat, he realized the pain in his legs and back had faded.

The rest of the school session went by very quickly for Teancum. With his schoolwork, starting a life with Hanni, his increasingly frequent appearances at the morning exercise formations with the commander and his soldiers, and helping Hanni with her volunteer work, time passed swiftly. Eventually, the weather started to change and the days grew shorter and colder. Teancum was getting ready to head out the door for school when he heard Hanni getting sick in the outhouse behind the bungalow.

"Are you okay?" he asked after he gently knocked on the door.

"I will be. You should get to class, don't want you to be late." She vomited again but tried to sound supportive.

He paused and thought for a second; something was not right. "Nonsense, you are sick."

"No, no I will be fine. Must be something I ate. If I need anything I will walk over to mother's house," was Hanni's reply.

Teancum felt badly but Hanni was insistent. "Are you sure? It's just a lecture today, I can stay here if you need me."

She opened the door to the outhouse and gave Teancum a brave smile. "See, I feel better already." Her eyes were watery and bloodshot, her face was flushed red and her long hair was in disarray, with much of her hair escaped from her hair tie and hanging in her face.

"Hanni?" Teancum was becoming genuinely concerned.

"'Really, I already feel better," she insisted while gently pushing him, with her open palm as she stepped from the outhouse. "You are going to be late and that simply will not do." She put on a brave face, and Teancum knew he was not going to win this battle.

"Okay, but you will promise to send word if you need me?" He felt there was something she was not telling him but he did not want to argue.

'Yes, dear. Now scoot, young schoolboy." She flung her hand shooing him away. "Before the headmaster comes looking for you."

Teancum gave her a gentle kiss on the cheek and he was off.

Hanni went inside and sat down at the little table near the cooking area. She took a small sip of water and closed her eyes to try to relax. There was a knock at the front door and Hanni could hear her mother call out her name as she let herself in.

"Hanni?"

"In here, Mother."

Hanni's mother walked in and took one look at her. Looking around, she asked with her silent gestures if Teancum was still in the house.

"No, he just left," Hanni responded.

"So?" Hanni's mother had a questioning tone in her voice as she put her hands on her hips and smiled.

Hanni looked up with happy eyes and a wide grin, "Yes, I'm pregnant."

The two of them spontaneously squealed in delight and embraced but Hanni was still weak and recovering from the visit to the outhouse.

"Did you tell him?" Hanni's mother asked.

"No, not yet." She felt a slight tinge of sadness. "I don't know how he will react. Teancum is so focused on getting through school and setting us on a path for success." Hanni took a deep, courageous breath and smiled at her mother.

"He is a good and loving man. How could he not be overjoyed at the news?"

"I know," Hanni responded. "I am just nervous and a bit overwhelmed right now. Are you going to tell father?"

"No," Hanni's mother shook her head, "that is your task." She thought for a second and continued. "I have an idea. How about we give the happy news at dinner on the Sabbath? They will both be at the table and we can enjoy the good news as a family."

"That's a great idea," Hanni responded. The two embraced and a few tears were shed.

"Now." Hanni's mother pushed her back slightly to look into her daughter's eyes, "If you are up to it, why don't we make a trip down to the market to see about a walking cart for the new child?"

"Mother!" Hanni gave her a look. "Any excuse to shop."

They both had a good laugh and Hanni went to wash up and change. She was feeling better and thought some time walking outside would help.

Dinner at Hanni's parents' house on the Sabbath was becoming more of a routine than a tradition. Everyone sat in the same seats, the tabletop conversation never really changed, and they rotated every week between four different meal choices: lamb, some type of chicken dish, thick soup with bread, and fish. First, the commander would ask Teancum how his school was progressing. Teancum would oblige him with a story or explanation of the week's learning. Then like clockwork, their conversation would turn to politics, or religion, or the weather, or half a dozen different topics. So, it was a bit of a surprise when Hanni wiped her mouth with her cloth napkin, then cleared her throat and told her father she had an announcement to make. Teancum and the commander both turned to look at Hanni with questioning looks on their faces. Hanni's mother was already beaming with anticipation and joy. Hanni's eyes were sparkling with excitement. The old commander stole a quick glance at his wife and saw the expression on her face.

She already knows what Hanni is going to say, he instantly concluded. He was no fool, he knew his wife and daughter better than anyone else. *They planned this*, he thought. *What could it be? Think!* He looked at the two women and saw the expressions they were sharing. *It must be a very happy announcement for the family…* Then he almost burst out loud, *She is pregnant!* He almost said it but caught himself so as not to ruin Hanni's moment. "Yes, my child, what is it?" The commander was playing it very cool, but inside he was screaming for joy. He wanted grandbabies around before he was too old or too broken to enjoy them.

Hanni stood up, putting her hand on Teancum's shoulder. "I don't know any other way to say this, so I'm just going to say it." She looked down into Teancum's eyes. "I am pregnant."

Teancum was stunned silent. He just sat looking up into Hanni's eyes, motionless and not breathing.

"Teancum?" Hanni called out. "Say something!" She was beginning to worry about his reaction.

"I'm going to be a father?" he questioned with almost child-like wonder.

Hanni nodded as the tears started to roll down her cheeks. She still did not know for sure how Teancum would receive their life-changing news. His silence and emotionless expression was quickly making her nervous.

Hanni's mother was also crying. She held her hands over her mouth to quiet the excitement she felt.

Her father remained outwardly stoic, sitting still at the head of the large table, watching as the deeply human event unfolded before him.

"I'm going to be a father?" Teancum asked again as he turned to look at his mother-in-law.

"Yes my dear, you are going to be a father." She could hardly control herself now. She was going to be a grandparent.

Teancum looked back at Hanni then stood up. He put his hands on her belly and gasped, "I'm going to be a father?" He looked at his in-laws then shouted with excitement, "I'm going to be a father!" Screaming with joy, he took his precious bride in his arms and held her tightly. Hanni gasped and Teancum realized he was squeezing her a bit too tightly and let her go. "I'm sorry, I'm sorry!" He apologized over and over as he tried to hold her more gently.

"It's okay," she reassured him while wiping happy tears from her eyes. Hanni's parents got up from their seats and came around the table to congratulate the new parents-to-be.

"How far along are you?" Teancum questioned. He was suddenly disappointed in himself that he had not recognized the signs and symptoms of pregnancy in his wife. His lessons so far had only generally covered child development and the birthing process. "I should have known."

"I visited the army surgeon last week and he said I appear to be two months along."

Teancum did some quick math in his head and smiled. "Seven more months? That will put the birth at the end of classes, before summer break ... Excellent. We can spend the summer together as a new family here and at the ranch, and then be ready for classes in the fall." He hugged her again. "Not only are you a perfect wife, but you will be a perfect mother too."

The happy news was equally well-received when they told Teancum's family the next weekend they had gathered together. Rachael dabbed tears of joy from her eyes while Saria and Pilio glowed with pride.

They were such a happy and beautiful couple, everyone they came into contact with knew they deeply loved each other. Teancum doted on his sweet, pregnant wife. When they were together, he was never more than three feet from her and was always ready with a kind word, a hug, or help with any chore. When he was away from her at school, or for any other reason, she was the foremost thought in his mind. It was not uncommon to see Teancum walking home from a long day at the university with flowers in his hands or a small treat for Hanni. He loved his wife and expressed his feelings every way possible. Over the months, several merchants at the bazaar came to know Teancum and Hanni. The smart shop owners saw how Teancum acted around his young bride and quickly learned her taste in gifts and food. They knew Teancum would often visit the markets as he walked home from school and they would hold things aside specifically for Teancum to buy for Hanni. Even though he could afford anything, Teancum was a wise shopper and would only select the best for her. In turn, Hanni respected and adored her husband. He was the single most important person in her life. The care and attention she gave him made that clear to everyone. She was his best friend and closest advisor. She would help him study and make sure he was fed and always had clean clothing. When she was at her work or visiting the markets, she conducted herself with quiet dignity and was the very definition of a virtuous woman. She tried to live a life full of grace. When the Sabbath came, Teancum dutifully followed her to the meetings, but he was too busy to commit to more. Hanni knew Teancum was a good man, and never chided him to share her belief. She confided in her mother, who told her faith cannot be harvested until it has grown ripe. "Take your time with him, show your faith through example and he will one day understand." If Hanni was impatient, she never let it show. Her testimony of the love of God was expressed in her words and deeds. She was kind and modest, always ready with a gentle hand or a smile that would brighten even the darkest of hearts. She was loved by all and tried hard to return those feelings. They grew together as a couple while waiting for the day to arrive for Hanni to give birth to their first child.

It was getting close to the end of this session of classes and Teancum was finishing a project with some of his classmates when the headmaster came into the classroom, followed by a young teenage boy who was wearing the uniform of a squire from the army base.

"Master Teancum?" the headmaster called out.

Teancum and those students with him all stopped what they were doing and turned to look at the headmaster.

Teancum stood up and responded, "Here, sir."

"A message for you from the army camp," he said, with a grin, as he motioned the boy to come forward to deliver the message.

The young boy stepped forward, came to attention and saluted. Teancum waved back. "Go ahead son, what is the message?"

"Sir...." You could tell he had been running. He was a bit out of breath. "With the commander's compliments, your wife has gone into labor. She has been moved to the army hospital. The commander and his wife await you there."

There was a shout of excitement from those who were with Teancum as he reacted to the news. Gathering up his personal belongings and uncharacteristically shoving them haphazardly into his bag, Teancum moved quickly toward the door. As he exited the room, he realized something, stopped and turned around.

"I don't think I will be able to meet tomorrow night to help finish the project," he said to his classmates in a rushed and concerned tone. They all shouted and waved for him to go and not worry about it. "Thanks!" he whooped as he moved through the doorway toward the building exit.

He ran the entire distance from the college to the main army hospital. It was not his first choice for medical care for his new family, but with Hanni being the daughter of the boss, they all got free medical treatment. Thanks to his studies, he knew enough about medicine now to keep up with what was happening around him so he could keep an eye on Hanni as well as her caregivers.

The hospital itself was not really equipped for the delivery and care of a new baby. This was more of a facility for the treatment and rehabilitation of wounded soldiers. So when a woman in labor came in for care, it was out of the ordinary. And with the garrison commander being the grandfather of the arriving child, this delivery was the event of the day. When Teancum finally found where Hanni was located, he entered the hallway to her room and found several hospital staff members, as well as uniformed military personnel, standing around and blocking his attempt to get to his wife.

"Excuse me! Please... May I pass?" Teancum tried to weave his way around bodies and get by everyone who was standing in his way, but the closer he got to the room the more crowded the passageway became.

He could hear Hanni crying out in pain and was becoming very frustrated that he could not get to her. Finally he stopped trying to work his way around the people in his way. He set his school bag down at his feet and bringing his hands up to his mouth, forming a funnel, for the sounds he was going to make, Teancum shouted at the top of his lungs, "Ladies and gentlemen!" Everyone in the hall stopped talking and turned to look at him. When he had everyone's attention, Teancum made a gesture with his hands to ask everyone in his way to part the hallway down the middle and let him pass, unobstructed. As he was waiting for those important people standing in his way to decide if they were going to move, the deep and booming voice of his father-in-law could be heard coming from the far end of the hallway.

"Make a hole, people!"

Without question, all the people in the hallway quickly moved up against the sides of the walls and opened a wide path for Teancum to walk down. At the far end of the human path, Teancum could see

Hanni's father standing in a doorway, waving to him. "This way lad, quickly now, or you will miss it!"

As he quickly walked toward Hanni's room, the people in the hallway realized who Teancum was. There were several apologetic whispers and nods as he passed. Teancum did not have the time or energy to respond. He was completely focused on getting to Hanni to be by her side.

"Father, is Teancum here?" Hanni cried out as Teancum reached the doorway.

"I'm here my love," he responded, as he shook the commander's hand and entered the room. The look in his eyes showed the gratitude he felt to the old soldier for intervening on his behalf. He moved up next to Hanni as she lay in the bed. Taking a seat by her side, he gently grabbed her hand and kissed her forehead. "How are you doing?" he asked.

"What took you so long?" she asked weakly.

"I am so sorry, Hanni. I ran as soon as I got word." He looked up at Hanni's mother who was standing at the head of the bed placing a cold cloth on her head. "Is everything going okay?" Teancum asked.

"She is doing just fine. She is strong, and the baby will be here very soon," Hanni's mother responded.

Hanni cried out in pain again, clenching down on Teancum's hand.

"The pains are coming faster now. It won't be much longer," a doctor spoke from the other side of the room as he wiped his hands on a clean towel. He moved into his position and examined Hanni's condition to check the progress. "Looks like someone is about to make a grand appearance. When you feel the next pain, I want you to breathe and push," he instructed Hanni.

It was not long and Hanni cried out again. "Breathe and push," Teancum spoke into her ear. Hanni took several quick breaths and gasped as she tried to push the baby out. This went on for several more minutes until the doctor announced,

"Excellent, well done. The head is almost out. One more big push!"

Hanni focused all her remaining strength and gave one last push. With the doctor's help, out of Hanni's exhausted body a new life emerged. She felt the extreme pressure release and collapsed back on the bed, exhausted, and covered in sweat. The doctor and the midwife did not say anything but hurriedly checked the baby. As they worked, looks of concern broke on their faces. They were moving more quickly.

Hanni could see the faces of the medical staff and the doctor, busily fussing with her new child. "What is it?" She looked at Teancum, her fear becoming apparent. "Is my baby okay?"

Teancum stood up and, still holding her hand, looked down at the new baby. He was a medical student. He knew what blue-colored skin meant on a new baby. He knew that the doctor and midwife were trying to get the baby's airway open and get her breathing. *Her...* he thought. *My child...it's a girl.* At the sudden thought of another loss in his life, a very deep and long-forgotten pain started to well up inside him.

"Teancum?" Hanni cried out. She could see the change of expression in Teancum's face. Her mother was trying to hold her down on the bed. Hanni's father was shifting his weight, moving back and forth. He had not felt this helpless in a very long time. Being a military leader, he was not used to standing by and watching events happen without his permission or involvement.

"Clear the room!" the doctor yelled out, as he struggled to save the new baby's life. This birth was going badly and he needed room to work. Two nurses moved forward to escort Hanni's parents out of the room.

"Teancum?" Hanni yelled out. "Tell me!" Teancum knew her fear was pushing her toward hysteria, but he could not take his eyes off of his precious child as the medical staff struggled to help her. He could feel the pain in his hand as Hanni squeezed tighter and started to cry. "Look at me!" She cried out and jerked on his arm. "Tell me what is happening!"

Teancum slowly turned his head to look at his wife. He knew it was taking way too long for the baby to get air and it was a matter of time now. This was his responsibility. He knew he needed to be the one to say it, to be the strong one for her, the rock she could anchor to when the reality of this devastating moment set in.

God, please help this child, Teancum pleaded with all his heart. He could not believe those words had erupted from his heart and mind. Teancum did not consider himself a religious man. He did not really believe in a higher power like his mother and grandparents did. But at this moment, he was willing to take a leap of faith and reach out to that unseen being that his family cared for so much.

"Hanni," he half choked as he tried to speak. The rest of the sad news was forming on his lips when the gasping cry of a newborn baby came echoing across the room. The cries were loud and strong. The baby was gulping air and screaming in a dramatic response to the sudden change of her environment. The unseen God that Teancum had reached out to moments ago manifested himself in the new cries of their baby girl.

Gasping, Teancum was overcome with emotion and relief. He felt as if someone had released him from a choke hold around his neck, and fresh air and blood could once again flow freely to his head from his heart and lungs. The tears were streaming down his cheeks. Hanni cried out with joy and excited laughter when she heard her new child's voice for the first time. Her parents came back in the room and were quickly by her side.

"Towel!" the doctor ordered. The midwife finished cleaning the baby and one of the nurses handed the doctor a large swaddling cloth.

Teancum held Hanni in his arms as he kissed her. "It's a girl," he said softly, while crying and beaming with pride and joy. "It's a girl!" he almost shouted to his in-laws as they stood at the head of the bed with their hands on Hanni's shoulders for support. They were emotionally exhausted and overwhelmed, but very happy.

"And a healthy one at that," the doctor added, as he handed the crying child to her mother for the first time. Time seemed to stand still for Hanni during these first moments with her baby. As soon as the child was placed in Hanni's arms, Hanni pulled her close, feeling the child's tender skin against her own. The child instantly stopped crying and fell asleep. Warm and safe, the little one instinctively knew she was close to her mother and relaxed into a welcome slumber.

"Congratulations," the doctor said matter-of-factly. He was a professional, but you could tell he was overjoyed by the happy outcome. This was a close one for him and he was quietly thankful for the hand of divine providence.

"Thank you, sir," Teancum said while holding out his hand to shake the doctor's.

"Yes. Thank you so much, doctor," Hanni added with deep sincerity. She dared not let go of her precious gift but instead offered a genuine smile of gratitude.

"It was my pleasure." The doctor took one last look at the baby and then at Hanni. "You two need to rest. The midwife and nurses will see to getting you cleaned up and then, after you have rested and she has something to eat, I will be back to check on you both." He stood up and looked at Hanni's parents. They both bowed slightly to him in acknowledgment of his fine work saving the child. He smiled and nodded his head in response.

"Father of the baby," the doctor grabbed the back of Teancum's arm and asked, "do you have a name for this little princess?"

Teancum looked down at Hanni. They made eye contact and she nodded her head, telling him she agreed with his choice.

"We want to name our first child in memory of my father," Teancum spoke as he looked around the room at those who had gathered to be with him and Hanni for this moment. "Kaila," he loudly whispered. He reached down and kissed his new baby daughter gently on the forehead, then his wife on the lips. Standing up tall and strong like a proud father he spoke again, "Her name is Kaila."

Hanni was only in the hospital's care for a few days. Considering Teancum was a medical student and her mother was close by, everyone felt she and the new baby would be better off at home resting than in a bed surrounded by wounded soldiers. While they were in the hospital, Kaila and Hanni were the new unofficial mascots for those brave men recovering from battle wounds. While she recovered, Hanni would be carried out into the courtyard to enjoy some fresh air and the soldiers would line up to see the baby and speak to a friendly face. They were all honorable, harmless men and ever so sweet toward Hanni. A soldier's life is one of separation from family, and these poor brave men were missing their own children. They found joy in seeing a baby and speaking to someone who was not a soldier or doctor.

The day they left the hospital, the wounded soldiers and medical staff who had come to know Hanni and Kaila, lined the halls and, those who could, stood at attention as Hanni was escorted to the main doors by Teancum and her parents. There was not a dry eye in the room as Hanni went past those brave men, acknowledging each one as she passed. She held little Kaila up so they could see her tiny face and sweetly whispered a thank you. Lining the hall was their way of saying thank you to Hanni and her family for the time they had together, and for Hanni and little Kaila, making them feel human while reminding them what their sacrifice was for.

Hanni would never forget the love and affection she felt for those men who gave so much for freedom. When Hanni was up and feeling better, she and little Kaila made several trips to the hospital to visit the patients. Years later, Hanni would arrange for Kaila and her little school friends to make weekly visits to the hospital to sing for the men or decorate the common areas of the hospital in holiday themes. Hanni pledged that as long as she had the ability, those men who were wounded protecting the Nephite people would never feel lonely or forgotten.

Little Kaila grew up fast and before long, she was the most popular person on the army base. Word had reached back to the soldiers of the sacrifice and dedication Hanni showed toward the injured men at the hospital and how Kaila would light up a room when she arrived. With Teancum away at school every day, Hanni would usually walk with Kaila to Hanni's parents' house. Along the way, Kaila would wave to the passing soldiers as they marched by. Most of the time, the soldiers would make it a point to stop and acknowledge her with a greeting or playful hand slap. They all had little sisters or young daughters, and they treated Kaila like the little princess she was.

Five years quickly passed. Teancum was finishing up his medical training and now was working part time as an assistant physician at the same military hospital where Kaila was born. Teancum was a gifted student. With his ability to remember everything he read or was taught, he aced all his tests and was going to graduate at the very top of his class. The hospital had already offered him a job working in the research department. His new job would include finding new herbs and plants, and refining them so they could be used as medicines for healing. At this point in his life, the only thing that could make Teancum happier was the news he got one morning as he was getting ready for work. Hanni was having morning sickness again, and this time, Teancum was more than ready to diagnose her symptoms. They counted up the days and realized the new addition would arrive close to Kaila's birthday.

"You making me a son in there?" Teancum joked as he held Hanni from behind, putting his hands on her belly while resting his chin on her shoulder.

"What if it's a girl?" Hanni questioned as she placed her hands over Teancum's, kissed him on the cheek and held on to her man's arms.

"Then we will just put it back in the oven until it's done cooking."

"Hey!" Hanni playfully gasped and turned around in his arms. "You take that back, mister."

"Teancum gently kissed her lips and spoke, "Boy or girl, it does not matter. You and Kaila are the lights of my life. I can only imagine how happy I will be with a new baby to love."

Those sweet words pulled at Hanni's heart. "You should go before you are late. You don't want them to give that job to someone else, do you?"

She tried to speak while choking back the tears and gently patting her love on the chest.

"No ma'am." Teancum winked while reaching for his shoulder bag. "I will be home a bit late tonight. There is a study group at the college and I wanted to make sure I had everything covered for the final exam next week."

"Don't forget, your mother and grandparents are coming for Sabbath dinner this week at my parents' home…no study groups or extra shifts on that day." She looked into his eyes. "Promise me?"

"I promise," Teancum said has he grabbed one last breakfast biscuit from the pan as he headed for the door. "I love you," he mumbled, with a mouth full of Hanni's home baked goodness.

"Daddy….!" Kaila called out as she ran up with a small blanket in one hand and a rag doll in the other. She held out her arms for a goodbye hug and kiss from her biggest hero before he left for the day.

"Goodbye, my little princess." Teancum bent down and gently hugged her.

"Goodbye, daddy," Kaila said and kissed him on the cheek.

Teancum stood up feeling like the king of the world. "I love you," he mouthed to his sweet bride and waved goodbye to them both.

"Goodbye, my love," Hanni mouthed back as she blew him a kiss. Hanni looked down at Kaila, who looked up at her mother, then put her thumb back into her mouth. "Let's get dressed and go see grandma. We have some good news to tell her." Kaila smiled then ran for her room to change clothes.

TROUBLE AT THE HOSPITAL

Teancum was excited to get to work so he could tell his co-workers the news of the new baby coming. As he was walking toward the hospital, enjoying the fresh morning air, shouting erupted and people ran past him. A wagon full of wounded men came racing by, followed by several more soldiers in full armor and weapons.

"What the…?" Teancum wondered out loud as he turned back to the direction from which the wagon had come. He turned just in time to see a second wagon coming right at him. The teamster was shouting for everyone to get out of his way. Teancum and everyone in the streets jumped out of the way. As the wagon passed, Teancum could see it, too, was full of wounded soldiers all heading for the hospital. There was a man in the back of the wagon trying to stop the bleeding from a bad wound on a soldier's arm. Teancum recognized the man as a co-worker from a different section of the hospital. The man doing first aid saw Teancum standing on the side of the road as he passed. He recognized Teancum and called out to him.

"Get to the hospital!"

"What happened?" Teancum called back.

"Lamanite attack!" the man shouted back as the wagon continued to barrel down the street. That was all he said. The wagon was moving too fast and it was clear that he had more important things to do than to continue the explanation.

The civilians were starting to scatter and run out of fear of a possible

Lamanite attack on the city. Teancum thought about his family and turned to run back to the barracks.

No! He stopped himself. *They are in the safest place in the city right now and I have a duty to perform,* he smiled to himself as he continued his thought, *besides, Hanni would just turn me around and send me to the hospital to help, anyway.*

Teancum was only about half a mile from the hospital and ran the rest of the way. When he arrived at the courtyard at the front entrance to the hospital, the scene before him looked like controlled chaos. To the untrained eye, it looked like pandemonium, with the wounded arriving by the wagon-loads, the injured screaming in pain, people running around shouting, and doctors working on their patients in the open. But to the staff of the military hospital, this was exactly what they had been trained to do. It was not chaos at all, but a well-organized and functioning triage, or response to mass casualties. As a military medical unit, they had drilled and practiced for this very event. Now was their time to shine. Every moving part was functioning as intended. Teancum slowed to a walk, then stopped at the edge of the grassy, open area, where the injured were being treated. Hundreds of stretchers and blankets were arrayed in the field, each containing a wounded soldier. Some lay still, others sitting up and still others writhing or crying out in pain. He was stunned by the sheer number of injured people lying before him. "I'm not a doctor yet," he murmured to himself, while questioning his abilities and purpose. "I still need to graduate." The magnitude of what was happening shocked him into silence. Unable to mentally process it all, he froze.

"Hey!" An older doctor, with salt and pepper hair, shouted at Teancum. He was frantically working on a badly wounded soldier. The soldier had a large wound across his chest.

Teancum had worked on injuries before, but nothing of this scale or intensity. Everywhere he looked, there was blood, cries of pain and death.

"You!" The doctor could not remember Teancum's name but he did know Teancum was from the university and was on his last week before graduation. "You... Student! Come here!"

Teancum blinked and swallowed hard when he heard the word student and looked at the doctor.

"Snap out of it and grab me a bag of bandages and a stitching kit!" He pointed to a table at the far end of the grassy area that had been set up with medical supplies stacked upon it.

"Yes, sir," Teancum's automatic response kicked in as he started to move forward. The more he moved, the more his mind cleared and he was able to concentrate on the task at hand. As he reached the area with the medical supplies, he grabbed several bandages as well as a stitching kit. He turned around to face back in the direction he needed to go. Teancum saw the sea of human suffering between him and his destination and he started to panic. He was gulping air and clutched the bag of bandages tightly to his chest. His vision was starting to cloud and there was a ringing in his ears. "What's happening?" he questioned to himself out loud. He could feel his legs start to shake and a cold sweat was beading on his forehead.

Breathe.

'Who said that?" Teancum turned around expecting to see someone standing right behind him.

Courage.

Teancum spun around again but no one was there. He knew that voice, he had heard it before. "Breathe?" Teancum questioned. He did a quick self-assessment. "Yes, I need air." He realized he was hyperventilating. He needed to slow down his breathing. Taking slow breaths, in through his nose and out through his mouth, Teancum was able to control his breathing. After just a few seconds he felt much better and more alert. "Courage?" was the next word out of his mouth. Teancum knew there was a wounded man in desperate need and he had the lifesaving tools in his hands.

You know more about the healing arts than any other member of you class. You are a doctor now. Go and save lives! The voice in Teancum's head was almost shouting the words of encouragement at him.

Teancum looked again at the madness and human suffering unfolding before him. "Courage," he spoke. Still clutching the bandage bag closely to his chest, he forced his feet to move one step at a time. He worked his way around the wounded lying on the grass, finally reaching the doctor.

"You are too late." The doctor stood up as Teancum arrived. He was wiping blood from his hands.

"I have the bandages and sewing kit," Teancum said while reaching out, trying to hand the items to the doctor. He looked almost relieved.

The doctor looked hard at him. "I said, you are too late. He is too far gone."

"But I have the bandages!" Teancum was not processing what was happening, he had been so focused on delivering the needed medical items. Fixating on his immediate task was how he was dealing with all of the horror around him.

"Son, there is nothing else we can do. He is as good as dead! We need to move on. Come with me." The older doctor impatiently grabbed Teancum by the arm and started moving towards the next injured soldier.

"No!" Teancum shouted and pulled away from the older man's grasp "I don't think you understand, I have the bandages and the stitching kit! We can help him now!" Teancum held the items out again for the doctor to take from him.

The older doctor had seen this many times before. The confusion, the lack of comprehension, the denial. This young medical student was in shock and needed to be snapped back into reality fast or he was going to be more of a liability than an asset. Grabbing Teancum by the tunic, the doctor jerked him close to his own face and spoke in a low tone so those around him could not hear what he was going to say. "We don't have time for this, so listen to me very closely. This is a mass casualty event. That soldier's injuries are too severe. It would take a team of doctors several hours and a tremendous amount of medical supplies just to stabilize him. And after that, there is only one chance in three he will make it through the night. With all that time and energy, we can save ten others who are not as badly injured but will surely die if they don't get immediate help." He backed away slightly from Teancum's face then continued in a softer tone. "It's simple combat math, son. Don't try to figure it out, it's just war. We need to save those we can save."

Teancum looked down at the poor soldier who was in and out of consciousness. His blood was everywhere. "Is there nothing we can do?"

The doctor looked back down at the soldier and then up into Teancum's eyes. He could hear the simple compassion in Teancum's voice and the sadness in his eyes. He knew in his own heart what the right thing to do was. "Give him some of the opiate extract for the pain, make him comfortable, and then let him go to his reward." The doctor looked around and saw another soldier close by with a bad wound to his leg. A nurse was desperately trying to apply a makeshift tourniquet. "I will be over there helping that soldier. Be quick and join me there." The doctor took the medical supplies from Teancum. He opened the stitching kit and removed a small vial full of a milky substance. "Just a few drops under his tongue is all he needs, understand?" He looked into Teancum's eyes for understanding.

"Yes, sir," Teancum responded while hesitantly taking the vial.

"Hurry now." The doctor spoke and turned to move on to the next injured warrior.

Teancum knelt down next to the dying soldier and opened the vial next to the soldier's head. The dying man opened his eyes and tried to speak.

"Shhh," Teancum said, trying to comfort him. "Medicine." He held the vial up so the man could see it. "This will help with the pain." He nodded slightly, there was gratitude his eyes as he opened his mouth to let Teancum administer the medication. Teancum put several drops under the man's tongue and told him to close his mouth and swallow. The man swallowed hard. About ten seconds later a wave of relief washed over his pain-wracked body. The dying man opened his eyes again and Teancum could see the tremendous relief from the pain on his face. He tried to smile at Teancum but took three short gasps for air and then his heart stopped beating. His eyes froze in place and what color was left in his cheeks quickly disappeared with the sudden loss of blood pressure. Teancum felt completely numb as he looked at the lifeless body before him. *Is it that simple?* He questioned in his mind. *Do you just stop existing?* As a medical student he had been around plenty of dead bodies in anatomy class, autopsies; he had even done a stint with the sheriff's office as they investigated crimes in the city and had seen the tragic outcome of criminal behavior. But this was the first time he was all alone watching someone in his care die right in front of him. He looked up at the carnage all around him and had a surreal moment. Everything was happening in slow motion as he watched those dedicated medical personnel work frantically to save as many soldiers as they could. He turned and looked at the doctor, who was having a difficult time holding the next wounded man down while attempting to apply the lifesaving tourniquet. Before realizing what he was doing, Teancum was on his feet, moving toward the doctor. He dropped down on his knees next to the man with the leg injury and held down his arms so the doctor could tie off the tourniquet and stop the free flow of blood from the large gash to his thigh. The doctor looked back to see who was helping him and realized it was Teancum.

"Do you still have the vial of the poppy extract?" He asked.

Teancum held up his hand, while still struggling to control the wounded soldier, to show the doctor he was still in possession of the medicine.

"Give him two drops," the doctor ordered. "Just two, no more."

Teancum held the vial over the man's eyes then spoke, "It's medicine for the pain. Let me help you." The wounded soldier understood, stopped screaming and thrashing about long enough for Teancum to uncork the vial and put two drops in his mouth. Almost instantly the soldier felt better and relaxed, lying down flat on his back.

"Come over here and quickly tell me what you see," the doctor ordered Teancum to move over by the wound to the man's leg.

Teancum moved and gave the wound a quick exam. He was in his element now. "The wound looks deep, but it appears to be only a muscular injury, no broken bone. The artery has been hit and will need to be repaired if there is any hope of saving the leg below the wound."

"Good, what else? Quickly, this is a triage, not a full exam."

"Yes, sir...." Teancum moved down to the soldier's feet then checked the pulse on the wounded leg. "It is weak but I can feel it." He then pinched the big toenail and counted the seconds for the color to return under the nail. "Four seconds to refill...There is still blood flow to the lower leg, but it's weak."

"So, what does that tell you?" the doctor asked.

Teancum thought for a second and looked back at the wound. He saw that even though the tourniquet was on, there was still some blood flowing from the injury. "We need to tighten the tourniquet and pack the wound with bandages. We have to stop the bleeding or he will die."

"Correct. Well done," the older man said. "See to it...Doctor."

Teancum felt a rush of emotion as he tightened the band around the upper thigh and then packed bandages into the open wound. He was doing it—he was being a doctor and helping someone in need. Wrapping the bandage-packed wound with a large strip of cloth, Teancum then made a mark on the injured man's forehead with a piece of charcoal.

"What's that for?" the old doctor asked as he supervised Teancum's work.

"It is a mark to let the surgeons know he has a tourniquet on his leg so they don't overlook it and can try to save the leg."

"That's good thinking. Is it something new they are teaching at the university?"

"Yes, sir." Teancum stood up wiping his hands on a large

rag. "Stretcher bearer!" Teancum called out and waved to two men moving quickly around the grounds. As the two men ran up carrying a stretcher Teancum gave them instructions. "He is a priority for surgery. Tourniquet on the right thigh and poppy oil for the pain."

"Yes, doctor," one of them responded as they both bent down to lift the wounded soldier and put him on the stretcher.

"Well done, doctor," the older man complimented Teancum. "Shall we?" He held out his hand inviting Teancum to join him on the next patient.

"Yes, sir." Teancum smiled, then moved past the older man, heading for the next wounded soldier in need of medical aid.

The rest of the day was spent moving from one injured man to the next. Teancum lost count of how many soldiers he assisted and how many died right there on the open, grassy ground. The staff of the hospital had done a heroic job, but they were clearly overwhelmed. When word got out the Lamanites had ambushed a column of Nephites and the wounded were at the army hospital, aid came from all over the city. Before long, large tents had been erected for shade from the hot sun, and food stations were preparing meals for the medical staff and those soldiers who could eat.

It was hours later and Teancum was applying a splint to a soldier's broken arm when he saw his father-in-law, the garrison commander, walking among the wounded and doctors. There was a very large man in full armor walking next to the commander, along with several lesser-ranking officers and attendants. The large man had a magnificent sword on his hip and Teancum could tell he was someone important by the defference Hanni's father was showing him. They appeared to be talking to the injured men as well as checking on those who could not speak.

"Do you know who that is walking with the garrison commander?" One of the stretcher bearers asked Teancum. He was in awe as watched them.

"No. Should I?"

"That big man is our chief captain," the man with the broken arm replied. "His name is Chief Captain Joshua and he is the garrison commander's boss. I don't see his son, Lieutenant Moroni, with him, though." The injured man looked around the grounds. "I wonder if he is among the wounded," the soldier continued as he grimaced in pain, then sat back and let Teancum finish his task. "That would be a shame. Moroni is a good kid; big and smart, that one is. He will make a fine leader some day."

Teancum glanced over to them again, then finished with the splint and gave instructions to the stretcher bearer. "He will be okay, just a broken arm. Move him to the shade tent and get him some soup and bread." Teancum stood up, wiped his hands and made eye contact with Hanni's father. He was exhausted, but Teancum knew he needed Hanni's father to see him working while trying to save the lives of the soldiers. He still felt, in the back of his mind, the commander and the other soldiers around him judged him to be less of a man because he was not carrying a sword. Waving to him, Teancum smiled and the old soldier smiled back. Teancum was about to move toward the next wounded soldier when realized his father-in-law and the others were coming his way. He tried to be casual about it, but Teancum was a bit excited. He would finally get the chance to show Hanni's father what he could do. Washing his hands in a basin full of hot soapy water, he moved a few feet to greet them.

"Teancum, how do you fare?"

"I am well, Father, but very busy. I am afraid there are many more that still need my attention," he spoke as he wiped off his hands with a clean towel to shake his father-in-law's hand.

"Son, this is Chief Captain Joshua. These are his men you're treating."

"It is a pleasure to meet you, sir." Teancum held out his hand to shake the captain's hand. The large soldier was abrupt in his tone and demeanor, and Teancum saw he had a bit of blood coming from the left side of his head and a small wrap covering the wound. "Would you like me to take a look at that?" Teancum asked as he pointed to the side of Captain Joshua's head.

"No, doctor," Captain Joshua responded, as he shook young Teancum's hand. Teancum almost choked when he heard the legendary war leader call him "doctor". "I will be fine. Thank you for taking such good care of my men."

"It is my honor to serve you and your men, Chief Captain." Teancum composed himself then stole a quick look at the hilt of the big sword Captain Joshua was carrying. "So that's the famous sword of Laban?" He questioned as he quickly changed the subject.

"The very one," Captain Joshua responded as he turned a bit so Teancum could get a better look at the hilt and scabbard.

"It is amazing that after so many hundreds of years it is still in such

fine shape," Teancum commented.

"The story says it was the finest blade ever made in all of Israel by master sword makers. Laban spared no expense." Teancum noticed everyone was looking at him and Captain Joshua as they spoke. He suddenly felt very out of place and thought he was being judged by the others for having such a casual conversation with the chief captain. Clearing his throat, he continued, "Thank you sir, for allowing me to see this priceless relic up close. I would love to know more about the history of that amazing weapon, but duty calls. Now if you gentlemen will excuse me, I have many more injured to see to. By your leave, sir?" Teancum faced the commander and requested his permission to continue his duties.

"Granted. Go with God, and help these men."

Teancum made a quick and courteous nod toward the chief captain then turned to move to the next wounded man.

"He is the boy who married little Hanni?" Captain Joshua asked.

"Yes sir. My wife and I were saddened when you could not attend the wedding ceremony. He is the grandson of Lord Pilio and Lady Saria. Do you know them?"

Captain Joshua looked surprised at the family connection. "I know Lord Pilio, and he is an honorable man." He turned to look at Teancum and watched him as he cared for the injured. Teancum was kneeling down and bent over a soldier and adjusting a bandage. "It looks like he is a fine young man, and he is from a noble family. My compliments to you on the match for your daughter."

"Thank you sir. He is a good boy." The commander felt a bit of pride as he and Captain Joshua watched Teancum begin to work on the wounded man.

After a moment of motionless silence, one of Captain Joshua's officers reminded him, "Sir, there are many more wounded inside the hospital. We should keep moving if you want to visit all the men before nightfall."

"Thank you lieutenant," he responded with a bit of sorrow in his voice. He turned to look at the bodies of the men who had died and were covered with sheets laying in neat rows away from the others. "The price of freedom was high today." No one responded. They all knew nothing else needed to be said.

It was well after dark and Teancum was still outside tending to the less seriously wounded. Every man was triaged as they arrived at the hospital, then put into categories according to the severity of their injuries. Those with mortal wounds, having no hope of recovery, were made comfortable then left to pass to whatever reward in heaven awaited them, based on the life they had led on earth. Those with serious wounds who could be saved with additional medical aid, like the man with the tourniquet on his leg, were stabilized and moved inside the hospital. Those men with wounds that could be quickly treated, and who were not in need of immediate advanced care, were seen, bandaged, and put under the large shade tents to wait for Teancum and his colleagues to return and render whatever additional attention they needed.

Teancum was under the tent cover and working by torch light, stitching a man's arm up when he heard Hanni's sweet voice.

"Teancum...?"

He looked up to see his wife standing there, with a bundle of fresh clothing under her arm as well as a basket of food and a small jug of juice in the other. She had been crying and looked relieved she had found him alive. "I was worried when you did not come home. Then the guards at the base said there was a Lamanite attack and I figured you were here." She smiled and came two steps closer. "I brought you a fresh set of clothing and some food."

Teancum suddenly felt so tired and lightheaded that his legs wobbled a bit. He realized he had not eaten anything since he had grabbed an extra breakfast biscuit early that morning. "Oh, my love, you're so sweet," He gestured with his hands. "I am almost done here, can you give me a few more minutes?"

"Of course." She looked around at the surroundings. There were blood stains, wounded men and used bandages everywhere. She went pale. This was no place for her to be standing. "I will be over by that tree when you're ready," she gestured with her head and bravely smiled.

"I'm sorry, my love," Teancum lamented. He understood she took a risk leaving little Kaila and coming here. He knew she was worried about his health and she was uneasy being around all the death, but he could tell she was putting on a brave face for him. "I will be right there." He smiled back. As she was walking off he shouted to her, "I think your father is still inside the hospital."

Hanni turned, "Mother said I should check on him if I get a chance."

Teancum nodded, telling her they would look for her father as soon as he was done. He finished with the stitches and had one of the nurses apply an ointment to the freshly closed wound. Washing his hands in a large basin full of warm water and aloe soap, Teancum walked over to the tree and hugged his wife.

"You look so tired," she said as she brushed his dark hair from his eyes.

"I am!" Teancum was shaking as he tried to eat some bread and meat from the basket Hanni had prepared. His body was revolting from the overload of emotions of the day and lack of food and rest. Hanni handed him a jug of water and told him to drink. Teancum took a large drink and handed the jug back to Hanni. He was very grateful for a wife who supported and understood him. He smiled and took her under his arm. "Thank you for coming and bringing me food." She smiled back and wrapped both of her arms around his waist and hugged him.

"I'm just happy you are safe. I know you need to help. It's your job and those poor men need you right now." She took a deep breath and continued, "So, what now?" Hanni asked. She was not complaining. Hanni was no sheltered, clueless civilian. Far from it. Hanni was experienced on how things in a soldier's life of sacrifice worked. Growing up in a military family, and with her long experience working with those most in need, she knew in a situation like this, with so many wounded and dying, it might be days before she saw Teancum at home. She just wanted him to know she would help him in his work to help others.

"There is a staff meeting in one hour to discuss the next steps. Your father should be there." He said as he looked into her eyes. "I will check on him if he is." She smiled back saying thank you with her eyes. After taking another drink from the jug he continued, "Stage one of this madness is over. All the wounded have been triaged and the most severely injured have been moved inside for follow-up care. I am hoping, if everyone is stable, we will start working in shifts and some of us can go home and get some sleep."

"That would be nice," Hanni said with a hint of sadness. Her husband was the youngest and newest doctor working in the hospital. She knew he would volunteer for the first shift so the others could rest. That was the type of man he was. She was proud of him and knew this quality was one of the many reasons she had agreed to marry him.

As she expected, Teancum did attend the meeting. After checking on the welfare of his father-in-law, he was the first to volunteer to stay and care for the wounded, allowing the other doctors to go and get some rest. To his surprise, the older doctor with the gray speckled hair also agreed to stay behind and help look after the men.

"We are both tired," the old doctor spoke to Teancum as they left the meeting. "This will work best if we stick together and check each other's work."

"Yes sir," Teancum responded, as they walked down the main hall. Teancum was starting to feel overwhelmed at the magnitude of his responsibility. Everywhere he looked there were wounded men in bandages lying on cots, sitting in chairs and spread out on the floor sleeping on mats.

The old mentor sensed Teancum's feelings and reassured him, "You can only attend to one patient at a time. Do your very best as quickly as you can and move on. No one can expect more than that."

"Yes sir. Thank you, sir."

"And quit calling me sir, my name is Jopper."

It was noon by the time Teancum was relieved of his duties, and started the long walk back to his small home at the army barracks. As if by some work of magic, Hanni was standing in the doorway, waiting for him as he arrived. She hugged him and helped him inside. Taking his bag and walking him over to the kitchen table, she sat him down in front of a hot bowl of thick stew and fresh bread with butter.

"I know you are tired, but you need to eat something before you go to sleep." Teancum tried to rebel and stand up to go to the bed, but Hanni pushed him back down. "Trust me on this one, mister. I have seen my dad come home too many times like this and skip food, only to wake up hours later sick from the lack of a good dinner. Now, doctor's orders— eat!" She pointed lovingly but firmly at the bowl and stood her ground. Teancum was way too tired to argue and picked up the large spoon. Scooping a heaping serving into his mouth, he slowly chewed and swallowed.

"I love you," he said with hot food still in his mouth.

"I love you too my darling. Now, there will be a basin of hot water and soap waiting for you out back. When you are done, wash up and then get to bed."

"Where is Kaila?" Teancum asked as he took another bite.

"She is taking a nap at Mother's house. When you go to sleep, I will go get her and bring her home."

After finishing the bowl of stew and getting a good scrub down, Teancum was in bed and asleep before his head hit the pillow. He slept deeply for hours and it was just before sunset when Teancum was jolted awake by a bad dream. He was dreaming about trying to help wounded soldiers in a far-off battlefield then finding his entire family dead in the middle of the chaos. Jerking and kicking the covers off, Teancum sat up. It took a second for him to remember he was safe in his own house. Hanni was standing near the bed, holding a wicker basket full of clean clothing. She was trying to be quiet as she moved through the room and was scared by Teancum's sudden awakening. She dropped the basket and shrieked, "Teancum, are you okay?"

Teancum looked at her and blinked several times, trying to focus in the dim evening light. "I'm fine," he said and waved his hand in the air.

"I'm sorry. Did I startle you?", she gently asked.

"No… Bad dream," he said as he rubbed his eyes while sliding over to the side of the bed to sit up.

She sat down on the bed, next to him, putting her arm around his shoulders. "Want to tell me about it?" She knew her father had bad dreams sometimes. She remembered hearing him call out in the middle of the night, or finding him standing alone in the front yard, staring into the darkness at nothing and everything all at once. She did not like it when her father would get that way and was concerned for her husband.

"I will be okay." Teancum kissed her forehead and patted her arm. "It's just my body rebelling at the mess of the last few days."

Hanni knew better, but she was not going to push the issue right now. She knew Teancum had been through a very traumatic event and needed time to process everything. Right now, he needed to feel safe and loved. She was quietly grateful for the experiences of being a military child and learning how to deal with the aftereffects of extreme trauma.

"Daddy!" There was the patter of little feet on the wood floor and Teancum smiled as he turned to see Kaila run and jump onto the bed. "Daddy is awake!" she cried out as she crawled across the bed and into Teancum's arms. Teancum held her close and felt her little arms trying to wrap all the way around his neck. "Where were you, Daddy? I was at Grandma's house all day and did not see you. Mommy said you had to help people?"

"Yes, my little angel. I'm sorry I was away. Daddy was helping sick people get better." He could tell Kaila had just had a bath. She smelled clean, her hair was still wet and perfumed by the scented soap that Hanni liked to use. "Are you getting ready for bed?"

"Yes, but I wanted you to help me with prayers," she said in her sweet way.

Ever since the episode in the delivery room, Teancum had taken a fresh look at the topic of religion. He had warmed to the idea of church again. Most Sabbaths, he could be found sitting next to Hanni and her parents in the pew. He even started helping Hanni with the humanitarian work she did for the church by offering free medical assistance to the very poor, the orphaned and widowed.

"Prayers?!" Teancum said as he grabbed Kaila by the waist and started to tickle her. She screamed with delight as she tried to fight out of his hold and wiggle away from him.

"Don't get her all excited this close to bedtime!" Hanni warned him. Hearing this, Teancum quickly grabbed Hanni's arm and pulled her down onto the bed with them and started to tickle her, too. Hanni cried out as the three of them wrestled on the bed, laughing and tickling each other for a few minutes until Teancum was out of breath. He rolled onto his back letting Hanni and Kaila hold him down by both of his arms.

"Okay, okay, you two win."

Kaila knew this game well. "Do you yield?" she questioned with joy in her voice.

"Yes, I yield to the two best warriors in the land. Please, show mercy!" Everyone knew what was going to happen next. Kaila then crawled up on his chest and looked Teancum in the eyes.

"Mercy is for the weak!" she cried out and started to kiss his cheeks while Hanni tickled him under his armpits. This went on for a few moments more until Hanni finally called a halt to the fun. Then they all laid on the bed, panting for air, enjoying this simple moment in their life.

"Ok, my princess, it's really time for bed now," Teancum spoke. "Let's say our good night prayers." Kaila got to her knees and brushed the long strands of disheveled hair from her eyes. Folding her arms and bowing her head, she then looked out the corner of her eyes for the prompt from her father of what to say. Hanni sat next to her and folded her arms to join in.

Teancum saw the look and knew it was time for him to speak. It took him a moment to recall the pattern of words. Teancum relxed and spoke softly. "Father in Heaven," Kaila followed along in her young voice, speaking the words Teancum was saying. "Thank you for this day and for all my blessings." He paused as she recited his words. "Thank you for my family and friends, for my health and safety, and for my home and happiness." As Teancum was speaking the words for Kaila to recite, he felt Hanni's hand reach for his and he held it in a loving grip as he continued. There, with his little family, Teancum felt almost overwhelmed with love. "Please bless me while I sleep and bless those who are protecting me while I sleep. Help me to always remember who I am and what I stand for. I say these things…"

She interrupted him with a whisper. "Daddy, I can say the rest by myself."

"Okay, go ahead." He was so proud of his little girl.

With a child's innocence, she finished her prayer saying, "Please help me remember who I am and what I stand for. I say these things in the name of Jesus Christ, Amen."

"Amen." Hanni and Teancum spoke in unison. Kaila gave them both big hugs and Hanni got up to escort her off to bed.

"Good night Daddy, I love you," her sweet voice echoed off the walls as she walked to her padded sleeping mat. Teancum was fighting back the tears as he listened to Kaila and Hanni talk as Kaila was being tucked into her bed.

"Mommy, I'm glad Daddy is home," she spoke in a loud whisper.

"I'm glad he is home too, little one," Hanni replied. "Now go to sleep. I love you."

"I love you, too, Mommy. Good night."

Hanni blew out the small single candle burning in the corner of Kaila's room, then walked back into the bedroom where Teancum was still sitting on the bed. "And you… What am I going to do with you?" she playfully asked with her hands on her hips.

"Truce?" Teancum playfully pleaded as he held his hands up.

"You're lucky I like you," Hanni responded, as she sat down on the bed next to Teancum. "So when do you need to be back at the hospital?"

"Tomorrow, at noon. We will be doing twelve-hour shifts until things settle down." He looked at his wife. He was not completely sure how she would react to the news of him being gone for so long each day.

"What about your final exam? Do they know you are not technically a doctor yet?" she asked.

"That never really came up. I just started to help where I could, and everyone, I guess, just assumed I was."

"What are you going to do? I don't want you to get into trouble," Hanni had concern in her voice.

"It will be okay," Teancum reassured her. "I was supervised by an older doctor and they really needed the help. I am going to say something when I get to work tomorrow to let them know I will need time off to finish my exams. I'm sure they will understand." He smiled at her to help ease her worry.

"Okay, you know them better than I do. I trust you to do the right thing," Hanni smiled back and laid her head on his shoulder. "Are you hungry? You were asleep for over seven hours."

"Yes," Teancum replied, "I am starving and dehydrated." He stretched and yawned. "But I could fall back to sleep and lay here until dawn."

"I have some leftover stew in the warmer and more bread," Hanni said as she stood up and pulled him off the bed by his arms. "Eat up. Then we can clean the mess, go to bed early, and both get a good night's rest." She felt it might be the last chance for a good sleep together for a while.

Teancum arrived at work a few minutes early the next day and was surprised to see so many wounded soldiers still outside, under the tents. They all had received primary care but many were still waiting for a place to go to get the follow up care they needed. Even though he had a full night's sleep, he already felt tired as he walked through the main entrance of the crowded hospital. He made his way to the main corridor where he was greeted by the older doctor he had worked with the day before. He was arriving also and waved Teancum over to stand next to him.

"Good morning," the older doctor smiled, putting out his hand for Teancum to shake. "I am sorry, but with all the confusion, I don't remember your first name."

Teancum took his hand and shook it with a firm grip as he looked the doctor in the eyes. Pilio had always been insistent that Teancum always look a man in the eyes when he shook hands. "Sir, my name is Teancum."

"Teancum, my name is Jopper, and you can stow that 'sir' business. Most people just call me Jop." They smiled at each other while they shook hands.

"Jop it is." Teancum released his grip on Jop's hand then turned to look down the hallway. "Any idea what's happening?"

"I have been through something like this a few times, and usually what will happen is the chief doctor for the last shift will give a briefing on how the last shift went. Then he will turn the responsibilities over to the next shift's chief physician. That doctor will then assign duties to the others and the day will begin."

"Oh, so I guess we stand here and wait?" Teancum asked.

"You *are* new," Jop smiled as he spoke.

"Don't tell anyone," Teancum replied, winking back.

"We will meet here in the main hall way for the briefing." They both had a quick laugh as others gathered to start the staff meeting.

The briefing began. The last shift's lead doctor was explaining what had happened over the last twelve hours while he was running the hospital. Teancum was more focused on the man's appearance and nonverbal expressions than on the words he was speaking. As he gave his briefing, Teancum could see the man was struggling just to move. He was far past the point of exhaustion— he moved as if his limbs were heavy rocks hanging from his torso. His eyes were sunken and dark bags hung under his lids, he had a two-day old beard and several blood stains on his medical coverings.

"Are there any questions?" he asked as he finished speaking. There was a short, silent pause, as the man looked over the medical staff gathered to run the next twelve hours. "No? Very well. Doctor Jop, are you ready to take the reins?"

Teancum instantly snapped to attention and turned to look at his companion. "You are the head physician?" he gasped.

"Yup, and guess who just became my assistant?" Jop smiled and winked as he handed Teancum the stack of parchments in his hands. "Okay, people, let's do everything we can to get those still outside either discharged or inside for further treatment." He spoke in a firm but commanding voice as he doled out the work assignments to his staff. "Questions? If not, let's get to work." Jop clapped his hands as a signal to dismiss those around him to see to their responsibilities. Teancum was still standing with both arms out, full of scrolls and parchments, and a puzzled look on his face. Jop turned to face him.

"But…I?" Teancum tried to speak but could not form the words. The position of head physician for the military hospital in the capital city of Zarahemla was a great honor and full of responsibility. Even more than the instructors at the medical school, he had complete power over Teancum's future. "If I had known…."

Jop held up his hand to interrupt Teancum, "You would have acted differently. I would never have known who you truly were as a healer." Jop took a step closer to Teancum so he could keep talking but hold his voice down so others, passing by, could not hear. "I watched you for hours working outside with those wounded men. You were impressive. You're a better doctor than half these people I have on my staff, and you have not even graduated yet." He smiled and patted Teancum's shoulders. "If you forget school and stay here to help me get through the next few days as my assistant, I will make sure you not only become a physician, but you will have your pick of assignments here. Deal?" He looked into Teancum's eyes for a sign of comprehension.

"Y…yes sir," Teancum stammered with a hint of uncertainty.

"Excellent. Now, take those files, put them in some sort of order, and then join me outside as I conduct my rounds." Jop slapped Teancum on his back as he walked past heading for the main doors, leading outside.

Teancum, still not fully comprehending what had happened, turned and watched as Jop walked outside. As his new boss left his view, Teancum smiled to himself, slowly starting to realize how lucky he was. Feeling a bit proud of himself, he headed down the hallway toward the staff office and tried to readjust the papers in his hands. In his fumbling they all fell out of his arms and spilled onto the ground covering the floor in front of him. Teancum ate a bite of humble pie as he gathered up the papers while the rest of the hospital staff walked around him.

The next few days were long and tasking for young Teancum. He was doing the job of both administrative assistant and attending physician at the same time. Working next to Jop was like a dream come true for him. Jop was meticulous and aggressive in his healing arts. He showed Teancum methods and medical techniques Teancum had never learned about in school. Teancum learned more about being a real doctor in those few days than he did in a year of study at the university. The time flew by and before long, all the wounded soldiers who could be transported were moved back to their own villages and cities. There they would receive any additional care they might need from their families and clansmen. It was Teancum's job to oversee the transfer process. He had to ensure each wounded soldier was taken care of and was physically ready to travel. He would meet with each one personally, conduct a full examination, and check to ensure the soldier was strong enough, mentally and physically, for a long journey in a wagon or on horseback. Teancum was fascinated by the individual life stories of those brave men and how they all ended up there at the hospital at the same time. Teancum knew Jop was going to review each discharge, so all the processes had to be flawless. The arrangements all needed to be appropriate for the needs of each soldier. Some of the discharged soldiers could walk and care for themselves, while others had crippling injuries that would require long-term care.

Teancum had heard Jop say, "They all just can't be loaded in the back of a wagon and then dropped off in the dead of night at their lonely little fishing village." As they started the process of moving the soldiers out of the hospital, Jop had instructed Teancum to draft his father-in-law and detail soldiers to escort and care for the wounded warriors as they were being moved back home.

Teancum made notes of Jop's instructions, but it was a struggle to keep ahead of the rapid pace.

It was on one particular day, when Teancum was making his arrangements for some soldiers, all headed home to the city of Noah, that he went looking for Jop for a final approval on his work. Teancum searched the hospital high and low but could not find his boss and mentor. After looking for several more minutes Teancum was informed by a medical attendant that Doctor Jop was last seen in the research lab. Teancum knew where the lab was, but he had not spent much time in that part of the hospital. He did know the quickest way to reach the lab from his location was to walk out of the main doors and go around the massive main building to the back door of the lab. This was fine with him; he needed the fresh air and sunlight to help clear his mind. Teancum had been working at the hospital long enough for others to recognize him and know him by name. The others all thought Teancum was a good doctor. He worked hard and had a great attitude about doing his tasks. This made him popular with the other members of the medical staff. He greeted several people as he walked and finally made it to the open door of the lab. As he entered the room, he could smell the overpowering stench of something burning and saw smoke escaping from the open door. Thinking there might be a fire burning, out of control inside the lab, Teancum dropped his paperwork and rushed to the door to see inside.

"Doctor Jop... Are you in here?" Teancum cried out as he moved deeper into the room trying to see through the smoke.

"Here, lad," Jop responded coughing and wafting smoke away from his face with his hands. He was chuckling under his breath as he pushed the window covering away from the opening to let more of the smoke out and sunlight in.

"Sir," Teancum said as he moved up next to Jop, "are you ok?"

Before Jop could answer, a voice from farther in the room called out. "Well, I guess we know now what happens when you heat that up!" There was a deep laugh as a man with half-burnt clothing, soot on his face, singed hair, and crazy eyes walked into view.

"Professor, this is the boy I was telling you about," Jop pointed to the singed researcher. "Professor, meet young Doctor Teancum." He pointed back to Teancum. "Teancum meet the professor."

The wily professor tried to brush off his dirty hands on his soot covered frock, then held it out for Teancum to shake. "I have heard so much about you…it's finally good to meet in person."

"I am afraid you have the advantage sir." Teancum carefully reached out for the professor's hand and shook it. With the smoke still clearing, he was unsure of his surroundings and suspicious of this new and strange person.

"Oh, a strong grip," the smoldering man spoke, in a jovial tone, as he gripped Teancum's hand and shook it up and down. "That's a good sign," he finished as he winked at Jop.

Teancum gave Jop a questioning look as if to ask, "Who is this guy?" Jop smiled, shook his head and snickered under his breath.

Once the smoke cleared, Teancum was given the grand tour of the medical laboratory. Originally, this section of the hospital was created to manufacture the opium pain drops and aloe ointments the hospital staff used on a daily basis for the care and comfort of the wounded. When the professor had been brought on board a few years ago to run the lab, he began to experiment with different combinations of plants and herbs. He had made some strides toward finding uses for his creations, but there was something missing from his experiments. He and Doctor Jop agreed they needed a fresh set of eyes to look at his speculative concoctions— a young, smart, and capable doctor with a knack for remembering all the vast combinations of mixtures, and who wanted to help find cures for the fevers and infections that killed so many. It was an answer to their prayers when Jop met Teancum. After the tour, Jop and the professor sat Teancum down and bluntly laid out their idea before him.

"Teancum," Jop started, "I am impressed with your capabilities. Your memory and attention to details are impressive." Teancum felt a little bit sheepish as Jop spoke. "You know that most soldiers don't die from combat wounds but from infections to their wounds as well as from sickness and fevers which spread through the camps." Teancum shook his head as he recalled his college training and lectures from those who had experienced just such an event. Jop continued, "The professor believes, and I agree, that with the right combination of ingredients," he waved his hand back behind him toward the lab itself and the different experiments bubbling, as they spoke, "a cure can be found for those things that kill the most....the rot of wounds and the camp fevers."

Teancum blinked in astonishment as he processed that news. "A cure?" he whispered, questioningly.

"Think about that, Doctor Teancum." Jop leaned in close to Teancum. "Finding a cure for the pox, or the red fever, or the infant cough. Think about how many lives we could save if we just found a way to stop the infections from battle wounds." Jop looked Teancum squarely in the eyes. "I know you were offered this job before, but things in your life have changed. We could use a good man like yourself. What say you?"

Teancum looked up at Jop. "Does this mean you want me to stop treating the wounded and stay here in the lab?" Teancum loved his job and he wanted to help those who were in need. Being stuck in a lab all day did not sound appealing to him.

"No." Jop sat back in his chair. "Of course not. You are a very gifted doctor and it would be a shame if you stopped practicing your healing arts. What we need is someone like you who can do both. Someone who has the intellect, who is capable of multitasking, who can serve both the medical needs of his patients and also track the ever-growing list of compounds in the lab. We need someone who can see a problem with the patient," he used his fingers to count as he continued, "then devise a solution in his mind, then create that solution in the lab, and, finally, chart and treat the problem with the solution. Frankly, son, you are the only person I have met who possesses all the requirements we need."

Teancum was still unsure and a bit overwhelmed. He needed time to think this through, but what he needed, more than anything, was counsel from Hanni. What they were saying was revolutionary and could change the face of medicine, but he had to be sure it was for him. "Let me speak to my wife and I will have an answer for you in the morning."

Jop looked up at the professor and smiled. "See," he said as he pointed to Teancum, "told you." Teancum was confused and started to speak. Jop held out his hand to stop him. "The good professor was concerned you were too young. He thought you might be hasty and reckless. I told him you would want to think it over and speak to your spouse before you made any decision. You continue to not disappoint, young Teancum." Jop had a wide smile on his face.

The only thing growing faster than Teancum's medical skills was his reputation among the Nephites. News spread of this young doctor in Zarahemla, who had harnessed the power of plants and herbs to heal the sick and snatch the life of his patients from the grasp of death itself. Teancum was discovering some very interesting compounds of plant extracts that showed promising results. In the right doses, he discovered some of the plant extracts could cause extreme pain, rashes, hallucinations and even paralysis. With one experiment, he found if he combined the extract from the castor bean with certain herbs and the venom of a poisonous snake, he could create a poison so potent that it would kill a large cow in only a few seconds. Realizing he had created a very potent weapon, he hid his findings from the others with whom he worked. He was a doctor, not a weapons craftsman. His efforts would be for healing only, not for war. He made notes of all of the plants and herbs he experimented with, and thought, as a whole, it was all just an interesting byproduct of his research into the healing properties of nature.

The more people he saved from the fever, infections or the pox, the greater his reputation grew. After only a few years, his healing abilities were known from one end of the land to the other. Medical professionals came from far and wide to learn from Doctor Teancum.

Teancum was a good and honest man who spoke the plain truth. People found that not only was Teancum a wise, well-educated physician, but he also understood a wide range of important issues like civil governance, economics, religion and education. Thanks to the life and teachings his grandfather Pilio had provided him at a very young age, Teancum was now one of the most knowledgeable men in all of Zarahemla.

As his young family grew in size, so did his influence among the

Nephites. Often Teancum would be called before the great council of the kings and asked for his advice or guidance. Eventually, Teancum was called to be a physician and counselor to the beloved King Mosiah. As counselor to the king, Teancum would have many deep conversations with his monarch, and the king would challenge Teancum's intellect like no other person ever had. As a counselor to the king, Teancum received access to many of the ancient writings and records of the great leaders of the past, both from the Nephites and from the Old World. Teancum loved his interactions with the king, so as often as he could, Teancum would go into the royal records room and open up the words of the great fathers and study for hours, so he could engage in further conversations with the king.

He watched as the king struggled with his sons and their negative behavior. It saddened him to see young men of privilege shame their father. He knew if it were him, Pilio would have taken him by the scruff and tanned his hide. Hanni often spoke sadly of the sons of Mosiah working diligently to destroy the church. "I pray for them every day," she said, "As I know their father does."

"Why?" Teancum asked once, while they were eating dinner together.

"Why, what?" she responded.

"Why pray for them when they are beyond hope? Who could possibly reach those spoiled brats? They act like they own the world already. I am truly terrified for the future of this kingdom."

"Silly man," she affectionately patted his cheek, "there is no one beyond saving. Not even you."

Teancum smiled back, but something about what she said troubled him, something far back in his mind and barely out of his vision. He knew it was there, but couldn't put his finger on it.

One day as he returned home, Hanni was beaming. "It happened, a miracle!" she said. "What kind of miracle?" Teancum asked, as he set his work items down and reached for his wife.

"Alma and the sons of Mosiah have been converted!"

Teancum inquired with a puzzled look. "Converted to what?"

"To God, of course," she said, folding her arms in mock exasperation. She told him of how they'd met an angelic being on the road, and Alma, son of the High Priest, had spent days in some sort of coma before reawakening and sharing his change of heart with all who would listen.

Teancum heard her report with some skepticism. "If there was a medical issue like all the princes of the Nephite kingdom in a coma at the same time, then I would have been summoned."

Hanni shrugged her shoulders. "Not everything needs an explanation. Sometimes," she paused and winked, "you just need a little faith."

The next morning King Mosiah called for Teancum. The king needed his advice for a perplexing issue.

"Do you know what happened to my sons recently?" He asked Teancum as they walked in the royal gardens together.

Teancum knew something happened that he could not medically explain and now they were somehow changed.

"Yes, my king. But I am still at a loss for words to explain. In my medical experience I..."

King Mosiah held out his hand and Teancum stopped speaking.

"I know what happened to them and it was not a medical emergency, that is why I did not send for you. They were touched by God and saved by his grace." He smiled and choked back tears of joy as he spoke. The king composed himself and continued. "I am getting old, as you know. The kingdom needs to be reassured the government will continue. Last night I offered the throne to Ammon, my eldest." The king stopped and turned to look at Teancum. "He refused the crown." Teancum was too stunned to speak. "So, I offered it to Aaron, then Omner, and then Himni." He smiled. "They all refused the crown." The king seemed lost in thought and continued walking. Teancum had to hurry to catch up. "They all have chosen to refuse their birthright and instead, will go as missionaries to the Lamanite people."

Teancum instantly saw the problem. "Your grace, with no heirs to the Nephite throne, what will you do? What will happen to the kingdom?"

"That is why I am speaking to you, Doctor Teancum. I could hand it to another, but what if my son, the legitimate heir, returns and demands the throne? You are a wise man and I have observed that you can see problems from a different perspective. I feel prompted by the Spirit of God to seek your counsel and advice on this issue."

Teancum wasn't sure what to think. He was growing more familiar with the church and its teachings. The birth of Kalia and Hanni's persistence saw to that. But he knew he had much to learn about the mysteries of God.

"You have been spending much time in the records vault. Have you any understanding from the writings of the past on how we might proceed with governing the Nephites without a worthy king?"

Teancum's mind leaped into action. He stood for a moment and pondered the problem and searched the corners of his mind for an answer.

"My king, without a rightful heir, there will be civil war for control of the crown. The rich will support one as king and the commoners will support another. Many people might suffer and die if the path of succession is not made clear."

King Mosiah nodded his head in agreement. "If our own history has taught us anything, it is that one evil king can bring an entire nation into bondage."

"Yes, my king. We must be careful to remember the people and the cause of individual freedom. You have been the champion of the people in this way." Teancum looked at his loving monarch with respect. King Mosiah's greatest legacy was being a true friend to the people. Teancum lowered his eyes, paced about, and continued to search his thoughts for an answer. He pondered the political writings of previous rulers, laws and strategies to maintain the monarchy. As he struggled. a thought came to him suddenly, an image of a page he had seen as a boy, from the scriptures his grandmother often read. Where did this thought come from, he wondered, it was so far afield from where his thoughts had been. He felt a warmth come over him, enveloping his body. This is the answer, a quiet voice whispered. Teancum opened his eyes and exhaled, wondering what had come over him. He shook his head and turned back to the king who stood looking at him with a slight smile on his face. Teancum couldn't help feeling the king knew this would happen. Teancum told Mosiah he remembered reading about the Israelite prophet Moses, and how he had heeded the advice given him by his father-in-law, Jethro. Jethro had helped Moses manage a very large and difficult group of people by suggesting that he needed to find righteous men who would help him govern the Israelites by using God's natural law as a guide, rather than trying to rule all by himself. The king patted Teancum on the back.

"I feel you have been inspired with the correct answer." He said. "Because it is the same answer the Spirit gave to me." They walked back to the gate in silence. "God has a plan for you, my son." The King said, suddenly as they parted. "You must trust His word. Go now, ponder and pray over how we should proceed. Return tomorrow and lunch with me. Then we will work together and chart a new course for this people." The king finished speaking then turned and walked back towards the palace. Teancum stood at the gate for a while trying to make sense of it all before turning himself back towards home. After a restless sleep and much time spent in thought, Teancum returned to help the king draft a proclamation to all the people of Nephi, to convince them to support their king in this bold experiment. King Mosiah would abolish the ancient practice of a king and ruling class. For the first time in all of Nephite history, the people would govern themselves.

"To truly understand the mind and will of God," King Mosiah would later instruct his people from his high tower, "one must know that all men are free and equal in the eyes of the law and in heaven. Men must be free to exercise their own agency. It is only in the true freedom of mind and body that man can comprehend the great plan of happiness set by our Father in Heaven. Men must be free to exercise their own agency. Therefore, I decree, from this day forth, all men are created equal. I decree that the reign of the kings is over. It ends with me. Until the great Jehovah himself shall personally rule as the Lord of Lords, this land shall be a land of liberty and justice and shall never be again subject to a monarch, so long as the people love and fear God. You will choose, by the voice of this people judges, or elected officials, who will govern by the consent of the people. By the laws of nature and the universe, not by the whims of one man. It is by the consent and will of the people, as well as the blessings of divine providence, this great nation will rise to the heights of prosperity promised to Father Nephi. "'If ye will obey my commandments, ye shall prosper in the land'". The wise king quoted from the writings of Father Nephi. "The majority of the people will, generally, choose what is good; but when the majority choose to abandon God's laws, then will you be visited with great destruction, as this people has seen before."

When the king was finished speaking, the community leaders realized much needed to be done to create a functioning government from nothing. Naturally, it was Teancum who was chosen by the voice of the people to be one of the first judges of this new and revolutionary form of self-governance. So now, with the added duties of helping to establish this new government, and being one of the most sought-after physicians in the city, Teancum was spending more time away from home than ever before.

With Teancum's constant work load, Hanni began to feel she needed a more stable environment in which to raise her family, rather than living around rough and rowdy soldiers. Before long, little Kaila welcomed a little sister into her world, and two years later a third sister came. With the arrival of a third child, they had outgrown the small cottage they were living in at the army barracks in the city. Hanni made the decision to move the family back to the ranch. She did not really ask Teancum his opinion on the matter. In her mind, this was what needed to happen, and she was going to make it so.

"We can keep the cottage so you will have a place to sleep when you are in the city working, but our home is going to be out there," Hanni pointed to the distant walls of the city and beyond. "You can travel… it's really not that far, any way." She was not raising her voice or making demands of Teancum. This simply was how it was going to be. "Your children are going to be raised in the same loving, nurturing environment that you experienced, not on an army post like my childhood." She put her hands on her hips and looked Teancum in the eyes. He had seen that look before and knew he was not going to change her mind. Teancum could think of a hundred reasons why they should stay in the city, but none of that mattered to Hanni, and he knew it. She had put up with too much already to be denied the great wish of her heart.

"I will bring home some shipping crates from the hospital tomorrow, so we can start packing," he smiled and surrendered his position to the gentle, but overwhelming force that was Hanni. In the end, it was really her happiness and the welfare of his children that mattered most.

Hanni knew Teancum loved her more than anything, but at that moment, she felt like the queen he had always called her. After her first visit to the ranch all those years ago, she yearned to live there and now her dream would be fulfilled. She squealed with delight, wrapped both her arms around Teancum's neck, hugged him tightly and kissed him on the lips.

"Just one thing?" Teancum asked, as he grunted under the enjoyable onslaught of emotions from Hanni. "You get to tell your mother we are moving, not me." There was a quick nervous laugh between them.

"Deal!" Hanni smiled back. She kissed her loving man again and left quickly to inform her parents and the children of the big change in their life.

CHAPTER TEN

THE RAID

The packing went as well as could be expected. Hanni was in charge of preparing the house and children for the move. She ran the operation like the daughter of a military leader— everything was happening on her schedule. Every item was accounted for, every crate was correctly labeled, and every piece of furniture was in position while waiting for the wagons to arrive. She even had her father detail a squad of army recruits to assist with loading the household items and lift the heavy things into the large cargo areas of the moving wagons. Teancum had cleared his calendar. He had two whole weeks off with nothing else to do but cater to Hanni's every whim. The day finally came when the wagons were all loaded and the kids were saying their goodbyes to their grandparents. It was Hanni's mother who was the strong one. Her father, on the other hand, was blubbering on like a child. He had known this day would come. He had dreaded it from the moment he and his wife had gotten the news that his only child and all his grandchildren would be moving away. He loved his little grandbabies very much and did not want to see them go.

"It's not forever, Papa," Kaila whispered in his ear as she hugged him tightly around the neck. The little girls had a special relationship with their grandfather. They were all trying their best to calm him down and reassure him they all still loved him and would visit soon. Hanni and her mother shared a moment as they watched the big, strong commander of the Zarahemla legion wipe tears from his eyes as he lifted each of the little girls into the passenger wagon. One last embrace with Hanni and

Teancum and they were off. There were several wagons loaded down with boxes of household goods that fell in behind the family wagon as they moved toward the main gate. Because of Teancum's unique status in the community as one of the new leaders, a cavalry squad was detailed to escort them safely to their destination. The sergeant of the squad was leading the way on his own horse and the rest of the horsemen dispersed themselves in pairs among the wagons.

The old commander and his wife stood on the porch of their home, watching the wagon train exit the military compound disappear around a street corner and out of sight. "Well…That's that," she spoke to her husband, who was still sniffing up the tears. Sensing the pain her husband was feeling, she wrapped her arm around his big bicep, then whispered into his ear, "Why don't you go and lie down for a while, you seem tired." She gently pulled on his arm to urge him to move back into the house. "I will get dinner going and make some of that sweet bread you like so much for dessert. I think you have earned it after today." Without even so much as a whimper in protest, he allowed her to walk him into the big sleeping room where she sat him down on the bed and helped to remove his heavy boots. He rolled over and was asleep before she could walk out the door and close it behind her. "Men!" she whispered to herself then shook her head and smiled. In that moment, she allowed one tear to fall. She loved her family too, very much, but someone had to be strong. She smiled again as she wiped it away from her cheek. *What would you do without me*, she thought as she walked away from her eternal love and started to prepare their dinner.

Creating a new government was much more time consuming than anyone one could have possibly imagined. Dealing with the diverse personalities of the other men and women chosen to be the judges was overwhelming, not to mention creating new laws, administering the proper functions of government, and finding an acceptable balance between religion and politics. Teancum's medical practice was really starting to suffer because he was devoting so much of his time to being a representative to the people in the great Council of Judges. He would not accept any new patients, and those he was seeing and treating suffered from his lack of time or ability to properly help them get well. A choice had to be made. Teancum chose to close down his medical practice and fully devote his time to the creation of this new government. He had trained his staff and replacements well, so the medicine he developed would still be available, but he was not going to be a doctor anymore. When the people heard Teancum had chosen to be a full-time judge, they celebrated his decision, and it made him even more popular with the masses. The constant praise and attention he was getting from the people of Zarahemla had bugun to affect him. He was soon forgetting important family dates, such as birthdays and anniversaries. He would be gone for days at a time from the ranch, and his young family was suffering from his absence. They were not suffering for any physical want; Lord Pilio made sure they had everything they could possibly need. No, the girls missed their daddy and Hanni missed her husband.

The seasons changed and one full year had passed from the time Teancum moved his family back to the ranch. As his status in the community continued to climb, his thoughts were drifting away from his family and toward the praise of men.

During the harvest season, the judges and the staff who served the people took several days off to attend to their personal crops. Teancum was not very happy about a cessation of government services for so long, but he understood that most people still needed to farm their own land to make ends meet. Hanni had sent him a letter, asking that he return to the ranch to spend the time he had with her and the children. Reluctantly, he agreed, but put off traveling home for three days while he attended important dinners and a festive ball celebrating the holiday season. Finally, it was time to leave and on that morning Teancum was dressed in a very expensive outfit with soft leather moccasins and a light colored cloak. It was the perfect attire for someone who spends most of his time indoors attending meetings or banquets.

"Remember sir," a slightly built male attendant said, as they quickly walked toward the main doors of the Judges' Hall. "You will need to be back before the Sabbath if you are going to attend the hearing on the irrigation matter."

"Back before the Sabbath…got it," Teancum spoke as they walked and stood at the bottom of the stone stairs waiting for his ride. "I feel as if I am forgetting something," he spoke to the attendant, as Teancum looked through his personal items. The full light of dawn was still several minutes away making it hard for him to see clearly.

"Sir?" The attendant spoke while holding out a cute little rag doll for Teancum to see. "It's Kaila's birthday tomorrow, that's why you are going back to the ranch sooner than planned."

As usual, Teancum had been too engrossed in political matters and paperwork to really pay any attention to those around him. Forgetting his child's birthday stung his conscience a bit and deep deep down he questioned what had happened to his mind. Shuffling the papers in his hands, he took the doll and winked at the attendant.

"Thank you," he sounded relieved. "Forgetting to take home a present would have meant Lady Hanni would banish me from my own house and send me to sleep in the barn."

His personal buggy arrived to take him back to the ranch. It was a very well made, wooden covered wagon with padded seats and a dedicated driver. As Teancum stepped up into the fancy coach, his attendant waved to two young Nephite soldiers on horseback. The two cavalrymen rode up to the side of the buggy and one of them spoke to Teancum through the open window.

"Sir, my name is Gid, and this is Teomner," the closest soldier declared in a very professional tone. "Due to the problems with the bandits on the road, we have been assigned to escort you to your home and stay with you until you return."

Teancum was completely lost in the contents of a parchment on his lap and paid no real attention to what the soldier had said. "Fine, fine," he absently remarked as he waved out the window and adjusted his position in the cushioned seat.

The two soldiers both looked at each, then down at the attendant.

"Thank you gentlemen," the attendant quickly spoke. "We are all counting on you to keep Doctor Teancum safe on his journey. I'm sure you will do your duty to the utmost." He spoke in a very officious manner to the armed men and then waved to the driver to start the journey. "Pleasant trip, doctor." He waved, directing his well wishes toward the open window of the carriage. He knew Teancum probably did not hear him, and if he did, he probably did not care, but he gave the salutation anyway. It was his job to be professional and courteous.

The driver gave the reins a slap and the buggy was off. Even at this early hour it took them longer than planned to work their way through the crowded streets of Zarahemla due to the influx of citizens moving in from the countryside. They wanted to be inside the city walls and safe from the bandits roaming unchecked across the land. This made everything inside the city, from shopping to travel, almost impossible at times. Finally, they reached the main city gates and passed the guards on watch without incident. The rest of the trip was uneventful. Teancum sat in his buggy, alone, and the two Nephite cavalrymen followed a short distance behind.

They were getting close to the ranch property when the driver noticed and pointed to something off in the distance. Teancum was sitting in the back of his covered buggy and looking over some important scrolls when the assistant driver leaned over the side and looked into the window.

"Sir?" he said with a bit of concern in his voice. There was a pause as the driver waited for a response from Teancum. When none came, he tried to hail the doctor again. "Sir?" he said with a bit more force.

"Yes, what is it?" Teancum asked impatiently. He was too engrossed in the words of the document before him to look up.

"There is thick black smoke rising in the distance."

Teancum put the papers down and looked out the window in the direction of the smoke. He knew this land better than most. He had been raised here. He had hunted, fished, and explored all over the mountains and valleys. He knew every family within fifty miles of his ranch, where every building stood, and what was down every road, path and game trail. So, when he saw the billowing smoke, he instantly knew what was burning and where it was coming from.

"The ranch... My family!" Teancum shouted up at the driver. "Go, go!"

The small buggy lurched forward and Teancum was pushed back into his seat as the driver slapped down on the reins, urging the single horse to pull faster. The two Nephite cavalrymen, acting as his escorts, galloped behind on their own horses.

"No, no, no!" Teancum shouted in a panic, as he quickly rolled up the parchments and scrolls, stuffing them back into the large shoulder bag he had at his side. Looking out the window again, Teancum shouted, "Faster!" The driver slapped the horse again with the reins. This poor animal was not bred for long, hard runs. It was more of a trotting horse and it quickly started to tire out under the demands to keep going hard and fast.

Teancum noticed they were slowing down and he shouted out the window again, "Why are we slowing down?"

"I am sorry, sir, it's the horse. She is faltering!" the driver shouted back in frustration. He knew Teancum was in a panic and felt responsible for not getting him home quicker.

"Stop the carriage!" Teancum shouted, as he kicked open the door and stood on the single metal step waiting for the horse to stop. When the carriage had slowed down enough for him to jump off, Teancum leaped and landed on his feet running toward his escort's horse.

"You!" Teancum pointed at Teomner, sitting atop a large brown mount. "Get down!" The soldier looked at his partner who quickly nodded at him to dismount.

"Get off!" Gid told his fellow soldier to get of his horse and give it to Teancum. It did not take a genius to figure out Teancum was frantic about the smoke coming from the location of his ranch and he wanted to get there as fast as possible. Taking the horse was the only option. No one was going to argue with Doctor Teancum, the head army doctor and Chief Judge of the 6th district of Zarahemla.

Teancum leaped up into the saddle and shouted down to the soldier who just gave up his ride. "Follow in the buggy!" Looking at Gid, still sitting on his own horse, Teancum commanded, "With me!" Then he kicked the horse in the ribs. The horse, carrying Teancum, burst forward and the second soldier urged his mount to follow.

Teancum pushed the horse to gallop just as fast as it could. Blazing down the wide merchant trail toward the ranch, he kept looking out the corner of his eye at the smoke billowing from behind the trees in the distance. "Father…?" Teancum whispered a prayer out loud. "Be with my family, please let them be safe!"

He rounded the bend, still moving at breakneck speed, heading for the main archway and gate. He could see the main house now and it was fully ablaze. The large barn doors were open and black smoke was gushing from the inside. He could also see dead animals lying in the open area, but no one was moving around the property. No one was trying to put out the fires or save what animals remained alive.

The house and barn are both burning. This was not an accident! Teancum thought as he got closer to the house. Concerned for everyone's safety, he looked back and saw his lone armed escort was keeping up with him.

He reached the main house and the horse refused to get any closer or move around the flames. It reared up and tried to back away from the heat and noise. It was useless for him to stay on the animal, so Teancum jumped from the horse and it ran away. Moving toward the front of the house, Teancum shouted for Hanni and his children but no one responded. He ran up on the wrap around porch as the flames and choking smoke shot out the windows. Teancum tried to get closer to the windows and doors, to find a way inside and search for his family, but the flames and heat kept pushing him back. Panicked, he screamed out again for his grandparents, his mother, for Hanni and the children. Then he heard a woman's scream ring out. It came from the back of the house. Teancum frantically ran around the house towards the voice. When he got to the side of the house closest to the barn, he found several of the ranch hands lying dead in the blood stained dirt. There was blood everywhere and it looked like they had been attacked and slashed with sharp blades. Teancum stopped in the middle of the bodies and did a quick search for any of his family lying among the dead. Not seeing anyone, he stood back up and shouted for Hanni again. The soldier who was with Teancum came up to his side.

"They were attacked!" Teancum shouted. "Pull your sword and make ready!"

Gid yanked out his trusty weapon and turned in a circle, looking for the threat which had caused this horror.

"I'm going around to the back!" Teancum quickly explained. "You check these men for survivors, then meet me there!"

"Yes, sir!" the soldier barked back.

Teancum took off again and ran around to the back of the large house. As he reached the back corner of the house, he went past a large wood pile set up for the cooking ovens and fire pit. He saw a small hand axe lodged in one of the chopping blocks and pulled it out to use as a weapon. Most of the fire was still contained in the front of the building, so Teancum had a clear unobstructed view of the back porch and yard when he turned the corner. Teancum's blood ran cold and his knees buckled. A hooded man stood over Hanni, with a bunch of her hair in one of his hands and a large sword in the other. She was on her knees, crying and grasping at the hand holding her hair. Their littlest child, Carra, was screaming and holding onto Hanni's waist as she too was being pulled by her hair. The hooded man was laughing and looking at something near the back door of the house. There was movement and shouting to his left side, and it caught Teancum's attention. Turning, he saw Pilio standing over Saria's body. She was lying at the bottom of the steps that led up to the back doors. It looked like she had been pushed down the stairs and had died at the bottom where she landed.

Pilio was swinging his great sword and madly cursing at two other hooded men. Those men were dancing around him, taunting him and dodging Pilio's sharp blade. The aged Pilio was frustrated and unable to put up a stout defense. The criminals hacked at Pilio's body and swatted him with the flat side of their blades in a cruel and contemptuous taunting. Pilio had blood stains on his loose-fitting shirt, and blood was flowing freely from a large wound on his head. He was hurt badly and kept losing his balance as he tried to fight off the younger men. Pilio mustered a wild swing with his sword and almost took the head off one off the bandits. The bandit's hood came off as he blocked Pilio's sword with his own, and Teancum could see the man had long hair and was missing a front tooth.

A flush of helplessness came crashing over Teancum. Who should he help? Pilio was slowly being torn apart by those two thugs and his grandmother lay dead at his feet, while his wife and smallest child were being dragged off by a third criminal. Teancum froze in complete fear and desperation, aggravating his broken emotions as he watched this human tragedy play out before him.

"Finish it!" the man holding Hanni called out. He jerked up hard on her hair and told her to be quiet.

Teancum looked back at Pilio and shouted, "Nooooo!" He watched helplessly as the long haired man Pilio was fighting ran his own blade into Pilio's chest and pushed it all the way through him until the point protruded from Pilio's back. Pilio dropped to the ground onto his elbows and knees and tried to crawl to Saria's body. The other thug walked up to Pilio, and, with a look of contempt on his face, kicked Pilio in the side and knocked him over. When Teancum shouted out, everyone turned to see him standing there with the small axe in his hand.

"Teancum!" Hanni screamed. Carra broke free and tried to run to her daddy.

Teancum raised up the hand axe and started to rush toward Hanni and little Carra. The bandit who had stabbed Pilio pulled his sword from Pilio's chest and ran to intercept the running child, as the second armed bandit moved toward Teancum. The second bandit got between Teancum and Carra, pointed his sword, forcing Teancum to stop moving forward. The first bandit scooped up the screaming child and tucked her under his arm.

"Whoa, big boy. Where do you think you are going with that axe?" the bandit closest to Teancum challenged.

"Let them go!" Teancum shouted as he almost burst into tears.

The three criminals all saw Teancum start to lose control of his emotions and laughed at him.

"Oh, you're not going to cry, are you?" The one holding Hanni spat. They all laughed again. Teancum was so overwhelmed with hate and desperation that he started to shake and stuttered as he tried to speak. "Le...let them g...g...go!"

The bandit with Carra in his arms walked over to Hanni and dropped her into Hanni's arms. "Keep control of her, or I will!" he shouted as he turned back to face Teancum.

"Teancum!" Hanni shouted, as she held onto Carra. "The girls, they are still inside!" The bandit holding Hanni tried to get her to stop talking. She struggled against his grip, scratching his face with her fingernail. In a fit of rage, he struck her on the side of her head with his knee, knocking her unconscious.

Teancum saw Hanni go down hard, and took two steps forward, ready to fight the evil men to the death. As he moved, the faint sounds of his other two girls crying out for help could be heard coming from inside the burning house. He stopped, cocked his head sideways, trying to hear better. Over the blaze of fire, he heard them call out again. This time yelling for their daddy to save them.

"What will it be, hero— us or your kids? Can't deal with both at the same time," the boss bandit taunted Teancum, as he let go of Hanni and her lifeless body fell to the ground.

Teancum readjusted his grip on the ax and shifted his weight. He had only seconds to act. Save his children or his wife? It was the realization of the worst nightmare a man could ever endure. Torn between the two things he loved more than life itself. He must sacrifice one to save the other. "God in heaven, help me!" he shouted out, pleading for guidance, help or absolution. Suddenly his thoughts went blank and his emotions went cold. "The girls... They are still inside." The image of Hanni mouthing those words played slow motion in his mind.

"Hanni made the choice for me." Teancum realized. He knew the two girls in the house would certainly die if he didn't save them. Hanni and Carra were still alive, and there was a chance for them to escape or be rescued. "There is no way she would ever forgive me for leaving her children to burn to death in order to save her. She is a true mother. She would be willing to suffer and die for her own children." He knew what he needed to do but he was not going to let this monster standing over his wife's unconscious body get away with what he was doing. Teancum was not very good at throwing the axe but he was going to try. He threw it as hard as he could at the man who knocked Hanni down, then jumped for the porch railing and climbed up to get to the back door. The criminal Teancum had been aiming at was not able to move out of the way fast enough, and the axe hit him squarely in the ribs but with the flat side of the blade. The man grimaced and grabbed his side in pain. The other two bandits started to follow Teancum up the stairs but the injured bandit called out to them, telling them to stop.

"No!" he shouted while holding his side. "Get the swag and bring the child!" He pointed to little Carra. "Idiots! People can see that smoke for miles; let's go before help arrives!" He did not know which one of his men started the fire, and he did not want to stick around to find out.

The two men looked disappointed, but moved at the orders from the bandit chieftain. They jumped down from the porch and picked up the heavy bags of stolen loot from the ranch. Another younger bandit appeared from behind one of the out buildings with several horses in tow. He was proud of his find and wanted to show the leader what he had stolen.

"Leave the horses!" The commander shouted in frustration. "This whole operation is getting out of control," he whispered to himself, as he looked at his inexperienced and bumbling followers. He spent three days hiding in the trees and watching this ranch with his recruits. He wanted them to learn the patterns and habits of the people from the ranch who worked the fields and tended to the flocks so they would know the best time to attack. "This is the Nehor way." He whispered to them as they observed several men and women leave the ranch and move to the many fields and pastures. "See how they leave in the early morning to work." He pointed for his newest Nehor hopefuls to see. "We wait until the majority of the men are away in the fields and then we make our move." He knew he would catch this rich family completely unprepared and still in their sleeping clothes, but now the deed was done and he was wasting time with foolish things.

"Amateurs!" he mumbled as he shook his head and winced in pain from the damage to his ribs. *They have so much to learn about the ways of the Nehor. It will be too easy to track us if we are riding them*, he thought. the leader bandit called out. "Come on! Get the child!" The fourth bandit let go of the ropes around the horses then walked over to Carra. She was still clinging to Hanni's body.

"Noooo!" she screamed as he pried her arms off Hanni and flung her over his shoulder. "Daddy! Help me!" She called out over and over again as the bandits headed for the edge of the thick forest.

When Teancum burst through the back door of the large house, he saw the flames were devouring the walls and ceiling of the front part of the house and moving rapidly toward the back. "Where are you?" he called out to his two girls as he moved around the kitchen and dining area looking for them. The smoke was making it impossible for him to see or breathe. He could not even imagine what his two older girls were going through.

"Daddy!"

Teancum heard them calling for him from their rooms upstairs. Covering his mouth and nose with the collar of his shirt, he quickly moved toward the main stairs leading up to the second floor. The well-built wooden staircase was still intact, but not for long. The fire was spreading more quickly than Teancum had estimated, and it was only going to be seconds before the stairs started to burn. Teancum tried to move up to stairs but the flames were flickering at him from the burning walls as he tried to climb. The heat, smoke and flames drove him back down to the main floor but he was desperate to reach the top and save his children. Looking around the large open room, Teancum grabbed a blanket from a chair and ran to the kitchen. There he found a big cooking pot full of water. Coughing from the smoke, he quickly doused the blanket with the water and wrapped it around his body and face. He then grabbed the pot and poured the remaining water over his head. Now wrapped in the wet covering, Teancum moved back to the staircase and saw the stairs were still intact, but he needed to move immediately. The smoke was thick and black and it choked him as he breathed. The wet blanket was helping to keep the flame and heat at bay, but Teancum knew he had only seconds before it would be too late. Braving the danger, he moved up the stairs and into the hallway leading to the children's rooms.

"Kaila! Ayla! Where are you?" he shouted, as he moved down the smoke filled hallway. He took a few steps and tripped over something lying across the hallway. Losing his balance, Teancum fell to the floor and was face-to-face with his mother, Rachael. Her lifeless eyes were gaping wide open and her body was lying as if she had been trying to crawl to the children, still trapped in their rooms. "Mother!" he choked. He reached for her face, but the cries of help from his children rang out again. Crying out in agony, he left Rachael's body and moved toward the sounds of his children. He reached the first room and found it empty. He quickly checked under the bed and in the small closet—nothing. Coming back out into the hall he called out again for his girls, but there was no response.

In the enclosed structure, hot air, flames and smoke were rising up, forcing the cooler oxygen-filled air down and away from the source of the fire. Teancum dropped to his knees and tried to move quickly down the hallway, but it was completely choked with thick, black smoke and flames coming from the corners and doorways. He was still wrapped in the wet blanket and holding a section of it against his mouth and nose to try to filter the smoke and keep breathing as he searched for his missing children. Reaching the main bedroom, where he and Hanni slept, Teancum entered and started to look around. As he was moving in almost pitch blackness, he bumped into an object on the floor that he knew should not be there. Reaching down he felt the long hair of one of his daughters.

"Daddy is here!" he shouted, as he grabbed for the child. He moved her closer to him and could tell it was Ayla. She was unconscious. Her hands and feet were bound. Teancum felt a pulse but it seemed she was not breathing. He knew she had only moments for him to start her lungs working again before it would be too late, but this smoke-filled environment was poisonous and she needed fresh clean air. "I got you... Where is Kaila? Kaila!" he shouted out. He realized the closer to the floor he stood, the less smoke there was so Teancum moved onto his belly and kept looking for Kaila. As he was searching, he felt Kaila's ankle and grabbed it. Pulling her seemingly lifeless body to him, he found she was in the same desperate shape as Ayla, not breathing and bound at the hands and feet. "Daddy has you both...I'm getting you out of here!"

Teancum took the wet blanket from his shoulders and wrapped it around his children the best he could. Scooping both of the girl's up in his arms, he tried to stand up. Grunting under the weight, he got to his feet and moved toward the door, holding his breath as he moved. Teancum knew he had to move quickly if he was going to save his two

older children and then help Hanni and Carra. He remembered there was one trained soldier outside in the front yard and one more should be arriving shortly. He was hoping with all the commotion in the back yard that those two armed escorts were already dealing with the bandits. If he could just make it to the stairs and out the back door before he ran out of air in his lungs or the fire blocked his escape route.

He was moving down the hall and could see the body of his mother where he had left it, near the opening where the stair landing was located, leading down to the main floor of the house. What he could not see was that the area underneath the wooden stairs and landing was fully engulfed in fire, and the structural integrity had been compromised. With his lungs burning for fresh air, Teancum ensured his children's faces were covered so they did not see the dead body of their grandmother. He stepped from the smoke-filled hallway and put all his weight, combined with that of his two daughters, on the landing. He felt a wash of relief as he was able to gulp some air and turned to move down the stairs when, a loud popping sound came from underneath his feet. The entire wooden staircase and landing shook and Teancum stopped moving and looked down.

"No!" he shouted, as what was about to happen became perfectly clear to him. What happened in the next few seconds would always remain a blur for Teancum. The human mind has a unique ability to block out extremely traumatic events from memory, thus allowing most of us to heal and function without reliving the crisis over and over in our minds. Some poor souls are burdened with a full recollection of tragedy and suffer for it, sometimes for years or even longer. Those who are exposed to prolonged distress, like soldiers involved in sustained close combat, law enforcers, or people who suffer from years of abuse, are most susceptible to remembering and reliving the trauma. But for Teancum, this next moment would remain forever shrouded from his thoughts.

Teancum knew the stairs were giving way under his weight. He could feel it as he tried to run down as many steps as he could before everything collapsed. But it was too late, the entire structure gave way. He, with his two daughters in his arms, came crashing down to the floor below and landed among the piles of wood and twisted metal. When they landed, Teancum was knocked unconscious, and the girls fell from his arms.

The next thing Teancum remembers was being dragged out the back door of the still burning house by his arms. He looked up and saw Gid, the young soldier who rode with him to the ranch, pulling him to safety. The second soldier, who Teancum had left in the buggy, was following close behind and he had the two girls, one over his shoulder and the other under his arm.

"Bring them over here by the woman!" someone shouted, and the two soldiers obeyed. Teancum was slowly coming back to consciousness and he tried to speak. Coughing and hacking up smoke, he rolled over and tried to stand, but he was light headed and dizzy.

"What happened?" Teancum gasped.

"You went in to save your kids and the stairs collapsed. You were trapped and we went in after you," Gid spoke, as he tried to keep Teancum from collapsing.

"My children!" Teancum spouted. "My wife…Where is my family!" He spun around, dazed and confused, trying to make sense of what was happening. His face and clothing were covered in soot and bleeding scratches marked his exposed arms and legs.

"Doctor Teancum," the soldier who was helping him out of the house pleaded with him, "please sir, sit down, you are injured."

Teancum saw the body of his wife lying face up a few feet from where he was standing. The old wagon driver had put his jacket under her head and he was holding her hand. Crying out for Hanni, Teancum shook free from the soldier's grasp and moved over to be by her side. With panic in his eyes, he looked into his wife's eyes. She was awake, but just on the edge of alertness. The driver laid her hand on her stomach and got up to give them some space. The second soldier, Teomner, set the bodies of the two girls still wrapped in the blanket down a few feet from Hanni.

"My queen…" he gasped. She loved that term of endearment and almost smiled when she heard it. He gently spoke as he brushed the hair from her face. He was trying to be brave but he was a doctor who worked with combat injuries. He saw right away that she was gravely hurt. The blow to her head from the bandit's knee had done fatal damage. As he looked at her face. He could tell her pupils were different sizes, the whites of her eyes were turning dark red and there was a clear fluid with a tinge of blood flowing from her ears and nose.

"The girls…safe?" she mouthed at a whisper that was barely audible. Her body was shaking.

Without even looking up to check on his children, Teancum nodded his head to say yes. "They are out of the fire." He tried to smile, but the despair was painted across his face.

"I can't feel my arms or legs," she whispered, without emotion. "Am I dying?" She looked for the answer in Teancum's eyes and instantly knew. He could not hide the painful truth from her. Teancum gently took her hand and felt the cold lifelessness in her touch. With more tears streaming, he brought her hand up to his mouth and kissed it.

"We will get you fixed up and good as new." He tried to mask his pain but he knew it was just a matter of time now. She was going to die. The old sorrow Teancum held deep in his heart began to surface. He closed his eyes and started to cry, great drops of salty tears.

"The baby?" Hanni questioned. "Is she safe?" Teancum did not hear her and continued to cry to himself. "The baby!" She gasped, with all her remaining strength "Where is my baby!?"

Teancum sniffed and looked up. "Carra!" he called out as he scanned the area for his youngest child. The fire behind him was roaring and the columns of smoke were blotting out the sun like a dark, swollen storm cloud. He looked over to where his other two girls were lying on the ground and saw their lifeless expressions with their hands and feet still bound. Their lips and nostrils were blackened from the toxic smoke they'd inhaled. The soldier who had carried them out of the fire had just finished checking for signs of life. Finding none, he sorrowfully covered both of their bodies with the blanket.

No! What is happening? Teancum cried in his mind. His frame started to tremble uncontrollably. He looked back down at his poor wife. "Hanni, I—" But he could not finish. His mind was collapsing under the weight of it all.

"My love." Hanni gently called out to Teancum. He continued to cry as he looked back down at Hanni. "Please don't cry." She was so weak now, her words were fading like a long forgotten dream. "Courage…" she gasped. There was a smile and then she was gone. A single tear rolled down her face as her eyes locked in the vacant, haunting stare of the dead.

Teancum froze in place. His mouth was open and air was coming out but there was no sound. "Hanni?" He called out after a moment. He was still holding her hand and he shook her arm. "Hanni?" There was a more desperate tone to his voice now. "Wake up baby. Please wake up!" He slapped the back of her hand and shook her arms a little harder. It was a coping mechanism. He knew she was gone, just like he knew his mother and two older daughters were gone. Pilio and Saria were also dead. His logical, educated, medical mind had been forced aside by the shock of the horrible events. His primal dark side was in command and he was fueled by pure emotions now. "Wake up!" He shouted, as he grabbed her lifeless body by her shoulders and shook her up and down, as if he could wake the dead. He lifted her into his arms and cried out, "No…Wake up Hanni!"

The other men who were standing nearby did not know what to do. They stood as silent witnesses to this unbelievably tragic moment in time. The two soldiers locked eyes and moved away from Teancum so they could speak without disturbing his mourning.

"You were here before me. Did you see anything?" Teomner asked.

"I saw a group of men running toward the tree line when I rounded the corner. That's when I checked on the lady and she told me where to look for Doctor Teancum." He pointed toward the distant forest to show his partner the direction the bandits were traveling.

"We should do a sweep of the area and ensure there are no more criminals or victims," the first soldier recommended.

Their conversation was interrupted by the sounds of a galloping horse pulling a wagon, coming around the house, stopping just short of where they were standing. Not knowing what to expect, both soldiers quickly pulled out their swords and readied themselves for a fight.

"What is the meaning of this? What has happened here?" It was Tum and two of the ranch hands who had just returned from the fields. They saw the dark smoke on their return and came as fast as they could. Defying his age, Tum came down from the wagon at a dead run and went right past the two soldiers like they did not even exist. "Master Teancum!" he cried out as he ran. The two soldiers watched him go by and then looked back at the wagon as the other two ranch hands dismounted and started to move toward Teancum.

"Stop!" One of the soldiers called out as he held up his hand. "Who are you all?"

"That is Tum, the head butler for the family and steward of this ranch," one of the hands responded as he pointed to Tum. "And we work here for him," he continued, as he ran off toward the ranch hands housing to search for his family. The second ranch hand was overcome with emotion as he surveyed the burning home. As he moved around to the back of the home, he spotted Lord Pilio and Lady Saria at the bottom of the porch stairs.

"Gracious mercy!" he wailed. "Lord Pilio! Lady Saria!" He moved in close but stopped quickly when he realized they were both deceased. The fire was still raging, and it would be only a matter of time before it reached the porch and burned the bodies. Out of respect for his loving master and landlords, the ranch hand quickly grabbed Saria's body and pulled her clear of the flames. Running back, he grabbed Pilio's body and dragged it over by Saria as burning embers started to rain down.

Tum was at Teancum's side and fell to his knees, when he saw Hanni and the girls lying dead on the ground. Crying out, he asked Teancum what happened. Teancum did not respond. He just held on to Hanni's lifeless body and sobbed great uncontrollable tears of anguish. Tum got up and moved over to where the two older girls were lying under the blanket. He was hesitant to pull back on the cover. Deep down, he did not want to know which two of Teancum's children were under there. Based on the size of the bodies, he had an idea but he needed to be sure.

"Kaila and Ayla," he whispered in utter shock. He saw their bound hands and feet and the soot on their faces. He looked back at the burning shell of the house and then at Teancum. He saw Teancum's clothing was torn and burnt and his body was covered in cuts and scratches. "He went in after you two, didn't he?" he whispered, looking down at the little ones.

"Tum!" The second ranch hand, standing by the porch stairs called out. Tum looked up and saw him waving for him to come over.

"Godspeed, my darlings." Tum said a quick prayer for the souls of the dearly departed and covered them back up. He walked over to Teancum and put his hand on his shoulder. Without speaking, he wanted Teancum to know he was there and standing ready to support him. Teancum continued to weep and moan, enveloped in his misery and rocking back and forth holding Hanni's body.

As Tum slowing walked toward where the ranch hand was standing, he realized he was looking at the dead bodies of his two oldest and dearest friends. He stopped just short of the bodies and stood looking down at them. Tum looked up at the burning house and the barn. He saw the other bodies of the murdered ranch hands and their families by the side of the house, the dead animals and the discarded personal property left by whoever had done this terrible thing. What does a man do or say when he discovers his entire world has been torn apart? Tum was in a state of shock and could not summon a response. He simply turned around and looked at Teancum. Then it dawned on him— where was Lady Rachael? Where was the baby? Tum did a quick visual check to see if she was about, but he did not see her. "Did you see little Carra?" he asked the ranch hand standing next to him.

"No, sir," he quickly responded.

"I will check with Teancum. You search the grounds," Tum quickly ordered. The assistant sprinted off, running for the outbuildings unaffected by the fires.

Tum looked down at the murdered bodies of his lord and lady. "There will be time to mourn later. I must find Rachael and the little one. I know you will understand." He quickly bowed one last time, out of respect for the great man and woman they were, then moved toward Teancum. When he reached Teancum, Tum found he was not crying anymore. Teancum was sitting on the ground, rocking Hanni's body in his arms as if he were holding a small child and trying to get her to sleep.

"My lord Teancum." This was the first time Tum, or anyone, had ever addressed Teancum this way. Even in this most sorrowful moment, Tum felt it was appropriate to acknowledge that with the passing of Pilio, Teancum was now the lord and master of this ranch. "There will be time for the dead, sir. We must tend to the living." He moved around to face Teancum and held out his hands. "My lord, please let me take her. We need to find Carra, she is missing. And what of Lady Rachael?" Although Tum was in the employment of Teancum's grandparents, and his job was to be of service to them and the family, as he was growing up, Teancum always looked to Tum as an authority figure. When Teancum heard the gentle but firm demand from Tum, he slowly released his grasp on Hanni's body allowing Tum to take her from his arms. Tum gently laid Hanni back on the ground face up. He then removed his outer coat and placed it over her face and upper body.

"Teancum," Tum questioned with a bit of boldness, "do you know where Carra is?"

"Carra," Teancum responded. "She is missing?"

"Yes, my lord . Do you know where she is…and Rachael? Where is your mother?"

"Carra!" Teancum wailed as he stood up in a panic. Looking around, he searched for his only remaining child. "Carra!" He called out again at the top of his lungs.

"Did you see her when you arrived?" Tum asked, as he tried to calm Teancum.

Teancum tried to relive the events of the past hour in his mind. As he remembered, the images flashed by in broken and chaotic scenes of fire, death, and pain. Then he focused on the last thing he remembered seeing before he ran into the burning house. It was Carra, holding onto Hanni's body, and crying out for her daddy. Then, the dead eyes of his mother flashed like the fiery flames he saw burning around her body.

"She…" Teancum spun around and looked at Hanni. "She was with Hanni." He looked up at Tum in horror. "I had to choose…" He choked and wept. "They were going to burn to death!" He looked back at the burning wreck that once was his home. "Mother…" he moaned and started toward the burning heap. "She was right here!" He turned back, remembering his child now. "Carra!" he cried out.

"Sir," Gid interrupted, addressing Tum. "There was a woman's body in the house. She was dead and we could not go back in to recover her from the fire." Gid gestured toward the burning house. He paused and then finished speaking. "The men who did this fled toward the trees, over there." He pointed so Tum could see where they went. "They were carrying several bags with them. I can't be sure, but one of them might have been carrying a child."

The blood drained from Tum's face as he heard these words. "Could you be certain?"

"What!?" Teancum spouted as he charged at the soldier.

"No, sir, I cannot be sure." The Nephite soldier backed up two steps. He knew Teancum was not in control of his emotions. This was not personal to him, but it was for Teancum. "I am sorry, but I had all this to deal with or I would have followed." He held out his hands to show Tum and Teancum all the carnage and destruction that greeted him.

"Not your fault," Tum patted the young soldier's shoulder. "You were right to stay and help here."

Teancum spun around and looked at the far tree line. "There?" he pointed as he asked Teomner.

"Yes, Doctor Teancum— where the two big trees are. to the left is where they entered the forest."

Teancum looked at Tum. "The trail that leads up to the ridge line," he spoke clearly. Having lived on the ranch for most of their lives,

Teancum and Tum both knew it well. They were also both thinking the same thoughts.

Tum nodded his head in agreement. "If they follow that path, they can reach the ridgeline above. From there, they can go anywhere and she will be lost forever."

The change on Teancum's face was instant and complete. He spun on his heels and moved over to where his grandparent's bodies lay. Stopping for a second, to look at them, he took a deep breath and moved to the porch landing. On the ground was Pilio's old sword, right where he dropped it when he was murdered. He picked up the weapon and walked back to Pilio's body. Holding it out in front of him, Teancum spoke, "I swear to you, Grandfather, with your sword, I will avenge you all."

He moved back towards Hanni's body where Tum was still standing.

"Give me your knife," he ordered. Tum pulled his knife and sheath from his waist and handed it Teancum. "I am going after her," Teancum spoke, as he tucked the small blade into his belt.

"But, sir—"Tum started to speak. Teancum held out his hand to stop him from finishing. Looking down at his wife and two daughters, Teancum bowed his head and closed his eyes, trying not to lose control. He continued to speak with his eyes closed, "You will see to them. Give them all a proper burial." He opened his eyes and looked at his old mentor.

"Of course, Lord Teancum."

"*Lord* Teancum?" Teancum snarled. His tone grew angry. "Lord of what?! A butchered family, a burnt-down house, stolen property, dead animals...." He paused and took a deep breath, his hands were shaking. "Don't ever call me that again." His voice turned hard and dark.

"The lord of this land lies over there next to his murdered wife." Turning, he looked old Tum in the eyes. "I let those dogs kill all of them and take my baby." Tum could feel the hate and anger radiating from Teancum. "Tum, you are in charge. Salvage what you can. Sell what you need to. See to the needs of the families of the slain ranch hands and give my family the honor of a proper burial." He took another big breath and tried to speak but no words would come out. There was nothing else to say. Teancum, alone, still dressed in his soot-covered fancy clothing and soft shoes, without food or extra water, and no way of knowing exactly where the bandits were heading, took off at a run toward their last known location with his grandfather's sword in hand. Tum, with the wisdom of his many years on this earth, let him go without saying a word in protest.

Teancum was almost to the trees when the two soldiers realized he was missing. They approached Tum and inquired as to his whereabouts when they saw him running into the forest.

"Let him go, lads," Tum spoke, as the two young warriors motioned to chase after him.

"Sir, he needs to come back. It's not safe in the woods," Gid spoke.

They both turned to look at Tum He did not answer them at first. The men watched him, wating for a response. Tum simply stared off at the receding figure of Teancum as he dissapeared into the trees. After he was out of sight, he finally spoke, his voice filled with sadness. "He is not coming back."

"But he is our responsibility!" Teomner barked in a retort.

"Teancum, the man you knew, died today with his family." He put his hands on their shoulders to keep them from continuing after Teancum. "Now, help me care for the living and honor the dead."

CHAPTER ELEVEN

PUSHED TO THE EDGE

The signs on the trail were so clear even a child could have followed the bandit's path through the woods as it cut along the side of the long ridge line. Teancum was making good time following the track. He was raised in these mountains, where he stalked and hunted all manner of game. But now, he was hunting men. The same men who murdered his family, kidnapped his only remaining living child, and destroyed his life. As Teancum moved through the brush and around the great forest trees, he realized he had grown physically and mentally soft and very complacent, living in Zarahemla. "The life of a rich and powerful doctor and judge of the people was a far cry from his hardy upbringing on the ranch," he thought, out loud, as he shook some mud from his expensive, but worthless shoes. The snags and branches of the thick undergrowth, had torn holes in his clothing. His knees, palms and elbows were bloody from falling down. But worst of all, he was getting very thirsty. Teancum knew these woods very well and knew there was a large stream, not far from the trail, at the bottom of the ravine, but he would need to leave the trail and climb down the side of the ridge to reach it.

Teancum thought about his options of either continuing to follow or stopping to hydrate and rest. The sweat from his face was stinging his eyes. *They are not making a very good effort to hide their tracks, and they will need to stop soon, anyway,* he stood with his hands on his hips, gulping air, and looking up at the late afternoon sky. *It's going to be dark soon.* Then he thought about his little child with those killers. *Be strong, Carra.* He

191

mentally asked her for forgiveness. *I cannot risk trying to catch up to you at night. If they take you off the trail, I could miss the signs in the dark and lose you forever.*

Teancum still had Pilio's big sword in his hand and he tried to tuck it into his belt. The belt was holding the weapon for now, but what Teancum did not know was when he tucked the long blade into his belt, he cut the inside of the belt, and it started to fray from the added weight and pressure of holding the sword in place. Teancum started to work his way down the side of the ridge and move toward the flowing water below. As he moved, he noticed the grade of the earth was changing and it was getting ever steeper, the further he got from the trail above. Using the brush and small trees as hand holds, Teancum continued working his way over the rocks and down the unstable ground. More than once, Teancum slipped and lost his balance, grasping whatever handhold he could find to keep him from falling down the side of the mountain. He was still several hundred feet from the bottom when he realized he had made a horrific misjudgment. He was standing at the very edge of an almost vertical cliff. Teancum gently positioned himself right to the edge of the cliff and looked over. Almost one hundred feet below, straight down, were massive jagged rocks and a raging river. He had moved down the one section of the ridge line that opened up into a sheer cliff and rapidly tumbling water. He was going no further and was no closer to getting a much needed drink of water. Taking a deep breath and desperately trying to moisten his parched lips with his dry tongue, Teancum gave himself a quick rebuke, *Nice job. Not your finest moment.* He looked over the edge one last time, then turned to try and work his way back up the side of the mountain, to hopefully find an easier way to the source of water. Teancum took several steps up the mountain when his footing suddenly gave way and he completely lost his balance. Falling to his side, Teancum hit the slopped ground and started to roll uncontrollably toward the cliff's edge. He twisted and bumped as he completely rolled over, three times, before he reached the edge. As his legs started to fly over the cliff face, he desperately reached out for any hand hold to save him. The tips of his left fingers barely grasped the branches of a small but stout tree growing out from between two large boulders and Teancum was able to hold fast and keep his body from continuing over the side. The momentum of the fall and tumble, combined with the damage already done to the belt from the sword blade, caused the belt to snap when Teancum grabbed the branch and the sword flung off of Teancum's hip, into the open air. Teancum felt the belt give way and turned his head just in time to see his grandfather's sword break free and fly through the air and clang off the rock face, before it plummeted one hundred feet down to the bottom of the raging torrent, lost forever.

"No!" He screamed as he reached helplessly with his right hand, in a desperate but vain attempt to somehow get the sword to come back up and into his arms. He cried out again as the sounds of his anguish echoed against the canyon walls and across the ridge line.

Further up the trail, the bandit leader held up his fist to signal for the others following him to stop. He had pulled the hood back from off his head. Out there, in the woods, there was no need to keep up the mysterious appearance. Looking over his left shoulder, he cocked his head back and forth trying to hear the faint sounds echoing through the trees. "Shhh!" He commanded. "Did you hear that?"

The others all stopped and tried to hear the sound he was referring to. They all stood still, silent for several seconds.

"What? What did you hear?" The youngest bandit asked his leader.

"Quiet, boy!" he barked back.

The wind was whispering through the trees and in the distance, song birds chirped a happy tune. But there was something else…a yell, an alarm, or cry for help? The leader could not be sure. The only thing he did know is he heard it and it meant they were not alone in these woods. He got a bit nervous thinking about being chased through the mountains by Nephite soldiers with just these new recruits by his side. Looking at them, he realized he needed a plan. *They are just civilians, pretending to be brothers of the Nehor clan. They are still in the trials and have not taken the blood oath and earned the right to call themselves Nehor.* He was growing disgusted at the quality of the new men coming into the brotherhood. "You," the boss criminal spoke while pointing to the youngest and smallest of the group. "When we reach the spot in the trail where we head off to the hideout, I want you to stay behind and watch the trail to see if we are being followed."

"Yes, sir…?"

"Was there a question?" He responded to the tone from the young bandit, with a bit of anger in his voice.

"Yes, sir. What do I do if we are being followed?"

"You surrender yourself to the search party," the boss said, sarcastically.

"But, I—?" The boy was confused and reluctant to say more.

"No! You do not surrender, ever!" He quipped at the boy. "You want to be a Nehor?" The other men snorted and giggled under their breath at the boy's naivete.

The young boy shook his head in affirmation to the question. He was embarrassed.

"You stay hidden and count the number of men searching for us. See if the men are soldiers or civilians. You will account for rank and how they are armed, if they are carrying packs or have mules and horses, lugging supplies, or is it a hasty search party, without the means to sustain a long search." The old bandit stopped speaking and looked at the other men with him. "They will not see the mark to indicate the point where we will exit this trail and follow a hidden path to our resupply location. It is a secret sign known only to the Nehors, and I will show it to you when we reach that point." He wagged his finger at the men to emphasize the next point. "Remember the blood oath you will take to join us. If you reveal our secrets to anyone who is not a Nehor, then we will take our pound of flesh… And I get to decide where from your bodies that pound will come from." He smiled an evil smile as he looked the men in their eyes. They knew he was not kidding and none of them had any intention of turning on the Sons of Nehor. They continued on, but every now and again, the leader would look behind him at the trail from where they came. His instincts told him something was not right.

Teancum struggled and gasped with exertion as he pulled his body back up and away from the chasm, then rolled onto his side. "What are you doing out here?" He cried out, chastising himself for being so unprepared and out of shape. He pounded the soft ground with his fist. The loss of Pilio's sword, a priceless hierloom, to a stupid mistake was devastating. He was already raw and disturbed from the events at the ranch earlier in the day. Now he could feel himself losing control. As he lay there crying and lamenting his situation, he looked back at the rocks where he lost his footing and almost fell over the side. There, sitting on a patch of grass near the edge of the cliff, was Tum's knife, still in its sheath. Teancum gasped when he realized the knife did not fall over the side like the sword. When he saw the weapon, he felt a glimmer of hope and quickly sat up. Not wanting to repeat the same mistake, Teancum braced himself against the rocks, reaching out with his right hand, to retrieve the knife. As it came within his grasp, he snatched the knife and pulled it close to his chest. Sitting back against the side of the mountain, he pulled the blade from its sheath to inspect it for damage. He did not see anything wrong with the metal or handle. He felt the edge of the knife with his thumb. He knew Tum always carried this knife and kept it well maintained, with a razor sharp edge. "Yes!" He whispered, when he felt the sharpness of the honed blade. The feel of this knife in his hands gave him a sudden spark of energy. It was surprising to him how something as simple as a well maintained knife could inspire him to continue on. With this, Teancum found renewed courage and returned the blade to its sheath. He picked himself up and started picking his way back up to the top of the mountain. "Carra is still their prisoner and probably has had nothing to drink either," he thought out loud as he carefully worked his way up the steep slope. "I am coming, my princess."

When Teancum reached the top of the mountain and found the trail again he realized the sun was starting to go down. Very soon it would be pitch black and impossible to continue traveling. "I can't risk starting a fire. The bandits might see the glow or smell the burning wood, then come back and try to kill me while I sleep." He considered his situation a bit more. "I don't have a tent or sleeping mats, and nothing to make a shelter, or the time to construct one." Then his stomach grumbled in protest of the lack of food. Grimacing, he patted his belly. "Or food." He thought about his child in the hands of the bandits and how she must be so hungry and scared. These images were more than he could bear so he focused his attention on something else. "I will find you tomorrow, Carra. They will pay for what they have done."

From his experiences in the woods as a boy, Teancum knew the last thing he wanted to do was sleep out in the open and on the bare ground. Looking up into the darkening sky, he knew he was quickly running out of daylight. He unhooked the bright metal clasp holding his dark colored cloak around his neck and over his shoulders. Pulling his cloak off, he started to search for a more suitable location to bed down for the night. A few feet off of the trail, Teancum found a large boulder with a semi-flat surface. Climbing up onto top of the large rock, he inspected it for anything that would impede his slumber. Brushing a few leaves and dead twigs from the top of the rock, Teancum was satisfied it would do for one night's rest. He laid down on the rock and curled into the fetal position. Using his arm as a makeshift pillow, he covered his body the best he could with the cloak and closed his eyes. The sun lowered behind the mountains and it quickly became very dark. Teancum was exhausted but could not fall asleep. His body was revolting against the constant punishment it had sustained over the long day, but his mind was moving like a well bred horse in a prize race. Every time he closed his eyes, the experiences, thoughts, feelings, and images he faced earlier in the morning haunted him. The scenes of horror would flash across his mind and his body would jerk him awake in response. At one point, Teancum got tired of trying to sleep, so he sat up and covered his shoulders with the cloak. He sat in silence, looking up at the stars and praying with all his might for God's intervention in his life.

Even though it was dark, the bandits were still moving down the trail, led by the older Nehor. He knew the way and could find the marker to the hidden turnoff for the hideout, even under the worst conditions. Poor Carra had been so traumatized by the events of the day her mind shut down and she had fallen asleep. Her little body was dangling over the left shoulder of one of the bandits and her hands were bound with a small cord. She had been unconscious for some time and the man carrying her was growing concerned for her well-being. He said something to the leader who quickly pointed out the hypocrisy.

"You kidnapped her, killed her family and burned down her home," he said, with a bit of sarcasm in his voice. The older bandit cocked his head to one side and gave the younger bandit a questioning look. "And now you are worried she might not be feeling well?"

"I just thought if she is going to be our prisoner, then—"

He was interrupted when the older man put up his hand to tell him to stop talking. "You are a Nehor, not a nursemaid! Put her down and check if you must."

The younger man slid little Carra from his shoulder and set her down on the trail. The jostling brought her out of her slumber and she opened her eyes. Rolling to her side, Carra carefully sat up and looked around at the large men standing over the top of her. In the light of the moon, the men could see her big blue eyes and the fact she was still dressed in her sleeping gown. Sitting there on the ground and surrounded by the bandits, Carra slowly looked into the eyes of each of the men. She held still for a moment, expressionless and still as a stone. The men, all standing around her, softened their posture and were smitten as they looked down on the innocence of the child before them. Then, without warning, she filled her lungs with a large gulp of air and screamed as loud as she could. The sudden burst of the screeching noise caught the criminals off guard and they all instinctively recoiled, taking two steps back. Carra ran out of air and stopped her screaming long enough to refill her lungs and started back up again. The older bandit was the first to snap out of the sudden shock and react.

"Stop her!" He shouted over her screams. Panicked, he reached out for Carra and tried to grab her. He knew from experience that sounds travel farther at night, and a little girl screaming would draw way too much attention if there were armed men searching for her. Carra rolled to her right and tried to get up as the bandit grabbed her by the waist and picked her up. She continued to scream and started to thrash about, kicking her legs and swinging her arms.

"Quiet!" The bandit demanded, but Carra was not going to obey. She continued to scream and the bandit covered her mouth with his big dirty hand. Despite his best efforts, her muffled cry could still be heard and the older bandit became angry.

"I said be quiet!" He demanded, then he smacked the side of her head with the open palm of his hand. Little Carra's eyes rolled back in her head and she went limp in his arms.

At first, the bandit thought he had killed her. He felt a sudden surge of regret for his actions. Not for the fact he just killed a defenseless child, but for the loss of extra income she would have provided the Nehors when he sold her to the slavers. He held her out, away from him, with both hands, and tried to inspect her condition, to see if she was unconscious or really dead. As he was looking her over, he saw her chest expand and her eyes twitch. "Good," he spouted, when he realized she was still alive. "That should keep her quiet." He held her out for the youngest bandit to take her from him. "Think you can handle her now?" the older bandit mocked the younger one as he took possession of the unconscious little girl.

"You didn't need to hit her so hard," the young man spoke, under his breath. He was a murderer and plundering criminal, but something deep inside him wanted to protect the child.

"What did you say?" the leader barked back.

"Nothing," the young criminal responded sleepily as he cowered and moved back a few steps, with Carra in his arms.

"Keep moving!" the leader barked. Frustrated, he picked up his pack and continued up the dark trail, snorting and cursing under his breath as he went. Not knowing what else to do or say, the other men trudged along following the experienced Nehor to the hideout. Carra was still unconscious and back on the shoulder of the young bandit.

Teancum was finally starting to doze off when Carra's bone-chilling scream echoed through the canyons and across the ridge line. Instantly he was awake and on his feet. Turning completely around, Teancum tried to get his bearings and figure out where the sounds came from.

"Carra!" he whispered. A father knows the sounds of his child in danger, and there was no mistake in Teancum's mind. That scream was from Carra, and she was closer than he thought. *A mile, maybe two*, he calculated in his mind. He knew he needed to keep going. She was alive and she needed him to come and save her from the monsters who took her. He quickly gathered his wits and with his cloak bundled under his arm, Teancum moved the several yards back to the trail. He felt so tired and so thirsty. His legs were wobbling under him and his back was aching from the fall down the cliff, not to mention the rock mattress, but it was his thirst that was most pressing to Teancum. His lips were parched and brittle from the lack of moisture and his head was pounding out of the need for water. He rolled his tongue around inside of his mouth and tried to get some saliva to form, but nothing was working. Cursing to himself under his breath at the utter lack of forethought he'd had when setting off after the bandits, Teancum wrapped the cloak around his shoulders and looked up at the stars for his bearings. He generally knew where on the mountainous ridge line he was, he just wanted the confirmation of the North Star to let him know he was heading in the right direction. *I am coming my little princess…daddy is coming to save you.* Teancum looked down at his expensive, but completely useless soft leather shoes and winced at the pain in his feet as he started to move up the trail.

Teancum was moving slowly, but he was determined not to stop until he had the criminals who murdered his family and kidnapped his child in his sights. The long night without rest and the lack of water were really affecting his mental state. He could feel what little stored energy he had left in his body quickly draining away as every step became a challenge.

His balance and coordination were off, and just walking in a straight line was a labor. While he moved down the darkened trail, he kept tripping and falling over unseen obstacles in his way. As the darkness of the thick tree canopy and solitude of the trail enveloped him, Teancum started to see and hear things due to exhaustion and lack of water. First, it was subtle movements in the shadows; he thought he could sense someone or something moving around the trees and large rocks lining the trail, but he wasn't sure of it. Then like fireflies, specks of light would flash around his peripheral vision, as a physical and physiological reaction to the extreme stress he was under. Teancum kept moving cautiously down the trail, trying not to let the unseen being know he was on to him. But he kept seeing movement or the streak of a dark form passing deep in the shadows of the night.

At one point, Teancum thought he had the upper hand on the unseen creature stalking him. He saw movement near a tree close to the trail itself, and he waited until he was close. Pulling the knife from his belt, Teancum lunged for the base of the tree and slashed at the air trying to wound his would-be attacker hiding in the darkness. "Ha!" he shouted as he stabbed and sliced around the large trunk of the ancient tree. But there was nothing there. Teancum paused to gather his thoughts. "I know there was something here… Am I losing it?" he questioned out loud. He knew for certain there was something there. He saw the flashes of light and movement in the blackness of the night. With the conflict raging in his mind, he held still for several seconds, listening to the sounds of the night. The duality of the moment was upsetting him. He wanted to hear his would-be follower moving in the brush, to validate his actions and prove he was not going crazy and seeing things. But hearing movement would mean there was a very real threat just out of sight and following him. As he stood motionless, the only sounds were his labored breathing and the crunching of the leaves under his feet as he shifted his weight. "Nothing…" He spoke out loud, as if to both console and chastise his inner voices. "There is nothing there." There was disappointment in his tone. Nothing there meant he was seeing things, and that was not a good sign. Taking a deep breath, Teancum calmed his mind and did a quick self-assessment. *You are exhausted and quickly becoming dangerously dehydrated. You have experienced sorrow and terror at an unspeakable level. You are emotionally raw and physically injured.* He twisted his aching back to try to loosen it up as he spoke those words. "You need rest but you can't stop." He thought about his daughter and her big blue eyes. "Of course you are nearing the breaking point, but you must keep moving," he reassured himself, like a good doctor sitting bedside, and urging a sick patient to keep fighting. The emotions were welling up again and a lone tear rolled down his cheek, brushing along his cracked lips. The images of his dead wife and children flashed across his mind. Teancum licked the tear and tried to wet his parched lips with the salty testament of his pain. His chin started to quiver as he desperately tried to choke back the flood inevitably coming. "Hold it together, lock it down! Your child needs you!" he said audibly. Taking several more deep breaths, he pushed the grief deep down inside his soul and tried to replace it with something else. He wanted to feel hate, or anger, even contempt, but the best he could do was find the courage to continue on. So, taking one step at a time, Teancum continued up the trail.

The sun was starting to rise on a long night for the bandits. They had kept moving farther from the scene of the crime and finally, with the new dawn, they reached the point in the trail where the Nehors had placed a hidden marking to indicate a branch in the main trail.

"You see that sign on the tree?" The old leader pointed to the large 'X' with a circle around it and a line running right down the middle. "That is the mark of the Nehor." He made sure everyone in his group could see it and understand. "You see that mark on a house, then it's a Nehor safe house. You see it painted on a wall, then the street is a Nehor Street. You see it on a judge's bench, then he is with the Nehors." The head criminal smiled and looked sternly at the men. "As a new brother in the Nehor clan, you will soon pledge your life to our cause. If that means we need to use your house, then so be it. If it means you beat a man down to make the rest of the neighborhood afraid, then you do it. If it means we use your family to further our cause, then that is the way it will be. If it means you lie or kill to protect a fellow Nehor, then you do it." He pointed his finger at the men and used anger in his tone to make his point. "And if you ever expose our secret signs and combinations to the world, then you and your loved ones are as good as dead." The other men with him could tell he was not joking. "That is what you will swear to do when you became one of us. Your oath is to put the needs of the brotherhood before your own— to commit your life, family and property to the cause.

In return, you have respect, wealth, protection and the reputation of the Sons of Nehor." He smiled and softened his demeanor. "You are family now, one of us." He moved closer and put his hands on the men and, like a loving father, he smiled at each one. He guided them over to the tree where the evil gang's marking was carved high up into the side of the trunk.

"Is she still asleep?" he questioned the young man who was carrying Carra.

The young man shrugged his shoulder and there was no response from the tiny captive. "Yeah, still out cold."

"Good. Let me show you how we care for our own." Pushing the thick brush aside and moving over by the base of the marked tree, he revealed a hidden path carved into the undergrowth. The path followed along the edge of the mountain and could only be seen from their current location. "Gentlemen, up this hidden trail is one of a series of established hideouts known only to the Sons of Nehor. It is well provisioned and some of our fellow brothers maintain these locations on a constant basis. If you are ever in trouble or need a place to hide, you can come to one of these." He looked back at the men with him. They all had a look of wonder in their eyes. He knew their thoughts and responded to their feelings. "Yes, the Sons of Nehor are better equipped and organized than any of those worthless civilians can possibly know." He paused for effect. "Very soon, we will reveal our true nature. Then the cursed judges, those who are not already supporting us, and those so-called Christian holy men will learn how deep the our reach goes."

There was more he wanted to say but now was not the time. The old leader still felt they were being followed and he needed to take steps to hide their tracks. "You," he pointed to the young man holding Carra. He never really bothered to learn their names. To him, they were just useful idiots, pawns in the great game to further the Nehor cause. "Give me the kid." Without question, the child was handed over to his thuggish boss who tucked her under his arm. "You and you," he pointed to the youngest and the one standing next to him. "Take a leafy branch from that tree across the trail, backtrack at least a half mile and then walk backwards, sweeping clean all traces of our foot prints. Be cautious and leave no reason for someone to follow. When you are done, you," he said, pointing to the youngest, "hide here, next to the marked tree, and watch the trail until dark. Do what I told you and watch for people trying to follow our tracks. When the sun is down, make your way up the hidden trail and join us at the top of the mountain." The older man pointed to the top of the mountain in the distance.

The young man nodded and looked at the new bandit next to him. The two of them moved across the trail into the thick woods to find the appropriate branch for their needs.

Teancum was really struggling now. With the sun up and the temperature starting to rise, the heat was adding to the already overwhelming effects of the duress he was under. Like a man walking to his death, Teancum labored with every step as he continued to climb ever higher up the mountainous, rocky trail and toward the unknown. The only thing keeping him moving was the thought of his precious, tiny child in the hands of those murderous outlaws. He trudged along at a slow and difficult pace for what seemed like hours, when suddenly the footprints in the dirt path disappeared. Teancum stopped and shook his head, trying to clear his mind. Confused, he looked around to ensure he hadn't veered off the main trail. Inspecting the ground behind him, he clearly saw the tracks and footprints he had been following, but in front of him they vanished. Then he noticed something very strange. As he looked closer at the ground, there appeared to be drag marks across the dirt, like something or someone had wiped the ground clean of the markings made by the men walking. Teancum blinked and shook his head again to clear out the cobwebs. "Why would they cover their tracks?" he asked out loud, as he knelt down to get a closer look at the ground. His cracked and dry lips moved as he slowly pronounced every word. "They must know I am following them. They are close and they are trying to lose me by clearing any sign of their movement." Teancum was now on both knees. He sat back on his heels and smiled. "I guess they don't know I hunted in these woods my entire life." He stood up, brushing the dirt from his pant legs. "I know this trail continues over the mountain and down into the great valley," he grunted. "They can try all they want to cover up their tracks. I know where they are going." As he shifted his weight, he winced in pain at the raw blisters forming on his feet. Those expensive, soft leather shoes were wholly inadequate for his current needs and he was paying for it. He hobbled around a bit on the trail, but focused again at the task at hand. "I am coming, my princess," he murmured.

The heat of the day was increasing and Teancum removed his cloak, then draped it over his shoulders. He thought about leaving it behind, but considered how the temperature dropped when the sun went down. If he needed to stay another night outside, he would want the covering to help trap his body heat and keep him warm.

Up ahead, the two bandits covering their tracks reached the large tree with the Nehor marking, and the younger one tossed the branch they were using to sweep the trail clean into the bushes. "I guess I'm stuck here until nightfall," he said with a hint of disappointment in his voice. "Don't eat all of the food," he joked to the other bandit, as that man found the hidden path behind the large tree and started up the Nehor trail.

"I will save you the dirty dishes to clean up. How about that?" the man snickered at the fledgling criminal as he walked away without looking back.

"Don't fall off the side of the mountain," the younger man responded under his breath. He was getting really tired of being picked on because of his age. He was a killer, and soon he would be a pledged son of the Nehor clan. He joined the clan so others would fear and respect him. Deep down inside his soul, he knew he just wanted to be respected and he wanted the reputation of the clan on his side to keep others from picking on him. He was tired of being the joke, but felt even now, nothing had really changed. When he was younger, he was smaller than the other boys his age. He did not grow until later in his teens, but by then it was too late. He was mocked and mistreated because of his size and had developed a sense of self-doubt because of the harsh treatment from others. He was angry— angry at the world. He knew with the Nehor, he could get back at all of them and punish the world for treating him like garbage. Taking a large drink from his water skin, he looked around and found his hiding spot.

Removing his pack, he set it down under a tree with a large canopy of branches reaching to the ground which made for excellent concealment. Sitting down on top of the pack, he opened a small leather bag and pulled out a helping of jerked meat. He put his back to the tree trunk and sat, slowly chewing on the meat, as he watched the trail in silence. "One day," he spoke out loud, "you will all see what I can become." He tossed a stick into the brush with a frustrated gasp. "I will be a feared Nehor commander, and no one will dare pick on me then."

"Where else could you go?" Teancum questioned out loud, as he scanned the horizon and the trail before him. "Zarahemla is the closest city, but it's behind me." Teancum looked back down the trail in the direction he had just come from. "This trail only leads to the great valley beyond the ridge line," he muttered, as he squinted toward the tops of the rugged mountains before him. He had been carefully following the swirl marks in the dirt that appeared to be covering up the tracks from the bandits. Every now and then, he would find a partially covered boot print or, if he was lucky, he would find a single full print that was missed by the person responsible for hiding the tracks. This section of the well-used trail was wide and uncovered. For the last hour or so, it had been completely covered by the large, old tree canopies, and almost choked out by the rampant underbrush. Now, Teancum was standing in a small meadow looking up at the sun, trying to get his bearings. As he stood in the open air resting and gathering his thoughts, he gently touched his lips and felt the cracks and dried, blistering skin. The almost complete lack of water was taking its toll. He was so very thirsty. His body was falling apart and his crisp, meticulous mind was going dim from the over-exertion, trauma, lack of food, water and rest. As he stood there, wondering if he had the strength to continue, Teancum felt a shift in the direction of the wind and a cool breeze blew across his face. He was surprised by the change in the weather and he looked in the direction of the wind. Off in the distance, there were storm clouds building and the sky was dark with moisture. "Rain clouds!" He smiled. He knew how much water this side of the mountain range got each year. "All I need to do is survive until it gets here, Teancum recited to himself, like he was giving a commentary on his actions. "I will have plenty to drink soon enough." Teancum found the courage to continue, at least until the impending storm arrived. He started to move down the path, but stopping had given his muscles a moment to seize up and his feet ached even more. Hunched over and walking like a man twice his age, he struggled and groaned with every step.

The wind was starting to pick up and the sky was growing even darker as the young bandit sat, alone and still on his pack under the tree branch canopy. "This is ridiculous," he spoke out loud in frustration. The coming storm was rustling the tree tops and the sounds of creaking branches rang out. The young man looked up at the darkening sky and the massive branches swaying back and forth in the strong wind. He could even feel a few drops of cold rain on his face. He knew it was only a matter of time before he was completely drenched. Sitting cold and still was not his idea of fun. Sighing he spoke out loud, "They are up there, out of the weather and eating roasted meat, while I am stuck here, hungry, bored and about to get rained on." He looked at the trail he was tasked to watch in secret. "No one is coming," he reassured himself. Sitting for a few moments more, he tried to be patient. Finally he took a deep, frustrated breath. "I have had enough of this," he whispered. He took out his water skin and removed the cap. Tilting his head back he poured down the last remaining liquid into his open mouth. The water came out too fast, and he gulped and coughed as the water made him choke. He held his hand in front of his face as he coughed several times to try to clear the water from his windpipe. "Stupid," he spoke out loud, as he tossed the empty water skin through the bushes and onto the trail itself. Chastising himself for the drinking mistake, he stood up and cursed again. He was confident no one was around, and he moved from under the low hanging canopy, trying to gather up his pack without concern for the noise he was making.

Teancum was still moving slowly up the trail when he heard someone cough in the bushes off to his right, just up the trail. He froze in place with his hand on the hilt of the knife tucked in his belt. Then, a water skin came flying out of the bushes a few feet from where he was standing, and the voice of a man cursing rang out. Instinctively, when he saw the water skin and heard the man hidden from his view, Teancum moved closer to the bushes lining the trail. He crouched down to make a lower profile and quietly pulled out his knife. He was hesitant to blindly attack whomever was making the noise. The sudden revelation he was not alone on the trail caused Teancum to cower and question why he was there. Quickly looking back behind himself, Teancum tried to plot an escape route, but it was too late. The bandit, with his pack on his back, stepped out onto the trail and bent over to fetch his empty water skin. Teancum was exposed, and unprepared for the fight that was sure to come. He had been mindlessly trudging along the trail for over a full day, and during all that time, he never given a thought as to how he would react if he came upon one, or all of the bandits he was tracking. He only wanted to find them, make them pay for what they had done to his family, and rescue his daughter. So, without a thought as to what to do next, he quickly pulled out his knife and held it out in front of his body. The bandit saw movement out the corner of his eye and slowly stood up, the water skin in his hand.

The two men made eye contact and the bandit instantly recognized Teancum as the same man from the burning ranch where he had assisted in the robbery, kidnapping and murder.

"Easy, man," the young bandit beckoned with his hands out to show he was unarmed. He could see Teancum had been physically shattered in the last few days. His clothing was torn and tattered. He was covered in dirt and streaks of blood, but it was his face and hollow, sunken eyes that gave away Teancum's true mental and emotional state. He looked desperate, scared, and wild.

"Take your pack off, slowly, and lay down on the ground face down," Teancum ordered in a hoarse, ragged voice, as he waved the knife around to show the bandit he meant business.

"It's not me you want. If you are here for the little girl, I can help you." The bandit pointed toward the side of the mountain. "I can show you where they are hiding."

Teancum forced himself not to overract at the mention of Carra. He refocused on the young criminal before him. *Don't trust him,* a voice from deep in his consciousness begged him. "The pack." Teancum was more firm but did not raise his voice. He was not sure who else was close by. He quickly scanned the surroundings and shifted his weight as he talked.

"It's just you and me out here. They left me to watch the trail for you." The bandit was trying to gain Teancum's trust. *Just keep talking, get that scarecrow close enough to knock the knife out of his hands. Then you can beat him down in a wrestling match,* he thought to himself, as he slowly moved closer to Teancum.

"Put your pack on the ground and get down!" Teancum slashed at the bandit's hands. He was getting too close and Teancum did not want to back up any more.

The bandit waited until Teancum made his last slashing move and the knife was pointed away from his body. *Wait for it… Now is your chance to show everyone just who you are and what you're made of.* The young criminal rushed forward, grabbing for the hand holding the knife.

Teancum did not see the bold attack coming and was caught off guard. Before he could adjust or get out of the way, the bandit had hold of Teancum's arm and they were struggling over control of the weapon. It was more of a contest of raw power than any type of martial skill. Both men were novices at hand to hand fighting, but they were equally determined not to lose. Grunting and pulling, twisting and pushing, they strained and struggled over the knife. Teancum still held it firm in his hands but the young man was slowly gaining the advantage. He was better rested, nourished and well hydrated and had not been exerting himself for the last twenty four hours, like Teancum had. But Teancum had the fire and indignation of a man who had watched his family viciously murdered. Reaching down into his inner strength, Teancum found the grit to overcome this assault and started to physically overpower the younger man. The bandit felt the tide turn in Teancum's favor as he started to lose the battle for control of the knife. Sensing things were not going well, the young criminal tried to push Teancum away and make for the hidden trail. His only hope was to run and try to get close enough to the other Nehors and call out for help. The terrified man had completely forgotten he had a short sword and other weapons on his own belt. He was panicked and unfamiliar with close combat fighting, so instead of turning and facing Teancum with a bigger weapon, he did what he had always done—run. Under this stress, his body and mind did what it was trained to do. Screaming and gasping for air, the cowardly bandit flung himself into the thick bushes and moved toward the marked tree and the hidden trail beyond.

Teancum quickly recovered from the push and was off like a flash after his foe. The instinct to chase came from deep in his primitive instincts. He was having a hard time controlling his actions as he became overcome with primal rage. He burst through the bush flailing his arms and screaming like a madman as he tried to catch the bandit.

The bandit took one last look behind him as he ran past the tree marking the entrance to the trail to the Nehor camp. Teancum crashed through the brush after the bandit, with fire in his eyes, while swinging the knife back and forth and screaming, "Where is my daughter!?"

The bandit let out a panicked yelp and turned around to move around the tree, but he failed to see the low hanging branch just on the other side of the massive trunk. The branch was not terribly thick, maybe the same diameter as a baby's arm, but it was the branch's angle, coupled with the speed of the bandit when he hit the branch that caused the damage. There was a loud whack as the branch hit him diagonally across his face, from the top right side of his forehead down and over his eye, his nose and his left cheek bone. The bandit's head snapped back and he fell backwards with the top of his small pack being the first thing to hit the ground. A giant gasp of air exploded from his lungs when he hit the ground, and the skin across the bridge of his nose split open from the impact; blood flowing freely down his face. Instinctively, the young criminal rolled to his side, trying to get to his feet. As he was moving, he felt the hilt of his short sword brush against his arm, and suddenly he remembered he was much better armed than the stranger chasing after him. Still stunned from hitting the branch, the bandit wiped the blood from his eyes and got to his knees as he tried to pull out his sword. Teancum closed the distance and hit the bandit with his shoulder at full speed before the bandit could unsheathe his weapon. Both men tumbled to the ground and Teancum was first to get back to his feet. The bandit struggled to find his footing, but his legs were weak and his mind was cloudy from the blow to the head. He succeeded in getting his sword out just before Teancum could get close enough to use his own knife. The bandit recklessly swung the sword out in front of him and shouted, 'Back!' several times, in an attempt to keep Teancum at a distance. Teancum could see the blood in the bandit's eyes was affecting his vision, and he was losing his balance easily as he swung the sword.

Wait for it, he thought to himself as he moved and dodged the wild swings from the young man. As they battled, the storm's intensity was increasing, blowing dust and shaking the trees and large ferns and bushes, making it even more difficult for the bandit's sword to find its mark. "Where is my daughter?" he shouted again at the bandit as he lunged just out of reach of the tip of the blade, then moved around a small tree.

The young bandit was desperate to finish this deadly encounter and he was trying even harder to strike Teancum with the sharp blade. "I will never tell!" he shouted back to Teancum as he struggled to see or even stand and fight.

Teancum waited for just the right moment. When he saw the bandit about to make his next move, Teancum charged. The bandit swung the blade across his body and at the last possible second, Teancum was able rush in close enough to trap the bandit's arm against the man's body. Using his own momentum, Teancum pushed the wounded bandit against the base of the large marked tree, pinning him between the tree and Teancum's own body weight. The bandit cried out in pain and tried to break free from Teancum's grasp and weight. Teancum knew he only had seconds to gain the advantage and he needed to know about his child.

"Tell me!" he grunted fiercely. He was doing his best to hold the bandit's arm against the man's body and keep him pinned against the tree. "Where is my daughter?"

The bandit was so overcome with pain and raw emotion, all he could do was scream out, gnash his teeth and growl in a gasp, "Never!"

Teancum could feel he was losing his grip on the younger man, but did not want to take the chance the bandit would escape his hold, run away, or turn on Teancum again with his sword. Suddenly, a flash of memory crackled across his mind. When he was younger, he was being instructed in the art of wrestling by a champion brought to the ranch by Pilio. Teancum remembered a very effective move for bringing down a strong aggressor. "We call this the hip throw," the instructor told young Teancum. He then demonstrated the technique and Teancum, the instant learner, quickly mastered the skill. In less than a second, Teancum remembered the move and shuffled his hips into place. Grabbing the bandit's hips and arm, Teancum flipped the man over the top of his head and onto the ground. He landed hard with a large thump, dropping his sword. Teancum fell on him, breaking some of the bandit's ribs. The bandit cried out in pain and tried to push Teancum off. Teancum rolled on top of the bandit and straddled his legs over the injured man's hips. Holding his knife in both hands over his head, Teancum screamed out as he tried to drive the blade downwards into the bandit's chest. The young man caught Teancum's hands and stopped the deadly movement. It was now a pure power struggle. The young bandit was pushing back against Teancum with all his might, desperately fighting to keep Teancum from stabbing him. But he was hurting badly from the broken ribs, and his strength was failing him. Teancum pushed down with all his might. He was reaching the point where if this struggle continued for much longer, total exhaustion was going to keep him from inflicting the lethal blow. He also knew this man might be his only source of information on the location of his daughter.

"Where is my child?" Teancum gasped as he fought the bandit. "Tell me!"

As he spoke, he pushed one last time with his entire body weight down on his blade. He felt the bandit's strength start to give. The blade was moving closer to the man's heart.

"No!" the bandit cried out, as he succumbed to the overwhelming pain from the injured ribs and the last of his reserve energy gave way. Teancum came crashing down on top of the man and drove the long blade of the knife deep into the bandit's chest, piercing the heart and delivering the killing blow. The bandit gasped three times then stopped moving. His arms gave way and his legs stopped kicking. Teancum was still on top of him, looking the bandit in the eyes, as he watched the life leave his enemy's body. Teancum had killed a man with his bare hands, and his only link to Carra's location. Teancum gasped as he realized he had just failed the only family he had left on this earth, again.

"Tell me!" he gasped as he shook the dead man. "Tell me where she is!" He was crying now. The flood of emotions came down on him like a stone dropped from a great height. "Tell me!"

Teancum let the lifeless body go and he slowly rose to his feet. Looking down at the body of the enemy, he pondered in his mind his sorry state. *What have I done? Am I a monster?* He rubbed his neck and sore arms. Despair was starting to overcome him. *Have I just condemned my child?* The cracks of lighting were bursting in the swollen storm clouds above him as he looked up into the sky. The large branches above him were swirling as the trees moaned under the unrelenting wind. Teancum knew this was going to be a very intense storm. As he stood motionless, trying to gain some measure of control over what was happening to him, a thought came to his mind, *Why did you run in this direction?* He looked back down at the dead man. *Why not run up the trail toward your friends? Why did you run into the thick underbrush and move toward the edge of the mountainside?* He looked around at the environment surrounding him. This thought intrigued Teancum. He slowly stepped around the fallen Nehor and looked closer at the ground. *I see other tracks in the dirt.* Teancum followed the impressions in the ground back to the trail and he stepped out into the open. *You all came off the trail right here...why?* He knew the others were not close or they would have come to the aid of their comrade. *Where did you go?* As he was looking around, he noticed a strange marking on the trunk of the large tree just to the right of where the tracks showed the men left the trail and moved through the brush. *What is that?* he questioned, as he got closer to the engraving. *I have seen this before...but where?* He searched his mind to remember where he had seen the symbol, but his extreme fatigue and lack of water were making it very difficult for him to concentrate. He got close enough to the marking on the tree to run his hand over the grooves carved into the wood and bark. *Man-made...someone put this here, but why?* Then he thought about the dead man still in the bushes. *You ran toward something or someone who you thought would make you safe and this marking is in the same location.* Teancum took several steps back from the tree and stood in the middle of the trail. *This is not some random marking on a tree. It's a symbol... It's telling someone on the road there is something unique about this tree.* He looked up and down the trail. *But what is it saying?* Teancum walked slowly toward the exact location where the footprints led into the underbrush. Following the prints back into the undergrowth, Teancum moved with purpose, scanning as he walked. He was unsure of what he was looking for, but there was some reason why the criminal ran this way, why the footprints from the others were leading him there, and the marking on the tree was on this specific location. As he was walking, it suddenly appeared right in front of him. He did not see it earlier because he was either running after the bandit or walking back out toward the trail. There was a section of the undergrowth which had been trampled, and some of the bushes looked like they had been slightly trimmed back. "Is that a path through the brush or the start of a game trail?" Teancum asked himself aloud as he stepped closer to inspect it. The dead body of the bandit lay only a few feet from the opening in the brush. Teancum stepped over the man and knelt down next to the body to get a closer look. A surge of energy bolted down his spine when he saw two different footprints in the dirt leading deeper into the brush. "This is a trail!" He sat back on his heels as he looked up the side of the mountain. "A hidden path, marked by the carving on the tree." He smiled as he figured it out. "You were running for this trail, to try and join your friends up the mountain," Teancum spoke over his shoulder back at the corpse. It was starting to get very dark and Teancum did not want to lose what little light was left in the evening sky. He stood up, moved down the hidden path, being careful not to make any noise or do anything that might alert the other kidnappers to his presence. Stopping after twenty feet, Teancum returned to the body of the dead bandit and grabbed him by the ankles. "Can't leave you out in the open for your friends to find you," he spoke as he dragged the lifeless corpse deeper into the woods. Stopping near a fallen tree, Teancum kicked some fallen leaves over the body and moved back to the trail head.

Teancum had been walking for several minutes when he suddenly stopped dead in his tracks. Looking down at his worthless shoes, he could see his big toe poking out of the top of one of them. The blood from the open sores on his feet had dried and formed dirt rings on the outside. The rough trail had taken its toll on his foot coverings and he was paying for it with his injured feet. Smiling and quietly chastising himself, he remembered the man he had killed had on more appropriate footwear, as well as a larger weapon and supplies in his pack and pockets. He realized he had left all of those things back on the dead body, and he snorted as he shook his head. *Should I go back for those things?* he questioned in his mind, as he looked back down the trail from where he came. *Or do I continue with the thought the others might be right around the corner?* While he was contemplating his predicament, a strong gust of wind blew across his face. In the traces of the breeze, Teancum could smell burning wood. He sniffed again, as he scanned the top of the mountain for clues as to where it was coming from. *It has to be them.* He took a deep breath for courage, and knew he could not afford to go back to gather the belongings from the dead criminal now. *They finally stopped and made camp.* He strained his eyes as he tried to look closer for a flicker from the fire's light. *I must be getting close.* Instinctively, he felt for the hilt of the knife stuck in his belt. He had already used it once today when he took the life of the young man at the base of the hidden trail. *Could I do that again?* He questioned his motives and abilities. He thought about his dead family and his tiny child in the hands of those who murdered her mother and sisters. As he tried to find the courage to go on, to continue toward the unknown and face death, emotions started to well up inside him. He tried to swallow them down and hide his feelings deep in his soul, but they were overpowering his efforts. He was shaking and bursting with fits of anger and sadness. "No," he whispered with authority. He was trying to control his own emotions. He balled up both his fists, and shook his arms, trying to break the hold his thoughts had on his body. *Focus!*, he demanded of his entire being. He knew he was going to pay dearly for repressing the release of tension and feelings that his body and mind desperately needed to get this out but now was not the time. *Focus!* He shouted internally. He was commanding his mind to deal with the task at hand. Slowly, with the help of deep, calming breathing, Teancum was able to gain control of his emotions and return to dealing with the task at hand, rescuing his child. Several large and cold drops of rain began to fall and Teancum knew this was a precursor to a powerful storm about to be unleashed any second. His mind was spinning, and he felt numb as he continued to move up the trail.

After several more minutes, Teancum froze in his tracks. He cocked his head to one side and strained to listen over the noise of the wind. *Did I just hear laughter?* He wondered. Then he heard it again, a man's laughter. It was coming from around a slight bend in the trail and on top of a ledge protruding out from the mountain, near the very top. *Get off the trail!* A voice in his head shouted to him. Without thinking, Teancum reacted to the warning and moved quickly into the undergrowth, crashing through the thick vegetation. Once he was safely off the path, and well inside the dense underbrush, he stopped for a moment to collect his thoughts and listen again for any tell-tale signs he had been discovered. No one came. When he felt the gathering storm had covered any sounds he was making, Teancum continued to move closer to the top of the ledge, but kept off the trail and hidden as best as he could. Within minutes, he had reached the cliff outcropping and carefully moved into a position behind a large mass of rock and ferns, where he could better see what was happening.

The storm was starting to intensify. The wind was much stronger now and lightning crisscrossed the dark sky in exploding bolts of pure energy. The following thunder shook the very ground and the rain was getting heavier by the moment. This side of the mountain range always experienced heavy rains during the season, and tonight was no exception. Through the bursts of light from the electrical storm, Teancum could see two of the bandits sitting on the ledge with their backs against the cliff face, sheltered from the rain under a large, heavy tarp fastened to long wooden poles and anchored to the side of the mountain. The third one was fussing with a fire which, even though it was mostly protected by the tarp, was still struggling to stay lit under the weight of the rain. Scanning the area around the bandits, Teancum saw his tiny daughter lying in the fetal position next to the wood pile facing away from him and not moving. From his vantage point in the trees, Teancum could not tell if she was dead or sleeping. Her crumpled body laid motionless in the mud. As he stood there, hidden from view in the rocks and dense undergrowth, he realized his whole body was starting to shake again. *This is not good*, he thought to himself, relying on his extensive medical training to diagnose his condition. He had been running on pure emotion for the last two days and now his body was rebelling. He knew he needed to either sleep or act quickly to rescue his daughter before his body and mind started to shut down on him. *First, your motor skills will start to decrease.* He could hear the logical, medical professional side of his consciousness speaking to the dark animal side. *Then your logic and thought processes will fail you. Lastly will come the shutdown of your internal organs.* He wiped the rain from his face as the calmer voices of his psyche continued to reason with his dark side. *Your body will revolt and collapse before you can cause any real harm. The question is, when and where will your mind and body fail you?* Looking down, Teancum realized he was still holding in his quivering hands the long dagger he had used to kill the lone bandit. *Then I need to move now and finish this before that happens!* The hardness in his mind responded. Resolved to do what he must, Teancum took in a few long, deep breaths, to try to calm his nerves and slow the shaking. The heavy rain helped him quench his burning thirst as he manipulated a large fern leaf into a makeshift funnel and caught the rain water, letting it slide into his mouth. Feeling a little better after taking a good drink, Teancum tucked the knife into his belt and refocused on the task at hand. "It will be totally dark very soon," he whispered, as he looked up into the night sky. The sun had gone down not long ago and black storm clouds were choking off what twilight remained. "I need to get in closer if I am going to save her." Teancum readjusted his position behind the bushes as he tried to figure out a way to sneak past those evil men and rescue the only family he had left on this earth.

He was wondering what the third bandit was doing around the fire when suddenly, the aroma of roasting rabbit reached his hiding place. Up until this moment in time, Teancum had lived a very privileged life. Growing up the grandson of Lord Pilio and Lady Saria, he had never really known what true hunger felt like, or how hunger could so completely affect a person's thought process— until he smelled the meat cooking over the fire. Teancum felt the saliva drooling from his lips and his stomach wrench in knots as he watched the bandit carefully sprinkle salt and turn the cooking meat on a spit over the fire. He suddenly felt cold and dizzy. There was a pounding in his head right behind his eyes, and he was breathing heavily. "Something is happening to me…, what is it?" He quickly realized something was very wrong and he questioned what it could be. Closing his eyes he tried to calm his body and reflect more on his medical education. "This must be the effects of stress and a lack of food." He remembered the teachings of his instructors about dealing with people who are affected by famine, war victims, or someone suffering from a lack of proper nutrients. *Yes, the shaking, dizziness and headaches… Of course! I need food and rest.* Teancum reflected more on his current situation. *My teachers told me the body does not react well when you are under extreme stress and lacking food, water and proper rest; I understand that now.* Considering this to be very useful information which may come in handy later, Teancum logged this into his memory. Knowing what was causing his body to react this way was very useful for Teancum. He knew, under the circumstances, it was natural and completely unavoidable. Now he knew what to expect if it ever happened again, and he could accept it, work around it and continue trying to solve the problem at hand.

As Teancum was trying to form a workable strategy in his mind, one of the bandits got up from his sitting position and started to walk toward his hidden location. Teancum grabbed for the hilt of the long knife tucked in his belt, and held his breath.

"Where are you going?" the older bandit called out to the man who stood up. Teancum saw the questioning bandit was much older than the others and seemed to be in charge.

"I need to use the bathroom," the walking criminal responded, with contempt in his voice. "Can I do that alone or do you need to follow me for this, too?"

As he walked away from the rain cover, Teancum could see this man had long hair and was missing a tooth. A shot of hot emotion burst across his mind as Teancum remembered this was the same man who killed Pilio.

There was tension in his voice as the bandit continued to walk toward Teancum's location, while fussing with the leather ties holding his breeches up. He was complaining about getting wet from the rain, the problems he was having untying the straps on his breeches, and just about everything else in his life. The man stopped a few feet away from Teancum and began to relieve himself on the bushes in front of him.

As Teancum tried to hold perfectly still, one of his past medical lessons flashed in his mind. It was the teachings about the human eye and its range of vision. Suddenly a plan of attack formed in his mind. *It's dark enough now, and if I quietly get in behind him as he walks back to the camp, and stay low enough, he will not see me and his body will block the view of the others from seeing me.* Teancum felt a surge of energy as he quietly pulled the knife out, holding it in his right hand. *I can deliver a death stroke to the standing bandit from behind then quickly move on the other two before they can react.* He had a working plan, now, but did he have the courage to execute it?

The bandit finished urinating and worked to re-secure the ties to his pants. *It's now or never, Teancum.* He tried mentally to encourage himself to make his move. *You must do this to save your daughter. She will die by their hands…or worse, live a life of slavery and pain if you don't act now.*

The bandit turned and started to walk back as a large bolt of lightning lit the cliff face like the noon day sun. The bandit stopped walking and looked up in the sky at the lightning.

Now! Go now! Teancum knew the clap of thunder would closely follow and cover any sounds of him moving from the trees and in behind the bandit. Crouching as low as he could, Teancum held the knife out in front of him as he stepped carefully and quickly toward the bandit. The burst of thunder shook the ground after the lightning; it was an awesome display of nature's power. The bandit did not expect such an overpowering sound and flinched from the explosion of noise while covering his head.

Teancum was single-minded in his actions. Focused, he ignored the thunder as he set himself perfectly behind the bandit and readied himself for the killing strike. As the bandit moved back toward the camp, Teancum could see the man's back. In an instant, his mind's eye could see the man's rib cage and lungs as if it was a medical display during one of his classes. He suddenly realized if he turned his blade flat, he could stab between the ribs protecting the lungs. With one of his lungs pierced, he would lose the ability to call out to his friends for help, but he also knew this move alone may not cause a fatal injury, or incapacitate the enemy fast enough. Then he saw in his mind's eye the man's kidneys below the ribs, resting on either side of his spine, in the lower back just above the hips. He knew there was a major artery attached to the kidney and the kidney itself is full of blood. A well-placed stab wound to one of the kidneys would be a death blow. It would be very painful and would give the man the ability to warn his friends before he died. *First the lung, then the kidney.* The voice in his head put it all together for him. Crouching low and ready like a jungle cat, Teancum moved closer to the bandit and readied himself for the killing strike.

"Wow, did you guys hear that?" The walking bandit recovered from the thunder and called out to his friends.

"No, we missed the entire thing," the older man responded sarcastically

216

while chucking a small piece of wood into the fire. "I guess we were too far away to see or hear anything." The man cooking the rabbit sat down by the older bandit, then the two men had a quick laugh at the third's expense.

Shaking his head and snorting at the response from his cohorts, the approaching bandit had no idea Teancum was positioned behind him as he moved toward the shelter.

There was another crack of lighting and explosion of thunder. Teancum was moving before he realized what was happening. Three small steps and he was at the man's back. With his left hand, he reached up and grabbed a large hand full of the man's shoulder-length hair to stop him from moving forward. At the same time, he drove his knife into the man's ribs. With the blade turned flat, Teancum felt it slide right past the protective bone and deep into the right lung. Stunned by the sudden and overwhelming pain, the bandit's body stiffened as he gasped for air. Quickly, Teancum pulled out the knife and drove it again into the man's lower back, right into his kidney. Pulling out the knife, Teancum let go of the bandit's hair and pushed him forward toward his unsuspecting companions.

The two other men were still sitting under the tarp when the third man fell face first into the fire, knocking over the metal cooking pots and spilling the hot food onto the ground. They both pulled their feet out of the way and looked up to see Teancum standing over them with a bloody knife in his hand. Teancum's eyes were wide open and aflame with rage, his body was surging with adrenaline, burning up any stored oxygen he had left in his blood supply. He was shaking again, and gulping air in large quantities through his mouth to compensate. He looked like a madman standing over their fallen comrade. It only took the two remaining bandits a few seconds to realize what was happening. They quickly recovered from the shock of seeing their partner suddenly fall dead and a wild man standing over his body. The closest one to Teancum moved to grab his sword while the other man, rolled to his left to make distance. Teancum instinctively kicked the closest man in the face, knocking him senseless, then stepped over him and tried to stab at the second man as he rolled away. The second bandit was temporarily stunned and landed next to the fire as the last criminal was able to move quickly enough to avoid Teancum's blade. *He is quick for an old man,* Teancum thought as he adjusted his feet and turned back to deal with the bandit he kicked. Teancum saw him sit up and shake his head while spitting out three broken teeth. This man saw Teancum looking at him and tried to lunge for his sword again. As the man moved, Teancum dropped down on his back with both knees. The bandit cried out in pain as Teancum felt several of the man's ribs break under his weight. Teancum was in the thick of bloodlust now. He had lost control of his emotions as the dark animal instincts buried deep inside every person's subconscious were now in full display. Screaming savagely, Teancum's arms flailed as he struck the man with his knife, in his back and neck, with wild and uncontrolled abandon.

The third bandit had rolled away from his weapons and began to search for something he could use to defend himself from the crazed attacker. Seeing a large branch by the wood pile, he moved to grab it. As he pulled the branch from the pile he bumped up against the body of Teancum's baby girl. She had been asleep and woke up to the noise and disruption. Looking around, she saw Teancum attacking the first bandit and cried out, "Daddy!"

Teancum heard her pleas and stopped his murderous onslaught. Turning to face his child, Teancum saw the last bandit coming at him swinging the large branch. At the final second, Teancum managed to get his arm up to try to deflect a blow to his head. The branch crashed into his forearm, splitting the skin wide open and knocking Teancum off the mortally injured bandit. The branch broke into three different pieces and the last bandit was again without a weapon. Teancum rolled off the dying bandit and still holding the bloody knife, he tried to stand up but the blow from the tree branch had jarred him and he was off balance. Seeing his strike with the branch did not stop Teancum, the old and cagey criminal dropped what remained of the branch to the ground and started to backpedal. As he was trying to make some distance between himself and the unknown assailant, he saw Teancum wobble on his feet and took advantage of it. Diving for his own pack, the bandit grabbed a long, curved knife from his own possessions and quickly jumped back to his feet.

The rain was getting heavier as the voice of his child echoed in his ears. Between the blow to his head, the rush of emotions, and the stress of the last two days, Teancum's mind was starting to fall apart. He shook his head several times and wiped at his eyes attempting to clear away the confusion and fog in his mind.

"Daddy!"

The panicked cry from his only living child was like a distant light in the mental darkness to which he was succumbing. He felt like he was underwater, like he was trying to move with all his might, but he was heavy and slow. Everything was fuzzy and moving in slow-motion.

"Daddy, please!"

Her voice, was clearer now, more distinct. He tried to focus from where it came. There were images flashing across his mind. Shadows and light, movement and contrast. He tried harder to focus and balance himself.

The last surviving bandit heard the child's plea for her father and it suddenly dawned on him who he was facing. He quickly changed tactics. Instead of facing the stranger in mortal combat, he moved toward the little girl. He was the last one of his gang alive, and this madman had single-handedly killed all the others. He did not know the stranger's skill-level at hand fighting and, considering he just took out two of his clansmen, and most likely the boy he left to watch the trail, he was not about to find out. He also quickly figured if this was the man's daughter, then he was the rich landowner and would probably pay a ransom for his child's return. He moved to the wood pile and grabbed little Carra by her hair. She screamed in pain, as he jerked her up to her feet. Her cry of agony brought Teancum out of his haze. He turned and saw the bandit dragging his child away from him through the mud. The poor girl desperately tried to reach out to Teancum with one hand while screaming, "Daddy, help me!" and holding her hair with the other.

Teancum took three steps forward and the bandit yelled out, "Back!" The man had his own knife in his other hand and waved it at Teancum. As the bandit moved the child farther from camp, he realized Teancum had moved and was now blocking the path back to the trail, his only avenue of escape. Teancum quickly figured this out and kept side -stepping to counter the kidnapper's move.

"Let her go!" Teancum shouted, as he held his knife out in front of him, pointing it at the old bandit. The way off the cliff was blocked now, so, in a panic, the bandit looked behind him. He could barely make out the cliff ledge and the open blackness below it. Smiling, he knew what to do. Jerking again on Carra's hair, he pulled her up to his face. "He will negotiate for your life when he sees you clinging to the edge," he smiled and whispered under his breath. The bandit took two more steps toward the drop off, pulling Carra with him. Teancum saw what was happening, and he knew he needed to change his tactics if he was going to save Carra. He had lost the element of surprise and the bandit now had the upper hand. Teancum knew he could not get any closer without risking Carra's safety. Quickly looking around the simple campsite, Teancum spied the exact thing he needed. It was a short hunting bow made of wood and bone, and a quiver full of black arrows leaning against one of the bandit's packs. Teancum dropped his knife and quickly picked up the bow and quiver of arrows. He looped the quiver over his shoulder and head and nocked one of the arrows into the bow string. He felt the tension on the string and wondered if this cheaply-made weapon would suffice. Teancum was an expert with his bow, but this was not one of Teancum's expensive steel bows or handmade arrows. He had left those in the smoldering ruin he had once called his home.

The bandit reached the edge and was looking over the side of the cliff and struggling to control Carra at the same time when the first arrow sailed past his head missing by less than three feet. The arrow cut through the rain and swooshed past his face, dropping harmlessly out of sight, lost forever into the blackness. The bandit could not believe his eyes as he turned around to see Teancum fumbling as he tried to load a second arrow. It looked like Teancum's left wrist had been slapped by the bowstring when he fired the first arrow. Between the pain to his wrist and the dump of adrenaline, he was having a hard time holding the bow still while he set the second arrow.

"Stay back! I'll kill her, I swear it. I'll slit her neck, then drop her off this cliff!" The bandit still had a large clump of her hair in his left hand, and with the other, holding the sharp blade of his long knife against her neck.

"You let her go!" Teancum shouted over the pounding rain. He was now full of hate and long past the point of exhaustion, so his words were garbled. He got the second arrow set and pulled back on the bow. He was trying to aim the arrow for the bandit's head, but the pouring rain was mixing with the blood from his head wound and getting into his eyes.

"Put the bow down and step back!" the murdering criminal demanded. "You shoot me with that arrow and I will take her with me." He jerked Carra up by the hair and moved her even closer to the edge. "Do it! Now!"

Carra screamed as she was shoved to within inches of the dark drop-off. "Daddy!" she cried out again while reaching for her father.

"Shut your mouth!" The bandit hit Carra in her back with his knee and brought the knife closer to her skin. Teancum readjusted his footing and tried to close the distance but the bandit saw him moving. "You think I'm fooling around?" He pushed the curved blade into Carra's skin causing it to bleed. Carra felt the cut on her neck and she cried out in pain. "Daddy! Please help me!"

"I'll kill you! I swear on my child's soul, I will kill you if you harm her!" Teancum was drunk with rage and had lost control. The bandit had seen this reaction a thousand times with all the people he had taken hostage or robbed. He knew he was winning the battle for control of the emotions. He knew this man would eventually make a mistake and let his guard down. Teancum was gulping for air and shaking, all clear signs his body and mind were reaching the breaking point. He was not a professional soldier who had been trained and prepared to act under this kind of stress.

The rain was coming down now in pounding sheets. There was so much water pouring down it was difficult to even breathe. Teancum's muscles were burning from holding the bowstring and aiming at the bandit. The blood was flowing freely down his forehead and into his eyes and mouth. The wet rocks were slippery and his legs were shaking from the exertion. This was it— he had reached his breaking point. The bandit saw the fire go out in Teancum's eyes and needed just one more push to get what he wanted. He jerked up hard on the child's hair and she let out another cry of pain.

"Okay, okay!" Teancum barked. He slowly released the tension on the bow string and pointed the arrow away from the bandit. "Just don't hurt her…Look, I'm putting it down!" Teancum dropped the bow and arrow on the rocks in front of him.

"Move away!" The bandit demanded as he pointed back to the area by his dead comrades. This allowed Teancum to get a much better look at the shape of the blade in the bandit's hand. The curved snake-like shape of the metal and the open mouth of a serpent on the hilt identified it as a Nehor assassin's blade. Teancum's body seized as his mind instantly flashed back to the shrine of memory for his dead father at the ranch.

If you see a man with a weapon like this, he could hear his grandfather Pilio's voice in his mind as he reflected on the past, *you kill that man. He is an assassin for the Sons of Nehor and this is their weapon. This blade killed your father.* Pilio would show it to young Teancum and recount the story of how his father was murdered. Teancum's memory had missed nothing; he knew every line and curve on the blade. Every bit of detail on the hilt, the weight, the length, how it felt in his hands, all of it was burned into his memory. *You kill them, Teancum,* Pilio's voice echoed in the rain. *You kill every last Nehor scum walking the earth!* His grandfather was a kind and peaceful man, but when it came to the Nehor brotherhood, Pilio was transformed to the young and brash soldier of his youth. They had taken so much and caused so much pain to his family. To Pilio, the Nehor were lower than insects and should all be exterminated.

There was another crack of lighting and burst of thunder. Teancum's heart, mind, and spirit were broken, there was no more emotion left in him. He stood frozen, facing the killer, who still held his child, unable to move. Then he heard his only living child scream again and everything went black.

"I said move over there!" the man holding Carra shouted as he waved the Nehor blade in the air.

"That's an interesting knife you have," Teancum said, completely void of emotion.

"What?"

"Your knife," Teancum pointed to the bandit's hand and spoke in a clear and even tone. "I have only seen one like it once in my life." He took two steps forward.

"Stay back, or I will kill her!" There was a hint of panic in the kidnapper's voice.

"Yes… I know you will. You're a Son of Nehor, that's what you do," Teancum responded calmly, as he moved back to where the bow and arrow lay. He bent down, picked up the weapon, and loaded the arrow back onto the bow string. As he set the arrow in the bow, another image flashed in his mind of the inner workings of the human body. The image focused on the right shoulder of a man and the bundles of nerves, blood vessels and tendons connecting the muscles which make the arm work. With all his years of medical training, he knew exactly what to do and where the arrow needed to impact.

The bandit moved the blade back to the child's neck. "Are you crazy? I will kill her if you don't stand down!"

Teancum took three more steps closer to the bandit and pulled back on the bow. "She was dead the moment you took her from her own bed,"

Teancum hissed. His tone was low and even. The bandit's eyes suddenly grew wide and full of terror as Teancum quickly took aim and let the arrow fly. The large, black, arrow split through the wet night air flying fast and true. It struck the bandit hard and buried its wide metal point deep into the bandit's right shoulder, exactly where the arm meets the chest. The damage was instant and blindingly painful. Teancum's arrow very effectively rendered the bandit's arm useless. The nerves and tendons controlling the movement of his hand and arm were all severed. Crying out in pain, the bandit dropped the large snake-shaped knife and let go of Carra. Carra felt the tension release on her hair and she tried to stand up to get away. Stumbling back to the edge of the cliff, the bandit quickly lost his footing on the wet rocks and started to fall over the side. Teancum saw Carra was still in great danger. He dropped his bow and moved to grab Carra away from him. Spinning and twisting his one working arm in the air, the bandit cried out and desperately tried to keep from falling. With one last grasp before he fell over, the bandit reached out and caught the corner of Carra's sleeping gown in his left hand. Her little body was no match for the forces of gravity. Whatever hope the bandit placed on using her as an anchor to keep him from falling were dashed as gravity took over and both of them went over the side. Teancum could see all this happening in slow motion. He was moving as fast as he could to get to her before she fell. Screaming, 'No!' and jumping at the last possible second, Teancum reached out and over the side of the high cliff in a desperate attempt to catch Carra. Against all odds, he managed to grab her arm just before she was out of reach. With his other hand, he frantically grasped for a handhold and dug his toes and knees into whatever nook or cranny of rock he could find, but it was useless. On the flat, wet rock surface, the incredible weight of both his child and the bandit was slowly pulling him toward the edge, Teancum was slipping toward his doom. Finally, just as his head and shoulders were dangling over the edge, Teancum was able to find and grasp a leverage hold in the rocks with his fingertips and stop his deadly progression over the ledge. Readjusting his legs to gain better control, he looked down and could see his child, screaming in pain and begging for him to save her. The bandit was still desperately clinging to the bit of nightgown in his good hand and kicking his legs to try to reach the cliff face. Teancum had her arm in his hand, but the rainwater and weight from both her and the bandit made the grip impossible to hold for long.

"Find a foothold!" Teancum shouted down to the bandit. "Stop jerking her around; I can't hold much longer!"

"Daddy, please don't let me fall! I don't want to die!"

"I have you, my princess… I won't," he groaned under the strain, "let you fall!" As the bandit kept trying to reach the cliff face with his legs, the nightgown was starting to tear away from her body. Teancum cried out under the exertion of holding both his daughter's and the bandit's dangling bodies with only one hand.

The bandit was able to find a small outcropping of rock and he got one foot on it. While pushing up on his foot, he pulled on the nightgown with his good arm and was able to balance himself on the tiny ledge.

Teancum felt the bandit's weight release from his hold and shouted down, "Let her go, Nehor!"

"Then what?" The bandit laughed and winced in pain. The pounding rain and booming thunder made it hard to hear. He looked up at Teancum as he held his balance on the rock and onto Carra's gown at the same time.

"Then you will face justice for what you have done!" Teancum bellowed.

"Justice? Whose justice? *Your* justice?" He laughed. "Your God's justice, the Judges?" His lunatic laugh echoed off the cliff face as he shook Carra by her gown. More of the fabric gave and she screamed out again. "I am a Son of Nehor and I only answer to my clan," the murderer shouted back in defiance. The old, wounded bandit winced again in pain and looked at the arrow still protruding from his shoulder. Looking around at his situation and then down into the darkened abyss below, the criminal suddenly became very calm and smiled. He had made his decision. Looking back up at Teancum, the two enemies made eye contact, and the bandit took a deep breath. "Let me show you Nehor justice." He smiled and pushed up on the one foot standing on the slight rock ledge. Letting go of Carra's gown he quickly reached up and grabbed a handful of her hair and violently jerked it down. Teancum felt and heard the bones in her little neck break. The tension in her arm suddenly loosened and her eyes rolled back into her head.

"Nooo!" he howled as he watched the last of his family die before his eyes. Still screaming, he looked over at the bandit.

"I pledge my life to the Sons of Nehor!" He shouted, as he let go of her hair and jumped away from the ledge. Teancum watched in stunned,

shocked silence as the bandit fell into the misty blackness, lost forever in body and spirit.

Crying out in uncontrollable pain, Teancum pulled the limp body of his dead child up and into his arms. Rolling onto his side he curled into the fetal position, clutching her lifeless body in his arms, and there on the cold, jagged cliff ledge, he wept as violently the unrelenting rains around him.

There is no accounting for the time Teancum spent on the rock cliff, clutching the body of his tiny dead child in his arms, screaming and wailing. The anguish and madness which circled his every thought and emotion was without mercy. It was like the storm itself, pounding him relentlessly while overloading his mind with bright hot flashes of despair and thunderous claps of soul-crushing pain. Teancum had no one left. His entire family had been murdered by those god-forsaken Sons of Nehor. First his father, so long ago, then the raid on the ranch, and now the last of his bloodline lay dead in his arms, murdered by a Nehor inches away from Teancum's reach. Carra had begged Teancum not to let her die, but he had failed her, his smallest child. He had failed them all. He had been too busy, too engrossed in his own pride and the affairs of men to be there for his wife and other children when the bandits came. In the end, he had failed to save his last child on the cliff. In the echoes of the thunderstorm he could hear her frail voice pleading to him over and over to save her. Madness gripped him as he finally sat up and looked around for the child who was calling for him, only to be again destroyed emotionally when he realized he was still holding her lifeless body. Everything began to spin and he collapsed.

Teancum was exhausted to the point of paralysis, and breathing was all he could manage. He lay on the cliff's edge, his thoughts swimming with the overwhelming guilt of complete failure, as the faint and almost unrecognizable whispers echoed in his mind. It was more of a feeling than a comprehension of words. The pain gave way to darkness and the words came again more clearly and more understandable. *Kill yourself. You have failed everyone, including yourself— the pain and suffering is not going to go away as long as you live. End it now.*

"No!" he cried out to his faceless tormentor. "No!" Only the darkness heard his cries. Only the storm bore witness to the pain.

What is the point of going on? You have lost your entire family, your home is in a smoldering ruin, your fortune stolen, and you will only be a burden to those who claim to care for you… Why fight it?

"You are wrong!" Teancum shouted back to the shadows dancing around him. Struggling, he sat up and turned his head to search the darkness for the voice. The thunder roared and lightning continued to crackle across the sky.

Who says I'm wrong, your God? Is this the same God who allowed an innocent child to die at the hands of a murderous band of thugs? Look at her!

Teancum looked down at the lifeless face of his daughter still in his arms. The rain had soaked her hair and the bright bursts of lightning showed the paleness of her skin. He was a physician; he knew what death looked like.

"No!" he cried out. "I must not blame God for this— I cannot!"

It's not God's fault, there was a hint of mocking in the tone from the dark and cold voice as it continued. *All of this is* your *fault.*

The tears came again in large drops as Teancum choked back his emotions. "Yes," he said, raising his face up toward the sky. "This… This is my fault." He pulled little Carra to his chest and held her tightly. "Why should I live, when the innocent die because of my failures?"

Looking back down at his child, he remembered her bright smile and deep blue eyes. *Gone forever.* The voice interrupted his memory. He gently rested his daughter's head on the rock surface and brushed the long, blonde hair from her face.

"Forgive me, my child," he begged, as he kissed her cheek one last time.

You know what you must do now? The voice was bolder and more demanding.

"Yes. I must atone for the lives lost because of my inabilities, my weakness, my failures."

And how are you going to do it? The dark presence boldly goaded Teancum to answer. He felt the presence closer now, almost standing right behind him.

"With my life," Teancum responded, while trying to stand up. His body was in bloody shambles. His clothing was torn and he had not slept in more than two days. Following the tracks in the jungle, dealing with the bandits and then being drug across the rocks while trying to hold his child from falling over the cliff, had left him covered in cuts and bruises. Everything hurt. Every inch of his body was in pain, but his heart ached the most. Struggling to move, Teancum winced and cried as he tried to stand up. "With my life," he said again, as he finally stood straight and looked out over the edge of the cliff into the black nothingness. He failed to even notice the rain had stopped.

Shuffling to the very edge of the cliff, a defeated Teancum looked to the eastern horizon. He could barely make out the first gray lights of dawn pushing through the rain clouds.

The start of the first day without your family, your fortune or your honor. Do you want to live through this? The voice was speaking in an almost conversational tone now.

"No..."

Then do it...Do it! A shout from the depth of his mind caused Teancum to blink several times and start to lean over the edge. Looking down to the bottom of the cliff, he could make out the trees and rocks below.

My love...? A familar whisper on the breeze blew past him.

"Hanni?" There was a spark of hope. He quickly stopped himself and turned to look back behind him. All he saw was his child's lifeless body, lying on the ground.

Your wife is dead, and it's all your fault. You failed her and your entire family. Now jump! the dark voice demanded.

Teancum's lips quivered as he once again felt the pain come rushing back. Turning his back on his dead daughter's body, he mumbled, "I'm so sorry... Forgive me." Holding his hands out to his sides, Teancum looked up and closed his eyes. Facing oblivion, he took a long cleansing deep breath, exhaled and whispered, "I'm ready." He then started to lean over the edge of the cliff, to accept his fate and fall to his death.

Daddy, look!

It was his daughter's voice...Carra's voice. Stunned, Teancum caught himself before he fell over the side and opened his eyes. Startled, he quickly checked his surroundings. Off in the far eastern distance, there was a speck of bright orange light no bigger than the head of a pin coming over the mountains and through the clouds. Teancum straightened himself up and focused on the light. For a second, he almost forgot what he was about to do and concentrated on the growing light coming from the east. The bigger the light grew the more he wanted to look at it. The more he looked at the light, the better he felt. Suddenly, the morning sunlight broke over the mountains and exploded across the valley with fire and color. The sun was no longer covered by rain clouds or hidden behind the great eastern mountains. It was announcing to every living creature who the master of the day was. The emptiness of the night had been defeated once again, and all things— darkness, shadows, the cold, the misery, all things shunning the power and majesty of the light— were sent scurrying to their hiding places.

Teancum was so overcome by euphoria at what was unfolding before his eyes, he began taking great breaths of air. A warm and fresh blast of wind blew into his face. The birds started to sing, as if on cue from the sun itself. Lowering his hands, Teancum took two steps back from the ledge.

What are you doing? The voice sounded different now. There was less confidence in the tone and a hint of desperation. *You want to live through your shame?*

Teancum started to feel the panic, pain and helplessness well up inside of him again. He took one step toward the cliff when a second warm breeze blew into his face. This time there was a scent of blossoms in the air. Teancum recognized the fragrance. It was a flower his wife had dearly loved; they were planted all over the ranch, they adorned the kitchen and great hall. Then he felt her presence. She was there, he knew it. Not in the flesh, but he could still feel her close to him, and his children too. Spinning around, Teancum expected to see them standing right behind him, but there was nothing. He started to get angry, but those feelings ceased as he felt Hanni's hand brush across his face. Only she had touched him like that.

'Hanni!" he cried out and turned all the way around again, checking for her presence by his side. Still nothing. "Why are you here?" Teancum thought he was going mad and this was the price he must pay for his failure. Crying great sobs, he yelled out, "God of my fathers… Help me!" Teancum wanted to run and jump off the cliff. He wanted to end the pain. The voices in his head, both gentle and dark, filled his thoughts with chaos and peace, warring with each other for control of his mind. Slamming both palms of his hands against his ears, Teancum screamed in pure agony, "This has to end!"

He turned back to face the edge of the cliff, stepping toward his doom when he had the unmistakable feeling of Hanni's arms around his neck and shoulders, hugging him from behind like she always did. Then he felt his daughters all clinging to him, one around his waist and one on each leg. Teancum was paralyzed with overwhelming joy. The euphoric feelings left him breathless and crying. He could almost make out the angelic forms of his young family surrounding him with love and devotion, doing all in their heavenly power to keep him from jumping to his death.

Live for us, Hanni's gentle voice rang in his ear. *Live for us and live for justice!*

Moments, frozen in time, flashed before his eyes. Growing up on the ranch, being with his mother, his grandparents, who loved him so much, the day he saw Hanni and spilled the drink in the dance hall, their grand wedding, the birth of his children. Like explosions of light and sound, these memories of happiness and joy unfolded before him. Teancum slowly backed away from the edge but not under his own power. Someone or something was gently moving him back from the edge of oblivion— back to reality, back to life.

Live for us… Live for justice. The sweet sound of Hanni's voice blew across his mind like a summer breeze. In the very far distance he could hear his daughter's' laughter ringing in the trees. They all called out, "We love you, Daddy." And then they were gone.

"Live for justice…" He mouthed the words, as his voice cracked from the horrors of the last few days. "I must live for justice." Mustering the last of his reserve energy, Teancum limped back to the campsite where the other bandits lay dead. As he moved, his head was spinning and he was becoming dizzy. He reached the campsite and stood looking at the dead bodies of the men who murdered his family. Looking back over his shoulder, he could see the body of his youngest child still lying on the rocks. His chest tightened upon seeing her lifeless form. Sharp pain shot from his heart and throughout his entire body.

You see this knife… You kill the man holding it. All Nehors are monsters and must be destroyed! The words of his beloved Grandfather rang out from the trees.

"How could this happen to them!?" He cried out. Teancum's mind searched for a rational thought to cling to, but there was nothing. At that point, everything started to whirl around him. Ten different voices were shouting at him now. Some in his mind and others coming from the shadows. He held his hands over his ears and screamed for the madness to stop. He gasped for breath, but instead bent over and vomited on the ground. Instinctively, he tried to stand and move away from the mess he had made and gulped for air, but after only two steps, his body collapsed and came crashing down on the wet, muddy grass. Teancum was unconscious before he even hit the ground.

CHAPTER TWELVE

A BLESSING AND A CURSE

The sun was starting its afternoon descent toward the western horizon when Teancum regained consciousness. Merely trying to open his eyes and focus his vision was an exhausting task. It took him several minutes to simply move his head. His tongue was glued to the roof of his mouth from the lack of hydration. Every bone in his body ached. After several more minutes of lying on his back and breathing, he was able to roll to one side and sit up. Bellowing in pain as he moved, Teancum tried to stand but struggled to find the strength. Looking around, he noticed one of the dead bandit's packs was not far from him. Rolling over onto his stomach, Teancum reached out and grabbed the shoulder strap of the pack and pulled it closer to him. Fighting back the urge to shout out in pain, Teancum rummaged through the pack, looking for anything that might be useful or help him recover from his injuries. He found, tied to the side of the pack, a half-empty water skin. Teancum gulped down the entire contents of the skin then violently coughed as some of the water went down the wrong way. Grabbing his ribs, he whimpered from the physical anguish. After he recovered, Teancum spilled the rest of the contents of the pack on the ground and sifted through them. Pushing some soiled clothing aside, he found a pouch full of dried fruits and nuts and took a large handful, putting it into his mouth. Chewing slowly, trying not to aggravate his chapped lips, Teancum savored the combination of tastes and swallowed hard to get it all down. It was surprising to him how much better he now felt after drinking all the water and eating just a mouthful of food. Teancum popped a second handful of the mix into his mouth, chewed and swallowed. Wishing he had another drink of water to wash the bits of food in his mouth down, Teancum rolled onto his other side to see if he could find an additional water skin. He could see one lying on the ground next to the fire pit, but it was too far away for him to reach. He would need to get up and move several feet to reach it. Frustrated he could not get up yet, Teancum rolled onto his back. He lay still, with his eyes closed, slowly breathing and quickly fell back asleep.

When he woke again, the sun was still high in the sky but it was closer to late afternoon. Teancum calculated he had been asleep for about two hours as he tried to sit up again. His sight was still blurry, so he blinked and rubbed his eyes to try to get them to focus. From the corner of his eye he caught movement in the sky. Using his hand to shield the sunlight from his eyes, Teancum looked up. He saw several large carrion birds circling above. He laughed out loud when he thought about how disappointed they must be, discovering he was alive and not going to be their evening meal. "Not today." he shouted and laughed to himself as he rubbed his eyes, trying to clear the fog in his mind. Suddenly, the image of his child's tiny, lifeless body lying on the rocks, with buzzards all around it flashed before him. Blocking all the pain he felt, Teancum was up and on his feet in a flash, moving as fast as his damaged feet and legs would go. After tripping and almost collapsing twice, Teancum rushed to her body, picked up the Nehor bow he had left lying on the ground the night before. He held it up high over his head and shouted while he shook the bow in the air, daring the birds to try to get closer.

After a moment, he realized the large birds had soared higher in the sky or left altogether. Lowering the weapon, Teancum turned back to look at the body of his child and considered his circumstances. He thought about the long climb up the mountain trail he had made to try to rescue her and the condition of his body now. "I don't know if I can take you with me, baby girl, but I can't leave you here, either," he spoke out loud to the body of his child, while keeping one eye on the large menacing birds overhead. His heart broke all over again, thinking about the pain of losing his family. Wiping the tears from his eyes, Teancum resolved to find a way to honor his child's death. "If the buzzards don't get you, then the forest animals surely will." He looked back at the camp and the stiff bodies of the dead bandits he'd killed the night before. "Don't really care what happens to you," he thought out loud, then looked back down. "But you, my little one. I will make a grand funeral pyre for you."

Resolved to honor the memory of his child the only way he could, Teancum walked the distance back to the camp and grabbed one of the bandit's blankets off the ground. He moved back to Carra's body, wrapping her tightly in the blanket. Teancum found a small hand axe stuck in a log near a large pile of wood. He cut several branches from a large tree growing near the side of the cliff, then covered her body with the branches. "That should keep the birds away while I finish building the pyre for you, my dear," he said as he brushed off the wood chips and dirt from his tattered tunic.

As he was walking back to the pile of wood to put the axe back where he found it, Teancum had a sudden moment of clarity. He looked at the pile of wood in front of him. Given the extremely remote location, it was a rather large pile of cut wood and neatly stacked. Teancum looked down at the axe in his hand. "And there was an axe?" he questioned out loud. Something was not right with this. He was still in a mental fog and extremely exhausted. He knew he was not out of danger and needed to treat his wounds, find food and more fresh water or he would soon be lying dead next to his daughter. *First things first*, he thought. Nursing his injuries, Teancum carefully moved over to where the bandits had set up the tarp to keep them out of last night's rain. Teancum found a large unopened water skin under a blanket. Checking its contents, he smelled the liquid inside and realized it was full of drinking water. "Thanks for the drink," he toasted the two dead bandits still lying on the ground as he took a big pull from the skin. Not knowing if they had carried any more drinkable water with them or when he would find a fresh supply, he capped the skin and rationed what was left.

Refreshed from the water, Teancum stood still, trying to clear his mind, but something still was not right about this place. He opened his eyes again and surveyed the area around him. For the first time, Teancum had a clear view of the location where the bandits had chosen to hole up. It was a wide and open rock face, maybe fifty feet at its widest. A several hundred-foot drop bordered on one side, and the incredibly steep continuation of the mountain rose up on the other. The path Teancum had followed up the mountain to get him to this campsite was more like a well-worn game trail than anything else. If he had not seen the bandit run from him and head up this way, he would have walked right past the trail. He saw there was only one way up and one way down.

That makes it easy to defend, he thought, as he made a mental note of the terrain. Then he noticed the cooking pots and metal meat spit with the half-cooked rabbit still on it. An image flashed in his mind of the fight he had with the bandits the night before, and how one of the bandits had fallen over the fire, crashing into the cooking pot and spilling the boiling contents all over himself. Teancum slowly walked over to the body of the bandit and saw the scald marks from the boiling water on the dead man's legs and hands. He was a physician— he knew what burn marks on exposed flesh looked like. "They were cooking dinner using metal pots and roasting meat on a spit," he whispered, while kicking the cold and dirty hunk of meat still stuck in the long metal spike. He looked at the fire pit and saw it had been hewn out of the ground then lined with large stones. The stones had black charring all over them. "This fire pit has been used before." He looked back at the wood pile. "This is not the first time the site has been used…." Then it dawned on him. *This place is a hideaway!* He felt a cold chill run up his spine. He picked up the axe, then tightened the grip on the handle. Teancum slowly turned around to take a better look at the bandit's camp site. His body still hurt, so any movement was slow and painful. Teancum looked over the grounds again with a whole new perspective. Teancum realized it was no accident the bandits came to this location. "This is a Nehor hideout."

Now he knew he could not stay, but he was in no condition to leave either. Teancum took a quick accounting of his injures by looking at the numerous cuts and bruises to his body as well as how tattered the bottoms of his feet were. Then he gingerly explored the injury to his head. He concluded he was in no shape to try to walk down the mountain or make the two-day journey by foot to civilization. *You will need at least two days to rest and recover before you can even think about walking out of here, mister.* His medical mind was in charge now and barking orders. Teancum was stuck in a place he did not want to be. Looking around at the sorry state the bandit's camp was in after the fight and thunderstorm last night, Teancum resolved to make the best of the situation.

"Yeah," he whispered, as he looked at the two bodies of the criminals he killed. Their bodies were starting to succumb to the effects of exposure and decomposition. "I need to deal with you two. If I am stuck here for a few days, I'm not going to smell your rotting flesh. And I bet if your buddies showed up, they wouldn't like the fact you are dead." Looking around, he remembered he was on a rocky surface, and there was no place to bury the bodies. He stood still, pondering what he could do to rid himself of the corpses. Then he remembered the third bandit at the bottom of the cliff. Smiling, he spoke, "Time to join your friend." Finding a section of rope attached to one of the bandit's packs, Teancum tied a quick knot around the first dead man's ankles then dragged him to the edge of the cliff. It was slow going and every step was painful, but he remained focused on the task at hand. Before he toppled the body over the cliff, he checked to see if the dead man had any useful items in his possession. He had learned his lesson from the first bandit he killed at the bottom of the trail. Teancum made a pile of the items then recalled, out loud, the things he found on the body of the bandit, "A few gold coins, some flint and steel, and a good belt." After he untied the rope from the legs of the dead man, he took off the man's shoes. Giving him a gentle nudge with his foot, the body spilled over the cliff, tumbling grotesquely to the ground below. Teancum did not look over the edge to see where the body had landed. He had seen enough blood and death already; besides, it seemed disrespectful. Coiling the rope and walking slowly to the next body, he smiled as he pondered a thought out loud, "You men burned my home and killed everyone I love. Why do I care?" He tied the second bandit's legs then started dragging him to the edge. The second man was not as big as the first bandit and Teancum was able to move him more easily. Checking this man's pockets, he found a few more coins and a small dagger. After he collected those items, and his shoes too, he sent the second body over the edge just like the first. Teancum stood still for a moment, looking out at the panoramic view of the vast green valley and span of distant mountains before him. So much had happened in the last twenty-four hours. He was bone weary. Teancum wanted to lie down and sleep for days, but he knew there was still too much he needed to do if he had any hope of surviving long enough to make it back to the life he once knew.

As he stood lost in thought, he heard the distant call of a mountain hawk in flight, and the sound of the predator bird snapped him out of his daydream and back to reality. Looking up, he saw several dark birds circling again in the sky and thought of his child still under the blanket and branches. Turning, he looked at the bundle not far from him and took in a breath of air for courage. "Okay, my little princess. It's time to send you on to be with God." Teancum was walking back toward the fire pit when he jabbed his foot on a sharp rock. The soft leather shoes he had been wearing when he took off after the kidnappers two days before had all but torn away from his feet. He hopped on one foot trying to relieve the pain. When he had calmed down, he tried on the two pairs of shoes he had taken from the dead men and found the pair which fit the best. "Another lesson learned," he thought, as he tried to walk around in a dead man's footwear. "Not the best fit, but much better than those things," Teancum lamented, as he took one last look at his expensive, but ruined shoes, then tossed them off the edge in a symbolic gesture. He stood still for a moment to log this experience away in his impressive memory, hoping he would never need to recall it again.

After a quick inspection of the ground around him, Teancum found there was a small depression in the rock surface near the very far edge of the cliff face opposite the fire pit. Teancum thought this would be the best place to build the pyre for his child. Using four fat logs from the big wood pile, the long wooden poles from the shelter, and the bandit's spears as cross sections, Teancum was able to make a fine raised bed on which to place the body of his child. He stuffed smaller sections of wood, branches and dried kindling under the bed, then larger split logs on top of them until the entire area under the raised bed was covered and ready for a spark. He placed a layer of green tree branches on the bed itself, then gently laid her body, still wrapped in the bandit's blanket, on top of the greenery. He knew the green wood would give off smoke when it was heated, but Teancum did not care. He wanted her spirit to mix with the smoke and fly high into the air. It was his last gift to his youngest child. Suddenly, he thought of something. "One last thing before I let you go, my child." Teancum pulled a long lock of her hair out away from her body, and with his knife, he cut it off. "I will put this next to your mother and sisters. Then you can all be together, I swear it," he declared as he held out the silky locks and made the pledge.

With preparations ready, all Teancum needed now was a flame to ignite the pyre. He walked back to the campfire the bandits had built last night, and using the metal tip of the axe, pushed over a log still in the pit. The fire had long gone out, but in the bottom of the pit Teancum found what he was looking for. A section of the log had broken off and it was still glowing red hot. It was no bigger than a robin's egg, but it would do the trick. Teancum took out his knife and scooped the red hot piece of wood onto the lid of the cooking pot next to the fire pit. Moving carefully and covering the ember with his hand, Teancum moved back over to the funeral pyre. He had a section all ready for the ember. Teancum had found an abandoned bird's nest. He knew it would make excellent fire tinder. He placed the glowing ember into the bird's nest, then gently blew air across the red-hot section. After several seconds of coaxing, white smoke billowed from the nest, then a small flame flickered to life. Teancum put the nest up into the stacks of wood under the raised bed and blew a little harder into the blossoming flame. With the aid of Teancum's added air supply, the flame jumped to life, spreading quickly across the tinder and dried brush he had placed in and around the smaller sections of wood.

Teancum stood back several feet as the fire spread quickly, engulfing the pyre. As he stood alone, watching the growing fire, he felt so empty, alone, and void of emotion. He was hollow inside. The only thing he felt was the heat from the flames as it reached high into the late afternoon sky. He watched as the dark smoke rose into the air and danced on the breeze. Orange sparks popped and flickered around the burning mass like fireflies. "Goodbye, little one. Daddy will always love you," he whispered. As Teancum stood his silent vigil next to the burning pyre, he lost all track of time and space. The large fire had continued to burn brightly as the hot sun set behind the western mountains and the sky turned from blue to purple and then the colors of sunset. When Teancum could no longer stand, he sat on the hard rock surface and continued to watch over the fire as it consumed everything in the pyre. Like a famished monster, the fire raged on and, before long, it started to dwindle from lack of nourishment. The sadness in Teancum's broken heart was accented by the hot flames, desperately trying to stay alive, but unable to find a reason to go on slowly flickered out.

It was now nearly dark, and Teancum was finished watching the fire. It had died down to a large pile of glowing embers. He had had enough. He stood up, slowly and carefully, wincing in pain, as his body was still complaining about the many injuries he had suffered these last two days. Teancum walked back over to the fire pit and picked up one of the light blankets the bandits had left. He whipped it in the air to free it from the dirt, then set it down on the rock surface next to the side of the mountain. Grabbing one of the packs, he moved it to the blanket, then sat down. Teancum took another handful of the nut and dried fruit mixture from the pouch he had found into his mouth and slowly chewed. His whole head ached as he tried to gently bite down and chew. He was able to swallow the mouthful and followed it with another long drink from the water skin. He put the cap back on the skin and laid his head down on the pack. Before he realized it, he was fast asleep.

The birds calling out their morning song brought Teancum out of his restless sleep. The nagging injuries were plenty to keep him from enjoying a full and restful sleep, but the nightmares and hallucinations were really driving him mad. His head was aching and his eyes were burning as he tried to open them to the morning light. He had fallen asleep on his left side. His shoulder and arm were numb from the weight of his body and lack of movement. Forcing himself to sit up, Teancum rubbed his left shoulder and tried to get his eyes to focus on his surroundings. His lips were dry and cracking and his tongue was again sticking to the roof of his mouth. *It must be from the lack of water*, Teancum concluded, as he kept trying to clear his head and get his eyes to work. He finally got some feeling back into his left arm and reached for the water skin. He popped the top and took a long drink. Putting the cap back on the skin, he coughed as some of the water went down the wrong way again. "About half left," he thought, as he shook the bag to see how much water was left inside. Teancum knew he was not going to make it with this limited amount of water. He needed to figure something out, and quickly. He also knew if he did not get the injuries to his body cleaned and dressed, the infections would kill him just as dead as dehydration. The head wound was still seeping blood but for the most part it had stopped and clotted over, but he was most concerned about his feet. "I'm not walking very far If I can't get them fixed," he laughed to himself, as he thought about all the things going wrong for him at the same time.

He sat with his back to the mountain and closed his eyes for a moment. He could feel the gentle breeze on his face. He listened to the sounds of the forest trees as they swayed back and forth in the wind. Everything was so quiet and still. He always loved the peace he found alone in the forest as well as the simple joy of sitting still and feeling nature all around him. He smiled at the irony of it all; he was truly alone, and the one time he did not want to be in the forest, here he was sitting and listening to the wind rustle through the trees.

After a few minutes of reflection, Teancum remembered the bag of dried fruit and nuts. He looked over to the pack where he left the bag of food, saw it had tipped over during the night, and some of the contents had slipped onto the ground. A colony of large black ants had found the bounty and were crawling all over the bag. One group of dedicated ants were even desperately trying to drag one of the pieces of fruit back to their home. "Hey," Teancum warned them, "get your own food." He picked up the bag, shaking it several times to get the ants off. He brushed away the few ants that were still clinging to the bag, making a quick inspection of the inside to ensure there were no more. Satisfied he was not going to accidentally eat an insect, Teancum filled his palm with the contents of the bag, then popped the fruit and nuts into his mouth. It was still very difficult for him to chew, but he was happy to have something to eat. He finished the first mouthful and poured himself a second helping. "Maybe, if I close my eyes and try not to think about it," he quipped, as he was looking at the food in his hand, "You will magically taste like eggs and breakfast meat." Snorting and smiling, he put the second handful of food into his mouth and chewed. "Nope," he mumbled with a full mouth. "Not even close." Teancum took a small sip of water to wash down the food and then tightly tied the bag of nuts and fruit so it would not spill again.

The soreness he felt today was worse than yesterday. Just trying to stand almost brought tears to his eyes. His feet were swollen and felt like he was walking on thorns. His head still ached from the blow he had taken during the fight. Groaning out loud, he managed to get to his feet and leaned back against the side of the mountain for stability. "Okay, let's figure this out," he whispered out loud. He was determined to find a way to get off the mountain alive.

Once he started to move around, the soreness in his body started to fade away, but his feet still hurt when he tried to walk. As Teancum was moving around, something on the ground near the cliff's edge was gleaming in the sunlight. It caught his attention and Teancum slowly moved toward it. When he recognized the object on the ground, his heart started racing and he felt white-hot anger inside. It was an uncontrollable and unconscious response to a learned behavior developed across the span of his entire life. At his feet was the Nehor assassins blade he had been holding against little Carra's neck before Teancum had shot him, rendering his arm useless and sending him over the edge of the cliff with Carra in tow. Teancum looked down at the blade, then over at the cold, black remains of the pyre for his child, and anger overwhelmed him once more. He reached down and picked up the weapon. Once Teancum had the knife in his hand, his first thought was how exact a replica, in every detail, this blade was of the one at the shrine on the ranch for his father. "Same weight, balance is the same…markings on the blade itself," he spoke as he inspected it and turned it over in his hand. "The same tool marks…almost an exact match in every way." Teancum was impressed the Sons of Nehor could craft such things. He thought about the broken and disfigured body of the dead assassin and his cohorts lying at the bottom of the cliff. Looking back down at the knife in his hand, he remembered all the pain this blade and its matching brothers had caused his family as well as the Nephite people. "Keep your instrument of evil!"

Teancum raised his hand to heave the long curved knife over the side, but just before he sent it flying into the sky, a thought came into his head. *Hold onto this, it might become useful.* Teancum slowly lowered his hand back down to his side. He looked again at the fire he built for his child's body and thought about the loss and tragedy which had befallen his life. He was surprised there was still emotion inside him as a single tear rolled down his face. His bottom lip started to quiver, so he gripped the handle of the blade tightly to release the frustrated feelings inside him.

Justice. The lone word came through the camp on the morning breeze and penetrated his very soul. He stood completely still and did not even breathe. Did he just hear that, or was he hallucinating again and going mad? He looked back down at the Nehor blade in his hand.

Justice, the voice repeated. Now he knew he had heard it. It was a man's voice. Strong and firm, but something about it rang familiar to Teancum. He had heard this voice before, but where? His sharp mind started racing through its memory trying to remember where he had heard it. Teancum turned around just to assure himself there was no one standing next to him. Then it dawned on him where he had heard that voice before. "The rocks by the crossroad… Courage!" He was excited now. "Father, can you hear me?" He was silent and still waiting for a response. But nothing came. It did not matter to Teancum. He was elated. "Yes, Father, I will. I will find justice for you and for our family." Teancum held out the long knife in front of him. "I swear to you, Father, on my honor, and on the memory of my children. Those who are responsible, the Sons of Nehor, they will know true justice by my hand."

There was a fire burning inside him now. A hot flame in his soul, a reason to fight and go on living. A single defining purpose to his life. Teancum was going to find the bandits and kill them all.

He tucked the curved Nehor knife back into his belt and started to walk carefully back to the fire pit and his bed. As he was walking, he noticed something was not right about a bush against the side of the mountain, not far from where he was sleeping.

What is this? he questioned. Still moving slowly, but with more determination, Teancum limped toward the bush. The closer he got to the bush, the more he was disgusted he had not seen it before now. *Just like the wood pile, and the fire pit, all hidden in plain sight. I guess the eyes see what they want to see.* This was another lesson he filed away in the back of his mind.

He moved up next to the large bush and realized the problem. *This bush is dead,* Teancum thought. *It has been propped up against the side of the mountain for some time… But why?* Teancum grabbed the bush with one arm and gently pushed it aside. As the bush slowly toppled over, it revealed an opening in the rock face, dug into the side of the mountain. The opening was about the size of a wagon wheel. Teancum took two steps back then crouched over to get a better view inside the opening. Looking inside, Teancum could see the opening went back about three feet and then it expanded into a large room. "It's some kind of cave," he whispered. The entrance was a rough circular shape and Teancum inspected the tool marks on the side of the entrance wall. "Someone dug this out." He squinted as he looked deeper into the opening. "Light… there is a shaft of natural light inside the cave." Teancum looked up toward the top of the mountain and thought, *There must be a hole or something near the top of the mountain letting in the light.* As he kept trying to look inside, Teancum heard the soft echoing of running water coming from inside the cave. When he heard the sounds of the water coming from deep in the cave, Teancum licked his dry lips and resolved to go inside to investigate. Looking around, then behind him, Teancum remained hunched over and carefully shuffled his way into the opening, exacerbating his injuries. After five or six short steps, Teancum was past the opening and was able to stand to his full height. The light coming in from the hole in the roof of the cave was weak, but improving. Teancum rubbed his eyes and blinked several times to allow his vision to adjust. It was much cooler inside the cave than out on the ledge. Looking around, he could not believe his eyes. He suddenly realized the great danger he was in by being there.

Stacked along the far wall of the cave were several wooden crates and liquid-filled kegs. Near the last keg was a large stalagmite hanging down from the cave roof with a steady flow of water dripping from it. The water was pooling in a naturally formed basin cut from the rock floor. Eons of constant dripping filled it with what appeared to be clean, clear drinking water. When Teancum saw the water, his body instantly reacted to his need for hydration. He took two steps toward the pool before he realized he was moving. He knelt down next to the water and took a small scoop in his hand. Bringing the scoop up to his nose, he sniffed the water to try to detect any rancid odors. Not smelling anything, Teancum took a small sip and let it sit in his mouth. The water was not acidic or salty; it had a slight, sweet taste to it. Swallowing the small amount, Teancum waited to see if his body would reject the water and belch it back up. Based on some of his research as a physician, Teancum knew that the water coming out of the rock was probably very clean, but if he was going to drink it in any quantity, it still needed to be boiled. In his weakened state, he was going to be cautious, and not drink directly from the pool. Teancum stood and looked over the crates stacked against the cave wall. The lids on the crates were not secured so Teancum lifted the closest one to see what was inside. This crate contained four large burlap sacks, and two of them were open at the top. Looking inside the first sack, Teancum saw a large quantity of dried fruit, and he found assorted nuts inside the second. Thinking back, he remembered the small pouch full of fruit and nuts he ate earlier. *This is the same stuff,* he thought. *This place is not just a hideout, but it must be a supply station as well.* He contemplated how hard it must be to get supplies up the side of the mountain and along the trail. Grabbing a large handful of the sweet fruit, Teancum filled his mouth and chewed as he moved to the next crate.

In the next crate he found assorted clothing and all manner of footwear. He looked down at his torn and bloody tunic and the shoes he took off the dead bandit. They were both in shambles and he could not wear them any longer. Digging through the crate, he found a pullover shirt, breeches, and a very sturdy set of walking boots conveniently his size. He removed the footwear from his feet and slipped on the boots. They were snug, but already more comfortable than the fancy dress shoes he had started out in. He smiled as he checked the fit of the shoes by shifting his weight. "Much better now." He knew he needed to hurry, so he removed the dirty shirt from his back, and, tossing the clean clothing over his shoulder, he moved on to the last crate. Inside the last crate he found first aid and medical supplies, bandage cloths, needles and string for stitches, wraps and jars of pastes and creams, including healing ointment from the aloe plant. He held up one jar and smirked when he realized it was his own concoction which had most likely been stolen from a patient. He also found soap for washing the wounds. Excited, Teancum knew exactly what to do with these items. *Finally, something I can do,* he thought. Rummaging quickly through what was inside the crate, he found what he needed to start the healing process on his many injuries. He made a pouch out of his old ragged and bloody tunic, then placed all the gathered medical supplies in it. As Teancum turned to walk out of the cave, he saw several weapons leaning against the rock wall near the entrance. Looking quickly at the different types of blades, spears, war axes, and bows, Teancum quickly grabbed a large hunting bow with a quiver of arrows, a short, single edged sword, and a spear. Tucking all of the items under his arms, he bent over and shuffled through the cave entrance, back out into the sunlight.

CHAPTER THIRTEEN

THEY SEE WHAT
THEY WANT TO SEE

At first, Teancum saw only large, black and blurry spots as his eyes adjusted to the light. But as he stepped from the cave and into the bright sunlight, he realized he was not alone anymore. His heart stopped as he looked over four large and heavily armed bandits who had arrived at the hideout while Teancum was in the cave. "Blast!" The word seeped past his lips like the exhale of a breath. They looked rough and wild, and were spread out and standing at the ready position with their dangerous-looking weapons. There were three additional older Lamanite boys standing close to one of the bandits. The boys were unarmed, panting for air and carrying large, heavy loads of supplies on their backs. Their hands were tied in front of them, and a rope was wrapped around their necks forcing them into a human train. The end of the rope was in the hand of the bandit standing closest to them.

Don't panic! The voice in Teancum's head cried out. *Quickly, think!* Teancum stood up tall and straight and cleared his voice. "Oh, good." He tried to sound relieved the men were standing before him. "You have arrived."

"Who are you?" a dirty-looking man with a large beard barked back at Teancum. He was holding a scimitar most likely stolen from a wealthy Lamanite.

"The name is Boaz," Teancum replied without thinking. He took some steps to his right, set the items in his hands down by the blanket where

247

he had slept. He was not sure who these men were and tried to play it off like he belonged there. Picking up the water skin he took a long drink to buy some time so he could think.

"Boaz, is it?" the bearded man replied, sarcastically. "Well, Boaz, you look like you got beat up. Suppose you tell me what you are doing here? Speak, or I will have you gutted."

"How did I end up here?" Teancum laughed and put the cap back on the water skin. He swallowed hard to try to control his fear. "It's kind of a long story... And yes, some men did try to kill me." As he shifted his weight and moved so that the Nehor assassin knife tucked in his belt could be seen.

They all reacted when they saw it. "Oh, sir, my apologies," the rough man begged pardon as he put his big weapon back into its sheath, waving for the other bandits to lower their weapons. "We were expecting someone else, and certainly not a brother of the High Order." The other bandits looked a bit confused, so the leader gave them a quick lesson. "Men, Boaz here is a brother of the High Order. That knife in his belt is their symbol. Only true Nehors can carry that blade. Sorry, sir," the man gestured and grimaced. "Fresh recruits, they don't know nothing. Just taking them to the Gathering Grove so they can swear their loyalty to the brotherhood."

Teancum was almost dumbfounded at his stroke of good luck. These men thought he was some sort of Nehor bandit royalty. His instincts told him to go with the deceit and keep playing it cool. He took another long drink of water and quickly ran the scenario in his mind. *If I play this right, they can help me get out of here... Well, if they think I'm the boss, then I better start acting like the boss.* Teancum put the almost empty water skin down, then spoke with authority. "So, who are you?"

"Name's Akin," the older bandit answered. "I have been with the Nehors for several years now. They have me running supplies between the hideouts and the city. I recruited these three men and they are helping me transport the goods. We captured these Lamanites wandering in the wilderness. Thought we could sell them as slaves and give the earnings as tribute to the Nehor high council."

"That will please the council greatly, I can guarantee it," Teancum responded, acting like he knew the Nehor chieftains personally.

Smiling, Akin was trying to impress Teancum. "Get those packs off those dogs and move the supplies into the cave," Akin barked orders and walked over to one of the captured boys. "You!" He kicked the slave as he was trying to get his heavy pack off. "Start a fire." Akin looked back at Teancum. "Of course, with your permission, Boaz sir?"

"That's fine, I need some hot water anyway to clean my wounds." Teancum started to move back toward his pack to pick up the medical supplies. "If this is going to work, you need to act more like a cold-blooded killer," he thought to himself, "and get me some hot food!" he barked, trying to appear arrogant and evil.

Akin nodded to one of the men with him, telling him to be responsible for feeding the high ranking Nehor. The captive moved over to the fire pit and spotted the half-cooked rabbit and turned over pots.

"Akin?" he called out as he pointed to the mess.

Akin walked over to the pit and looked at the pots and rotten meat still on the cooking spike. Teancum felt fear rise in his stomach.

"Boaz, have you seen this?" Akin asked.

Quickly Teancum continued the ruse, "Yes, it's disgusting. I come here to rest and heal from fighting Nephite soldiers on the trail only to find this camp in such disrepair." He pointed to the wood pile. "No firewood," then over to the cave entrance. "and the cover for the cave is missing. I was surprised there were supplies still inside." Teancum acted like he was getting angry. "If I find out who left this camp in such a state, I will personally have them skinned."

Akin still thought Teancum was an established member of the Brotherhood and he really wanted to make a good impression. "Get this place squared away!" he yelled and waved his hands at the other men. They did not know any different so the other men reluctantly moved. After bossing the others around and shouting instructions about what needed to be done, Akin turned to look for approval from Teancum. Teancum knew what was happening and he gave him a wink and thumbs up.

Got to keep up the impression until I can find a way out of here, he thought, as he gently moved his injured body. *I am in no shape to fight, let alone sneak away.* Teancum sat down and went to work on the injuries to his feet. *Going to need you two in good shape if I am going to make a run for it,* he thought as he applied the healing salve and a light wrap to the bigger sores. As he was working on his feet, Teancum kept a close eye on the other bandits wandering around the camp. One false move and he would be discovered and killed outright. Teancum finished with his feet and took another big drink from his water skin. He knew it was only a matter of time before he was discovered. With this in mind, he slowly moved the weapons he had found in the cave closer to him. Teancum then went to work on the large wound to his head.

After Akin got the others moving and working, he wandered back over to where Teancum was sitting and watched as Teancum tried to clean off the dried blood from his head wound and apply the aloe cream. Akin winced as he watched Teancum work around the injury. "Sir, if you don't mind, can you tell me about your run-in with the Nephite soldiers? Are there more out there? Are they close by....?"

"Not to worry... Akin, is it?"

"Yes sir, Akin, named after my father."

"Well Akin, it was a small squad of five young soldiers and they were lost on the trail. I came across them and told them I was a merchant heading for Zarahemla. They asked if they could join me, so I had no choice but to play along. The first night I poisoned their leader and that forced the other four to take turns carrying him, so they were all exhausted the next night, or so I thought." Teancum smiled and pointed to the wound to his head. He smiled as he continued the lie. "When I made my move, they put up a stronger fight than I was ready for, but I got them all."

Akin looked puzzled. "You say you were on the trail heading to Zarahemla. I walk these trails all the time. I did not see any signs of a struggle."

"That's because, Mr. Akin," Teancum pulled out the Nehor blade. "I am very good at what I do." He pointed the tip at Akin. "Are you questioning my honor?"

"No, no sir." Akin quickly attempted to apologize.

"Because if I remember correctly, you said you were responsible for the care of the hideouts along this trail." Teancum looked around and over his shoulders at the camp, and the men who were working and listening to their conversation at the same time. He needed to establish dominance over Akin. "This place is in shambles. How do I know this ransacked camp is not your fault and you are trying to cover it up?"

Teancum's verbal misdirection of the topic worked. Akin was on his feet and begging with his hands clasped in front of his body.

"Please, sir, you must believe me. I am a good worker and loyal to the Sons of Nehor. When last I saw this camp, it was clean and prepared for our brothers to use."

Teancum stood up. "Well, then, Akin," he advised menacingly, while he put the assassin's blade back in his waist belt, "you need to get to work and get this camp back in to shape."

"Yes, sir!" Akin exclaimed. He quickly turned back to the men behind him and shouted orders. "You dogs get this place cleaned up. You, more firewood. You," he pointed to another man, "get those provisions stowed in the cave...and someone get Boaz some hot food!"

Teancum smiled to himself as he sat back down, contemplating the situation. *I think they have bought it, but I wonder how long I can keep this up before I am found out,* he thought. Trying not to focus on the possible danger he was in, Teancum instead spent the rest of the morning working on healing and resting. He did keep his eye on the far edge of the cliff where he had pushed the bodies of the dead bandits over the edge. If one of those other Nehors happened to look over the edge and see the bodies lying far below, he might not be able to talk or bluff his way out of the next set of questions. *I will need to keep them occupied and focused on other things until dark.* He stood up and cleared his throat loud enough for everyone to hear. They all stopped what they were doing and turned to look at him. "So, when will I get some food?"

Akin stepped up to answer. "We have no fresh meat, but we will have a pot of cooked beans ready soon, sir."

"Akin," Teancum pointed out, motioning toward the trail leading away from camp, "those woods are full of animals. Send your men out to hunt some game."

Akin pointed at the two of the three men who were closest to him. "You and you, get bows and hunt some meat. Now!" He clapped his hands together several times to motivate the men to move. The order to go out again to hunt for food was not taken well. There was some grumbling and rebellious attitude coming from the two men chosen to do the task. "You will keep those comments to yourselves, if you know what's good for you," Akin dramatically bellowed, while rocking back and forth on his heels with his hands on his hips. He looked over at Teancum to see if his display of Nehor style leadership had been noticed. Teancum, ever mindful of the charade he was playing, gave Akin an approving nod. When Akin saw the acknowledgement he beamed and smiled from ear to ear.

Teancum saw Akin's reaction. *You are going to be easy to manipulate,* he thought. *No wonder the Nehors have you doing a thankless job like maintaining their hideouts. You are not very bright and you will do anything for a morsel of praise.* Teancum logged this bit of useful information into the back of his mind and went back to tending his wounds.

It was still early when Teancum woke the next morning. He was reliving the events of the past few days in his mind as he slept and had been jolted awake when, in his dream, he was falling from the cliff where he had pushed off the other Nehors. Gasping for air and looking around in a panic, Teancum clutched his chest as the muscles tightened and he felt real fear well up inside him.

"Are you alright, sir?" One of the Nehors asked as he moved close to Teancum. It was his turn on watch and he had been sitting next to the fire with a light blanket wrapped around his shoulders when he heard Teancum rattle around in his sleep. There was a light morning breeze and Teancum felt a bit cool.

"I'm fine," Teancum responded as he blinked several times and tried to focus. "Do you have some water?"

The man handed Teancum his personal water skin and Teancum took two big drinks. Capping the water skin, he handed it back to the Nehor and said, "Thank you."

"Bad dream?"

"I'm fine," Teancum responded, annoyed, rubbing and shaking his right arm. He had been sleeping on it, and it felt numb and weak.

The fire guard looked at Teancum for several seconds and moved back to his seat by the fire without saying a word. Teancum wondered if he had offended the man and started to say something to reassure him his rude response had not been personal. But then Teancum remembered this man was a Nehor and would not think twice about killing anyone, including him and his children. In this moment, everything in Teancum's world changed. The lack of focus and pain was suddenly overshadowed by pure hatred and spite. Teancum was instantly reminded that less than a week ago he was a successful and rich judge in the city of Zarahemla, with a loving wife, three daughters and an extended family who all adored him. Now he was alone, homeless, and a broken man in mind, body and soul. It was all because of people like this man sitting by the fire with his back to Teancum, wrapped in the blanket and staring into the burning pit without a care in this world. Teancum was suddenly white hot with rage; he could feel the blood beginning to boil in his veins. Shaking, his chest expanded and contracted as his body burned oxygen. Before he realized he had moved, the large assassin blade was in his hand and he was on his feet. Visions of plunging the serpentine blade deep in the back of the wakeful Nehor played over and over in his mind. He had taken three careful steps when he stopped and looked over where the other men had been sleeping. Something was not right. A bed roll was empty; one of the men was unaccounted for. Startled, Teancum quickly checked his surroundings, but there was no one else up and moving.

"Boaz?" a voice from the edge of the bushes called out.

Teancum turned toward the sound of the voice and saw one of the other Nehors walking out of the tree line and tying up his britches. Teancum instantly realized the man was coming back into camp after relieving himself in the privacy of the undergrowth. He must have gotten up when Teancum was asleep and made his way into the brush without waking anyone. At the same time, the man in the trees had called out, the fire guard turned around and saw Teancum standing not ten feet away from him with the large assassin's blade in his hand. The fire guard was startled at the sight of Teancum behind him with the knife and he quickly stood up, pushing the blanket off his shoulders, and took three defensive steps away from Teancum. As he moved backwards, he accidentally kicked over a large cooking pot, causing it to clank several times as it hit the ground.

Oh no, Teancum thought as he suddenly realized he had been caught. *This is bad!*

"What's all the racket?" Akin bellowed as he sat up, and pushed his blanket off his body and rubbed his eyes.

Teancum and the two Nehors all stood in silence looking at each other.

"I'm not sure what's happening, boss, but it looks like Boaz was going to shank Tiptu while his back was turned." The Nehor by the tree line spoke first, pointing to Teancum, then pulled out his own short sword. The other sleeping men started to stir and wake from the noise.

Teancum felt the panic start to well up inside of him. There was no way he could fight four armed men.

"Boaz, what are you doing?" Akin pleaded. There was no way Akin wanted to accuse a ranking member of the brotherhood of something as sinister as trying to murder another Nehor without permission from the criminal council. Akin was up now and moving slowly toward Teancum with his hand on his sword's hilt.

Get angry! Those words shot across Teancum's mind as he looked around. *Turn this around on them!* Teancum stood upright, pointing the fancy assassin blade in his hand at the Nehor who had been in the bushes. "You can try to cover up your friend's mistakes as much as you want, but I saw what he did and I know the truth," Teancum stated, then turned and looked at the fire guard. "You lost control of the security of this camp and let a wounded man sneak right up next to you." The face of the fire guard went white as cotton as the blood drained. When Teancum saw the unconscious reaction on the face of the fire guard, he knew he had just tricked them again. Wanting to keep up the deception, Teancum continued in his persona as Boaz, the Nehor assassin.

"Akin!" Teancum shouted as he turned again to face the bandit leader. "What kind of rabble did you bring for the Nehors?" Teancum pointed back toward the fire guard with the blade. "I can barely walk and I managed to get close enough to stab him in the back. And you!" Teancum turned to chastise the Nehor who had caught him trying to stab the fire guard, "You accuse me of attempting murder instead of getting angry at your friend for not doing his duty and remaining vigilant while on watch!" The contempt in his voice and fire in his eyes were all for show. He knew if this did not work he was a dead man. Teancum was not sure where the next phrase came from but it made an impact on the others. "I am a Nehor assassin of the High Order!" He almost shouted while bouncing the blunt edge of the snake shaped blade off his chest for effect. "If I wanted him or anyone of you dead, you would already be done for!"

"What? Wait, no— I was alert! I was keeping an eye out for..." the fire guard stumbled with his words as he suddenly realized he was being accused of dereliction of his duty and now he was the focus of the encounter.

Teancum raised up his hand to stop the guard from continuing his justifications. "I will deal with you in a moment," Teancum spoke like a disappointed father. "But first," he turned back to Akin, "put those weapons down and step closer. I don't feel like yelling."

All of the men instinctively relaxed their postures and put their weapons down. "Look Boaz, I am sorry. But from my angle it appeared you were going to try to hurt him," the Nehor near the tree line spoke as he moved closer to the center of the camp.

"No, this is my fault." Teancum pushed his tone to an even more disappointed pitch and tucked the assassin blade back into his belt. "I assumed you all were more seasoned Nehor men." He turned to face Akin. "Akin, you are presenting these men before the brotherhood for acceptance. They are your responsibility. Clearly they are not ready or prepared. I hold *you* responsible and expect you to get them trained up in our ways." Teancum moved back to his own bedroll like he was the boss. "Since I am still too injured to travel, and I am in no hurry to leave, we might as well get started now." He changed his tune from disappointment to being slightly annoyed. "I will observe the training and give my opinion when needed." He carefully sat back down on his sleeping mat while looking up at the men standing before him. They all had a "*What just happened?*" look in their eyes as they all turned to face Akin.

"Sir— Boaz, I…?" Akin stumbled under the sudden pressure.

"Don't know where to start?" Teancum bellowed back interrupting Akin. "Let's start with breakfast. I want roasted rabbit." Teancum stared at Akin fiercely. Akin blinked several times and realized he was out of his element. He had been around other assassins, but had never interacted with one on a personal level. He knew they were not to be trifled with and surrendered to his better judgment. He also was hoping that someday his hard work in maintaining the trails and hideouts would pay off, and someone of influence within the Nehor hierarchy would recognize his contribution to the cause. That person of influence could be this wounded assassin, and he was not going to blow his chance.

"You heard the man! He wants rabbit for breakfast!" Akin turned and spat as he ordered the other men to accommodate Teancum's wishes. They all cowered and moved to do their assigned tasks, all except one. The Nehor who was using the bathroom when he saw Teancum make his move toward the fire guard stood still in a defiant posture. Akin saw the man standing like a stone and walked up to him.

"What are you doing?" Akin challenged in a whisper.

"How do we know this guy is for real?"

"He has the Nehor blade; a token of an assassin of the highest order," Akin responded. "You don't just find those lying around."

"Well, how do we know he did not steal it or take it off a dead brother?"

"Really?" Akin challenged. He wanted so desperately to be liked by the Nehor bosses he was willing to argue the point with his recruit. "Then how did he know this was a safe place to come and recoup? And if he stole the blade or killed a fellow Nehor, why is he hanging around?" Akin looked the young man directly in his eyes. "No, he is the real deal and we need to listen to him if we want a chance of advancing up the ranks." Hearing Akin say these words, the young man knew exactly what Akin's motivation was in supporting the mysterious and wounded man who was called Boaz.

They stared at each other for several seconds, then the young man nodded his head and took a step back. "Okay," he replied in a strong whisper. "But I will be keeping my eye on him." He gestured with his eyes toward Teancum. Akin turned his head slightly and looked back to where Teancum was lying down. He was relieved to see the Nehor assassin, was fast asleep. However, Akin did not know Teancum was wide awake and fully aware of his surroundings. Teancum was faking sleep and peeking through his eyelids, watching the interaction between Akin and the young Nehor.

I will not be able to make my break and escape down the mountain with him watching over me, Teancum thought to himself. *I am too injured to flee or fight. I hope I am not going to need to kill him.* This thought broke across his mind like an arrow in flight. Teancum started to feel the hot anger toward the Nehors bubbling up inside of him. All the pain and suffering he had endured at the hands of those murderous dogs was beginning to manifest itself again. He felt the blood pulsing through his veins and his heart racing in his chest. He was fighting the urge to jump up and start swinging his new sword, while taking his chances with those new recruits. But then a completely different feeling came over him catching him off guard. *Why is there so much hate and sorrow in this world?* Teancum saw the face of his beloved wife smiling at him, along with the haunting figures of his small children dancing and laughing around Hanni, while waving to him to join them. Then he saw them all lying in a pool of their own blood and the Nehor killers standing over them, rejoicing over their murderous deeds. His heart broke all over again. Teancum could not stop the tears from flowing, so he rolled to his side in an attempt to conceal his anguish from the rest of the men. *Maybe I have gone mad?* he questioned in his own mind. Teancum was slipping back into the deep despair which almost took him a few days ago. It was in this moment the strong male voice that had spoken to him in the past rang out in his thoughts. *Courage... Justice.* It was not much, but it did provide Teancum enough comfort to find the strength to face another day.

The training Akin provided the young recruits was so basic Teancum could have done it himself, had he known the topics. Fire starting, navigation, the names of the different trees and shrubs, basic first aid, all simple things for someone who had learned to live off the land, as Teancum had when he was a boy. But for these new recruits, who were mostly city dwellers, there was a sharp learning curve. The unfortunate Lamanite boys who had been taken prisoner by Akin and his band spent the day gathering and chopping firewood and improving the camp. This was no easy task. They needed to be bound together with a long rope and guarded to keep them from trying to escape. Akin had his men take turns watching the Lamanites. Two of the men would learn a skill while the other two would supervise the Lamanites. That evening the Nehors were sitting around the fire eating as Akin was recounting the day's events. The Lamanite boys were forced to huddle together, sitting in the dark not far from the cavern opening.

"All this learning stuff is great, but when are we going to be taught about Nehor business?" one of the men asked Akin with a mouth full of food.

Akin stole a glance at Teancum before he spoke. Teancum gestured for Akin to address the men. "The business of the Nehors is a closely guarded secret. Before you can become one of us," he gestured back at Teancum, to make himself feel as important as a mighty assassin, "you will need to prove your loyalty to the brotherhood."

"How do we do that?" One of the younger men, sitting on the opposite side of the fire from Akin asked.

"First, you must learn our ways; then you will be tested," Akin responded quietly.

"What kind of test?" the first man responded.

"Well," Akin reflected for a moment and continued, "my test came many years ago when I was a much younger man." He snickered a bit and continued while wiping his hands and clearing his throat. "I helped my brothers rob an army pay wagon on a mountain pass north of the capital." Akin winked and smiled as he remembered the events.

Teancum's heart went instantly cold as he heard these words. He knew the story of his father's death by heart and the investigation which had taken place after his murder. He knew his father was attacked on the mountain roads north of the city while he was guarding a pay wagon.

"Tell us more." The words almost hissed out passed his lips as Teancum dug for more details. He did not need a reason to kill Akin. Teancum knew Akin and his companions were all working for the Nehors which, in Teancum's eyes, marked them all for death. But hearing Akin continue to speak and recount the events of his father's murder to the other men made Teancum's very soul cry out in vengeance.

"Then the crooked army officer and the headmaster's assistant took off after the wounded soldier, and, whoa, was the headmaster mad about how that turned out!" Akin shook his head and joked as he recalled the events which took place after Kail fled from the robbery. "He was yelling and cussing up a storm about the incompetence of the army officer we had working for us. A lot has changed from the old days. We do a much better job now of checking who we let into the brotherhood, don't we, Boaz?" Akin looked at Teancum for an answer to his question and saw nothing but fire and rage on Teancum's face. "Boaz, are you okay?" Akin asked with concern. Pain was the dominant emotion rushing from Teancum's essence. He was trying to hold the façade he had carefully created and maintain his composure. After all, he wanted those criminals to think he was Boaz, a trained killer. But Akin was retelling the story of how his father had been murdered.

"Were you one of the bowmen who shot the soldier as he tried to escape?" Teancum slowly asked, his hands were shaking now. There was a rhythmic pounding behind Teancum's eyes as his heart surged the scalding blood through his veins. Teancum stared into the fire as he waited for the answer.

"No," Akin responded, feeling a bit puzzled. "I was too busy doing my assigned duty of gathering up the swag. They did not trust me with a bow and quiver of black arrows." He chuckled nervously. "I was too young and dumb at that point in my life."

Teancum snorted when Akin said he was too dumb. "You spoke of the headmaster, the one who set this plan to rob the pay wagon in motion; is he still alive?"

"Yes," Akin returned, although he was still a bit confused at the question and the demeanor the high assassin was taking. "He is now the Grand Master of all Nehors. But didn't you know that?"

Teancum thought quickly. "I know the Grand Master, but I do not know all his stories."

"Well," Akin said as he tried to lighten the mood a bit. He could tell the man he knew as Boaz was upset about something. "Boaz, you should come with us to the Grand Council for the Feast to the Fallen. Everyone will be there, including the Grand Master and most, if not all, of the Nehor council." As he was speaking, Akin looked squarely at each of the other men attempting to give the impression he was smarter and better informed about the Nehors business than they were.

The knowledge that the leadership of the Nehor brotherhood would all be in one place at the same time piqued Teancum's interest. He could get a firsthand look at the inner workings of the Nehors. Maybe he could learn enough about them to help stop the scourge of crime plaguing his country. He quickly snapped out of his brooding and tried to pry more information out of Akin. "I would love to, but with these injured feet, I am not going anywhere anytime soon."

"Nonsense," Akin joked. "The feast is not for another week, and the walk to the Gathering Grove is not far from here. A day and a bit at the most." Akin seemed a bit confused as he answered. *Odd, he should know that,* he thought to himself as he looked at Teancum. Shaking it off as unimportant, Akin moved on.

"True," Teancum said as he saw the look in Akin's eyes and tried to change the narrative. "That should give me plenty of time to heal, with you leading the way." He nodded toward Akin, "I can concentrate on taking careful steps without worrying where we are going."

"You see, boys," Akin slapped the back of the closest Nehor candidate. He could not believe his good fortune. A member of the High Order had just appointed him to lead the group to the Gathering Grove. "We are brothers now, and brothers stick together."

Teancum raised his cup to salute Akin and the rest of the bandits sitting around the fire. He was getting good at lying, and it almost scared him how well he used his new skills of deception. *I could really do some damage to this evil clan if I could get closer to the leadership and learn their ways.* He smiled to himself as the words "justice and courage" came to his mind again.

Two more days of ointments and care and Teancum's feet were on the mend. He was up and walking now, but taking careful steps while moving slowly. His feet were not the only thing still bothering him. Most of his body was injured in some way from the long trek through the forest, as well as the fight with the first set of bandits. What was really surprising to Teancum was the fact he had gotten this far using the deception of being a Nehor high assassin. The rest of the group accepted it and continued on without question. What also surprised him was, regardless of how many times one of the group had moved to the edge of the cliff to look out at the wide valley below, no one had looked straight down and seen the mangled bodies of the men he had killed just a few days ago. But Teancum was not about to let his guard down. He always had a weapon at the ready to defend himself if the truth was ever revealed.

The morning of day four, with the new bandits as his companions, Teancum was greeted by them standing together by the early fire as they waited for the water to boil in the big iron pot for the tea.

"How do your legs feel this morning, sir?" Akin quizzed Teancum.

"They are getting stronger every day," Teancum responded as he stretched and moved his tired and sore bones.

"Don't mean to be pointing out the obvious, but if we are going to make it to the Gathering Grove, we will need to set out tomorrow morning at the latest," Akin whispered as he leaned in to speak to Teancum in confidence.

"I am aware of that, Master Akin." Teancum tried to sound condescending and unconcerned. "I will be ready to travel by dawn." Teancum pointed toward the men who were slowly waking. "Finish your lessons and ready them for travel. Come dawn, we will be on our way."

As they left the camp the next day, the stout walking boots he'd found among the Nehor supplies stashed in the cave allowed Teancum to keep up with the other bandit recruits for most of the morning. They left the hideout in excellent shape, moved out and onto the main trail, well before dawn. The three young Lamanite boys were lagging behind even though they did not have the heavy bundles of supplies to carry. Whispering among themselves, they figured they were on their way to an awful fate. They tried to resist the best they could by pulling at the leash around their necks while walking as slowly as they could.

"Keep moving!" One of the bandits took the knotted end of the rope they were using to pull the Lamanites and started to whip the boys with it.

"Akin, what is the problem?" Teancum bellowed in his best angry voice.

"It's the cursed Lamanite brats," Akin responded. "They are malingering and slowing us down. But it does not matter, since we are almost there." Akin pointed to a lone rock spire jetting out from the side of the mountains to the west of the trail. Teancum assumed he was pointing to the rock formation to indicate the Gathering Grove was close by with the formation as a visual clue to its location. Teancum stopped on the side of the trail overlooking a canyon to try to get his bearings. He had been hunting and exploring the woods near his home for most of his life, but he had never traveled this far into the wilds. As he was looking out over the expanse, a second set of bandits came up the trail and were met by Akin. Akin recognized one of the other men and called out to him. They met on the trail and Teancum watched as the two men shook hands in a very peculiar manner. Akin then turned to the recruits and said, "Did you all see the hand sign we just did? It is the Nehor greeting. If you are unsure the person you are speaking to is a Nehor brother, then you shake his hand like so." Akin demonstrated again for the others to learn. Teancum's mind absorbed everything he was seeing as he memorized the motions and sequence of the greeting. "Here," Akin spoke again as he grabbed the leader of the other group of men by the shoulder and moved him toward Teancum. "I want you to meet Boaz. He is a member of the High Order of assassins. He is walking with us to the Gathering Grove." Teancum suddenly felt apprehensive about meeting other members of the Nehor clan. He tried to avoid eye contact, but it was unavoidable.

"Boaz, was it?" the new man questioned, as he reached out with his hand to give the secret shake to Teancum.

"Yeah," Teancum half-heartedly responded as he extended his own right hand. The sequence of the handshake was simple enough, but Teancum focused to ensure he got it right. Teancum finished the shake and noticed the new man was looking down at his waistline and at the hilt of the serpent blade stuck in his belt.

"I have never seen one of those up close. There are so few of you, and we know so little about you." The man smiled as he looked back up into Teancum's face. "Wait a moment... I know you." He pointed at Teancum. "Your face is very familiar to me." Teancum could see the wheels turning in the man's mind as he tried to remember where they had met before. Teancum knew if he did not quickly change the subject the man was going to remember who he was.

"Aren't we running behind because of these slaves, Akin?" Teancum questioned condescendingly as he turned to look at Akin.

"Yes sir, we should get moving," Akin responded without giving it a second thought.

Refusing to give anyone more time to look at his face and perhaps remember that, not long ago, Teancum was once a very important person in the capital city of Zarahemla, Teancum moved past the men and to the front of the group. He gestured for them to follow him and he continued to walk the path toward the obvious stone formation in the distance.

Akin and the man he had greeted looked at each other questioningly. Shrugging, they continued as one big party to follow the odd Nehor assassin down the trail.

For all the mystery and secrecy surrounding the Sons of Nehor, Teancum was sure he would not be able to find the hidden gathering place, and he would need to find a way to have Akin show him the location. As he walked ahead of the others, Teancum was trying to form a plan in his mind when he rounded a bend and caught the first wafts of the scent of burning wood and meat being cooked over a fire. Teancum stopped for a second and sniffed at the air. He felt the breeze on his face and knew the direction to the camp. *Must be close*, he thought to himself. Then he heard the faint clanking of metal and the sounds of men speaking and laughing. *Very close now.* Teancum looked back down the trail at the simple men climbing up the well-worn path behind him. *I might be able to fool them into thinking I am a ranking Nehor leader*, he turned back looking down the trail toward the direction of the smells, *but if I walk into camp like this, they will figure me out almost instantly. I can't have Akin telling everyone he meets about his new friend, the mighty assassin.*

Teancum knew then what to do. "Akin!" he called out. "Bring up the slaves and walk with them into the camp. Everyone should know it was you who captured them, and it is you who will be selling them and giving the money to the council."

Akin smiled and moved quickly toward the front of the line of Nehor men with the Lamanite boys in tow. "Excellent idea, Boaz," he agreed with enthusiasm. Akin was a man who was always looking for a way to improve his status with the Nehor leadership while drawing attention to himself. Walking into camp with captured Lamanites, as well as being accompanied by an assassin of the high order, would do the trick. "Keep moving," he snarled as he pulled on the rope lead holding the boys together.

Teancum moved to the side of the trail, smiling as the rest of the men walked past him, following Akin the rest of the way into camp. As soon as the last man walked past, Teancum fell in behind him, except he began taking smaller steps which made him drop back.

One of the men in the party turned back to look at Teancum and saw his progress was slower than the rest. Teancum waved his hand to tell the man to keep going and that he would be alright. The trail took a sharp left turn and started to follow the side of the mountain. Teancum could see smoke from cooking fires and the roofs of huts in the distance and knew this was the last section of the trail before they reached the bandit camp.

"Halt!" An unseen voice called out from the bushes. Akin held up his hand to signal for everyone to stop walking. It was totally unnecessary; he did it in such a flamboyant way he looked like a fool, but Akin was trying to impress people. He wanted to look like he was the captain of this group.

"Who goes there?"

Teancum was trying to look past the men on the small trail to see if he could spot the location of the unseen sentry. They were in a long, single file line, and all of those heads in his way, combined with the thick undergrowth lining the trail, made it almost impossible for him to see much of anything.

"I am called Akin, and these men are with me," Akin paused, then continued, "I stand ready to give the sign and symbol to enter this Nehor holy ground."

"Step forward, alone and unarmed," the voice in the trees responded.

Akin handed his spear to the man behind him, then undid his equipment belt, laying it on the ground. He took several steps forward and stopped. Teancum watched as Akin drew something on the ground in front of him with his feet. After he was done, a man in full armor stepped out from behind a boulder and walked up to Akin. The armored man looked down at the symbol Akin drew and held out his hand. Akin shook the hand performing the ritual confirming each were members of the clan. The armored man turned around and nodded, telling the other armed men who were hiding in the bushes and behind rocks, they were welcome.

Got to make my move, Teancum thought, as he watched the proceedings in front of him. Akin and his band were waved forward. Teancum started walking with them. *Now's my chance to sneak away from this lot,* he thought. He was getting ready to duck into the thick underbrush when a guard came up behind him and smiled. Teancum was stuck now, and his only recourse was to walk into the camp like the rest of Akin's recruits. He was still the last in line, and as he reached the armed sentries, he smiled and saluted. Expressionless, the leader of the Nehor guards locked eyes with Teancum and watched him like a hawk as he moved past. Teancum swallowed hard and kept moving, acting like he belonged there. He kept the handle of the assassin blade covered with his cloak. *Don't need anyone seeing this and asking questions*, he thought. Not long ago, he was a very popular person in Zarahemla. It was possible someone in this camp might recognize him and then his cover would be blown. Teancum ran his hand over his growing beard. The last time he shaved was the morning he left the capital to go to his ranch; it had been some time now. The hairs were starting to come in, but it was not yet a full beard. Pulling up his cloak, he tried discretely to hide his face as he walked with his head down, not making eye contact with anyone.

As he moved past the guards, the foliage thinned out and Teancum was able to see the grove itself. He stopped walking as he got to the open ground, taking it all in. Looking around, he realized the people who established this place knew what they were looking for. The grove was simply a large outcropping of land on the side of a steep mountain. The ground dropped away sharply on three sides, with thick forest lining the sloping ground and a sheer rock face to its back. There was a small waterfall coming off the rocks, forming several limestone pools of water just below it, providing fresh water to the camp with areas to bathe and clean. There were several large huts as well as a barn, horse corral, bakery with a large clay baking oven, and a metal working shop. "This is a working village," Teancum thought to himself. He saw women doing chores, children playing and men repairing buildings and constructing new ones. As Teancum was taking in the environment, Akin whistled and gestured for him to follow. "I will be with you shortly," Teancum waved and spoke. Although he had acted like the submissive one coming into camp, he had to keep Akin thinking he was a cold-hearted killer. Akin looked hurt that the great assassin Boaz would not be joining him and surged off with his head down like a sad child. *I will need to be very careful*, Teancum thought to himself, as he slowly moved around the outskirts of the Nehor village. *Akin and his men are the only ones who know me as Boaz. I need to do everything I can to keep a low profile.* Teancum pulled his cloak up again and bunched it around his shoulders to try to hide his face the best he could. *Everyone here thinks everyone else is a Nehor. They won't look twice at me if I just act like I belong here.* Moving slowly, trying not to look out of place, Teancum continued walking around the open area. There were a few vendors displaying food and other items for sale. Teancum stopped next to an apple cart. *I have not had a fresh apple in quite some time,* he thought to himself as he examined the fruit in his hand.

"You are welcome to it, my lord ," a sweet voice came from behind the cart. There was a young boy, maybe twelve years old, tending to the cart.

"Really?" Teancum was puzzled as to why the boy would give him a free apple.

"Yes, my lord. Everything here is free. The Grand Council provides for all of us, and we live to serve them. No money is exchanged. We all do our part and they decide how we are rewarded. My job is to give away apples to the men of the clan." The boy reached out and took the apple from Teancum. He gave the apple a good rub with his cloth and handed it back. Teancum was still confused as the boy continued to speak. "Someday, soon, I will take the test and the oath to become a real Nehor, but until then, I do my duty and serve the council." He smiled up at Teancum and went back to his seat.

Not wanting to draw any more attention to himself, Teancum gestured his thanks to the boy with the apple in his hand and moved along. *Interesting concept,* he thought to himself as he took a big bite of the sweet fruit. *Get an entire group of people dependent on the good graces of the leaders and you have slaves for life.*

"Boaz, hey Boaz!" Akin was bellowing out for Teancum to turn and acknowledge him from across the camp. Teancum grimaced as he turned to look at Akin. Akin had a large mug of ale in his hand. He was waving for Teancum to come join him and his men at the open air tavern. Teancum waved to Akin, telling him he would be right there.

I need to get away from those men, Teancum lamented. *Their stupidity will get me discovered and killed.* As Teancum turned away from Akin, he saw a small table set up as a display. On the table were several fresh herbs and spices, along with the tools and bowls needed to mix and create concoctions. There was an old lady sitting next to the table. She looked older than anyone Teancum had ever seen. Her weathered face and tattered clothing gave Teancum the impression she had lived a hard life. Teancum moved closer to the table. He recognized several of the plants.

Some of them he had used in his experiments as a doctor, trying to find cures for the fevers and poxes which made the Nephites sick. There were a few plants he did not recognize. Before he realized what he was doing, his inquisitive mind took over. Teancum asked the old lady what they were and how they were used.

"That one is blackroot," she answered his first question about a strange, twisted bunch of roots.

"I did not think you could find blackroot this far north?" Teancum questioned.

"Can't. That's why it's five gold coins for half a measure. But these snakes make me give it away," she waved her hand in the air in frustration and spat on the ground in contempt. Teancum could see her eyes were almost completely white and she did not look directly at him when he spoke. She was blind and from the looks of it, had been for some time.

"I am told blackroot is good for pain," Teancum continued.

The old lady smiled and cackled, exposing a mouth of missing teeth. "Mix it with a pinch of ground sage and cloverleaf and put it in a tea, and you could stitch up a belly wound."

Teancum smiled. She knew what she was doing. "Let's hope neither of us will need to do that any time soon," he said, as he looked over the remaining items on the table. Then he spotted something on the table…and it made him freeze and gasp. A small bowl containing a few multi-colored beans. He almost choked out loud but caught himself and stiffened. "Castor beans," he whispered.

The old lady, whose other senses were heightened due to her blindness, could hear the change in Teancum's breathing patterns. She could sense his movement and hear his voice. "Yessss," she hissed like an old snake, "castor beans. If you know about blackroot, then you must know about castor beans." There was an evil note to her laugh. "Very few people know what they can do."

Teancum had a flashback to his time as a doctor, working on research for the cures, when he had discovered castor beans and what they can do. "Yes, I know about those things." The one thing he refused to tell his superiors, the one thing he swore he would take to his grave, was the recipe for the incredibly deadly poison he had accidentally created. He knew if they found out what he had created, they would steal his mistake and turn it into a weapon. Castor beans were the main ingredient for the deadly toxin. There they sat, like tiny nightmares in a hard shell, just

waiting for someone to unleash them. Then he realized sitting right in front of him was everything else he would need to awaken the monster from its sleep. The grinders, the mixing bowls, the measuring cups and the teapot… Everything he would need to recreate a good serving of death.

He looked behind him and saw Akin and the other Nehors enjoying themselves and drinking ale. Then he looked around the small community and saw other Nehors shopping and eating, visiting with friends and attending open air lectures on the necessities of the criminal life. These men were all murderers and pillagers. They were the scourge of the Nephites; they reveled in the culture of death, swearing eternal hatred on the peace-loving people of Christ. They had done more damage to the Nephites than even the Lamanite armies in the past years. The image of that moment, with a cursed Nehor shouting out his testimony to the Nehor Clan after he had killed Teancum's little child as he fell to his death flashed into Teancum's mind. The blood ran cold in his veins and Teancum looked again at Akin and his men. Time slowed as he focused on the movements and sounds those barbarians were making. *These animals and their supporters were responsible for the deaths of hundreds, if not thousands, of innocent men, women and children.* The voice in his head came to him again, *And yet, here they are, immune from the laws of men and of God, enjoying the day without a care in the world.* Teancum was growing hot with anger. The now-familiar hate was building inside him again. *They should know fear, not their victims. They should know true justice, they should be afraid— not the innocent whom they prey upon.*

"Justice," he mouthed. There was the word again, racing through his mind like a stallion at a full gallop.

"You okay, sonny boy?" The old woman was rocking back and forth as she spoke. "You are breathing so hard you are either looking at the prettiest girl you ever saw or a man you want to kill." Teancum swallowed hard. she was very perceptive and he was going to blow his cover if he did not get control of his emotions.

Trying to hide behind the mask of a Nehor assassin he answered back. "I fear no man, and you are the prettiest girl I've seen all day."

The old woman cackled and howled at his remark. "Sonny boy," she gasped between fits of laughter, "you are a smooth talker! Not too bright, perhaps, but a smooth talker." She waved with her hand. "Take what you please. Those Nehor dogs don't pay me for it anyway." Teancum joined in her laughter, then reached for the bowl of deadly beans along with a small stone bowl and hand pestle grinder and some herbs. As he was doing this, she reached out and grabbed Teancum by the arm. "I don't want to know who you are and what you're doing with those beans; you hear me?" She had a firm grip on his arm and a tone of determination on her lips. She had survived so far in this world by giving the appearance of a harmless blind woman, but she saw much more than people realized.

Teancum took the items he needed and stuck them in his satchel. "Thank you," he whispered, as he put his hand on her shoulder.

"You're welcome, sonny boy. Come back anytime." She instantly lost the hardness in her voice and fell right back into the sweet, harmless old woman routine.

People see what they want to see. Teancum again learned this important lesson. She was a hard woman playing the part of a helpless one to gain an advantage in life. Living in this environment full of killers, one would need to find an angle to survive.

CHAPTER FOURTEEN

THE WITCH AND HER OPTIONS

He knew what he must do, but Teancum needed privacy to make the poison. He walked toward the open air tavern where Akin and his men were sitting and drinking. They were the only ones who could ruin his cover, so they needed to be silenced— not bribed or bargained with.

"Boaz!" the men all chimed together and raised their mugs as Teancum walked up to the tables where they were sitting. They were all filthy and stunk from weeks without a bath. The tavern was no more than a few tables under some shade trees with a shack where the bartender could house the kegs of ale and jars of wine.

"Did you come to finally join us?" Akin asked.

"I did." Teancum was really playing his part now, slapping the men on the backs and laughing roughly with them. "But I need to relieve myself first." He acted like he was looking around desperately for the facilities.

"Outhouse, behind the tavern," Akin spoke with a slight drunken slur as he poked his thumb over his shoulder in the the general direction of the wooden structure.

"Don't order any more drinks until I return. The next round is on me!" Teancum raucously told the bandits. They all cheered and raised their almost empty mugs and goblets again, in celebration of the good news. Teancum had been waiting for this moment from the very second he emerged from the supply cave, coming face-to-face with Akin and his men. They were murdering Nehor scum, just like the ones who killed his family. With the news Akin was a part of the killing of his father Kail,

Teancum had no problem setting the next few events into motion. *Relax*, he told himself as he started to move toward the outhouse. He could feel his hands start to shake and he was breathing harder. *Don't draw attention to yourself. You are just some guy going to the bathroom.* He reached the outhouse and gave the door a gentle knock. No one answered so he stepped inside. "Sweet mercy," Teancum gasped as he closed the door behind him. The air was so foul he had to breathe through his mouth just to keep from vomiting. He cracked the door open and tried to shoo some of the large black flies out and let in fresh air. "Not the most sanitary conditions, but I will make do," he whispered, as he removed the small stone bowl and pestle grinder from his satchel. He then brought out the few castor beans he had taken, putting them into the bowl. "This will not be an exact dosage, but this is all I have to work with," he muttered to himself, as he grunted and strained to mash and grind the hard beans into a fine powder. It was as if he was justifying the rudimentary manner and method he was using to concoct the poison. "I cannot extract just the meat from the seed and boil it down into a liquid," he continued to murmur to himself, "so, I will add the herbs for a sweet taste to mask the bitterness of the bean shell." After a few more moments, Teancum had crushed and mashed all the beans and the herbs together. What he had created filled the bottom of the stone bowl with a fine gritty powder. Being careful not to inhale or touch the powder, Teancum covered the bowl with a cloth and gathered up his belongings. "Now, how do I get Akin and his men to ingest this?" he asked himself. But as soon as he said those words, he remembered he had told them he would buy them all drinks when he returned. "Yes," he whispered. Smiling, he took two steps toward the tavern when a rush of emotion hit him. *Wait! What am I doing?* He stopped walking, standing next to the smelly outhouse for several seconds. *This is a very deadly poison. I can't just kill them in cold blood.* As he stood holding the powder filled with death, the face of his little Carra flashed in his mind's eye as she smiled at him. Then, he saw his beloved wife in the hands of her killers, and his two older daughters left to die in the inferno which had previously been his house.

Justice… You are my justice, the voice from beyond spoke, breaking the stillness.

Like a parade of tragedy, face after face of those who had been murdered or harmed by the Nehor in their quest for power and wealth flashed in his mind. He did not know those people, but he could hear

their cries, their screams, their agony; they all called out to God for help
and succor.

*You are my justice. These cowards hunt the sheep, and you are my sheepdog.
Make the flock safe again.*

There was a loud, rhythmic thumping in Teancum's head as the blood
pounded in his temples. A chill went down his spine and the hairs on his
arms were standing on end. Something was happening to him, physically,
something even he could not explain with his medical knowledge. "Make
the flock safe again…" He mouthed those words over and over. "My
actions can help to make the flock safe again. I can hunt these wolves
and make them afraid of the sheepdog— Yes!" he exclaimed out loud.
Quickly realizing what he had done, Teancum looked around to see if
anyone had heard him. Holding his breath, he scanned his surroundings.
Concluding no one had taken notice of his strange outburst, Teancum
checked under the cloth covering the powdered poison. "Still intact." He
smiled and started to move toward the front of the tavern. "The drinks
are on me, boys."

Teancum went to the bartender's location behind the bar, ordering full
mugs of ale for Akin and all his men. "I will take it to them," he said, as
he stopped the bar attendant from carrying the full mugs to the tables.

"Help yourself." The bartender was too busy to argue with someone
who wanted to carry the heavy load of alcohol to a group of smelly
drunks. Handing the tray to Teancum, he moved away. Teancum set the
tray down.

"Need to get a better hold on it," Teancum smiled as he spoke. The
man turned and walked away. He had other customers who needed
his attention.

With his back to Akin and his men, Teancum carefully removed the
small stone bowl from his satchel and removed the cloth cover. Carefully
he shook a small serving of the deadly powder into each mug, trying to
make sure they all had a fair portion. "All but you." Teancum withheld
the substance from one mug in particular. It had a small dent in the rim
so Teancum would know which mug was not poisoned. Satisfied he
had delivered the toxin in equal measure, Teancum quickly put the bowl
and cloth back into his satchel and lifted up the tray. "Gentlemen!" he
shouted with enthusiasm, "Who is thirsty?"

They all cheered and reached for a mug. Teancum walked around
the tables handing out the mugs, but being careful not to give away the

only one without the poison. When he had handed out all the mugs, he reached for his own, then raised it high in the air. "Join me in a toast to our good friend Akin!" They all raised their glasses. "Because of him, we are all here today! To Akin— salute!"

"To Akin!" they all shouted, clanked their glasses together and then drank deeply.

Teancum only pretended to drink from his glass. He did not like what alcohol did to him. He knew he would need all his wits about him if he was going to make it out of this place alive. He watched out of the corner of his eye as those dirty Nehor scum consumed the poison and were none the wiser.

It was not long after drinking Teancum's poison, Akin and his men started to feel the effects. They assumed it was from the quantity of ale they had drank. Most of them wandered off to bed. The violent cramping and vomiting would start late in the night. No one else would really be concerned about it, knowing Akin and his men had been drinking that day.

"Serves them right for being so drunk," one guard said later to another as they stood fire watch by the large burning pit in the center of the camp.

"Should we fetch them a healer?" They could hear the men retching and calling out in pain.

"No," the first guard responded to the question "It will teach them a lesson about over-consumption. As the Grand Master says: moderation in all things." They both laughed as they listened to the men continue to vomit. The true nature of the Nehor clan was on full display for Teancum. As their own brothers lay in pain, the others did nothing but laugh at their misery. Teancum knew now, more than ever, he must rid the world of these monsters.

The organ failure started soon after, followed by the bleeding. By dawn, all of Akin's men were found dead in their own gore, laying together where they had tried to sleep.

The alarm was sounded and several people gathered to see what had happened. Teancum played the part and acted like he was upset about his friends being found dead.

"Move out of the way!" A shout went out, from behind the people who were standing around the dead bodies. Two well-armed men with spears and shields walked through the crowd, making a path for a third man to walk through. The third man was middle-aged, clean-shaven, and had on a bright red robe covering his black leggings and a matching blouse. Around his neck hung a large gold medallion. Teancum could see inscribed in the center of the medallion the symbol of the Nehor, with an eye in the center of it.

"What has happened here?" he demanded from no one in particular. No one answered. Most just looked away or lowered their heads. Teancum thought it would help him look insolent if he spoke up. "Sir, these are my friends. They were drinking last night and fell asleep here. They were sick during the night, but we thought nothing of it."

The man in the red robe stared hard at Teancum for several seconds. "Fetch the oracle!" He called out. A few minutes later, Teancum saw two more guards helping the old lady who had given him the castor beans walk toward the scene. His chest got tight as he felt a twinge of panic shoot up his spine. She was the only one who knew what this type of poisoning looked like.

"Tell me the condition of the bodies," the old woman asked, as she was led up to the location where the bodies were found. She was weak and unsteady on her feet. One of the guards grabbed a wooden stool for her.

"All the men are lying on the ground as if they were sleeping; there is no sign of combat wounds. They all look like they vomited during the night and blood is coming out of their noses," the red-robed man responded.

"Are they missing any property?" she asked as she adjusted her position on the stool. Teancum could tell she was not comfortable.

"No, Madame." The red-robed man answered, turning to look at one of the guards who had found the bodies. The guard responded, "It appears as if they still retain all their possessions."

"Not a robbery. And their skin color? Are they cold to the touch?" she questioned, as she fumbled with the beads hanging around her neck. She was turning her head in different directions as if she was trying to hear better or see past her blindness.

"White as the mountain snow, and just as cold," the same guard responded, as he reached out, touching Akin's arm.

"Who found the bodies?"

The man in the red robe turned to look at Teancum, gesturing for him to step forward and speak.

Taking a deep breath, Teancum moved closer and slowly spoke, "I did,

Madame."

There was a hint of a smile on her face. She recognized his voice, knowing instantly what had happened to the bodies. Teancum saw the change in her expression. He dared not move to see if anyone else could tell she had figured things out. He held his breath, waiting for the old woman to speak. Would she expose him as the culprit? It seemed like hours before she said anything. She held her head still for a great while, then took a breath.

She pulled out a small leather bag and manipulated it in her fingers while rocking in the chair and chanting some unknown words. Suddenly she stopped and shouted, "This is a pox, a curse on these men!" She gestured in the direction of the dead men. "The gods have condemned them for their disloyalty to the clan." She pointed toward Teancum's general location and continued to speak. "He survived because he was loyal to the gods— leave him be. Burn the bodies and think no more on it." She concluded and tried to stand up but was assisted by the guards who supported her. Teancum felt a wave of relief come over him. He wanted to get close to the woman and whisper a thank you, but he was stopped by the man in the robe.

"Who are you?" the man with the red robe asked Teancum.

"Boaz," Teancum responded as he looked past the person speaking to him and saw the old woman being escorted back to the huts in the market place. He was not going to get a chance to say anything, so he returned to his deception. "Akin recruited me to join the brotherhood." Teancum pointed down at the body of Akin lying in the grass. "I traveled with him to this place so I could take the pledge." The man in the robe looked hard at Teancum, as if he were trying to read Teancum's thoughts.

"And what did Akin tell you about this place and who we are?"

Using his perfect recall, Teancum was able to recite many of the things he had heard Akin tell the other men while they were being instructed in the ways of the Nehor. He spoke as if he were a student, not an observer. As he was speaking to the man in the robe and the others who were with him, a few more people came up to see what had happened, one of them was the guard leader who allowed Akin to pass with his recruits. Teancum remembered his face and stopped speaking. "And he was the one who met us at the edge of the Gathering Grove. Akin vouched for us all and he let us enter," Teancum pointed to the guard leader.

The man in the red robe turned and looked at the guard inquiringly.

"It is true, Grand Master. I remember Akin and this lot," he spoke roughly, without any sorrow for the dead men at his feet.

"Well," the Grand Master turned back to Teancum, "it would seem fate has spared you the same ending as your traveling companions. Unless you are feeling ill as well?"

"No Grand Master," Teancum tried to seem humble as he bowed slightly before the leader of the Nehors. "Fit and ready to learn the ways of the Nehor Clan."

"Very well. Burn the bodies and all their possessions. If they had been cursed and infected with a pox, we don't want it to spread," the leader shouted for all to hear. "The events of the day will continue as planned." The Grand Master spun on his heels and walked away from the scene without another word.

"You," Teancum was bumped on the shoulder by the guard leader, "help load the bodies on the wagon."

"Yes, sir, right away." Teancum could not believe how his luck had held out. He was not about to jinx it and was more than willing to assist in disposing of the only clues of his true identity.

True to the Oracle's instructions, once the bodies were disposed of, the conversation about Akin and his men stopped completely. It was as if nothing had ever happened. There was no funeral, no procession or words spoken over the bodies, no marked grave, just an effort to clean up the mess and dispose of the evidence any of those men had ever lived or were a part of this clan. This was very disturbing for Teancum. *These people are so callous and hard-hearted even the mysterious deaths of their own men didn't trouble them.* He reflected as he stood far off, watching the fire consume the bodies and all trace of his poisoning. *Emotionless monsters!* He shook his head as the simple village returned to business.

It was almost noon when the fire died down enough to not require tending anymore. Teancum and the other men who had set the fire and stayed to tend it nodded at each other and left in their own directions. Teancum grabbed some bread and cheese from a food cart and headed toward an open building where classes were being taught about the Nehor ways, when a voice came from behind him.

"Loyalty to the gods?" Teancum froze in place, his mouth half full of a piece of bread. Teancum slowly turned and was face-to-face with the Grand Master of the Nehors camp. His heart skipped a beat. "I wonder what one has to do to find that kind of favor with the gods of the Nehor… Hmm?" He smiled when he spoke, but Teancum could see treachery behind his eyes. Swallowing hard, Teancum tried to speak, but the leader of the band of thieves held up his hand to tell him to stop speaking. "I do not mourn Akin's death. He was a simpleton, but he did supply us with very useful recruits from time to time." The Grand Master reached out and grabbed Teancum's' shoulder. Feeling his arm muscles, the red-robed man continued, "Strong and tall— you are fit. Were you a soldier?"

"No, sir." Teancum meekly spoke. Before he realized it, he was speaking; the words just came out. "I was a student, trying to become a physician." Teancum tried to catch those last few words before they came out but it was too late. When word got out he was a trained doctor someone would recognize him for sure.

"A doctor!" The Grand Master slapped Teancum on the back. "What a fine addition you will make to the brotherhood." Teancum was getting very nervous now. His plan to infiltrate the Nehor culture and learn how to stop them was a bust. He needed to make his escape, and soon, or he would be just as dead as Akin. "What kind of doctor are you? Do you treat wounds, deliver babies, work with the animals?" The evil leader was pressing for more information, but trying to be subtle about it.

Teancum saw this as an opportunity to create some distance between his last statements. He shook his head, "I was still studying when I was caught selling the medications for extra money and cheating on my exams. My family disowned me, and I lost everything. That is when Akin found me."

The Grand Master smiled again and Teancum could see very clearly the leader had evil in his thoughts. "Were you going to the classes?" the Grand Master asked, motioning for Teancum to walk with him toward the classrooms.

"Yes sir, I was heading there now." Teancum was stuck. He could not try to leave now with the supreme leader of the Nehor clan standing right next to him.

"What is it you hope to gain from being here… Boaz, is it?" Teancum's mind raced back to one of the lessons Akin taught the new recruits while waiting on the cliff. He remembered Akin explaining the Nehor pride themselves in being a family and caring for each other when you think no one else will.

"I want to belong to something," Teancum answered. "I lost my family, and my purpose." Not wanting to make any more mistakes or say something that would turn on him, Teancum left the conversation there.

"Well," the leader responded, with a hint of joy in his expression. "You will find both here among the Nehor brotherhood." He guided Teancum toward one of the open air classrooms where an instructor was giving a lecture to a group of new recruits. When the Grand Master walked into the area, the instructor stopped speaking and turned to acknowledge the leader's presence in the class.

"Good afternoon, Grand Master," the teacher spoke, giving a respectful bow.

"Good afternoon to you and your class," the leader responded.

There is no way this guy is the leader of a murderous gang of cutthroat animals, Teancum thought as he listened and watched the leader interacting with the class. He walked around, greeting the students, and shaking their hands. He even knew some of their names. *He has the ability to act casually like this, and still command the Nehor, and then order the deaths of defenseless civilians.* Teancum paused as he thought to himself. *What audacity! This man is dangerous, very dangerous.*

"Class we have a new recruit. His name is Boaz and he possesses some training in medicine." The leader introduced Teancum to the class. The public introduction made Teancum cringe a little. He was hoping to learn what he could and just disappear without anyone remembering him. "What are we learning this afternoon?" The leader smiled and looked right at the instructor.

"Well, sir," the teacher cleared his throat, moving from behind his simple speaking stand, "I was just starting my lecture on how the Christian faith is a false religion designed to eventually enslave the masses, and how, through the teachings of our martyred father Nehor the Wise, we can all become enlightened as to the true nature of the gods."

"A true, favorite topic of mine." The red-robed Grand Master sounded truly delighted. He turned toward Teancum. "Boaz, I will leave you in the fine care of the instructors. We will speak again, I am sure of it." He smiled at Teancum and Teancum could clearly see the menace in the leader's eyes. Teancum felt there was more going on than he was aware of and he needed to be very careful now. "As you were, class," the leader addressed the group, then turned and walked away, flanked by his guards.

"Please... Boaz, is it? Come, find a seat— you have not missed anything. I was just getting started." The instructor gestured toward an empty seat near the side of the gathered students. Teancum slowly moved toward the seat as the instructor picked up on his lecture where he left off. "As you recall, I was telling you all about how our dear father Nehor was murdered by the coward Gideon, who was in the employment of the Christian leader and puppet master, Alma."

Teancum sat all afternoon, listening to the tripe the Nehors were trying to indoctrinate into their newest members. Unlike most of the simple folks who occupied the camp, Teancum was highly educated. Not only had he been taught by the master tutors and mentors his grandfather, provided him as he grew up on the ranch, but he was also a trained physician, lawmaker and common judge in Zarahemla.

Teancum knew the truth of the encounter between Alma the Great, the Prophet of God, and Nehor, the Anti-Christ and father of this criminal band. He knew Nehor had murdered Gideon, the great hero of the people of Limhi. Although the Sons of Nehor had been a secret society from before he was born, it was only a few years ago their leader had made public his attempt to overthrow the legitimate government and destory the church. He also knew first-hand of the pain and sadness the followers of Nehor had inflicted on the Nephite people. Now he was biding his time until he could exact justice on those who sought to murder, plunder, and destroy. Teancum knew, just like everything else in his life, the more he understood a subject, the better prepared it made him. So, now that Akin and his men were gone, the coast was clear. Teancum was going to play the part and learn as much about this organization as he could, so someday he could dismantle it and destroy the Nehor forever.

Teancum attended classes for the next few days. They were teaching everything from the history of the Nehor movement, to how to establish a new false identity, to the study of economics. He thought some of the more difficult classes were useless, considering the level of education among those gathered and the purpose for having this village, until he attended the class covering the manipulation of the education system. There he learned it was all about how to manipulate and blackmail local educational leaders, as well as how to establish criminal control over those who manage the educational affairs of a town or village, and not about empowering the uneducated.

As he sat in class listening to the instructor, it was a shock to discover the Nehors were trying to control the minds and ideas of the next generation. The teacher explained by changing the narrative of Nephite history and values of the youth this would help the Nehor clan gain power in government. The more Teancum learned about these bandits, the greater his contempt and anger grew. *They are brazen and open about how they are trying to destroy the Nephite people and the Christian church*, he thought to himself as he sat alone eating his dinner a few nights after his arrival. *This is more than just a bunch of thugs bent on murder and plundering. This is evil on a level I have never considered before. They are trying to raise up an entire generation accepting of their provisions and hate. If the children are indoctrinated in this filth, then when they are adults they will believe the Nehor lies and vote to destroy freedom and the church.*

Sitting facing several other Nehors as they ate their meals, he watched as they laughed and carried on among themselves as if there was nothing wrong with what was happening here in this camp. The fire in his soul was kindled and his anger continued to grow. Teancum was sickened to the point he almost could not swallow his food. He struggled to maintain control over his emotions and not blow his cover. By taking small bites and drinking plenty of water, Teancum managed to finish his meal. He quickly got up from his table and moved away from the dining area. He needed some air, and he decided a walk toward the tree line would help calm himself before the mandatory evening gathering around the main fire in the center of the camp. Every night, the leader in the red robe and others in the Nehor leadership would come speak to the new recruits, encouraging them to continue their instruction, then explain to them how valuable they were to the Nehor cause. Teancum would watch as they all sat around the fire as the ranking leadership of the Nehors tried to make the new members feel like they were part of a family.

Teancum was now skirting the edge of the tree line looking for a place where he could simply sit and be still for a few moments before he needed to face the madness again. As he was moving, he heard voices in the darkness. Whispers were coming from the back of one of the huts. He stood still for a moment, trying to hear what they were saying, but he could only make out a few words. Relying on his hunting skills, Teancum moved very slowly and quietly toward the sounds. As he got closer to the hut, he could see it was the leader in the red robe and one other high ranking Nehor who he had not seen in camp before. They were huddled together, making sure no one could hear them speaking.

CHAPTER FOURTEEN

"I'm telling you that man is not who he says he is," the unknown Nehor was insistent as he spoke. "I don't know why he is here. Maybe he was sent by the judges to find us out. A spy!"

As the man spoke, Teancum recognized his face and voice. He knew this man, but from where? Panic suddenly swept across his mind as he understood they were talking about him. hen he remembered where he had seen this man before. He worked for the Sheriff of Zarahemla. He was one of his main deputies, assigned to work directly with the judges in Zarahemla. When Teancum realized this high-ranking law enforcement official was really a Nehor in disguise, his blood boiled red hot. He felt for the handle of his hidden knife in his right hand and pulled it out.

"Shush!" the man in the red robe hissed, as he heard the fabric of Teancum's clothing rub as he pulled out his knife. The two stood still, listening for any more faint noises coming from the trees. Teancum held his breath and was as motionless as a statue as he watched the Nehors react to his lapse of judgement.

After a few seconds the quiet was broken. "Just an animal," the new Nehor waved, as he spoke.

"What do you recommend I do?" The leader asked, as the two returned to their conversation.

"Kill him now!" the new Nehor insisted. "Regardless of his reasons for being here, he is a threat."

"True, but what if he is here because he wants to join our cause?" The leader was now playing the devil's advocate.

"Is one man worth the risk?" There was a pause. "I will do it— right now, no cost."

"You would kill someone for free?" the leader was almost surprised at the gesture from the evil officer. "He must really be a threat. Very well, but not now. Wait until later. Kill him in his sleep. Make it look like a robbery, so I can instill some fear in the rest of the recruits." The leader lowered his brow and looked directly into the eyes of the Nehor. "I will pay you anyway, but no mistakes this time."

The Nehor nodded his head and then turned to walk away, leaving the leader alone with his thoughts. The leader stood for a few seconds thinking to himself. He smirked and started to move away from the hut, but stopped suddenly, looking into the darkness toward where Teancum was standing. Teancum was hidden behind a large tree and was barely peeking out from around it, but the leader was looking right at him.

Teancum froze again. He did not want to make any movement or sound to give away his position. He waited for what seemed like hours as the Nehor leader stared directly at him. Teancum knew the leader could not see him in the dark, but he felt exposed and desperately wanted to run away. He knew if he moved an inch or made any sounds, he would be exposed, and the leader would immediately order his men to hunt him down, so he held as still and quiet as if he were made of stone. After several more moments, the Nehor leader broke his gaze, then moved around the hut toward the main part of the camp. Teancum held still for a few minutes longer just to be safe. Then, when he felt it was safe, he slowly moved backwards and deeper into the thick forest, near the edge of the cliff.

What am I going to do? he asked himself, as he sat on a log, trying to figure out his next move. *They are going to try to kill me in my sleep tonight.* He paused as he said those words to himself, again. "They are going to try to kill me, tonight…" he smiled as he sat upright. "They don't know I know their plans. I know who it is and when he will try." A tingling sensation shot through his body as he worked out the problem in his mind. "I can lay in wait for the assassin, then take him out when he comes for me." Then Teancum remembered he was in a camp full of killers. "I will then need to escape….not just escape, I will need to cause a diversion so I will have time to make a clean getaway, making sure no one is following me." As he sat there on the log, thinking and softly speaking to himself, there was a snap of a twig right next to him. Startled, he jumped to his feet turning to see the cause of the noise.

"Good evening, Boaz. What are you doing out here at this time of the night?" It was the leader of the Nehor. He had moved through the woods like a ghost making his way right up next to Teancum.

Teancum was stunned when he realized who was standing right next to him. *Don't give away anything!* The voice in his head screamed at Teancum as he choked back his fear, "I was just collecting my thoughts," he responded.

The Nehor leader stood motionless for several seconds, just staring at Teancum. There was a different look in his eye than when he was walking around camp greeting and talking to the others. He was cold and focused now, like a great cat about to pounce on his prey. "Gathering your thoughts, you say?" He took two steps forward toward Teancum.

Teancum could see the leader had both his hands behind his back. *He is holding something— a weapon!* Teancum's inner voice was shouting at him now, as he tried to stand up.

"Boaz, do have a seat. There is something we must discuss."

Without thinking, Teancum sat back down on the log, adjusting his seat so he could face the leader while putting his hands down on the log for support.

"Boaz, Boaz..." the leader spoke in a condescending tone, as he stood in front of Teancum. "My child, you have been very busy in camp this week, haven't you?"

"Yes, sir." Teancum tried not to sound scared, but he was. As he tried to adjust his sitting position, he pushed down on the log and felt the rotted bark start to give way under his left hand. That was when a flash of images shot across his mind. Images from his medical training, specifically his knowledge of the human eyes and their delicate nature. How if an object or some type of debris gets into the eyes, it can cause temporary blindness and great pain. Before he realized it, Teancum was digging his fingers into the rotten wood.

"You have been very busy here in the trees tonight, haven't you?"

"Yes, sir." Teancum was more assertive now. He was finding his courage again as he quietly gathered more of the wet and rotten bark and wood from the log.

"You disappoint me, Boaz— if that is your real name." the leader passed back and forth in front of Teancum. He stopped, looked back at Teancum and smirked. Teancum remained silent and motionless. "No answer?" he continued to pace. "It is a shame we can't at least be honest with each other, now. There really is no point continuing the games, is there, Doctor Teancum?"

Teancum remained expressionless while locking eyes with the Nehor leader. He was not going to give this murderous thug the satisfaction of seeing him panic. Teancum watched as every single thing about the man in the red robe changed. He almost instantly became dark and sinister looking. The expression on his face changed to a scowl and his eyes burned with evil intent. Even the pitch of his voice dropped as he continued to speak.

"Why are you here?" It sounded more like a challenge than a question.

"Your men..." Teancum half choked as he spoke, "They murdered my entire family." Teancum did not want the Nehor to see his emotions but he could not help it. This was the first time since the tragedy he had spoken of it to another person. Now he was addressing one of the ringleaders, "You people are evil and must be stopped."

The Nehor leader let out a contemptuous snort. "Yes, we are evil." There was a gleam in his eye as he continued, "But you will never stop us." He smiled a wicked smile and brought his right hand out from behind his back. In his hand was one of the snake-shaped assassin blades. "Our roots grow deeper in the Nephite lands by the day."

Teancum saw the blade and the blood began to pound through his veins, into his chest and head. He looked up into the face of the Nehor. A flash of light shot through Teancum's mind. He saw the Nehor's veins and arteries running up and down both sides of his neck. Teancum also saw the wind pipe, muscles and nerves connecting the head to the rest of the body. He knew exactly what he must do and exactly where he had to strike.

"You would risk killing a sitting judge?" Teancum spat back in a low but hard tone. "You would risk the righteous indignation of the Nephite people and the wrath of the army?" He curled the handful of wet tree bark into his left fist. "I am well-known and well-respected. I am from a very wealthy and powerful family. My father-in-law is the garrison commander of the armed forces of Zarahemla. You cowards murdered my wife and children!"

"Shhh...." the Nehor held out his left hand trying to quiet Teancum. "You are just embarrassing yourself now," he said. "You are not that important, and I am not afraid of you or the Nephite people." There was contempt in his voice. He acted like taking the time to kill Teancum was a bothersome distraction for him. "We have bribed or blackmailed most of the important people in your government, anyway." He brought the long curved knife up as he continued to speak. "You will not be mourned or missed."

Teancum knew it was now or never. As the Nehor took one quick step toward him, Teancum flung the large wad of rotten bark and wet tree bits into his face. The mash of moist debris hit the Nehor between the eyes as he cried out and swiped with the knife at the last known location of his prey. Teancum ducked under the knife attack, rolling forward to his feet. The boss Nehor wildly swiped back and forth with the assassin blade as he frantically tried to clear the muck from his eyes. When Teancum came to his feet, he had his own long blade in his hand and moved, swiftly, toward the Nehor. Bobbing and weaving like a prize fighter, Teancum moved around the wild swipes and thrusts of the Nehor blade. The Nehor leader did not call out for help and Teancum was not going to give him any chances to. With lightning speed, Teancum dodged another series of wild, uncontrollable stabs and slices, then took his blade and drove it into the side of the Nehor's neck. He could feel the blade of his own knife hit the bones of the spine, then he roughly jerked it out. The Nehor gagged and spat as blood poured from the internal wound into his throat and down into his lungs. He dropped the knife, grasping with both hands at the lethal damage done by Teancum's blade. Staggering and choking, the dying Nehor commander gave Teancum a look of sheer astonishment as if to say, *How did you move so fast and strike with such skill?* He had clearly underestimated Teancum. He backed off a few paces, knife in hand, crouching at the ready to deliver a second blow if it was necessary. The Nehor tried to reach out for Teancum, but instead he collapsed as his knees gave out under him. Teancum watched his enemy fall to the ground and roll over in a last desperate attempt to survive. With one last gasp, the Grand Master gave up the ghost and was silent.

Teancum, lost in the moment, stood as still as a marble statue. He started to lower his weapon and relax his posture when he suddenly realized there was a dark shadow outline of a second person standing next to a large tree behind where the Nehor was standing before he fell. The fright of knowing there was a witness to this event had Teancum moving like lightning toward the unknown observer. He grabbed the unidentified person by the arm and brought his blade up to strike. At that moment, he realized the person in the moon's shadow was the old lady from the market who had given him the castor beans. Physically, she was no threat to Teancum. He slowly lowered his weapon.

"What are you doing out here?" he asked, as he pulled her around the tree and out of sight from the camp.

"The question is—" she forcibly whispered, as she looked up into his eyes, "what are *you* doing?" She diverted her gaze, looking at the lifeless body of the camp's leader lying in the dirt not ten feet from them.

"How long have you been standing there?" Teancum needed to know what she knew. He was not about to kill an old woman, but he needed information from her, and quickly.

"I saw everything… Doctor Teancum," the words hissed past her lips, as she looked back at him then gave an evil smile.

"I thought you were blind!" he gasped.

"You thought many things, young man."

He was shocked. She was not blind at all and she knew everything. She was the prime witness to his poisoning of Akin and his band of robbers. She watched his deadly assault on the Grand Master. She even knew his true identity. She held all the cards and was in complete control of his future, except for one small detail. Teancum felt the handle of his long knife in his right hand. He held fast to the weapon and slowly brought it up.

Kill her! It was the dark voice he contended with on the cliff. It was subtle and not so arrogant this time, but it was goading him to commit the unpardonable crime.

"No!" The word came out of his mouth so loud it almost shook him as he spoke it. Teancum blinked several times trying to re-focus.

"I am no threat to you," she spoke, as if she could perceive his thoughts. "I am also not a Nehor." She started to move toward him. "You should push the body farther down the hill to hide it." She pointed to the motionless form at Teancum's feet. "It will take them some time to realize he is missing, and even longer to find the body if you put it down there." She was next to him now and looking him in the eyes. It was very dark but Teancum could still make out the weathered outlines of her face and the light in her eyes. "Here, take these," she handed him a small bag.

"What is this?" he asked, almost wishing he had not asked the question.

"The remains of my castor bean collection," she smiled, again. "They are having cold mush for the communal breakfast in the morning. The men eat first." She lowered her head, raised her brows and put the bag in his hand, tapping it lightly with her fingers. "I assume you don't kill women and children?" Teancum's face drained of its blood when he heard those words. She was giving him enough poison to kill every murderous Nehor man in camp, as well as telling him how to do it.

"How do you know such things? Why..." he whispered. "Why would you give this to me?"

She smiled, again, then slowly turned to walk back to camp. "Balance." she said, as she looked back at him. "Without evil, you will never understand true goodness. But with too much evil, goodness can be wiped out." She stopped moving, standing still in the night air. "My work is done. The fight is now yours, young Teancum. Be a ghost to these monsters. Be what scares them in the night— be the only thing they fear.

As the scriptures say, there is a time and a season for everything under heaven. A time to plant," she pointed to the bag in his hand. "a time to reap what you have planted." She turned and started moving through the trees, back into the lights of the candles and fires of the encampment. After a few more steps, she stopped again, "Hurry back...before you are missed." Then she was gone.

"What is happening?" Teancum asked out loud. He was shaking, but it was not cold and he was not hungry. "Adrenaline." Always the physician, he spoke to himself, as he took several calming breaths. The fight with the Nehor boss and then dealing with the ghoulish old woman had put him in a mental and physical spin. He felt the weight of the bag of beans in his hand. Shaking them, he could not focus his mind around what she was telling him to do with the beans. Out of frustration, he set the bag on the ground. Not knowing what else to do, Teancum grabbed the feet of the dead Nehor leader, pulling him toward the steep decline farther into the woods. He reached the decline, then gave the body a shove. It rolled down several feet and then went over the edge of the surrounding cliff. While slowly moving back to the original location, Teancum noticed the heavy body left a drag mark in the dirt and leaves. There was also a blood trail leading from the edge of the decline back to the log where the Nehor had died. As quietly and quickly as he could, Teancum covered up the trail of evidence, hoping it would be good enough to keep those looking for their boss from finding him before Teancum could figure out his next move.

Confused and lost, Teancum sat on the log for a moment, trying to gather his thoughts. The stress of dealing with the crimes against his family, the injuries, the fighting and killing, the events in this evil camp—all of it was weighing him down to the point of surrender. "What are my options? I could make a run for it." He looked around again to confirm he was still alone. "They know who I am, now. Surely they will hunt me down when they realize I have killed their camp commander." His shoulders slumped as he continued to think. "But I can't stay here, either." Doubts and fears will kill a soldier just as quickly as an arrow. Teancum knew this from the time he spent with his father-in-law, but what was he to do? The situation seemed hopeless. What Teancum did know was he needed to heed the advice of the old woman and get back to camp. If he was going to have any chance of surviving the next twenty-four hours, he needed people to see him around the fire so he had an alibi. Resolved to face his fears, he grabbed the bag of beans and started moving from the dark woods and headed toward the front of the hut when he stopped himself. *This is the same location where the old woman was seen coming out of the trees. If anyone is watching, they might get suspicious if I return from the same direction. I need to find a different location to re-enter the camp. Someplace where it won't seem so unusual for me to be in the shadows of the trees*, he thought for a second. Then it came to him, "The latrines...." Teancum smiled to himself at his ability to be clever. Moving deeper into the dark woods, Teancum quietly made his way around the outskirts of the camp toward the general location of the male latrines. The only way to access the camp from the outside was along the narrow mountain path, so the Nehor leaders only posted sentries there. The rest of the camp was surrounded by the cliffs and drop-offs. Teancum took advantage of this fact, moving quickly, but quietly through the trees and undergrowth. As he approached the male bathrooms he paused for a moment to listen for sounds and check for signs of movement. Feeling confident he was alone, Teancum walked back into the light of the huts and fires while he pretended to be re-fastening the ties on his britches. To the casual onlooker, it appeared he had finished his business and was returning to the warmth of the evening fire.

Teancum casually took two more steps into the light. Looking down at his hands, he suddenly realized he had the blood of the Nehor leader all over him. In a moment of absolute panic, Teancum froze in fear. He was undone. *There is no hiding this evidence. Everyone will know he is the man who killed the leader.* He started to shake again, but not from adrenaline.

"Everyone, quiet down and listen to me!" a strong voice rang out, from Teancum's right side. He thought for sure the voice was going to call out for his arrest and judgement. Closing his eyes, Teancum slowly reached for his knife. If he was going to die tonight, he was going to take a few more Nehor with him.

"The camp is now in lockdown and we are going dark!" The voice had a face— it was the head sentry guard who met Akin and his band on the trail as they entered camp. "There is a large force of Nephite soldiers in the valley below. We don't know why they are here, and we are not taking any chances." He was in full armor, along with several additional men who were standing next to him. They were ready for a fight.

Teancum's heart skipped a beat. *The Nephite soldiers can help me return home,* he thought as an emotion he had not felt in some time crept into his soul: hope. *I must find a way to escape and join up with them.*

"Until further notice, this camp is on lockdown. No one comes in or leaves, and no sounds. Douse all fires and lamps. Unless you are on the security detail, everyone is confined to their quarters." He looked at the stunned faces around the fires. "Obey without question, that was your pledge." He was snarling now, like an angry dog. "You all know the penalty for disobedience! Move!"

Everyone in camp was up and moving. Lamps were covered, fires doused, huts and shops closed tightly, and the common area was emptied in a matter of seconds. Teancum stood motionless observing the events unfolding before him. He had been sure it was going to be his last few moments on earth. He thought everyone was going to see him covered in blood. But, now the only light to indict him was from the crescent moon above. All the people in camp who would have condemned and executed him were now scattering and hiding for their lives. *I must get free of this place and find the soldiers in the valley!*

"You!" It was the head sentry guard barking at Teancum. "What are you doing?" He was a ways off from Teancum and distracted by the chaos surrounding him. With the confusion and lack of light, he did not see the bloodstains on Teancum's clothing. "Where are you supposed to be?"

Teancum felt the weight of the castor beans in his left hand, and answered without thinking. "Sir, I am on cooking duty in a few hours, and was headed to the mess area to start preparing meals for tomorrow."

"Fine." The guard leader waved his hand in a dismissive manner toward Teancum. "No light or fire until I sound the all clear. Is that understood?"

"Yes sir." Teancum quickly started to walk toward the cooking area while he tried to remove his blood-stained coat.

"Wait!" The guard called out. Teancum froze and closed his eyes. He realized there was no escape this time. He held his breath and readied himself for the inevitable. "What's in the bag?"

"The bag?" Teancum gasped as he finished rolling his coat up to hide the blood. "Why, just some nuts I gathered to use as flavoring for the food in the morning." He held the bag up and gave it a slight shake. "Gives the meal a nice buttery taste." He smiled as he tried to distract the guard from looking at his blood-covered coat with the bag of castor beans in his other hand.

The guard walked up, and while staring Teancum in the eyes, he took his right hand and squeezed the bottom of the bag, twice, slowly.

"See? Just nuts," Teancum smiled, trying to come off as a simple man who just wanted to do his assigned responsibilities.

Teancum had not shaved since he left the burning wreck of his ranch home, those many weeks ago. Behind his beard, he tried to hide his true identity, but right now, he felt like the head guard was reading his every thought and knew exactly who he really was. There was a long pause, and Teancum tried to avert his eyes, making himself seem harmless. When he did, the guard let go of the bag. "Off you go. If there is fighting to be done, try not to get in our way."

"No...no, sir," he stammered his words to keep up the appearance of a weak person. As the guard moved past him, he bumped his shoulder against Teancum's in a silent show of disrespect. Teancum watched as the guard met with his comrades, pointed to the camp entrance, then disappeared into the night. The camp was completely dark. Most of the others had cleared out. Teancum needed to move fast if he was going to get his poison ready for the breakfast and still deal with the corrupt deputy who had been assigned to kill him.

Teancum snuck into the kitchen area and found the sugar pot. He knew the men would be hungry after a long night standing ready for a Nephite attack and they would be heaping sugar onto their cold breakfast mush. It was too dark in the hut for Teancum to see clearly. He knew he needed some light. He closed the door, then quickly put a large tarp in front of it to keep any light from escaping. Then he lit a wooden wick on some of the cooking embers, and touched the wick of a small oil lamp. The lamp provided just enough light for him to work. In the kitchen he found everything he would need to grind the raw castor beans into a powder. Using a grinding stone, he easily crushed the entire contents of the bag in a matter of minutes. He then poured about half the contents of the large sugar pot into a second bowl. Then, he refilled the original pot with the ground up beans. "Big pot for the men," he spoke to himself, as he formulated the plan. "Smaller bowl for the women and children." He set the smaller bowl down, behind some flasks and kegs near the back of the cooking hut. "If I volunteer for kitchen duty, then I can monitor the distribution of the poison, ensuring the women and kids don't get any." He paused as he contemplated his thought process. "I am not like them…" He saw the bodies of his family in his mind, his mother, wife and children, his elderly grandparents, all dead because of the Nehor.

He remembered the laughter as the robbers killed his grandfather. "I am not a monster." He remembered the thoughts and feelings he had on the cliff face where the last remnants of his old self died with his youngest child. *Justice!* The word rang out again from deep in his subconscious. "Tomorrow...." he whispered, "there will be justice."

The camp was as quiet and still as a graveyard as Teancum emerged from the cooking hut and carefully made his way back to his sleeping bunk. He moved through the market and common areas like a thief. He came to where the majority of the single men were assigned quarters. There were several long log structures with canvas covers where rows of men slept. Most of the men were stationed out in the woods in defensive positions, waiting to see if the Nephite soldiers were coming to attack. Teancum, still being fairly new to the camp, was not yet assigned watch duty, so volunteering for kitchen help was not out of the ordinary. Moving by moonlight, Teancum rounded a corner and as he started to approach his assigned cabin, he caught movement out the corner of his eye and heard the faint sound of metal clanking against armor. He froze, then carefully moved backwards into the moon shadows of the canvas overhang nearest to him.

"This one," an unknown voice rang out in a loud whisper, "he sleeps here." It was the corrupt deputy and a second, unknown man in the armor of the Nehor guards. Teancum had almost forgotten about the conversation he had overheard earlier this evening and the threat to his life. He silently cursed himself again for not staying focused.

"Are you sure?" The deputy questioned the guard.

"Yeah," the guard responded, almost insulted that he was being questioned, "I'm sure."

The evil law man gave the guard a hard stare, holding the gaze for a moment. There was an unspoken battle of wills going on between the two men, some unknown disagreement which had not yet resolved itself. "No more mistakes!" The big deputy waved his finger in the face of the guard. "Stand watch." He then pointed to the corner of the cabin where he wanted the guard to wait for him. The guard was insulted but moved as he was ordered.

Teancum watched from his vantage point as the deputy moved to the entrance of the sleeping cabin. As he went to pull back the tarp cover over the entrance, Teancum saw him reach for something hidden behind his cloak and tucked into his belt. The deputy stepped inside the door and Teancum caught the gleam of a Nehor assassin blade in the man's left hand.

You kill the man holding that blade, the voice of his grandfather rang out in his mind like the rush of a mighty wind. Images flashed across his mind of the blade that killed his father and the one in the Nehor's hand as he held it to his child's neck. *This man walks freely in the halls of the Judges and is influencing the people who govern the Nephites. He is trusted and respected by the very people he pledged to destroy.* Teancum could hear his grandfather almost begging him to kill the Nehor assassin. Teancum could feel the hot blood pulsing through his veins and his legs started to shake. He caught himself starting to pant, as the breath in his lungs was burning inside him. *That man is a Nehor assassin and he went into this tent to murder you. He is a coward, a traitor, and a killer.*

Teancum knew what he had to do. Everything suddenly went cold and still in his mind. Teancum's vivid eidetic memory sprang into motion. Suddenly he could see the camp in his mind's eye, from the perspective of a bird flying overhead. He saw the sleeping quarters and the disgruntled guard standing watch. He saw the cooking area, the simple market and the classrooms. His vision suddenly focused on the open area near the classrooms where a rack of spears and other weapons were set up for training. They were simply made, but effective weapons the recruits would use to learn the skills of a Nehor. Teancum realized he was not far from the weapons. Smiling to himself, he carefully moved through the shadows and around the back side of the crude building. Being much more deliberate in his movements, Teancum made his way to the training area, grabbing a stout spear from the rack. Quickly checking the weight and balance of the weapon, he found what he was looking for and made his way back into the shadows. Moving back to the corner of the building where he had first hidden from the guard's view, Teancum spied around the edge of the wall and could see the guard in the moonlight. The man had his back to Teancum and was not being attentive to his surroundings. He felt safe in his environment, knowing his fellow Nehors were on the perimeter or watching the trail for any Nephite infiltrators. He also assumed the man the deputy was going to kill was fast asleep, in his bunk and no threat to him. Teancum watched the man for a second. As he was watching, he could see the image of the man's heart beating in his chest. Teancum knew what a spear strike to the guard's heart would mean— almost instant death. He had to move quickly and very quietly. Any possible chance the guard could shout out an alarm would mean doom for Teancum. He scanned the grassy ground leading up to the guard and saw nothing he could trip on or disturb that would alert him.

I need to go quickly, before the deputy realizes I am not in the sleeping cabin and comes back out. Teancum felt the tension well up inside him as he watched the guard and waited for his moment to attack. He was gripping the shaft of the spear so tightly his hands started to tingle. Crouching down low in the darkness, he watched as the guard aimlessly wandered around the outside of the large sleeping cabin, turning and changing his position with randomness. "No movement I can predict..."Teancum whispered to himself, as he watched his prey like a great cat. He glanced at the bunkhouse opening where the deputy walked in. *I need to make my move.* The guard stopped pacing and turned his back to Teancum. The guard reached up toward the sky and started to stretch and yawn out loud. *Now! Go now!* The voice in Teancum's head barked at him. Keeping low and out of the man's sight, Teancum moved toward the guard with the spear point out in front of him. He stopped short, then made a quick and low whistle. The guard was startled and turned around to see what was making the noise. He froze in fear when he saw Teancum before him. He tried to call out but Teancum expertly drove the sharp point of the spear right into the man's chest, piercing the heart and shutting down the engine of life. The guard fell backwards with a thud and Teancum moved past him and out of sight of the door to the sleeping cabin.

Now what? he asked himself, as he repositioned his body to be ready for the evil deputy to exit the sleeping lodge. Teancum looked down and saw the guard had on a dark-colored cloak.

The mind sees what it wants to see... The voice in his head reminded him of this fact. Teancum reached down and unlatched the cloak from around the neck of the dead man. Pulling hard and fast, he brought the cloak from under the guard's body, then quickly wrapped it around his shoulders. Pulling the hood up and over his face, he then grabbed the dead man's arms, pulling the body next to the cabin and out of sight. Teancum then picked up the dead Nehor's ornate spear from the ground. It had a large flat spear point with bird feathers and bright ribbon wrapped around its shaft. Hoping the deputy would not give him a second look, Teancum stood up, assuming the position of a lookout while waiting until the assassin re-appeared.

He did not need to wait very long. Only a few seconds went by when the corrupt man poked his head out from the canvas cover. "What's all the racket?" he demanded, in a barking whisper. "Are you trying to wake the dead?" The assassin only gave Teancum a glancing look. The cloak and spear did the trick. "He is not here, and there is an empty bunk."

"There is something you should see over here," Teancum spoke in a low, registered, whisper gesturing toward the dead guard's body in the darkness.

"What is it?" The Nehor assassin responded abruptly, as he flung the canvas cover open and stepped out, the snake-head blade still in his hand.

Teancum lowered his head to keep his face hidden under the hood of the borrowed cloak and pointed down. "There is a body back here…it might be the guy you are looking for."

The deputy rushed past Teancum and bent down to inspect the face of the dead man lying in the weeds next to the back of the sleeping cabin. It only took him a second to realize he had been tricked. The face of the dead man belonged to his fellow Nehor. The corrupt deputy knew he had been duped and spun around with the assassin blade at the ready, but he was too late. Teancum ran the spear right into his chest. He was aiming for the man's heart, but he moved at the last second, the metal tip pierced the Nehor's left lung while severing a major artery. The pain and damage to his lung was an overwhelming shock to the man's system. He gasped for air as he wildly slashed at Teancum with the snake-shaped blade in his hand. Teancum kept the man pinned down with the pressure he put on the spear, then stepped on the arm swinging the large knife. Teancum knew the more the Nehor struggled, the more damage the sharp metal buried in his body was doing to his organs. With all his bodyweight on the arm with the knife, Teancum squatted down next to the dying man, covering his mouth so he could not cry out. All Teancum needed to do was keep his distance from the assassin's knife and hold him down. Fate would do the rest. After a few more seconds of futile struggle, the corrupt deputy started to succumb to his injuries. He looked up at Teancum as he struggled for breath and his body went limp. Teancum moved his hand away from the man's face.

"I know you, Teancum." the man mouthed in a gasping whisper. Blood frothed from his mouth as he tried to speak.

"Teancum is dead." He spouted back in a defiant but low tone. "Your Nehor brothers killed him and his entire family weeks ago." Teancum pushed and jerked a little bit on the spear shaft causing bolts of pain to shoot through the dying man's body. "I am the angel of death, come to avenge his blood. I am the hunter now— you and your clan are the prey." Teancum twisted the spear shaft in his hand spinning the sharp blade inside the Nehors body, then violently pulled it from his chest, causing even more fatal damage. The dying man crumpled over into the fetal position. "But don't worry," Teancum continued in a casual tone, as he checked his surroundings. "By this time tomorrow, many more of your murdering dog brothers will be joining you in Hell; I will personally see to it." Teancum picked up the assassin's blade the Nehor had dropped on the ground, then moved to where he could see the dying man's face. He stood motionless as he watched the evil and traitorous Nephite take his last few breaths and pass to the next world. As he stood there, he realized he felt nothing for the two Nehors he had killed, nor any remorse for the leader whom he had also killed a few hours before. He looked down at the expertly crafted knife still in his hand. *What have I become? Am I no better than them now?* He was becoming outraged at himself for not finding any sign of remorse in his heart for what he had done. "Curse them all!" He spoke out loud and raised up his arm to throw the assassin's blade deep into the dark woods behind the cabin. He stopped himself just before he let the weapon fly. Looking down at the two bodies, he quickly formulated a plan. *I can stage it to look like these two had a fight and killed each other. This will cause quite a bit of controversy in the camp in the morning and take the attention and suspicion away from me.* Teancum liked this idea. He took the assassin's blade and drove it into the chest wound of the Nehor guard, then put the ornate spear back into the guard's dead hand. The tip of the guard's spear he put next to the wound on the evil deputy's chest to make it look like they stabbed each other during a heated fight. Inspecting his handiwork, Teancum smiled. *Between the Nephite army in the valley below, the two dead men here, the poisoning of the men of the camp, and the missing leader, there should be plenty of distractions to help me escape.*

There was still the matter of the blood all over his clothing and hands. Teancum left the scene of the crime, walked slowly and carefully around the sleeping cabins, to ensure no one was up who might have seen what he did. He went to the wash area, removed his top shirt and britches. Quietly, he splashed cold water all over his face and hands to get the blood off his skin. Teancum then took his soiled clothing wrapping them into a tight bundle. If there had been a fire burning, he would have just tossed them into the flames destroying any evidence of his involvement. With no fires lit, he was stuck with the blood-stained garments. Thinking for a second on the problem a solution came to him, *I will toss them over the cliff behind the sleeping area.* He smiled again at his problem-solving skills. *By the time someone finds them, I will be long gone. This night and the coming dawn will be just a cursed memory for those Nehor who survive.*

Teancum carefully made his way into the woods, walking the several yards into the bush until he reached the cliff face. He gave the bundle of bloody clothing a toss over the edge. Teancum watched the clothing disappear into the blackness of the depths below him as he stood there for several seconds, pondering the events so far. As he was standing there, he realized he was getting very cold. He had stripped down to just his underwear and sandals. He still had some of the cold wash water on his body. "I need fresh clothing," he whispered to himself as walked back to his meager possessions stowed under his cot.

Teancum tried to sleep but the lingering adrenaline still in his blood stream and the thoughts of what he had done, as well as what he must do in the morning, made sleep almost impossible. So he lay face up, awake and fidgeting until he could take it no longer. He got out of his bunk and quietly gathered the things he would need for the day. Tiptoeing past the sleeping men, Teancum exited the bunkhouse, walking briskly toward the cooking area. He tried very hard to act like he did not see the two dead men on the ground, along the side of the long sleeping cabin. *Let someone else find them,* he thought to himself. *Get to work in the kitchen; it will be a good cover story.*

Teancum made it to the kitchen as the head cook arrived. "I have kitchen duty today," Teancum said in response to the cook's inquisitive look. The cook, old and stooped from the rigors of camp life, shrugged his shoulders and entered the kitchen. He was just grateful for the help.

"No fire to warm the water. Cold mush again," the grumpy cook spoke out loud, as he went for the large metal pot holding the remains of yesterday's breakfast.

"I will get the sugar," Teancum volunteered as he went for the large bowl containing his deadly mixture.

The cook nodded his head in agreement as he measured out portions of the cold mush into smaller bowls for the guards and men standing watch. "Cut up some of the apples, and then fetch the salted pork from the root cellar," he barked at Teancum in a gruff tone.

Teancum continued to work and wait for the day shift guards to come for their breakfast before they relieved the night shift. Slowly, by themselves or in small groups, the men of the camp wandered into the dining area, gathered up a bowl of cold mush, a few apple slices and a measure of salted meat. Teancum watched as several of the men of the Nehor clan took a helping of the deadly concoction, then sprinkled it on their morning meal. *Not everyone is taking the sugar*, Teancum thought to himself, as he watched what was happening. *But enough are.*

The men of the day shift quickly finished their meals, then left to relieve those Nehor who stood watch for the Nephite army all night. With Teancum hovering like a hummingbird, the murderous Nehors who had been standing the night watch filtered into the dining area and were served the same breakfast. These men were in a grand and jovial mood like they had just returned from a drunken party and were continuing the celebration there at the breakfast table. Some of them were even bloody. *They did battle with the Nephites*, Teancum concluded as he moved away from the tables, making some distance from the Nehors. *They must have ambushed a patrol from the camp or something.* His mind wandered to the scene of the attack, and the wounded Nephites in the valley in need of a doctor. It made him hate the Nehors even more. As he continued to watch his victims eat the poison-laced sugar on their mush, he made another observation. *Not everyone came to breakfast,* Teancum noted, *and not everyone wanted the sugar for their mush.* He did some quick calculations in his head. *More than half the men at arms ate the poison. I could not measure each dose, but all of them will be sick. If at least a third of the men get sick enough to die, that will cause enough of a distraction for me to escape down the mountain and find the army.* There were some women and children starting to enter the dining area. Teancum quickly grabbed the large sugar bowl from the table. "Let me refill this," he said in a cheery tone. He carried the contaminated bowl to the outhouses, then dropped the bowl with the entire contents down into the foul mess below. Hurrying back Teancum pulled out the smaller bowl of sugar, placing it on the serving table. Stepping back, Teancum felt a combination of dread and satisfaction. He was proud his plan seemed to work so well. He also felt sorrow over what he had to do to stop the Nehor and escape with his life.

Be the ghost that haunts them, the words from the mysterious old women echoed again in his ears. He swallowed hard. *It's a waiting game now*, he thought.

He did not have to wait long. Because Teancum could not measure out exact portions of the toxin, some of the affected men had greater exposure than others. Those men felt the effects first, coming on fast and strong. By the time someone realized the entire camp was at risk, three men had already died, their bodies lying in the open. The camp leader was missing, so there was a vacuum of authority. People began to panic, and as in every situation where evil men are present, a physical struggle over control and leadership unfolded.

Teancum remained at a distance, working in the kitchen watching it all unravel. "If the poison does not kill them, then the fight for command over this village will," he whispered quietly to himself. More men died. Finally, amidst the chaos, the guard-force leader asserted his dominance, taking control of the situation.

"Bring the witch forward," he called out as he held his ground, barking orders. Two men under his command fetched the old woman who had been such an asset for Teancum.

"A gloomy day indeed," she cackled with joy in her tone, as the guards rushed her up to the communal fire pit. Everyone in the village was in a panic. People were either dying from the sickness or from the struggle for control of the Nehor village.

"What do you know of this madness old woman? Speak the truth or I will burn it out of you!" The new, self-appointed leader was not in the mood to be put off. He pulled a glowing red hot poker from the big fire, holding it out in front of him in a threatening manner.

The old woman pulled her arms free from the guards' grasp. "A curse rests on this place," she called out. She held out her arms, twisting them back and forth in front of her, then started chanting. The villagers and Nehors stopped what they were doing as they watched, in amazement as the old woman continued to sway and chant while speaking a strange language. "Death has come for this place… The universe is not in balance and you must pay for your sins. Mmm…" She stopped swaying while lowering her arms. "You are all going to die! The Ghost is coming, he's coming for you all!" She opened her eyes and pointed to the man with the hot poker. "He is coming for you," she cursed him under her breath. "Flee from here and never return!" She screeched loudly. The entire village gasped and the leader took two steps back. As she was speaking, she glanced toward Teancum, making eye contact with him. The guard force commander saw this and looked at Teancum.

Teancum was standing off to the side, away from the crowd, watching what was happening from the background. *Amazing*, he thought. *She is good.* He looked over the gathering. *She has them completely convinced... Fascinating.* His analytical, scientific mind took over as he began to study the moment, as well as the effect it had on the people of the small village. If he had stayed in the moment and not allowed his mind to wander, then he might have avoided what happened next.

The old lady was looking the villagers over, trying her best to invoke a high level of fear. She knew her age and weathered appearance was enough to scare some of them. So she was trying to evoke dread in others with her fierce gaze and overly dramatic demeanor. "Your leaders are missing, your warriors are dying... Flee, before the Ghost finds you!" she glanced again at Teancum, but he was oblivious to what she was saying. The new leader of the Nehors, however, was not oblivious. He suspected something was not right. He had been high enough up in the command structure of the Nehor leadership to know her rantings were a sham. He knew the Nehor leaders were cunning and devious. They used things like religious mysticism and crowd manipulation to influence the majority of the Nehor supporters, or the ones they called the 'useful idiots'. He knew the old woman had no real magical powers, but it kept the panicked villagers in line. So when she started spouting against the clan, he was suspicious. When he saw her look not once but twice at the new man, he reacted.

"You!" he shouted, as he started to forcefully walk toward Teancum. Teancum snapped back to the present, blinking to shake his mind back to life. "You, kitchen help!" the angry leader shouted, "Seize him!" Two more guards ran past the leader, heading right toward Teancum.

In a panic, Teancum turned, trying to run toward the woods and the edge of the cliff surrounding the majority of the village. He had run about ten yards when his legs were suddenly tangled up by a strange object. It was three long sections of rope with weighted ends. The object completely wrapped around his legs binding them together, and holding him fast. He fell hard. Trying to curl up his legs so he could free himself, he saw the guards were too quick. They ran to his side, taking Teancum by the arms. The Nehor guards yanked Teancum to his feet. One of them held his arms behind his back, while the other loosened the rope snare around his legs. Teancum watched as the guard took the ropes off his legs. He recognized the rope contraption as being the same thing he had seen hanging off the equipment belts of more than one Nehor. He wondered what it was but had never found out— now he knew. "Neat trick," he spoke to the guard as the man continued to untangle his legs.

"It's called a bolo," the Nehor guard responded in a matter-of-fact tone as he untangled the lines from around Teancum's legs. "Works well when you are chasing down traitors," the guard smiled a wicked smile as he stood up, showing off the device. Teancum could see the guard was sweating, his eyes were bloodshot and he was starting to breathe heavily.

"He is sick," Teancum thought to himself. He ran the man's face through his memory, but could not remember seeing him at breakfast. *No matter... He is showing the symptoms and will soon be incapacitated.*

"Bring the witch!" the leader commanded, as he walked up to Teancum. Another set of guards seized the old woman, then moved her toward Teancum and the leader. "I don't yet know what devilry this is, or how you are involved." He got very close to Teancum's face as he continued speaking, "But I intend to find out." he spouted. "Bind his hands."

The two guards standing next to Teancum reacted to their orders, forcing Teancum's hands together behind his body. Teancum knew if he was arrested, he was going to die. He needed to act, and quickly.

"How dare you handle me this way?" the old woman challenged. "When the other Grand Masters hear of this, you will be whipped." She jerked her arms out of the guards' hands and moved to be face-to-face with the new village leader.

"Why do I need to worry about the other Grand Masters? Why not the one who rules this camp," the man demanded, in a flat tone with a smile. "Do you know something of the whereabouts of our dear leader?" He was on to her and she knew it.

The two stood in a silent power struggle for several seconds, eyes fixed and locked on the other. "I do know where your dead leader is," she slowly spoke, as a smile formed on her face. There was another woman screaming in the distance as another murdering criminal fell from the effects of Teancum's poison. The boss guard turned self-appointed leader, turned to look in the direction of the screaming. "He has gone to his eternal reward, like that man there— and like you!" The old woman shouted as she reached for the leader's knife tucked in his equipment belt. His attention was drawn to the wailing woman and did not see the old one reaching, until it was too late. She had the blade out and with all the force her tired body could muster, she rammed it deep into the new leader's chest.

The two guards who were holding Teancum let go of his arms, then rushed to aid their leader. The old woman was instantly overwhelmed by brute force as the other guards hacked and slashed at her small frame with their weapons.

"Be the Ghost!" she screamed, before succumbing to the onslaught.

Teancum heard those words, and without a thought as to the outcome, took off running through the camp.

"After him!" One of the older guards standing over the dead body of the witch and his boss shouted while pointing with his sword. There were only three guards left in the area who were healthy enough for a foot chase. Teancum realized he was running blindly and turned toward the kitchen. The guards were close. Teancum burst into the kitchen. There he found one dead guard, slumped over one of the dining tables, dead from the laced food. There was a spear next to the body and the man had a long knife sticking out of his belt. Teancum grabbed both, then moved toward the cooking area.

"I need a distraction," he muttered in a panic as he entered the cooking area. There was a small fire still burning in the large cooking oven as well as several large pots and bowls lying about. Teancum made a quick scan and spied what he was looking for. Grabbing a jug full of oil, he removed the top, then splashed most of the oil over the walls and counters. Next, he took the lid off the oven, exposing the flame. He was about to break the jug over the oven, igniting the entire building, when the guards who were chasing him burst in. Teancum smiled at the guards, who paused to try to figure out what he was doing. He took two steps back from the oven, then smashed the jug on the oven. Burning oil went flying in all directions. Teancum moved back from the flames, then hurried out of the back of the kitchen, as the entire cooking shed erupted in a mighty swoosh. The guards who were chasing Teancum dove out of the door, onto the patio where the eating tables were located.

"The smoke! The Nephites in the valley, they can see smoke for miles!" someone yelled, as the building was engulfed in flames. The thick black smoke was rising, leaving a dark indicator of the Nehor presence for all to see. It was absolute pandemonium as people came to help extinguish the fire. The sick and dead were everywhere, the new camp leader had just been assassinated by the witch, Teancum was loose in the village, and now there was a burning building to contend with.

Teancum ran past the outhouses and back into the wood line near the cliff's edge. He stopped to examine his handiwork and was pleased to see he was not being followed. *The fire has distracted them*, he thought. He could hear people shouting about the amount of smoke and how it would give away their hidden location. "More fire!" he mouthed and smiled. Then he saw the body of the old woman who had helped him. *Thank you*, he spoke through his thoughts. *I will be the Ghost*. Teancum still had the spear and long knife with him. He worked his way through the woods, past the location where he had killed the camp leader and on to the men's barracks. He checked to make sure no one was inside the barracks, then quickly set them on fire, staying just long enough to ensure the fire ignited properly. He made his way back into the trees.

"Look, the sleeping quarters!" a teenage boy cried out from across the camp. People stopped what they were doing and turned to see. A second fire at the opposite end of the camp meant only one thing— the stranger they were looking for had set it. Some of the villagers left the burning kitchen, moving to the barracks to try to stop the spread of the fire to the other buildings close by. Teancum took advantage of the opportunity to make his way back toward the only exit from the village and down the mountain. Teancum was moving fast through the trees and brush near the edge of the cliff. He had finally reached the exit point when a guard working on the kitchen fire spotted him.

"There!" he shouted and pointed as Teancum crossed an open area, running toward the hidden path. The guard dropped his water bucket and reached for his spear.

"No!" A second guard yelled as he grabbed the first guard's arm. "We need to douse the flames and reorganize before we can hunt him down. There is only one way down the mountain…we can track him easy enough. Right now, we need to put out those fires before an army patrol sees the smoke." There were only about a dozen men still healthy enough to fight the fires— they could not spare a single one. The first guard agreed and went back to work fighting the fires.

CHAPTER FIFTEEN

THE GHOST SOLDIER

Teancum was at a dead run now. The branches and long leaves lining the trail going down to the valley slapped at his face as he drove his body hard to escape. *Get to the valley and find the army*, he kept telling himself over and over, again. Trying hard not to lose his balance, Teancum continued to move with great urgency. He saw the distant camp fires from the Nephite encampment last night, so he had a general idea of where to locate the army. He kept moving down the marked trail, hoping it would lead to a route back to his Nephite brothers and away from the pursuing Nehors. As he moved, his inner thoughts turned to the old lady, her last sacrifice and the words she uttered, 'More than one Grand Master!' Teancum was trying to work the problem out in his mind as he kept up the pace. *The Nehor cancer is deeper than I thought.*

Teancum had been moving for quite some time before he finally slowed a little, and was now traveling at a brisk jog when he reached a trail crossing his path. He stopped at the crossing, trying to be quiet for a few seconds, to see if the Nehor were on his tail. All he could hear was his blood pounding in his temples, and his hot breath as he gasped for air. He knew it was useless even to try to listen while shaking sweat from his eyes. *They are coming. Even if I don't hear them, they are still coming. Take the trail to the right*, he told himself. He did the calculations in his mind and figured that direction would be his best chance of reaching the Nephite army encampment. Teancum wished he had had more of a chance to gather some items to help in his escape. *No water, no fire starting kit, no blanket...* He did an inventory of his meager items in his possession, "My knife, a spear," he looked down at his feet and smiled, "and a good pair of rugged shoes." He knew how to find drinking water as well as how to start a fire. He had his grandfather to thank for those skills. He was concerned, if he had to face the Nehor before he could reach the army, he would not be prepared for a fight against more than one opponent. "Run hard and live another day," he panted. Then he turned down the path leading to the right of the cross road.

Teancum ran for another thirty minutes before he reached the edge of the small clearing where the Nephite soldiers were camped. Teancum waited for a second at the edge of the clearing to survey the landscape. *Funny,* he thought. *No guards or roving patrols?* As he looked out over the clearing from behind a large tree, the wind suddenly changed direction. He caught the unmistakable odor of death. He was an experienced and skilled physician and had been around death before. The blood, the gore and bloating flesh of a rotting corpse has an unforgettable smell. He realized no one was moving around the camp. No soldiers, leaders, camp attendants, not even horses, nothing. Teancum felt a cold chill run up his spine. Without thinking, he left the safety of the trees and started to move into the camp. He returned to his doctor mode, looking for survivors. The large carrion birds present in the mountains had already started in on the remains of a bloated horse near the first set of small tents. As Teancum walked past, he waved his stolen spear in the air to shoo the birds away. The hungry birds squawked as they took flight, circling above until the stranger passed by. Teancum saw the flagstaff still standing in the center of the camp ground, with the colored banner flapping in the gentle breeze. He had seen this banner several times in the past. He lived for many years on the army base, inside the great city of Zarahemla where he had seen many regimental colors. But this one, with its solid gold outlined in black, had stuck in his mind because of who it represented— the Cadet Corps. He stood still for a moment, trying to make his mind focus. "No... Oh please, no!" He begged for this reality to not be true, but as he cast his eyes to the ground, there he stood surrounded by the bodies of murdered children. Young boys between the ages of twelve and sixteen, all volunteering their summers to learn the skills of a Nephite soldier in hopes of one day joining the army as a junior grade officer. "No!" Teancum screamed to the heavens as he dropped his spear and knelt down next to the closest body. Checking for any signs of life, he found none, then moved to the next. Still nothing. He continued checking the bodies of the young boys, but to no avail. They were all dead, the leaders too— older soldiers, past their prime physically but still able to lead, teach, and inspire the next generation of warriors. Teancum could tell the older men had tried to save the children. They had put up a valiant defense, but they were overwhelmed by the Nehors. As Teancum was examining the bodies, he started to realize there was a pattern developing with the wounds that were inflicted on the boys and their mentors. "Stab and slash mark to the front and back," he whispered as he checked one boy. "This one had both his arms chopped off," he said of another. He looked at the body of one of the adult leaders and saw arrow strikes to both the front and back of his chest. "Attacked from both directions at the same time." Teancum checked his surroundings and saw the battle take place in his mind's eye. "Simultaneous attack from there and there." He was working out the logistics of the Nehor assault in his mind. "Full charge… No mercy." He stood up and looked all around him, picturing the scene of these boys moving around camp without a care, then suddenly being ripped apart by those Nehor monsters. He could almost hear the screams of the dying boys and the clash of metal. *They cut through this camp like a hot knife through butter.* Then he remembered the jovial mood the night-watch soldiers had been in when they came back into camp for their breakfast. *They came down into the valley to spy on the Nephite army, only to find they were dealing with children and old men.* He felt overwhelming anger and knew what the answer was even before he voiced the next sentence. "Instead of giving the cadets a wide berth and just letting them pass, they attacked and viciously murdered children." He lowered his head. "And you celebrated your cowardly feats at breakfast." The corner of his mouth started to curl up in a bit of a smile as he pondered his next thought, while reflecting on the images of the criminals and murderers eating the poisoned mush. *Justice.*

"This way!"

Teancum heard a Nehor call out in the distance. They were on his trail, coming down the path leading to his location. He looked around for help and found only the dead staring back at him. Their soulless eyes called out to Teancum for revenge. Teancum had had enough of this running and hiding. He was done pretending to be someone else, trying to work around the evil Nehors. They had caused too much pain and sadness to be excused or allowed to exist anymore. With fresh courage, he grabbed a stout sword from the cold hand of one of the dead Nephite leaders tucking it in his belt. Moving to one of the camp's weapons racks, he grabbed a short bow and a full quiver of arrows. Looking back at the trailhead, he formulated a quick but deadly plan. *I will give them a taste of their own medicine. Let's see how they like being ambushed.* Teancum threw the strap of the quiver over his shoulder and then slung the bow. As he moved toward the trees and the path, he grabbed three spears off the ground, taking them with him.

"Here, more footprints!" A second Nehor voice called out. Teancum could tell they were getting closer. He had to hurry if he wanted to be set and in place before they arrived at the Nephite camp. He entered the thick brush and dropped the bow and arrows near a large rock off the trail. Then, quickly checking the path, he bolted across, and set himself behind a bush with the spears. He could see the end of the path and the camp from his position. There he waited for the murderers who were hunting him to arrive. "What are you doing?" he whispered as he held tightly to the wooden shaft of one of the spears. He was trying to work out the problem in his mind. *How many are coming? How well are they armed? What if someone surrenders? Do I still kill him?* A voice inside was trying to talk him out of his lethal plan. *Just run!* He almost dropped the spear and bolted for his life, but then he remembered all the dead children in the camp before him. An image of the grieving mothers who had lost their sons to the Nehor evil burned in his mind. *No!* The braver voices of his conscience prevailed. Stand and fight. *These cowards murdered your children and those boys in the camp. They must face justice.* Teancum settled back down behind the large bush, holding tightly to the spear in his hand. It was only a matter of moments now, before the Nehors came into view. He took deep, calming, breaths while trying to focus on the present moment.

Strike hard and move fast. Keep moving and press the attack… Always attack, the voice in his mind was giving him last minute advice. *You know better than most how to bring a man down. Do your duty.*

Teancum heard the pounding of sandaled feet and the heavy breathing of men coming from over his left shoulder. He knew he was hidden from view, in the brush, so he dared not move or it would give away his hidden location. As the men ran past him, he counted the bodies in his mind. "One, two, three," he swallowed hard. "four, five, six… Seven." The men stopped running and stood at the edge of the clearing, almost in a straight line leading from the tree lined path. "Seven against one…." He felt a thrill of fear run down his spine. Teancum closed his eyes and let out a silent prayer. *Lord God, please guide my hand and help me rid this land of the cursed Nehor. I send them back to you now!*

Is that the same God who let your child die on the cliff? The dark presence took advantage of the moment, trying to put doubt into his mind. Teancum almost felt insulted as he rose to contend with the men of the Nehor clan. *No!* he shouted in his mind at the darkness. *The men before me now, they murdered her. In just a few seconds, they will face God to answer for their crimes.*

Teancum put one of the spears in his right hand and the other two in his left. Keeping low and moving as quietly as the night, he worked his way up and around the bush.

"Do you see him?" One of the men asked as they all stood in the open, panting for air and scanning the surroundings for any sign of Teancum. None of them even thought to check behind them. If they had, they would have seen Teancum, spears in his hands, creeping up behind the last man in the line. As Teancum moved closer to the back of the last man, he had another vision of his medical training. He saw inside the base of the man's skull where the spine joins the head. He knew the point was very weak and vulnerable. If he pushed the tip of the spear into this exact location, it would cause instant death. He remembered the training from the weapons master his grandfather provided him during his childhood, and firmly gripped the spear in his right hand.

"Spread out and search the camp," the leader of the Nehors shouted, while pointing with his sword. Teancum knew he needed to act fast. He took two big steps in order to close the distance between himself and the last man in line. Stopping and planting his feet, Teancum propelled himself up, with the spear in his right hand, driving the sharp tip directly into the base of the man's head. The man gasped and fell forward under the pressure of the thrust from the spear. His body was limp as it fell over the next man in line, knocking him to the ground with his dead friend on top of him. The rest of the criminals turned to see what was causing the commotion. Teancum grabbed one of the other spears from his left hand and flung it at the next man standing in line. The spear hit that man in the center of his chest. He cried out and fell over with the spear sticking out of him. The other Nehors instinctively backed up and Teancum took his last spear and drove it into the side of the man on the ground trying to get out from underneath the weight of his dead companion's body. Teancum had almost instantly reduced the fighting capabilities of the Nehors by half, but there were still four armed men to contend with, more than a match for any trained soldier.

Before the others could react, Teancum dove into the bushes on the opposite side of the trail, to where the bow and arrows were hidden.

"In the bushes! Go!" the Nehor leader shouted to the rest of the men. Two of the men stood still, their minds frozen as they tried to process what had happened. The leader moved to his right and the last man, who had been the first to enter the clearing, moved to the left. Teancum was up on his knees, had the first arrow nocked and the bow drawn. He was surprised at how efficiently he was moving while making the bow ready to shoot. He could see the remaining Nehors through the ferns and branches. He saw the two men still standing in the open, confused and trying to make their bodies react, while the other two men were moving to outflank him. *The ones moving are the priority*, he told himself. The two standing in the open were a threat, but not as great as the ones who had overcome the shock of the ambush and were reacting to Teancum's actions. Teancum quickly scanned the men moving opposite of each other and saw the one who had been first in the clearing had a bow and quiver of arrows slung on his back. The Nehor archer was moving quickly at an angle, while reaching up and behind him to grab one of the arrows with his right hand. Teancum's medical mind flashed a spot just under the exposed armpit of the criminal archer. Teancum realized if he hit that exposed spot, both of the man's lungs and his heart were in perfect alignment for his arrow. Teancum quickly pivoted, took a true aim, letting his first arrow fly. It shot out of the brush like a bolt of lightning, hitting the Nehor archer as he was moving, right in the soft spot of the arm pit. The man's body jerked and seized from the pain and fatal damage caused by Teancum's arrow. He came crashing face first into the dirt and stopped moving. As if he had been training for this moment all his life, Teancum pivoted back to face the two men still in the open. In less than two seconds, he pulled a second arrow from his own quiver, sending it flying toward the next man to come into his view. This arrow hit the second Nehor in the center of his belly, driving it deeply into the organs. The criminal let out a pained cry and dropped to his knees. *Without any expert medical attention, this type of wound is almost certain to be fatal*, Teancum told himself, as he gave a running, emotionless commentary on his actions.

Teancum loaded a third arrow and scanned for the Nehor leader. The leader had reached the relative safety of the tree line and Teancum had lost sight of him, so he turned his attention back to the last man still in the clearing. By this time, this Nehor's mind had caught up with his body and he realized what was happening. Dropping his own spear, the last exposed criminal turned and tried to run into the center of the camp to escape. "Not this time," Teancum whispered, as he took an extra heartbeat to nock the arrow into the bow. He let the arrow fly. It cut through the air with a rushing sound, striking the last Nehor in the back above the beltline and left of the spine. The man fell hard, rolled to his side and crawled behind a Nephite tent. "Blast!" Teancum spat, as he tried to load another arrow before the Nehor moved out of sight. Out of frustration, he shifted his gaze, recklessly aiming his next arrow in the general direction of the leader who had disappeared into the brush, letting it fly. To his astonishment, when the arrow flew into the darkness of the trees, he heard the arrow impact something, then a man cried out in pain. "I got him!" Teancum shouted in surprise, as he jumped to his feet, pulling his sword from his belt as he ran toward the sound of the man he had just wounded. He came crashing through the thick undergrowth, weapon in hand, ready to meet and deal with the man he hit with his unbelievable shot. What he found instead made him pause. His arrow had embedded itself deeply in the bark of a large tree, but there was no injured man. "Blast!" Teancum gasped again. He knew he had been tricked and had fallen for the Nehor's ruse. The sun was behind him and he caught a gleam of light from something shiny quickly moving on his right side. Instinctively, Teancum ducked under the slash of the Nehor's sword then turned to his right to face the attacker. As he moved, Teancum slashed back with his own sword at the man's thigh, cutting a wide gash across the outside of his leg. The attacker recoiled in pain, hopping two steps back, while holding his own sword out in front of him.

"I am going to kill you and leave your bones for the rats and bugs," he hissed at Teancum, as he tried to move to Teancum's side on his injured leg. He was clearly in pain. His bravado was not covering that fact.

"Murdering scum." Teancum spoke back as he held out his own sword in a strong defensive position. "You are not leaving this valley alive."

Teancum took a quick look at the wound to the man's leg. It was a deep cut and bleeding badly. He was thankful for finding a very sharp, well-made blade to defend himself. Teancum knew all he had to do was wait his enemy out and the loss of blood would do the work for him.

"That's a bad wound." Teancum spoke as he pointed at the wound with his sword, continuing to keep his distance from the Nehor. "I must have hit the vein."

The Nehor unconsciously clamped his right hand down on the wound. He could feel the blood oozing out of the gaping wound and down his leg. "It's nothing. I had a horsefly bite worse than this." The defiance in his tone was not masking the truth very well. He knew it was a bad injury. He also knew if he did not get help soon, he was going to be in real trouble.

Teancum moved to his left and then back to his right. The wounded Nehor tried to mirror his actions. He could barely put any weight on the injured leg and almost lost his balance trying to stay in front of Teancum while holding up his own sword. The Nehor was starting to sweat and his color was draining from his face. He was dying.

"Not much longer now," Teancum said, as he checked his surroundings. He had almost forgotten about the wounded Nehor who'd crawled behind the Nephite tent. Teancum did not know if he was alive or dead. He certainly did not need the other man sneaking up behind him. Teancum looked at the man to his front. The Nehor was swaying back and forth now, but there was still fire in his eyes. Teancum made a quick medical assessment of the man's condition. "You are going to pass out any moment," he observed, all the while still trying to keep the wounded man preoccupied with his movements. "Then you will lose so much blood, your heart will stop beating and you will be dead." Teancum took several steps backwards then lowered his sword. The Nehor tried to follow but his leg gave out and he finally collapsed. "You are no longer a threat to me," Teancum asserted, as he tucked his sword back into his belt.

"Why… Why not just kill me?" the dying man gasped.

"Why let you slowly die and not just finish you off? The same reason I poisoned all those men yesterday!" Teancum responded in a frank tone. "It's simple, and it answers both questions. I wanted helplessness to be the last emotion you and your fellow clansmen felt before you go to your final reward. I wanted you, in some small way, to feel what the Nephite people have felt from your actions." There was no emotion in Teancum's voice as he spoke to the dying man. He was done with feelings and rationalities.

"Who are you?" The Nehor weakly asked, as he tried to look up. These were his last words. Teancum pondered this question as he stood still, watching the wounded man slip out of life and into the next world. His body was no longer able to sustain itself with such a loss of blood.

Who am I? Teancum asked himself as he looked for the bandit who had crawled behind the tent. "Let's find out." He spoke out loud as he moved into the clearing and toward the tents.

The Nehor behind the tent knew he was badly hurt. The arrow shaft had broken off at the point where it had entered his back. He tried to pull out what remained of the arrow lodged in his body, but with the amount of blood mixed with mud on his hands, as well as the location of the injury, it was impossible for him to get a firm grip. As he tried to stand and move, crippling shocks of pain went shooting down his legs and across his back. He fell back to the earth, gasping for air and shivering in agony. The best he could do was drag his body along the ground, hoping he could reach the relative safety of the trees before Teancum came for him. His vision was starting to get fuzzy and he could feel his surroundings start to wobble. "Not like this…" He urged his body forward trying to survive long enough to get help. "I am not going to die like this." he gasped. He had managed to pull himself along the grass until he reached a large wagon near the edge of the clearing. It was a military supply wagon that the corps of Nephite cadets had used to transport their tents and supplies into the field. It was empty and detached from the team of oxen which had pulled it. The Nephites had left it on the outskirts of their camp. The bandit thought he could use it to hide there from the man who was hunting him and so quickly killed his companions. He grimaced in pain as he crawled in the tall grass toward the back of the wagon. He heard the echoes of his leader confronting the mysterious Nephite a few minutes before, but now everything had gone silent. *I will wait here until things settle down*, he thought. He had completely lost the use of his left leg now and was pulling himself along with only his arms.

He dragged himself along in the grass until he made it to the wagon. Reaching up and grabbing the wooden wagon wheel, he started to pull himself under the bed. Without warning, Teancum's arrow struck in the center of the back of his hand. The sharp tip of the arrow drove completely through the muscle, skin and bones of his hand, pinning it to the wood of the wheel. The wounded Nehor bellowed in blinding pain. He tried to reposition himself so he could break the arrow and pull his hand out, but the pain and damage from the arrow in his back was denying him full function of his body. Looking at his hand, he realized it was an expert shot, intended to harm but not kill him. Exasperated, he cried out and looked to see the source of the second arrow. "What... What do you want from me?" He screeched at the unseen assailant. He could not see Teancum, but the arrow in his hand was proof enough Teancum was close by.

Teancum had fired the shot, then quickly dropped to the dirt and high grass to get out of the sight of the wounded Nehor. When the man called out in pain, Teancum knew he would be distracted, so he quickly moved to the tree line. He made it before the Nehor turned around to scan the area behind him. Unable to see Teancum, the Nehor tried to free himself. Teancum saw this as an opportunity to get closer to him. Remembering his hunting and tracking skills developed as a boy, Teancum quietly moved in the trees until he was next to the edge of the forest. He watched as the Nehor struggled to wobble the arrow back and forth until it loosened enough to finally free the arrow from the wagon. He broke the shaft and gingerly pulled it from his hand. The wounded criminal curled the injured hand into a ball against his chest and whimpered as he turned on his side with his back to Teancum. Ever so slowly, Teancum moved out from the trees, making his way toward the Nehor. Crouched like a cat, he rose up, placing his feet with such care he made no sound as he moved. The bandit was crying while trying to stop the bleeding from his hand. "Who are you?" He shouted again, whimpering in pain. As he moved forward, Teancum felt the excitement rising up inside him, like on his first hunt when he had killed his first deer. His belly started to quiver and his breath was labored.

Was I lucky, or am I just good at this? The psychology of the moment had his head swirling as he closed the short distance between the trees and the injured bandit. Teancum moved right in behind the Nehor, then rose up to his full height. He stood motionless as he watched the man at his feet try to scan the camp for his tormentor.

"Where are you?" He whispered between sobs of pain.

"Right behind you." Teancum hissed.

The man jerked he head towards the sound of Teancum's voice, crying out in complete horror. "Don't kill me, please don't kill me!"

"I wonder…" Teancum speculated, as he stepped around to face the Nehor. "Did you grant the same gift to the victims of your crimes?"

"I'm not like them!" He shouted as he waved his uninjured hand toward where his companions lay. "I am not a killer." His eyes were wild with fear. Teancum took a sick pleasure from the man's fear.

"Now now." Teancum drew out his long knife as he continued to address the wounded man, "I remember sitting in the classes in the village back there," He pointed behind him toward the distant smoke still rising from the smoldering ruins, "where they told me a true Nehor can convince anyone his lie is the truth. They showed me the way to evoke emotions in others with my facial expressions and way of speaking." Teancum had a '*Got you!*' look on his face as he stared down at the man.

"No! No, I am not like that. I only work for them to pay the bills. I am not a killer or robber," he replied.

"Yet, here you are. You came down the mountain with your friends to kill me," Teancum responded.

The expression on the bandit's face slowly changed from helpless and innocent to angry and contemptuous. "You think you understand everything," he hissed, as he lowered his brow, glaring at Teancum. "But you will never defeat the Nehor. We are too powerful." The man tried to raise up his body to gain some advantage over Teancum. "We will hunt you to the edge of the earth for what you have done here."

All the pain, all the sadness, all the hopelessness and anger which had been locked up inside of Teancum came boiling up the moment he heard those words. "How dare you speak to me that way?" Teancum knelt down, putting the tip of his knife against the bottom of the bandit's jaw. Pushing up until the very tip of the blade had entered the man's skin, letting a drop of blood run down the razor-sharp metal. "It is you and your clan who will be hunted." The bandit winced at the pain of the knife to the bottom of his jaw. He could see in Teancum's eyes, something had changed inside him. He looked more like a predator than a human now. Teancum was burning with the desire to drive his knife into the skull of the bandit and be done with him, but something was keeping him from finishing the job.

Look, the guiding voice in his head spoke, *look around you.*

Teancum blinked several times, then stood up. The bandit was relieved from the pain of the knife point and he crumpled back down to the ground. Teancum took two steps backwards, then started turning around in place. He was not sure what he was looking for but he had learned to listen to this voice. He saw them again. The bodies of all those boys and their leaders, slaughtered by the Nehor for doing nothing more than camping in the wrong location.

Justice, the voice spoke again.

"Justice," he echoed. At some point in every person's life, there should be a defining moment where their destiny is revealed. This was Teancum's moment. He understood now, his purpose and meaning. "I am the hunter now…" Teancum whispered. "I overcame a squad of armed Nehors on my own." Looking up, he could see the distant smoke from the village. He shook his head in acceptance. "Plus, all those up there, I killed them using my medical knowledge." He lowered his head and nodded, understanding his purpose. He knew at this moment he could not return home. He was a changed man. His old life was behind him, and his new purpose was made clear before him.

Be the Ghost that scares them. The image of the old woman who saved his life flashed in his mind.

"The Ghost." He smiled to himself then turned to face the Nehor. "I like that."

"What?" the man spat in a defiant tone. He could see Teancum looking at him and smiling. Teancum walked over to the wounded man, pushing his face into the dirt.

"Make it quick," the Nehor puffed, resigned to his fate.

"Quiet!" Teancum barked. He pulled up the man's shirt to expose the section of arrow still sticking out of his lower back. Teancum made a quick assessment of the injury. "I can't tell the extent of damage the arrow has caused unless I do surgery."

"What?" The Nehor was confused and tried to turn himself back over.

"Hold still." Teancum forced him back down onto his chest, continuing his medical work. "I am going to remove the arrow point. Whatever damage it has done is beyond my ability to fix." He cut the Nehor's water skin away from his belt, then poured some on the wound. Brushing some of the caked-on blood and dirt away from the wound, Teancum was able to expose the broken tip of the arrow shaft. "I am going to need to move some of the skin away from the wound to help get the arrow out." He shifted his weight and sat down on the backs of the Nehor's legs causing the bandit to let out a gasp of pain. Teancum pulled

out his knife. "You might feel some slight pressure." There was a hint of sarcasm in his voice. He cut the edge of the wound to make the opening larger so the arrow could more easily be extracted.

"Agh... Please stop!" the criminal begged, as Teancum cut into the man's flesh. Teancum grabbed the broken arrow shaft and tried to pull it out. It was buried deep in the flesh and muscle. "Nooo.... leave it!" the Nehor howled. The man screamed shrilly as Teancum gave a second tug on the shaft while using his fingers to make some room in the wound. This time he was successful. The remaining part of the arrow was dislodged from the man's back.

"Not as much blood as I thought there would be." Teancum almost seemed pleased with his work, then looked around for what he needed next. "That is a good sign. Don't go anywhere!" He patted the top of the man's head while jumping off him. The Nehor bandit lay still, moving in and out of consciousness from the pain and loss of blood. Teancum moved quickly toward the rows of small cadet tents, poking his head inside the first one he came to. He reached in, grabbing the blanket and sheet off a cot then moved back to the spot where he left the wounded Nehor. Teancum took his blade, then cut the sheet into long strips. He took the first strip, packing it in the wound in the bandit's back. Then he took the next strip and wrapped it around the man's waist. He took the last strip, folded it into a heap, and then put it on top of the wound. Teancum took the two ends of the section of sheet wrapped around the man's waist, tying a quick knot over the wound and heap of cloth, creating a pressure dressing.

"Here." Teancum dropped the blanket next to the wounded man. "This will keep you warm until you are strong enough to get up or the others come for you." The wounded Nehor looked up at Teancum in confusion. "I will find you some water," Teancum continued as he turned and walked back into the center of the camp. The Nehor was perplexed as he watched Teancum search the camp for the items he needed. Teancum returned a short time later with a water skin and a ration of bread. He dropped the items in the dirt at the side of the bandit.

"Why? Why help me?" His voice was weak was hoarse from screaming, and his eyelids were half closed. But Teancum could see the bandit was genuinely questioning Teancum's motives. He could not understand why Teancum bothered to heal him after he'd killed the others.

Teancum stood up straight, looking around at all the dead boys and their aged leaders. He took a deep breath, then looked back down at the wounded criminal. "I want you to deliver a message to the rest of your clan." Teancum paused, then continued, "I want you to tell them I am coming for them. Tell them they are no longer safe in the forests and mountains. I am now the hunter and you are my prey." Teancum shifted his weight on his feet and continued, "You saw what I did to your camp last night. You also saw what I did to your friends this morning." He gestured behind him toward the bodies of the man's companions. "You animals took everything from me— now justice will find you." The bandit could see the fire in Teancum's eyes as he continued to speak. "I have nothing to live for except this one motivation. You tell them, if I see a Nehor, or anyone supporting your evil ideas, I will kill that person. You will all know what true fear is now. The Nehor will never again know peace. From this day until the end of days, the Nehor are now the hunted. I will show no mercy."

The passion in those words left no doubt in the mind of the wounded man that Teancum meant every word. He was afraid to ask the only question on his mind, but he knew he had to. "They are going to ask if I know your name. Who are you?"

Teancum looked off in the distance and was lost in thought for a few seconds as he tried to figure out what to say. He knew he did not want to give them too much information. He knew the more mysterious he was, the larger the myth would grow. Then suddenly it came to him. The answer to the great and last question. He gave a slight smile as he knelt down to look the helpless clansman square in the eye. "You tell them I am Death, I am Vengeance, I am Justice— I am the Ghost Soldier!"

v

V

CHAPTER SIXTEEN

THE HUNT BEGINS

Teancum left the man there by the wagon, then wandered the camp for a few minutes, gathering up what supplies he thought he would need. He knew he needed to hurry; he had no idea if more Nehors were on their way or if real Nephite soldiers were coming to the cadet's camp. Both parties would kill him on sight. He also learned from the lessons in the Nehor training village not to leave a trace. The Nehors would kill him for the deadly deeds he already performed, and the soldiers would think he was responsible for the massacre of the children and hang him from the nearest tree; staying put was not an option. He needed to move quickly if he was going to survive. He hated leaving those dead children's bodies exposed to the wilds of the forest. It was one more reason to kill any evil Nehor he found.

With his fresh supplies, Teancum headed off into the woods. He wanted to make good on his quest to confront all the Nehors, but he did not know where to start. He walked for about an hour in the woods until he came to a small brook running with fresh mountain water runoff. He sat down on a large rock, next to the water, and took off his pack. Looking around, Teancum could still see the dark smoke from the smoldering Nehor village coming from the back side of the large mountains in the distance. "People can see the smoke for miles," he spoke in a whisper. "Any Nehor within a day's walk of this mountain will see it and know it's coming from their encampment." Teancum looked up into the sky to check the position of the sun. "Still a few hours of sunlight left." He checked his surroundings. "This is a good place to camp for the night. I should explore and see if there are any trails or mountain paths nearby. I can stay off the trails, watch to see if there are any Nehors coming and going from the camp. I can follow them, either ambush them in the forest, or see where they go in order to gain more intelligence on their operations." He felt as if he was justifying his actions to an unseen person. Smiling, he moved his pack over to a small depression near the back of a large rock, then began setting up his camp.

Teancum worked on the camp to make it as sound as he could with the time he had left. He gathered up some firewood and set up a small burn pit. The kindling and tinder were arranged so that when he returned, all he needed to do was put steel to flint and he would have a fire. All his water skins were filled. His personal belongings were set in such a way he could easily find them in the dark if he needed to make a quick getaway. When he finished rigging his camp, he left to search for any clues of additional Nehors in the area. Teancum decided to search, using the terrain as his guide. He did not want to lose his bearings and miss his camp site in the dark; until he knew the lay of the land a little better, he was going to keep the dominant land mass he called the Nehor Mountains and the small stream where he was camped close by. Before he left, he placed a large branch across the stream bed on both sides of his camp. Next to the branch, at the edge of the stream, he placed three round stones in a triangle. This way, if he had to follow the stream bed back to his camp in the dead of the night, he would see the branch blocking the way as well as the markings to indicate his camp was close by. He did not want to lose his bearings and walk past his gear and simple food supply. "I am going to need to think this through if I am to survive out here and hunt them at the same time."

Keeping his back to the mountains, he followed the stream bed down the gentle slope for about twenty minutes. He was traveling light with only one water skin, his long knife, and a short hunting bow and quiver of arrows. There was the ever-present pouch of dried fruit bits and nuts in his knapsack, along with his flint for fire starting, as well as a measure of stout cord. He was hoping to find a small game trail in order to set up a rope snare for his dinner. He also had a section of earth colored cloth he lifted from the cadet camp. He had the cloth up around his neck and shoulders. He was going to use it to cover his head if he needed to hide in the thick forest. He continued to follow the stream as it butted against an escarpment of rock making a sharp turn to the right. He stopped, set up a snare trap near a game trail leading to the water, then continued. He was moving lightly and slowly, like a hunter, crouched forward, his bow nocked and at the ready. As a boy hunting in the woods near his estate, Teancum had learned to scan through the trees for movement and stop and listen every so often for any out of place sounds. As Teancum turned to follow the path of the stream, he stopped and pivoted his head to strain his ears. He heard nothing, so he continued for another hour, stalking through the trees and undergrowth.

The trees started to thin out. The ferns and large bushes gave way to more grass and thinner shrubs. "A clearing," Teancum whispered, as he stopped to assess his surroundings again. He reached the edge of the clearing and scanned the open area. There was a wide gap in the trees with a pond in the middle fed by the steam he had been following. *Can't go out there in the sunlight,* he thought as he looked at the sun's position in the sky. *Not much time to look around if I want to get back to camp before it's completely dark.* It was his first day of his new life. He was pretty sure this section of the forest was devoid of Nehors. *I should head back.* He agreed with his own assessment, then melted back into the woods. On his way back, he checked his small trap, finding a ground squirrel tangled in it. It was not dead but it was completely helpless in the noose of the trap. Teancum quickly killed the small animal and picked up his snare. "Not much, but more than I had a few minutes, ago." He smiled at his morsel of food then continued toward his camp. He arrived back at his camp shortly before sunset. He lit the fire, and the squirrel was quickly skinned and put over the small fire on a wood shank to cook. "Maybe tomorrow I will find some Nehor," he whispered as he ate his dinner. A short time later, he was fast asleep, dreaming of better times with his family. As he dreamed, he was jolted awake by the images of them being murdered. It was nearly dawn and the forest was still and calm. Teancum got himself ready for the day. He spent most of the day exploring the forest in a different direction than the previous day. Along the way, he shot a rabbit with his bow. By the time he got back to camp in the evening to cook it, he was starving and salivating at the thought of broiled rabbit for dinner. Overcome with hunger, he cleaned the bones of all meat and chased it down with a full water skin, fresh from the stream. As he sat in camp, with a full belly, and tending the fire while watching the sunset light dance among the trees, his thoughts started to drift again to his family and happier times. Before he realized what was happening, Teancum fell into a deep sleep. His exhaustion caused him to stay in the same position all night. At dawn, the screech of a wood owl startled him awake. He sat upright, sword at the ready. It took Teancum a few seconds to fully awaken and come to his senses. Everything was right where he had left it the night before. The only difference was the fire had gone out and the bones of the rabbit he had eaten were missing. The tracks in the soft dirt revealed some creature had come into camp sometime during the night, stealing them right out from under Teancum's sleeping nose. Teancum got up and stretched his sore body. He made himself ready for another day of hunting Nehor and left the camp. It was another day of useless effort as he searched a different section of the woods and had the same results, no sign or contact with his enemy. He returned to camp in the evening with another squirrel as well as some wild onions and greens he found along the way. "I am wasting my time out here," he said out loud, as he tried to rekindle his fire and cook his simple meal. "Think Teancum… you are smarter than this." He spent the rest of the evening running over his options in his mind. *I need to get closer to them*, he thought, as he sat chewing his meal by the fire's light. *That is the only way to ensure contact. I can't wander around the forests hoping to run into a lone Nehor… But where do I go?* He thought about his condition.

Go where you know they will be. It was the voice in his head which had guided him in the past.

Teancum nodded in agreement and smiled. "The cadet camp— I will start there."

The sun was starting its downward descent behind the western mountains when Teancum reached the outskirts of what remained of the boy's camp. Storm clouds were forming and he could smell rain in the air. "I'm going to get wet if I don't find some cover," he muttered as he looked up into the sky. He watched the camp for any sign of movement from his covered position for about an hour. From the looks of things, the Nehors had come through, taking everything of value they could find, but had left the bodies exposed to the elements. Even the wagon where he had left the wounded Nehor was gone. He started his search there, looking for any signs to help him figure his next move. He saw the pool of dried blood and the broken arrows from the wounded bandit. "Wagon tracks head off in that direction," Teancum noted, as he followed the ruts made by loaded wagon wheels in the soft ground, with his eyes. *They are headed back toward the Nehor Mountains…* The stench of rotting bodies was overpowering his sense of smell, and he covered his face with a cloth from his satchel as he continued to look around.

The condition of the camp was starting to affect him; the bloated bodies, the twisted and contorted faces of the young victims, the dead eyes all staring back at him. He turned to react to the whispers in the wind as cries of panic and pain echoed through the valley and surrounding trees, but there was no one there. As he continued walking, it was becoming too much for him. He started to get weak, then the landscape began to spin. *What is wrong with you?* He demanded an answer from his subconscious. The logical portion of his brain was being overpowered by the basic primal instincts. He wanted to run, to be clear of this horror, and away from everything reminding him of the madness caused by his hated enemy, but he could not move. Everything continued to spin. He was losing control and he knew it. He felt the blood drain from his face, then his legs gave out. It was too late, he went down hard on his knees and elbows. *Weak from hunger, dehydrated.* His physician's mind raced to diagnose the problem. *Emotional overload… Too much—breathe!* Teancum tried to take in air to help calm his mind, but the smell of death overtook him. He vomited what had remained in his stomach.

"Get up! Move, get out of there!" The warning voice inside him was shouting to do something other than stay in the center of this emotional toxic spill. Teancum pushed off with his toes and lurched to his feet. He stumbled and wavered but managed to reach the tree line without falling. Moving on instinct, he found where he had stored his provisions, grabbing for a waterskin. The cool, fresh, water helped tremendously in calming his nerves and clearing his mind. Gulping the liquid and gasping for air, he closed his eyes to clear his thoughts and calm down. As he was breathing, images of his own family lying dead on the grass of his estate burst into his mind's eye. The bodies of his children and wife were in the same condition as those boys in the field before him. This was too much for him, and Teancum cried out in pain. "Nooo!" he pleaded as he covered his eyes with his hands, begging the powers of heaven to remove them from his sight. Teancum lost his balance again and fell backwards over a log. He landed on his back and curled into the fetal position, sobbing. While he lay there, wallowing in his own pain, he eventually fell asleep. While he slept, Teancum had a vivid dream. In the dream, Teancum was flying high over the mountains and valleys of the forest.

He could see everything from the perspective of a great eagle. He saw the destroyed Nehor camp, as well as the open meadow where the cadets were murdered. He could see the many trails and roads crisscrossing the region. He even saw the mighty river Sidon in the far distance as it snaked across the land, emptying into the great sea. Then he saw the main merchant road. It was the largest and most heavily traveled road in all of the Nephite lands. It connected all the major cities to the capital Zarahemla and was a several days' walk away. He could see where he was and the location of the merchant road. The voice in his soul spoke to him through the dream. *There— start your quest at the road. You will find your prey there.* Teancum remembered very little about the rest of his dream when he woke several hours later.

It was still a few hours before dawn. Teancum was awake now and in much better control of his emotions. He even felt encouraged at the thought of finally having a direction to travel and a goal to achieve. He knew he was not ready for the journey, but needed to prepare himself with food and supplies. "I could spend months hunting game, smoking meat and making skins. Then, finding a way to fashion weapons out of raw materials, all the while making sure not to get injured or sick. Or," he looked over his shoulder, back at the remains of the camp behind him in the clearing, "I could see what was left." This meant going back into the camp and scrounging for whatever the Nehor did not take. He did not like this option, but the thought of spending an entire season preparing for his campaign against the bandits was even more dreadful.

He took it slow at first, working his way around the bodies and broken equipment. Teancum made it a point to not look the dead in the eyes as he moved. "You will be avenged… I swear to you all. Just let me pass in peace." Those words gave him a measure of comfort as he continued with his scavenge of the camp. A length of rope here, a discarded blanket there, a stout pack and even a pair of good sandals in his size. The more Teancum combed through the camp, the more useful items he uncovered. A cooking pot, left next to a cold fire along with a hand axe. "Very useful, indeed," he whispered as he inspected his new axe. After about an hour of looking, he had outfitted himself quite well. There was no food to be found, but there was another water skin and more clothing. He gathered up any loose arrows he could find along the way putting them into a quiver. They were of different sizes, some were the smaller ones, used by the boys, and a few were the large black arrows, the trademark of the Nehor. With his pack full of gear, Teancum bid a final farewell to the fallen, then moved back into the woods. "I should return to the original camping spot to organize my gear. At least there is good water and some game for food." Teancum headed out back toward his spot. He was carrying much more weight this time so it took him longer to reach camp, but he made it well before dark. He had his new bedroll out and a fire lit in no time. Teancum left his camp to set a few snares for food then returned knowing he was going to sleep hungry. He spent the next few days checking, packing, and rechecking and repacking his equipment. He was trying to find the balance between necessity and comfort. He experimented with different configurations and ways to carry his gear. He knew each of his simple items were precious and valuable to him in a place like the uncharted forests and mountains. *Not many markets out here,* he thought as he held one of the woven blankets in his hand. *Leaving you behind is not an option, so I need to find a way to make you fit.* There was another reason Teancum was not in a hurry to leave—the game he was snaring was plentiful. Each day, he was successful at capturing food. Between the fresh meat and the wild greens and roots, he had plenty to spare. The more he ate, the better he felt. The better he felt, the more he slept and healed in body and mind. He was still feeling the effects of the original confrontations with the bandits who killed his family. Every day spent healing was one more day he would have to deal with the clan of thieves and cutthroats, but he knew it would not last. He needed to get on with his mission.

Two weeks after returning from the camp of the murdered cadets, Teancum struck his small encampment and headed toward the main merchant road where he could watch the people coming and going between the great cities, looking for signs of the Nehor. It was a few days' walk, but Teancum knew if he kept traveling west, away from the Nehor Mountains, he would eventually find the road. He met the road on the fourth day of moving and set up an observation post overlooking a wide stretch of the road from a vantage point on a hill. He did not need to wait long before a small caravan of goods, being carried by two wagons, came into view. The man leading the train looked like a Nephite in his late forties, which was old for Teancum's time. He was accompanied by two teenage boys. *Probably his sons,* Teancum surmised to himself as

he munched on some jerked meat. Teancum left his gear, taking only
what he thought he would need in order to follow the wagons from a
distance. He wanted to see if the Nehor would make a move on the
travelers. Teancum had been following the wagons for about two miles,
when he saw them suddenly stop. The boys jumped from their wagon
and ran to their father. Teancum moved closer and saw a black Nehor
arrow protruding from the older man's chest. The boys were holding his
wounded body and crying. As he moved closer, readying himself for a
fight, Teancum saw men in dark cloaks step out from the shadow of the
trees, confronting the boys. *Nehor!* Teancum instantly knew what was
happening. The bandits gave no warning or chance for the merchant to
surrender his property. They shot the man in cold blood and now were
closing in on the helpless boys. Teancum was incensed at the complete
disregard for life these Nehors demonstrated. His own bow was loaded.
He moved through the trees like the wind itself to get close enough to
make his arrows count. The boys were begging the Nehors to spare their
lives, but the bandits laughed and killed the first one with a spear thrust.
The second bandit moved to finish off the father with his long knife
when he was hit in the back, right between the shoulder blades with
Teancum's first arrow. The bandit tried to gasp and call out, but the arrow
had penetrated his heart and he fell forward, mortally wounded. The two
other bandits turned to see where the arrow came from when the second
one was struck in the neck with Teancum's second arrow. Teancum had
fired the arrow while running; he had actually been aiming for the chest.
Just as good, he thought, as he watched the second bandit fall next to his
partner. The third bandit had the spear and was making himself ready
for a fight. He moved behind the second boy and held out the spear in a
defensive posture. Teancum dropped the bow, pulled out his short sword,
moving forward to confront the last bandit.

"Who are you?" the bandit shouted. There was panic in his voice. He
tried to grab the second boy to use him as a human shield, but the boy
was aware enough to fight back. The young man started to kick and
punch at the bandit, forcing him to loosen his grasp. The boy felt the
murderer's grip relax so he dropped to the ground, rolling away from
the fray. Teancum pushed forward to strike at the bandit but the bandit
backed away two steps, bringing up his spear. He thrusted the spear at
Teancum. Teancum jumped left, then right, avoiding the spear point and
countered by slapping the spear away from the bandit with his sword.

The bandit recovered and tried to thrust again, but Teancum grabbed the spear shaft just below the metal point and pulled hard. The bandit was off balance as his hands, still gripping the spear, came forward. Teancum chopped down with his sword on the fingers of the left hand, cutting three of them cleanly off the hand. The bandit bellowed in pain, letting go of the spear. Teancum tossed the spear to the side and moved in to finish off the murdering scum. The wounded bandit curled his damaged hand in close to his body, then dropped to his knees, begging for mercy.

"I yield, I yield!" he cried while trying to hold out his good hand as a sign of surrender and care for his injured hand at the same time. "Take me to jail so I can get medical attention. Hurry boy," he chuckled and sneered at Teancum. This Nehor knew his fellow clansmen had corrupted the good-natured folks of the Nephite nation so completely that the law-abiding citizens were now preconditioned through the farce of political correctness to provide the best medical treatment available to prisoners and criminals, all while forgetting the veterans, the victims and those who were truly in need. This Nehor tried to take advantage of the deceit, thinking Teancum was some kind of lawman or soldier.

"I am not here to arrest you!" Teancum barked back as he moved to where the boy was, helping him to his feet. "See to your companions," Teancum gestured. The boy blinked several times and looked back at the wounded Nehor. "Not to worry." Teancum put his hand on the boys shoulder. "I will deal with him." The boy moved to check on his family while Teancum turned back to the bandit.

"If you don't take me in to get medical attention and see the judge, then you can't charge me with a crime," the criminal laughed, consumed by his contempt for the law which had been corrupted by evil.

Teancum smiled and casually walked toward the criminal. He stooped next to the wounded man, who was expecting to be helped up, then slapped him with the back of his hand, knocking the Nehor to the ground.

"You filthy animal!" Teancum barked. "You speak of the law as if you abide by it and honor it!" Teancum pushed the criminal on his back with his foot, then pointed his sword. He put the tip of the heavy blade against the Nehor's chin until the tip stuck into the flesh just enough to cause two drops of blood to ooze out. The bandit's eyes were wide with fear.

"Wait!" He tried to speak, but the movement of his mouth caused more injury to his chin. He grimaced from the pain, but held tough.

"Something you wish to say?" Teancum challenged. The man closed his mouth, carefully shaking his head. "No? Very well then, I will do all the talking now." He pulled back his sword to expose a good-sized gash on the man's chin. "You and your clan are now an endangered species. I am the sword of justice, I answer to no one except God and I have nothing to lose. You murderers have taken everything away from me and my fellow Nephites." Teancum gestured toward the boy behind him, who was dealing with the death of his father and elder brother. The wounded bandit looked past Teancum at the boy. He could see, maybe for the first time, the depth of sorrow he had caused. A crushing fear weakened his knees as he looked back at Teancum, seeing the level of commitment in Teancum's eyes. "I am sparing your life so you can share this one message with your fellow Nehors— death is coming." Teancum locked eyes with the criminal, then raised his voice. "If I see a Nehor, I will kill him. I see anyone supporting the Nehor, I will kill him. I find a building used by the Nehor, I will burn it to the ground. I am what you fear most. I am hunting you and your friends now. I am the Ghost in the night." Teancum stood up straight, looking down on the man as the man cowered before him. "Death is coming for you all...and Hell will be your reward!"

Teancum finished his speech, then moved to one of the dead bandits. He took out his long knife and cut the shirt off the body of the dead man. He walked back to the trembling bandit, tossing the shirt at his feet. "Bind your wounds," he ordered. "You have one minute to be ready to move." The criminal quickly wrapped the shirt around his bloody hand as best as he could. He was in no position to argue with this crazy man who had killed his two friends and bested him in a fight. As he was tying off his wounds, Teancum moved to be with the boy. "Where are you headed, son?" he asked in a gentle tone. He already knew nothing he could do now would ease the pain the boy was feeling, but Teancum tried to sound compassionate.

"The city of Bountiful," the boy replied, sniffing back the tears while gesturing toward the road as it wound into the horizon.

"I will help you bury them. Then, in the morning we will get these wagons to Bountiful together." Teancum put his hand on the boy's shoulder. "Take all the time you need." Teancum turned back to address the bandit. "On your feet, you scum." The man was struggling to stand. "Remember," Teancum pointed at the missing fingers, "I have marked you for all time. There will be no mercy for you if our paths cross again."

"What about my friends? Who will bury them?" he asked, in a pained gasp. The man was still bleeding, but the cloth wrapped around his hand helped.

"Run, you dog!" Teancum pulled out his sword, pointing it at the clansman. "Run, before I forget I let you live and I finish the job." The man did not need to be told a second time and bolted for his life. "Run like the dog you are!" Teancum shouted after him, as he watched the man disappear into the trees. "Go tell your masters the judgement day is here!" Teancum could hear him crashing through the brush. He stood still until he could no longer detect any signs of the bandit moving in the forest. Smiling to himself, Teancum put his sword back in his scabbard then walked back to the boy.

"Okay son, let's get these bodies up on the wagons and get them turned around." There was no response. The boy was frozen, staring at the lifeless forms of his father and brother. Teancum had to repeat himself to get him to look up.

"But sir," the boy finally looked up, "you said we were going to bury them and then continue on to Bountiful."

"Yes, I did," Teancum said calmly, keeping his eyes locked on the boy and placing his hand on the lad's shoulder. The boy was in shock, Teancum needed him to focus on his words, not the horror of the moment. "I wanted the criminal to hear me say it, too. If he is going to seek revenge, he will be looking for us in the wrong place." Teancum smiled at the boy. He did not expect one in return.

"Home is that way?" Teancum pointed down the trail from whence they came.

"Yes, sir. Zarahemla."

Teancum took a deep breath and let it out. "I will help you get the bod—" Teancum looked at the boy's trembling lips and stopped himself. "I mean, your kin back on the wagons, then you can get the teams turned around while I retrieve my gear from the woods." He looked up at the sun's position in the sky. "These are still very dangerous forests. I will help you drive them back to the gates of the city, but that is as far as I will go."

The boy said nothing in response. He just blinked, accepting this as his new reality of life.

Teancum and the boy spent the rest of the day in silence, each sitting alone on one of the wagons. The boy alternated between periods of shock and grief. Teancum's heart broke for him. He knew the boy could see the outlined forms of his dead family members under the light blankets they were wrapped in. But there was another, more pressing worry growing in his mind.

As they traveled toward Zarahemla, Teancum grew more and more anxious. He was not ready to face his old life. The closer they got to the Nephite capital city, the more he wanted to jump from the wagon and run away, but he held his calm for the boy's sake. Life was going to be hard enough for him. Clinically, Teancum understood the psychology of the trauma the boy had experienced at such a young age, but he also knew the shattering loss and grief he felt. It was all he could do not to let it drag him back into his own thoughts and pain.

They continued to travel until sunset, then made camp in a large field, next to the road. There was still no communication between the two as they ate the food set aside for the trip by the merchant's wife, and then made their beds. The horses were hobbled and the wagons were parked side by side. Teancum set up his bed under his wagon, but the boy chose to sleep on top of his load of goods in his wagon. Teancum fell into a restless sleep but was jolted awake in the middle of the night by the grief-stricken cries of the boy. He did not know what to do, so Teancum sat up and shed tears of grief of his own as he listened to the boy weep for the loss of his father and brother. Would this pain ever end? No answer came from the night.

The sun rose the next morning in a hot rage. Teancum squinted as he came out from under the wagon, checking the surroundings. The boy had already gathered the horses and hitched them to the wagons. It looked like he had not slept a wink, but had been up all night crying. His eyes were red-rimmed and bloodshot. The haunted look on his face nearly made Teancum break. Teancum wanted to say something, but he could not find the right words. The boy looked up, and Teancum nodded in acknowledgement of the efficient way the boy had readied the teams. They mounted the wagons and started off again. After a few more hours of quiet travel, they came over a small rise and the massive walls of the city of Zarahemla came into view. Teancum pulled his wagon to a stop, setting the brakes. He knew this was as close as he wanted to get to civilization right now, so he jumped down, walked to the second wagon, and looked up at the boy.

"Tie a lead from the back of my wagon to your horses, then take the reins of the lead wagon. The city is there, you will be safe from here." He pointed down the road toward the main gate. "This is where I leave you."

Teancum looked up at the tormented face of the young boy. He knew there was little else he could do. What he needed now was a safe place to grieve with family supporting him. All the things that were taken from me, Teancum reflected inwardly. "You still have family in the city, yes?" he asked the boy. The young man nodded his head to say yes. "Go to them and let them help you. This can still be a good life for you— live it for those who cannot." Teancum gestured to the covered bodies of his brother and father resting in the back of his wagon. A flash of Hanni's smiling face suddenly streaked across his mind. Why now? Teancum wondered. He could feel those now-familiar emotions welling up inside him as a lump started to form in his chest and his eyes burned. He understood the pain the boy was feeling and wanted so much to comfort the lad. Or was Teancum wanting someone to comfort him? The thought was more than he wanted to bear, so he pushed back from the wagon. "Go, go now," he half-choked his goodbye, and waved the boy on, while fighting the urge to completely fall apart.

The boy silently stared at Teancum as he watched the stranger who had saved him fight back his own tears and anguish. "Are you okay?" were the first words spoken by the boy since the event.

Teancum was surprised by the boy's interest in his own emotional state, he turned and faced him again. "Yes…" he cleared his throat then stood up tall. "I will be okay." He shook off the emotional pain like raindrops gathering on his cloak. His voice wavered, but grew stronger.

"I will be fine, but you must go now."

He pointed again at the city in the distance. Teancum could see other travelers and merchant caravans coming on the road. He did not want to be spotted by someone who might recognize him.

"What should I say happened?" The boy asked.

Teancum took a moment to reflect. Looking around again, he gathered his thoughts, then answered, "Tell them the truth. Tell them your father and brother died protecting you." He took a step closer to the child. "You tell them the Ghost came from the trees, killing the Nehor bandits, then helped bring you safely home." He took yet another step, his voice rising. "Tell the people they don't need to live in fear anymore of the bandits and Lamanites who raid and pillage outside the walls of Zarahemla. The Ghost will protect them now; the Ghost hunts the criminals now." Teancum looked the boy in the eyes. "Can you tell them that?"

"Yes, sir," he nodded as he spoke.

"Very well then… Godspeed, son."

"And to you, sir."

The boy nodded and smiled for the first time. "Will you hunt them for me and my family, too?"

"Every time you hear of me, know I do my duty for you too." Teancum bowed his head as he spoke. The sign of a servant speaking to his master.

The boy nodded his head in acknowledgement, then waved goodbye to his protector. Teancum moved off toward the closest stand of trees at a quick jog, spear in his hand and his heavy pack across his back.

The boy's story of murder and protection spread quickly through the city. Soon, many others began to share similar rumors, dead Nehor bandits and the man responsible loose in the wilds. Soon, he wasn't even a man, he was the legend of the Ghost Soldier. As Teancum continued his mission of justice and revenge, the legend only grew and grew. There were also survivor's tales, told in hushed tones over Nehor fires in the deep woods. Teancum often saved one alive so he could warn the others. Whispers spread throughout the city marketplace. There were sightings and evidence of the Ghost Soldier's deeds: bodies of bandits found, criminal enterprises destroyed, buildings known to belong to the Nehors burned to the ground, civilians rescued by a shadow, a politician exposed. Teancum was everywhere and nowhere at the same time. Just the mention of the Ghost Soldier was enough to scare the Nehor, but not enough to stop them murdering for gain.

Teancum continued to hunt and stalk his prey. He lived like a predator in the cover of the trees, killing with such efficiency the Nehor leadership thought for sure there was a dozen men hunting them. Every mistake Teancum made was an opportunity to learn and grow stronger. Every wound and scar he suffered was a physical reminder of the pain those loathsome men had inflicted on the Nephite people. All the hunger, thirst and fatigue he endured was like a battle cry for his soul. The rain, the cold, the heat, all of it changed Teancum from a man into something else. He became something primal, something dark and dangerous— not just to the bandits, but to himself. He grew cold and empty. After a while, he lost all feeling. He started to take chances and risks greater than the reward. He would boldly attack several Nehor at once in daylight, or expose himself needlessly to injury, just to feel something— even if that feeling was the rush of death all around him. The weeks turned into months, the months into years. He hunted, fought, and destroyed, leaving devastation in his wake. Teancum had no contact with the outside world other than his dealings with the Nehor or a chance encounter with a victim he rescued. Otherwise, he was alone.

Completely alone.

Any man could learn how to kill, but Teancum turned it into an art form. He trained his body to be a weapon. He learned to use anything as a device for destruction. He crafted weapons designed to kill quickly and efficiently: poisons, traps, snares, the sword, the spear, his bow, sturdy sticks, long staffs, his knives and hand axes; all of them were lethal extensions of his body. He could kill with his hands and feet using strikes, kicks and blows to damage vital areas of the body. He learned how to overpower someone using leverage as well as his brute strength. He could run all day, climb the side of a cliff, swim across any river and swing from ropes and branches. He had become a one-man army, and expert assassin— the Ghost Soldier.

Teancum became less aware of the passage of time as the months wore on. He was living each day, hand-to-mouth, with only one goal—kill the Nehor and make them pay for all the suffering they had and would cause. He was growing haggard in mind, body and spirit. It was only a matter of time before something had to give.

The end of the summer planting season was drawing to a close. The days were still warm but the nights were getting cooler and Teancum noticed the migratory birds had begun to return to the wetlands from their mating grounds in the north. He had been trailing a small group of Nehors all morning. He'd discovered them the day before and kept his distance to see if they would lead him to a larger group or a hidden Nehor camp. They were moving quickly through the heavy brush, skirting the main road leading to Manti and Lamanite lands. Like a jungle cat, Teancum was taking his time and stalking his prey, waiting for the right moment to strike. The day had passed uneventfully and it was getting close to sundown when the Nehor band unexpectedly stopped near a thicket of trees and held very still. Teancum spied on the men from his vantage point behind a cluster of large rocks, about one hundred yards behind. They were whispering and pointing at something deeper in the bush. Teancum's worn, dirty cloak provided effective cover as he held perfectly still.

"What are you up to?" He whispered to himself. Then he could smell the unmistakable scent of burning wood. *Travelers must be camped beyond those trees.* He had seen this scenario before and could predict the Nehor's next move. The Nehor had discovered a campsite and were scheming as to how they would rob the travelers around the fire. *Who would be camping this far from the road, this late in the season and this close to the Lamanite lands?* Teancum wondered. "Doesn't matter." He whispered to himself as he slid down off the rocks and dug through his heavy pack for the items he would need to deal with this new threat. *Those Nehor dogs will all be dead soon, anyway.* Deep down, Teancum felt concerned with the realization that the idea of killing no longer affected him. But the urgency of the impending Nehor attack required him to suppress his feelings and focus on what he needed to do next.

It was almost dark now. Teancum looked up, the sun had completely dissappeared behind the western mountains and several stars began to dot the dark purple sky. Up ahead, the four men sitting around the fire were in a good mood as they laughed and enjoyed the roasted meat cooking over the open flames. They had several pack horses tied to a long rope fastened between two trees and their burdensome bundles were stacked neatly on the ground beside the animals. The men were armed with spears and swords but had not assigned anyone to stand watch. It was as if they were unaware of the infestation of Nehors in these mountains or their close proximity to the Lamanite lands. Or maybe they did not care.

Teancum watched as the Nehors split up and moved quietly through the woods around the camp. One bandit moved close to the horses while another moved all the way around the camp and crept within striking distance of the men. The last bandit waited with a large bow in his hand on Teancum's side of the campsite inside the small clearing. *The signal for the archer will be the first strike by the thug closest to the campers.* Teancum played the scenario out in his mind as he readied himself to strike. He had seen it many times before. Although there were only three Nehor against four armed campers, the Nehor knew if they quickly killed two of the campers then the other two would be so overwhelmed by what was happening that they could be easily captured.

Moving in complete silence, Teancum maneuvered himself directly behind the Nehor archer. The man was completely focused on his companions and Teancum quickly sent him to his eternal reward with a knife thrust through the base of his skull. Teancum gently lowered the dead man to the ground and picked up his Nehor bow and quiver of black arrows. Loading the bow and pulling the string back, Teancum took careful aim and waited for the exact moment to loose the arrow. Teancum spotted movement in the bushes near the campers and let his big arrow fly. The arrow zipped inbetween the Nephite men gathered around the fire, startling them with the flash of movement in the firelight and a rush of air on their faces. The arrow struck the advancing Nehor in the dead center of his chest as he emerged from the trees. The impact of the massive arrow stopped the Nehor in his tracks. He held motionless for a few seconds with his eyes wide open in painful surprise. His mouth was gaping open while he stood with his axe high above his head. The campers sat startled for a moment, then jumped to their feet and grabbed for their own weapons. Before the victims of the Nehor ambush could ready themselves for the attack, the Nehor with the black arrow sticking out of his chest fell backwards and landed flat on his back with a thud and gasp of death.

"You fool... You shot Samson!" The third Nehor shouted in disgust as he emerged from the trees near the horses, waving his short sword. He had no idea Teancum had killed his two Nehor brothers.

Teancum quickly loaded the longbow and shot a second arrow at the remaining Nehor. His aim was slightly off and the black arrow struck the Nehor high in his right thigh. Teancum cursed his aim and knew in his clinical mind the arrow had struck in an area with soft tissue only. It was a painful, but not an immediately life-threatening wound. He knew the man could still escape and he needed to move quickly to prevent him from reaching the men around the fire. The last thing he wanted was a hostage situation. He had the briefest memory of that night on the cliff, Carra, the Nehor and the bow. It came and went like the lightning flashes that had surrounded him, but struck him like a blow from a club. NO! He screamed in his mind, You will not escape justice! The Nehor recoiled from the arrow's impact and dropped his sword. Grabbing at the shaft of the arrow, the wounded bandit looked in the direction it came from with pain and contempt in his eyes. Like a nightmare coming to life, Teancum sprang from the cover of the thick brush and charged at the wounded criminal, screaming his war cry, his hands filled with his own lethal edged weapons. The four Nephite men around the fire cringed in shock at Teancum's sudden appearance, but thankfully did not interfere. They moved into defensive positions but seemed to quickly understand the wild man, who had suddenly emerged from the trees, was saving their lives. They watched, mouths hanging open, as the wounded Nehor cried out in pain and tried to flee from Teancum. The bandit turned to run back into the forest, but the arrow in his leg was keeping him from moving fast enough to escape his doom. Teancum quickly caught up to the Nehor and struck him in the back of his head with the blunt end of his own hand axe. The Nehor crumpled from the impact to his head and fell down hard.

"Get up, you scum!" Teancum snarled as he grabbed a thick handful of the man's hair and yanked him to his feet.

"Please... I surrender." The wounded man begged in a groggy haze, trying to orient himself. He could barely walk. Teancum jerked his head upwards and shoved him back towards the campfire. He landed in a heap, knocking over their packs and partially spilling their dinner. The bandit rolled onto his back, hands held out to ward off Teancum, eyes wide with terror.

"Mercy... Please, have mercy!" The Nehor bellowed as Teancum loomed over the man.

"Do you know who I am?" Teancum demanded of the bandit as he kicked him in the side.

"Yes... Yes I do." The injured prisoner gasped in a muffled cry. Blood was running down the side of his neck from the blow to his head. "You are the Ghost Soldier."

"You know who I am, and still have the gall to ask for mercy?" Teancum questioned, his voice betraying his outrage. "You were warned what would happen to any Nehor I found in these woods. And still you tried to rob and murder these men?" Teancum was standing over the Nehor as he spoke and pointing with his knife at the four Nephites across the fire from him. Thus far they had stood in shocked silence, hardly believing the events of the last few moments. There was a moment of quiet, the only sound was the labored breathing of the Nehor bandit. Then one of the Nephites stepped forward, the oldest of the group. Teancum tensed, and shot him a quick glance. Have I misread the situation? Are these Nephites a threat? He wondered.

The Nephite man who stepped forward looked at Teancum with a calm intensity. Teancum saw something familiar in his face and body language. He thought he recognized him from somewhere, but could not remember.

The Nehor broke the silence. "I had no choice, I was forced into this life..." Teancum's attention snapped back to the bandit. "I was in debt..." the man gasped, "I asked them for help... My child was sick..." He looked around to see if any of the men about him were listening to his pleas.

"Lies... All Nehor lies!" Teancum growled, raising his knife. "Die like the coward you are!" The bloodlust began to take hold again, his rational mind pushed to the back as a raw, primal anger screamed for the man to die.

"Wait!" The man who'd stepped forward held out his hand and called out to Teancum.

Teancum stumbled in mid-stroke. Like the warm, gentle embrace of a loved one, something seemed to physically stop his arm. Teancum looked up at the man who called out, dumbfounded and searching for the reason he paused. "This man is one of the Sons of Nehor and would have killed you without a thought, just like he's killed so many others. He deserves justice for his crimes." He shouted.

"He is wounded. He is no longer a threat to you... Or us." There was a calming, peaceful tone in the man's voice. "Justice will come for us all one day. Please lower your weapon." The unseen force took hold again, Teancum lowered his large knife and stepped away from the Nehor.

The man speaking to Teancum was clearly the oldest of the four men. His head was covered but there was a peaceful power radiating from him.

"As long as even one Nehor still has breath in his lungs, they are a threat to all of us." Teancum tried to sound angry, but he could feel the rage draining away as the unknown man moved slowly towards him.

"Doctor Teancum... Is that you?" asked one of the other men. He was standing on the opposite side of the fire from Teancum and the wounded bandit. The Nephite who first spoke to Teancum stopped and took a longer look at the face of the wild man under the dark hood. It had been a very long time since Teancum had heard someone say his name.

Something is not right. How can these strangers know who I am? He wondered. Was this a Nehor trap? He instinctively took two steps back, turned his head to either side to check his surroundings and brought his knife up towards his chest.

"It is you, isn't it?" One of the other men now spoke. He held both of his hands out to show Teancum he was unarmed and meant him no harm. Teancum's head began spinning in confusion. "How... How do you know who I am?" He angrily demanded, "Who are you, is this a trick?" His senses were on alert, scanning the surrounding woods for threats. If this was a trick, he was in deep danger, possibly surrounded. He started to step back, the familiar rush of adrenaline pouring into his body, readying him for attack.

"Doctor Teancum, please, no tricks. It's me. Omner." The first man to recognize him removed the covering from off his head and smiled. "Do you remember us?" He pointed to his companions each in turn and continued in a gentle tone.

"Himni, Aaron and Ammon?" He spoke their names as he pointed to them. They all in turn removed their head coverings and exposed familiar faces. Teancum's mind was racing to identify those names and faces from his past. During his time spent focused on killing the Nehor, he had locked his former life deep inside his soul to avoid the pain of his loss. "You were a friend and advisor to our father, King Mosiah."

Teancum remembered them now. The darkness in his mind suddenly parted as he saw flashes of light from his former life. He did know these men. They were merely boys the last time he'd seen them but he now remembered they were the sons of Mosiah. He had been in their household, as he'd met and counseled with the king. "I know you." Teancum whispered.

Teancum also knew them when they were a scourge to the people of his mother's church. Hanni had spoken of praying for them, as did the whole church. Did the boys know that? Hanni said God had heard and answered their prayers, as he answered all the prayers of the righteous. The king's sons had been horrible people. They were bullies; mean, spoiled and cruel. He tolerated them and their actions out of respect for their father, the king. Teancum remembered when they'd unexpectedly had a change of heart. It was said by the faithful they saw a heavenly messenger and were rebuked for their wrongdoing. In response, they devoted themselves to the Christian faith and to missionary work. At the time, Teancum was still a bit skeptical about messages from heaven, but he had seen a complete change in their demeanor. They had traveled around the land, begging forgiveness and righting the wrongs they had caused. People had rejected them as frauds and spit upon them and chased them out. But, they had never retaliated, never used the power they held through their birth to make others listen. After the change, he had grown closer to them and was very courteous when they expressed their newfound testimonies to him. Teancum was there when they all refused their royal birthright and left to do God's work among the Lamanites. He felt, like many others, they were going to certain death.

He felt overcome by a wave of suppressed emotions as he looked into a familiar face for the first time in years. "Prince Ammon." Teancum whispered and slightly bowed to the same man who asked Teancum to wait before he killed the Nehor. The gentleman in him instinctively came through even though he was dirty and in rags.

"Doctor Teancum..." Ammon spoke respectfully as he stepped forward and extended his hand in greeting. "You have no idea how overjoyed I am to discover you are still alive." As Teancum touched Ammon's hand, he felt a tidal wave of love and peace envelop his entire body. "Our hearts broke when we received word of your family's murder and that you had disappeared into the forest. Our family..." He gestured back to his three younger brothers. "We lamented for months." Ammon put his left hand on Teancum's shoulder. "The entire Nephite nation mourned for your loss. Search parties were sent to try to find you and those responsible for the horrific crime." He paused to make eye contact with Teancum. "Have you been out here in the mountains the entire time?"

"The Nehor..." Teancum tried to speak more but was overwhelmed by his emotions. He had not spoken to anyone of his loss and pain before now.

"They killed them." He pointed accusingly at the wounded man still on the ground trying to associate that man with those who murdered his family. Laying in the midst of camp, forgotten, the bandit had pondered crawling to escape, but couldn't bring himself to move. He stared at Teancum, stunned by this outburst of sudden emotion. A moment before, he thought he was going to die, now his accuser was starting to break down. Something tugged at the Nehor's heart, he felt emotions begin to surface he had thought were no longer possible.

Teancum fought to control himself as tears came unbidden. He was becoming frustrated that he was so emotional. Fits of sobs and gasps for air shook his body.

Ammon could feel the suffering and hear the agony in Teancum's voice as Teancum sputtered out the events of the last two years of his life. Like the sudden release of a flow of water, Teancum felt helpless to stop an overwhelming desire to share with someone, anyone, what had happened. He let his emotional guard down for the first time in longer than he could remember.

The sons of Mosiah led Teancum back to the fire and salvaged some of their food and water. Teancum ate and drank in silence, trying to understand what was happening to him. Aaron expertly removed the arrow from the bandit's leg and bound his wounds. Teancum noted with a smile his skill in treating the wound.

"You do realize that if you try anything, he will kill you." Aaron spoke to the bandaged Nehor as he tied him to a tree with a stout rope and gestured towards Teancum.

"I am not like the others." The bandit responded, eyes downcast. His lips trembled as he seemed to be mouthing words to himself. Is he… praying? Teancum wondered.

"You owe us your life. Don't make us regret it." Himni said as he set a plate of food and cup of water down next to the bandit. After securing the prisoner, two shallow graves were dug and the two dead Nehor were laid to rest. Ammon offered a prayer for their souls.

"Oh great merciful Lord, we are sorry to take the lives of these, thy sons, and would not send them to thee unprepared if we could. Please have mercy on them, and upon us, who love Thee and seek to do thy will."

Teancum stood by, silently. Those men did not deserve respect. If it had been anyone else doing the praying, Teancum would have left the bodies to rot and stormed off. His family had been given no such respect. He squeezed his eyes tightly to drown out the sudden image of his wife and children laying in the grass, unmoving, covered with cloaks. The pain was so intense it took his breath away. He could not and would not forgive. Justice needed to be done!

Justice does not belong to you, a voice said softly, like a whisper in his mind. His eyes snapped open and he thought he saw Hanni, not unmoving, but smiling, holding out her hands. "Live for us", she mouthed the words. He shook his head, it wasn't real, it couldn't be.

He looked at Ammon, who had ceased praying and was looking intently at Teancum. He turned, the others were staring at him, as well. Teancum turned away from them, surprised at the sudden impression that came to him. Please, come home, the voice again spoke.

They finished burying the bodies and turned back to the camp. Omner stoked the fire and they sat around the flames in silence. Teancum seemed to feel they were waiting for him to speak. The smell of the cooked meal took his mind back, and he felt for a moment he was back in his home, without a worry or care. Home. It felt so far away. Could he ever go back? Aaron offered a prayer of thanks and they finished eating.

"So you have been out here, hunting those criminals, by yourself... This entire time?" Himni asked. Teancum nodded his head as he continued devouring some of the meat and bread they had given him.

"You have not been back to your ranch, or to Zarahemla?" Aaron questioned as he cleaned his hands after helping with the graves and sat back down near the fire.

"There is nothing to go back to." Teancum's voice was cold and low, but somehow, he didn't believe himself.

He took a long drink of water and lowered his head. "Besides, how do I explain all of this?"

"All of what?" Ammon asked. There was true questioning in his tone.

"There is a reason that criminal tied to the tree called me the Ghost Soldier." He pointed at the wounded Nehor who was clearly in great pain.

"There is a reason he knows who I am." Teancum was again surprised he was speaking so freely, but he wanted, no, he needed to tell someone, have someone tell him this had all been worth it, that he'd made some kind of a difference. "I have done things... Things that would make even the murderous band of Nehor fear me."

"I have heard some of the stories." Himni chimed in. "We all have. The Lamanites, they spoke of a vengeful spirit who fought for the weak. Others, a cold-blooded assassin. Some said you were made up, a thing to frighten children... a ghost."

Teancum remembered Himni as the shy one and slow to speak in a gathering. He usually just followed his brother's lead. Teancum was impressed he was speaking up and being his own man now. "We have all spent a great deal of time among our brothers the Lamanites and the tales of the Ghost Soldier are known even among them. They seem to fear you as much as they fear the Nehor."

"And what do you think?" He said to no one in particular. They glanced at each other. Himni stood and looked at Teancum squarely. "I have seen the worst of humanity, and the best. I believe that no one is past saving, not even them." He pointed to the Nehor. "Not even you, Doctor Teancum." Teancum tried to think of something to say, but the injured bandit began to thrash around. Teancum jumped to his feet, assuming the man was trying to escape.

The wounded man called out for more water. His leg wound was still bleeding and the blow to his head was aching. Teancum rebuked him and told him to quiet down. The sounds of the man suffering had made him go cold again. "What of all those who are suffering because of what you and your clan did to them?" He bellowed at the prisoner. It was tensely quiet for a few moments and the sons of Mosiah exchanged glances.

"Maybe you could help heal him?" Ammon asked in a still voice.

"I am so far removed from my days of medicine and politics. I could never go back." The Ghost Soldier sighed and was suddenly lost in his own sadness. "I am a killer now. My old life is past and gone. I am cursed to live what remains of my life as a scavenger, hunting and clawing in the wilds for every breath."

They all looked at each other again and smiled. Teancum, always the watcher, observed the nonverbal exchange.

"What?" He asked.

Aaron, Himni and Omner all looked at Ammon and each of them nodded. Ammon cleared his throat and turned to look Teancum in the eyes.

"Doctor Teancum, I am sure you remember us in our youth? The troubles we caused, the people we hurt and offended, the souls we turned from God?" Teancum nodded slightly. "We, along with Alma the Younger, were truly horrible people." Teancum looked into the eyes of the four brothers sitting across from him. Even in the dim light of the fire he could see their pained expressions.

The bandit cried out in pain again. Himni and Omner both stood and moved towards the injured prisoner. One gave him a drink from a small flask of water as the other inspected the wounds. When they were done both men placed their hands on the man's head and said a prayer over him. He instantly ceased his thrashing and raised his eyes to theirs, weeping, thanking them, and thanking God for his relief. Why does he smile? Teancum wondered, troubled by the thought the bandit might have been helped, in some way, by God.

"You should listen to what our brother Ammon is going to say." Omner said as he patted the bandit on the shoulder and both brothers moved back to the fireside.

"We found a path out of the darkness and into the light of God's grace." Ammon continued. "We were given a choice and shown the way that would lead us to our salvation or to our eternal damnation. We all chose the better way." Ammon smiled and waved his hand towards his brothers. "Even after all we had done, if even we can find favor again in the Lord's eyes..." Ammon then pointed at Teancum. "So can you." Then he pointed at the wounded Nehor. "So can he."

The Nehor was acting like he was not listening to the conversation around the fire. When he heard those words he looked up with a questioning face.

Teancum sat pondering in silence for several seconds.

"How does a person like me and like who you all used to be... How do I find favor and forgiveness for the things I have done?" Teancum asked. As he looked down, there was still blood on his hands, so much blood.

"The first thing you must do is forgive yourself." Omner spoke. All of the brothers nodded their heads in agreement. "What you have been through; the attack on your family, living out here hunting your enemy... It is impossible even for me to comprehend your level of sorrow and pain." Omner sat up a little straighter as he continued speaking. "But remember, God did not send you to earth just to watch you fail. There is a plan and reason behind everything He does. Our job is to try to be the best person we can be regardless of what is happening to us."

"But some of us will never find forgiveness." Teancum looked over in surprise. It was the Nehor speaking. "I did what I had to do to help my family. I pledged my life to the clan." His voice trailed off as he continued. "How do I come back from that...?"

"You are a Nephite. Do you know the stories of what we did in our youth?" Aaron asked.

"You are the sons of King Mosiah. Everyone knows who you are and what you did."

"We all were given a second chance. We all were forgiven of our sins. If we can find peace and a new path to walk, anyone can."

Teancum remained still and considered that for a while as he continued to stare into the fire. As they all sat there lost in their own thoughts, Himni got up and checked on the wounded Nehor. He inspected the rope that was holding him to the tree and checked the bandages on the wounds.

"Speak the truth to me." The bandit whispered. "You all found forgiveness and another way to live?"

Himni smiled and nodded. "Yes. It was not an easy road, but we are forgiven."

The criminal smiled a weak smile and nodded back. "I am not like the others. I don't want to do this anymore."

The words radiated within Himni's soul. He knew this man was telling the truth. He nodded his head at the Nehor and stood. Himni walked back to the fire and spoke as he looked down at Teancum. "He is no longer a threat to anyone. We will take him to the sheriff in Manti. He will answer for his crimes."

"Come back with us." Ammon softly asked Teancum. "This life is not your path back to God."

"I'm not ready." Teancum quickly answered like he was planning to say it. Long ago, he had convinced himself that his old life was dead and had built up too many walls around his heart against any other thought.

"There are still many people in Zarahemla who love and care about you." Ammon continued. Teancum felt the love Ammon had for him in those words and he started to choke on his emotions. "I'm not ready..." He whispered.

Wanting a way out of this conversation Teancum continued. "I think I just need to rest, it's been a long few days and I have not slept well. Do you mind if I share your fire tonight? I will take my turn at the watch."

"Fair enough." Ammon responded, but he was not ready to end the conversation just yet. "We are all ordained missionaries now."

He stood and gestured to Teancum. "May we give you a blessing before you sleep?"

Before he realized what he said, Teancum agreed, but immediately felt foolish for doing so. He purposefully had not allowed another human get that close to him in almost two years. Teancum was very uncomfortable when the brothers all stood up, formed a circle around him and put their hands on his head to pronounce the blessing. He tried to focus on the words Ammon was praying but his head was swirling with thoughts. Teancum heard words like 'comfort' and 'healing', and a phrase that spoke of forgiveness, the plan of happiness and that his family was together with God. But what really caught his attention was when Ammon spoke of God's desire for Teancum to stop being a wolf and to now be a sheepdog. He told Teancum that he was not one of the criminals who infested the woods, and happiness could be found if he sought the welfare of the flock, and not his own desires for revenge.

The blessing concluded and Teancum felt something he had not felt in a very long time; peace. A warm calming peace seemed to release the tension in his back and neck. It was the same feeling he'd had when he spoke to the King about changing the government from a monarchy to a republic.

The answer the spirit gave to me. The voice of the King came into his mind. He tried to stand but his legs were weak and his head felt like it weighed fifty pounds.

"It's okay, Teancum." Aaron spoke as he helped Teancum stand. "These have been trying times for you. You are safe with us, you should get some sleep."

Teancum nodded his head in agreement. He could not remember the last time he felt so tired. "My apologies, thank you for your kindness. Something has come over me." He looked the brothers in their eyes and saw they were beaming with happiness. "I will still take my turn at the watch." Teancum assured the brothers as he laid out his bed and arraigned his meager belongings. "But I must try to sleep."

"You have felt this way before." Ammon reminded Teancum. It was as if he had some insight into Teancum's mind. "The spirit of God is one of peace and calm. He is trying to tell you something."

"What is he saying?" Teancum meekly spoke before he could think about what was happening. His logical mind would have stopped the conversation, but something was moving deep in his soul.

"That is for you to ponder, pray and ask for yourself. We are just the messengers." He smiled and gestured to his brothers. Patting Teancum on the shoulder, Ammon moved to gather more wood for the fire.

Teancum paused for a moment to reflect. He started to feel the effects of exhaustion and lay down face up on his mat with his pack as a pillow and his long dagger clutched in his right hand. "I want to know more. Let me rest a little while and we will speak more of this in the morning." His voice trailed off as he finished speaking and was asleep moments later.

The brothers smiled at each other.

"Did you all feel that?" Aaron quietly asked his brothers. They shook their heads in agreement. "Teancum is destined for great things." Omner spoke next as they all looked down at him. "The Lord has great expectations for him."

"He has suffered greatly." Ammon continued. "But this has been a refining fire for him. If he hearkens to the will of the Father, these experiences will make him a powerful leader for good."

That night Teancum was wracked with dreams in a fitful sleep. In his dreams he could hear his dear wife crying out his name in anguish and asking, "Why Teancum? Why are you continuing on this path of revenge? This road will not lead you back to us." Then he saw his three beautiful daughters, also dressed in white, walk up to her side. His heart sang out when he saw his family together again. In a softer and sweeter tone, his loving Hanni continued, "We miss you and are waiting for you. Follow God's light. It will lead you home and back into our arms." She took a step forward and reached out her hand as she concluded, "I love you. And I will love you forever. Live for us! Live to be with us!" Teancum's heart raced as he tried to reach for the loving touch of his wife's outstretched hand. But she and his daughters quickly vanished as his dream moved on to a vision of his younger self sitting on his Grandfather's knee.

Young Teancum was listening as Lord Pilio taught him principles of the laws of Moses and how a follower of God only sheds blood in defense of freedom and his family.

"Never do the armies of the Lord take the offence." Pilio instructed him. "Blood is shed only to free the oppressed and keep the family safe."

Teancum watched as his younger self looked up into his grandfather's eyes. "I was wrong, Teancum," Pilio continued to speak to the boy. "Anger is not the right path. Fight if you must, but be a man of goodness, not hate."

That scene faded and he was suddenly back at the rock formation near the crossroads of Zarahemla. He was standing in front of the male figure he saw there those many years ago who spoke to him about justice.

"You have been hunting the wolf so long that you have become one of them, and you forgot who you were meant to be." The figure spoke in a voice that echoed in Teancum's mind. Teancum had a questioning look on his face. "What am I meant to be?"

"A sheepdog," was the response.

Then he dreamt he was a sheep and his flock was being chased by a pack of wolves. He felt fear only a victim could feel and saw a lone sheepdog standing ready to defend the flock. As he ran past the strong guardian who was standing ready to protect the flock from the predators, he felt so much honor and relief knowing the sheepdog was there to keep him and his family safe.

It went on like that all night, dream after symbolic dream, until, right at the crack of dawn he was jarred awake by the screech of a large owl sitting in the top of tree near the campsite. Teancum jumped up, knife at the ready, scanning the area for a threat. After a cautious moment he realized he was safe and lowered his weapon. That was when he discovered the brothers had risen before the dawn, loaded their animals and left. He had been sleeping so soundly that he did not hear them pack and leave. He quickly looked over at the tree where the Nehor was tied and saw he was gone also. Fearing that he had escaped in the night, Teancum went to the tree to inspect the ropes to see if he could find any sign of where the man had gone. When he looked at the section of rope he saw that it was coiled neatly on the ground. It was still in one piece and had not been cut.

"They took him." He whispered.

Not knowing what else to do, Teancum moved back to the smoldering fire and gently coaxed it back to life. He found that the brothers had left him some of their food and he quickly ate a simple but filling breakfast. As he sat on a log, chewing his food, Teancum pondered over the last twenty four hours of his life. "The dreams, the feelings I had when I heard the words Of Prince Ammon, can it all be true?" He swallowed hard and drank from his waterskin. His powerful memory recalled a moment with the sons of Mosiah from years before. Alma the Younger, their companion during those troubling times was trying to convince Teancum and others that they were true converts to Christ.

"My soul hath been redeemed from the gall of bitterness and bonds of iniquity." Alma's words came back to him like someone was standing behind him quoting from scripture.

Teancum looked around and reflected on how beautiful the morning was. There was a gentle breeze and the birds were singing. He had a full stomach, plenty of fresh water and although he'd experienced fits of dreams, he felt rested from the night's sleep. For the first time in a very long while, he felt at peace with himself and his surroundings. He liked that feeling. He finished his meal and gathered up his sleeping roll and pack. His mind was heavy with thought as the events of the previous night played over and over in his head. What are the odds I would meet all the sons of King Mosiah in one place, at the same time? He kept trying to make logical sense of it all. They all know me and I know their past. They have found peace and happiness... Why can't I?

With his belongings secured and the fire extinguished, he shouldered his heavy pack and made his way back towards the mountains. He may have been moving through the woods, but his mind was elsewhere.

Teancum knew this part of the forest very well. He had spent many months hunting the Nehor and Lamanite bandits that preyed on the travelers and farm folk in the region. After walking for about an hour he stopped for a drink of water, and to refill his waterskins from a natural spring that was bubbling up among some rocks. Teancum knew it was relatively safe there. He dropped his worn pack and spear while kneeling down beside the edge of the small pool to dip his hand into the water. The surface of the water was still and the sun was in just the right position as he leaned over the water to drink. For the first time in a very long time, Teancum saw his own reflection in the water's surface. He recoiled at the sight of himself and spun around, knife at the ready. He thought some wild man had snuck up behind him and was looking over his shoulder. It took Teancum only a few seconds to realize that grizzled, gaunt, dirty man in the reflection was actually himself. He looked again, marveling at his appearance.

"Has it really been that long?" he asked himself, as he stroked his thick beard and brushed the long strands of dirty hair from his eyes. Then he looked down at the blade in his hands. It was the snake-shaped Nehor assassin's blade he had been carrying for so long. You are not one of them. The words of Prince Ammon repeated in his mind. Why do I still have this? He questioned his own actions. This is nothing but a symbol of hate and evil. I need to let this go. Suddenly the familiar flush of warmth and calm enveloped his being. He wanted to keep that feeling and knew it was time for him to move on before hate would consume him entirely and he would become lost in the wilderness, physically and emotionally.

He thought for a moment on what to do with the Nehor knife. He did not need it to fight with, he had plenty of other weapons. If Nephite soldiers found him with it, he might be mistaken for an assassin and hanged. "We don't want that." Teancum snorted and spoke silently. Then it came to him.

"Yes." He spoke out loud, happy his mind was still sharp. Looking around he realized that this spot by the spring was the perfect place. Reaching for his pack, Teancum removed a small spade that was strapped to the side of his pack and began to dig in the ground. He quickly made

a hole in the moist dirt about three feet deep and stopped. Taking the Nehor blade, Teancum paused for a moment. He stared at the symbol of hate for quite some time. As he looked down at the blade, images of the past two years flashed across his mind. The suffering, the pain and hunger, the anger, hate and contempt he felt for his fellow man. The loneliness and sorrow for his lost family. Everything dark that drove him to this point in his life, he imagined himself dumping into the hole with the knife. As he slowly lowered the knife into the hole and let go, he felt a weight lift from off his shoulders and pressure release from around his heart. This is what healing feels like. He heard the words of Doctor Teancum, the renowned physician and judge counsel the wild man standing and staring into a hole in the ground. The words from the doctor were light and full of hope. The words made the wild man in his mind want to heal.

After a moment a slight smile broke across Teancum's face and he pushed the dirt back into the hole, covering the blade. He tapped the loose dirt a few times with his foot and stepped back. Looking up into the bright mid-morning sky he felt the warmth of the sun and could smell the flower blossoms Hanni prized so much.

"I miss you my darling." He whispered when he caught her scent on the breeze. Instead of feeling sad at thinking about his lost love, a notion of reassurance boosted his essence. Holding still he pondered over how he had come to this point. After a few minutes, he opened his eyes and checked his condition. "I'm a mess," he declared out loud, as he inspected his tattered clothing and saw clearly, for the first time, just how scarred, dirty and broken he really was. He also felt how bruised and damaged his spirit had become, and knew he needed to heal. He was so tired, so very tired. The choice was made. He took a deep cleansing breath and shook his head as he spoke aloud, "It's time to go home."

TO BE CONTINUED

INSPIRATIONAL ART

Invite true Christian heroes to serve as role models in your home with these full-color, fine art prints.

AUTHOR: JASON MOW

After serving a mission for the Church of Jesus Christ of Latter-day Saints, Jason joined the U.S. Army and served as a Paratrooper. He advanced through the ranks to the position of Team Sergeant for the Army's elite Special Reactions Team (SRT). He has experience and training in joint counter narcotics operations, protective services, counter terrorism, weapons and tactics training, and deployments to hostile areas.

After the Army, Jason began work as a civilian Police Officer. Jason has worked as patrol officer, gang detective, narcotics detective, street crimes detective, and spent several years on SWAT as an operator and instructor. He is a certified police instructor in firearms, defensive tactics, tactical driving, and patrol rifle operations. Jason has twice been awarded the Law Enforcement Medal of Honor for gallant bravery in the line of duty and was recognized as the Community Services Officer of the Year for his department.

In addition to the military and police training, he has a Bachelor's Degree in Education from Northern Arizona University and has graduated from the Arizona Law Enforcement Academy, the U.S. State Department International Narcotics and Law Enforcement program, and the United States Army Military Police Academy. He is also a POST certified police instructor.

In 2006, Jason took time off from his Law Enforcement career and worked as a Civilian Contractor for the U.S. Government in Afghanistan. He worked at the National Police Academy in Herat as the lead instructor. Jason also worked as the personal mentor for law enforcement operations to several regional Afghan government officials. He embedded with the US Army and traveled with small specialized teams of soldiers to remote locations throughout Afghanistan.

It was in Afghanistan that the first ideas for what would become the War Chapters series began to form. After a rocket attack on his base in Herat, he turned to the scriptures and found comfort in reading about the experiences of Captain Moroni. He wrote these scenes as they played out in his mind all throughout his time there.

Jason volunteers his time and skills doing humanitarian work, conducting personal recovery operations, medical aid, and security, in response to natural disasters around the world. He has deployed to assist during Hurricane Katrina and the earthquake in Haiti.

ILLUSTRATOR: GABE BONILLA

Gabe grew up in Southern California, and was one of those kids who was always doodling instead of studying. After serving a mission in Chile for the Church of Jesus Christ of Latter-day Saints, Gabe enrolled at Ricks College (now BYU-Idaho) and studied art and illustration.

Gabe transferred to BYU and continued his education there, eventually graduating from the BFA program in illustration. While at BYU he met his wife, Nicole Carson, also a Southern California native and graphic designer. They formed Bonilla Design & Advertising and have been working from a home studio for the last 16 years while raising their six children.

Since BYU Gabe has worked primarily as a graphic designer, but always enjoys a chance to get paint on his fingers. He recently switched to painting digitally on an electronic drawing pad. All the illustrations for The War Chapters Series were digitally illustrated.

In his free time, Gabe enjoys cycling, racquetball, and anything in the outdoors including sleeping under the stars, hiking a new trail, or shooting a few targets.